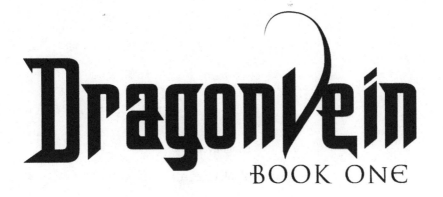

BOOK ONE

BRIAN D.
ANDERSON

Dragonvein

Book One

Copyright © Brian D. Anderson 2015

Published by Longfire Press

For my son Jonathan.

Books By Brian D. Anderson

The Godling Chronicles
The Sword of Truth
Of Gods and Elves
The Shadow of Gods
A Trial of Souls
Madness of the Fallen
The Reborn King

You can follow Brian D. Anderson @
http://briandandersonbooks.blogspot.com/
https://www.facebook.com/TheGodlingChronicles
https://twitter.com/GodlingChron

PROLOGUE

(Lumnia – End of the Age of the Five Kingdoms)

THE MUFFLED ECHO of footfalls running at a desperate pace roused Jonas from his sleep. Moments later the door flew open to reveal Lorina, Lady Illyrian's personal hand maiden. She remained there in the doorway, holding her sides and gasping for air. Jonas regarded her through bleary eyes. She was far too old and overweight to be chasing about in such a way.

He frowned. "Have you no manners, woman? I'm in my nightclothes." He looked over to the window. It was still dark. "What time is it?"

Lorina held up a finger as she continued to catch her breath.

"Out with it," he pressed. Still shaking away the lingering cobwebs of sleep, his eyes moved across the chamber to where his robe was folded neatly on a broken crate. "Well, if you're not going to speak, you can at least fetch me my robe."

The woman glared, then with surprising speed, took three steps to the crate and heaved the robe at Jonas. It hit him squarely in the face, further fueling his irritation.

By now she was sufficiently recovered to speak. "Get dressed. They have found us."

"What?"

In an instant he was out of bed. The bite of the cold, stone floor quickly encouraged him to put on his slippers. "Are you sure?" But the fear in her eyes told him the answer. "How long do we have?"

"Only minutes," she replied. In spite of the hard emotionless expression perfected by many years of practice, tears streamed down her plump cheeks.

"Where is Lady Illyrian?"

"In the basement." She turned to leave, then paused, looking over her shoulder. "Bring your sword."

The door closed behind her with an ominous boom.

Jonas tore through his pack, hastily donning a shirt and trousers and nearly toppling over while pulling on his boots. His hands trembled as he attached his sword to his belt. He had used the weapon only once before, and even then, not very well. He clenched his fists, cursing himself for such a display of fear. He must be strong. The enemy was coming and his mistress needed him. He took a deep breath, steeled his wits, and left the room with even, deliberate strides.

The barren halls of the dilapidated fortress were cold and dimly lit, with the rotten doors and rusted fixtures along the walls making the gloom seem deeper and even more depressing. Once, long ago, it had been a mighty castle built for the defense of a kingdom that stretched for hundreds of miles in all directions. But that was another age, and the kingdom had long since fallen, its lords and ladies lost to time. The fortress was now a forgotten relic, unfit for human habitation and used only by bandits and smugglers.

He had argued that they could find more suitable accommodations; a place where his mistress could at least lie on a soft bed and have a hot meal. But he knew his objections were foolish. They had been fortunate enough already to have made it this far unmolested.

The smoke rising from Dragonvein Manor as they fled on that first fateful night was still etched in his memory. They had watched helplessly while the place he'd called home for most of his life burned to the ground. And he could see the tears in Lady Illyrian's eyes as she looked back at the brightly glowing flames silhouetting the tall spires and proud walls that had housed a hundred generations of the

Dragonvein family. The vivid recollections brought a lump to Jonas' throat.

Upon nearing the stairs that led to the basement, he saw Lorina waiting for him. She was holding a brass lantern in her right hand and a small dagger in her left.

Jonas nodded curtly and waited for her to lead the way. Just as his foot touched the first step, a loud boom reverberated off the stone walls.

Lorina gasped. "They're here. We must hurry."

They moved down the stairs as quickly as they dared, but the wet stone was covered in slime, making the descent treacherous. Jonas frowned. Right now, neither of them could afford to injure themselves. Suddenly, he was keenly aware of the sword hanging from his side. It felt heavy and awkward and was pulling him off-balance.

A few steps from the bottom, his fears very nearly materialized. Lorina's feet slipped from under her and she fell sharply backwards. Only by making a desperate grab forward was Jonas able to catch her just before her head struck stone.

Completely forgetting the etiquette of expressing appreciation, she pulled free of his hold and set off down a long hall lit only by a few flickering torches. Along the way, the tiles were broken and the ground littered with refuse. Even with danger lurking so close behind, Jonas could not help but be repulsed by the rancid odor.

They hurried through a series of passages before arriving at a wrought iron gate. The metal hinges screeched in protest as Lorina pushed it open, causing Jonas to wince and cover his ears. She allowed him to pass through before picking up a thick chain and lock from the floor. Wrapping the chain around the bars and through a metal ring protruding from the wall, she snapped the lock shut.

A wooden door a few yards further down was slightly ajar, allowing the dim light of cheap tin lanterns flickering inside to escape. Jonas ran the rest of the way and pushed the door completely open.

The small chamber was moldy, and in his opinion, ill-suited for the magnitude of the activity taking place within its walls. In the center, Lady Illyrian was kneeling on a circular black rug, the twelve symbols of Arkazhi sewn in pure gold thread all around its border. Her purple satin ceremonial robes were tied at the waist by the golden Rope of Making: a gift given to her by her late husband. Jonas had never seen her wear it before. The full realization of what she was doing then struck him.

Her auburn, shoulder length hair was damp with perspiration, causing it to seize into tight little curls. Her alabaster skin was flushed, and the extreme exertion of the spell she was casting could be seen by the multitude of tiny veins protruding from her slender neck. With closed eyes fluttering as if in a dream state, her body began to sway rhythmically from side to side. In her hands she clasped a blue *rajni* stone about the size of an apple. It glowed and pulsed with the tempo of her movements.

"*Trinity* save us," Jonas gasped. "She can't be serious."

He heard the boom of a door being kicked in as the enemy searched the fortress above. Time was running out. The chained iron gate would slow them, but not for long.

Fear was now showing on Lorina's face. "She is *very* serious," she stated, at the same time moving quickly to the other end of the chamber where a small basket rested in the corner. After a quick glance at her mistress, she put away her dagger and lifted out a bundled cotton blanket.

Jonas knew very well what she was holding in her arms. Panic gripped him. "No! She can't do this!" he cried.

Another boom, followed by a loud crash told him that the enemy was drawing closer. He prayed that it would take time for them to find the stairwell. He looked hopelessly around for an escape that he knew for sure did not exist. They were trapped. There was only one way in and out of the basement.

Lady Illyrian, oblivious to everything around her, began to mutter the forbidden charm. Just a few feet away, a blue light blinked into existence.

As Lorina moved back across the chamber to Jonas, the soft cries of the young lord could be heard from within the blanket. She passed the child to him, as though handing over the most priceless of jewels.

"Why wasn't I told of this ahead of time?" Jonas demanded. "I could have…."

"Old fool," Lorina snapped. "There was no plan. We are trapped, and there is no longer any other choice. She began the rites just after I was sent to fetch you."

Harsh shouts and the sharp barking of orders sounded from above. Jonas tried to guess how close they were now. He looked across at Lady Illyrian, who was rocking even more intensely. The blue light had increased to the size of a dinner plate and was beginning to spin. Swirls of black merged within, making it appear an ethereal vortex of pure magic - untempered and powerful beyond human understanding.

Lorina reached inside the folds of her dress and pulled out a small amulet, together with a coin purse. Jonas' mind reeled as he recognized the amulet. It was a blue *rajni* stone set in a superbly crafted silver dragon's claw.

"What the hell are you doing with that?" he demanded.

Lorina did not bother to reply. Instead, in one swift movement, she placed the amulet around his neck. Had he not been holding the baby, he would have snatched it off in an instant. She then attached the purse to his belt and checked his sword.

"Stop this!" he commanded.

The magical tempest had now doubled in size.

Lorina slapped his face hard. "*You* stop, damn you!" Her eyes blazed, though her lips still quivered. "They'll be here in moments. We are to take Weslyn to Earth and protect him. There is gold in the purse, as well as instructions on how to return when the time is right."

The shouts, together with the stomping of boots and clattering of swords, were becoming much louder. They had obviously found the stairs. Lorina responded to this by once again reaching into the folds of her dress, this time producing a tiny glass phial that she threw hard against the closed door. The phial shattered, instantly creating a cloud of red smoke that settled just in front of the entrance.

"That won't hold them for long," she said. "We must enter as soon as the portal is big enough."

Jonas recoiled at the thought. "We can't leave Lady Illyrian. They'll kill her." He wanted to plead with his mistress, but he knew she could not hear him. The terrible magic she was wielding had blinded and deafened her to all but the task at hand.

"Break it down!" he heard a harsh voice command from very close indeed.

Almost immediately came the crashing and clanging of men battering away at the iron gate.

Lorina looked to the door, then back at Jonas. Her jaw tightened and she pushed him toward the portal, which by now was almost large enough to pass through. "Go!" she ordered.

Reluctantly, Jonas moved closer, stopping a few feet away to assess things. If he ducked low he should just be able to squeeze through, but in doing so he might risk harming the baby. Regardless, that was a risk he would be forced to take in a matter of mere seconds. He heard the gate come crashing down and men storming along the passage. Only moments later, a solid kick from a booted foot had the ancient door bursting into splinters.

Two men in black plate armor, the red raven of the emperor's guard splashed across their chest, stood in the doorway glaring menacingly through their steel helms. Towering behind them was General Hronso, his gold, chain-link veil revealing only his penetrating gray eyes.

In spite of the danger, Jonas glanced down at the tiny pieces of broken glass scattered about across the floor and smiled.

Drawing their swords, the two soldiers stepped over the threshold. It was as far as they made it into the room. The moment their boots crunched over the remains of the phial, violent flames erupted, consuming them instantly. Their horrified screams were still filling the chamber when Hronso jumped back, narrowly avoiding the trap himself. He cursed loudly.

Jonas looked again at the portal. Only a few seconds longer and it would be large enough for him to enter without risk to the baby.

"Give me the child!" roared the general.

The flames barring his way were already becoming a little less fierce.

"You will have nothing," screamed Lorina. Drawing a dagger from her sleeve, she hurled it with all of her strength.

With astonishing speed, Hronso reached out and caught the

weapon in mid-air. And though his mouth was covered, Jonas could see the sinister smirk in his eyes. Before Lorina could react, the dagger came flying back at her. With an ominous thud, it buried itself deep into her chest.

Jonas looked on with horror as she fell to her knees, clutching desperately at the blade. She looked back at him with tears streaming down her face, then slowly slumped to the floor.

The flames were now almost low enough for Hronso to safely enter the room. Jonas knew he must act fast. He moved closer to the portal.

"No!" Hronso's voice bellowed out, the sound echoing off the walls. He was already reaching for a long leather whip attached to his belt.

Holding the infant close, Jonas tried to leap into the blue light. But it was too late. The whip snaked out and wrapped itself around his left ankle, jerking his leg sharply back. He was only just able to extend his arms sufficiently to keep himself from falling on the child and crushing it. The impact as he hit the ground forced the breath from his lungs, but still he managed to keep his wits. Stretching out as far as he possibly could, he pushed the baby forward just far enough for it to enter the portal. There was an enraged cry from behind and the whip tightened. Consoled by the thought that he had at least saved the child, Jonas felt himself being dragged relentlessly back toward the remaining flames.

He closed his eyes and readied himself for the pain. But just as he began to feel the heat on his boots, the whip became slack. He looked up and saw Lorina, the bloody dagger in her scorched hand. She had cut him free.

"Go!" she pleaded. "Go before it's too late."

Their eyes met for a fleeting instant in a look that conveyed a thousand different emotions. Jonas then scrambled and crawled his way back to the portal.

With one final backward glance at his liberator, he threw himself into the spinning blue vortex.

CHAPTER ONE

(1944 Carentan, France)

E THAN MARTIN HUDDLED beside the ruined wall of what he imagined had once been a bakery. Now it was a bombed out ruin. The slimy mud caking his boots was so thick that they made a squishing sound every time he moved. He looked around and sighed, wondering what the town of Carentan might have been like before being reduced to rubble.

The sound of German 88's thundering in the distance, along with the crackle and pop of small arms fire, was so constant that he scarcely noticed it any longer. At least for the time being it was far enough away for him to catch some shut-eye. He glanced at his M1 Carbine and frowned. It was covered in the same gray mud as his boots. He'd need to clean it before Sgt. Baker saw him again, otherwise there would be hell to pay. Besides, the last thing he needed was for his weapon to jam at a vital moment.

Ethan leaned his slight frame against the wall. The cleaning job could wait until morning. The Krauts weren't likely to advance in the dark, and even if they did, the sound of panzers on the move should be enough to give him plenty of warning. He removed his helmet and ran his hands through sandy-blond hair, feeling the bits of dirt and grime sticking to his scalp and doing his best to brush them loose with the tips of his fingers. How he longed for a shower and a real bed, but no one had any idea when such luxuries might next be available. He put his helmet back on and sighed.

Just as he was drifting off, the crunch and scrape of boots approaching caused him to crack open an eyelid. But he knew who it was without looking. Markus James was his best friend. Actually, Markus was his *only* friend. None of the others in his company liked to be around him. He had gained a reputation for being bad luck, and there was a fair bit of justification in that belief. Three times he had miraculously survived what should have been certain death while all those around him had perished.

The first time was on D-Day. His *stick* had been dropped into the middle of God knows where. German anti-aircraft guns had spooked the pilots so badly that, when the green light came, their evasive tactics had taken them miles away from the intended drop zone. He'd seen five of his fellow paratroopers cut to shreds by ground fire during their descent. In fact, by the time he landed in the muddy field, he was the only one in his squad still alive. Since then, sections of their platoon had been ambushed twice while on patrol, and both times he was the only survivor. Luckily, Markus hadn't been with him on any of these occasions. He didn't think he could bear it if he was made to feel responsible for his friend's death.

"Wake up, mate," Markus said, his voice a bizarre combination of British and New Yorker accents.

His parents had moved to Manhattan from London about five years before the onset of the war. Markus had done his best to shed his strong London accent in order to avoid teasing from the other kids, but this only made him sound even more foreign than before. So, unfortunately for him, the teasing continued, even after enlisting in the Airborne.

During their training days, Markus discovered by chance that Ethan had lied about his age in order to join up. Ethan had pleaded with him not to say anything. He was only sixteen when he enlisted, and had turned seventeen a few days after that.

Markus had responded by laughing. "If a skinny little whelp like you can get into the Airborne, then I suppose God wants you here for some reason. And who am I to argue with the Big Guy?"

From that moment on they became firm friends. Moreover, Markus made it his mission to watch Ethan's back. Rarely was one seen without the other being somewhere close by.

Ethan was from Brooklyn. Or at least, that was his guess. His parents had adopted him as a baby. His adoptive mother was unable to bear children, a fact that nearly broke her heart. She desperately wanted to give her husband a child, and his father, who owned a bakery in Bay Ridge, could not bear to see his wife unhappy. Ethan had often wondered if his adoption had been far more for *her* happiness than for his. For sure, his father was uncomfortable around children and always had difficulty in showing his emotions.

His mother was quite the opposite, and doted on Ethan constantly. Not that his father ever treated him unkindly. In fact, they didn't even tell him he was adopted until he was twelve years old. And by then it didn't matter. His father told him that he was found wrapped in a blanket on the boardwalk in Coney Island. There was no note or anything else to give a clue as to where he was originally from.

His father had died of a heart attack three years prior to the war starting, so he and his mother moved to the South Bronx to live with her older sister. And though at first she still tried her best to be a good mother, the death of her husband was more than her heart could bear. She became increasingly withdrawn, eating little and rarely emerging from her tiny bedroom. Before long she had wasted away to a point where she could hardly stand without assistance. Ethan tried to ease her pain, but only succeeded in eliciting angry outbursts and wild accusations that he had always hated his father and was glad that he was dead. He knew she didn't mean it, but when war broke out, he thought it might help her condition if he was no longer around for a while. At least, that's what he told himself. The truth was a little more direct. He was hurt and angry, and the Army was the only escape he could think of.

He looked up at his friend. "Come to watch over me?" he asked with a smirk.

Markus settled in and tossed a half loaf of stale bread onto his lap. "If I don't, who will?" He held up two fingers and grinned devilishly.

Ethan took a deep breath while tearing off a hunk of bread. "Two? How do you figure that?"

"Once in the bar and once in the barracks?"

Ethan frowned. "I'll give you the bar...but I could have taken Lenny."

Markus laughed loudly. "Lenny would have beaten you bloody if I hadn't stopped him."

"Lenny's a big jerk," he muttered.

"Lenny's a *dead* jerk," Markus added. "Remember? He bought it on D-Day."

Ethan suddenly felt guilty for speaking ill of the dead. "Yeah. I remember." He looked over at Markus, who was still holding up two fingers. "Okay, okay—two," he admitted.

They ate quietly, then settled down and tried to get some sleep. The sun had not yet set. Even so, if the pair of them had learned anything about being in combat, it was that when you had an opportunity to rest, you sure as hell took it.

But the respite was short-lived. Ethan's eyes snapped open. The all-too familiar sound of German tanks approaching from the east had him scrambling to his feet.

"We have to go!" he shouted.

But it was already too late. Shells were exploding in the streets that led back to the rest of their platoon.

Markus stepped in front of Ethan. "Follow me!" he ordered. He could see the tension in Ethan's eyes. "Don't worry, mate. We can make it."

They bolted forward, hoping to get beyond the shelling range by sheer luck. It was a risky strategy. The already severely damaged buildings along the avenue were now being pounded anew. Dust and tiny bits of brick flew through the air, biting spitefully into the exposed flesh of their faces like a swarm of angry hornets. With the brim of their helmets the only thing protecting their eyes, they lowered their heads and pushed on. Each new blast created a shock wave that drove nearly all the air from their lungs and turned their legs to jelly. At times, merely remaining on their feet became a major achievement.

4

Then, all at once, it stopped.

Not willing to question their good fortune, Markus picked up his pace. But Ethan, who had always possessed keener eyesight than his friend, reached out and grabbed his collar, jerking him to a halt. A short way ahead, from behind the corner of the next street, the long steel barrel of a panzer was slowly peeking its way out. They could now hear orders in German being shouted both in front of them, and from not too far behind.

With no other options, they ran full speed back the way they had come and threw themselves flat behind a high pile of rubble.

"We're right in it now, mate," Markus panted.

Ethan could only nod in response.

Markus reached over and gave his shoulder a squeeze. "Don't worry. We'll be fine."

"I'm not worried," he replied unconvincingly.

They scanned the area for a better place to hide, but there was a major risk of being seen whichever way they headed. However, if they stayed where they were so close to the road, once the infantry followed the tanks, someone was bound to spot them.

The shelling resumed, hammering the town just beyond the panzer they had nearly run into. Ethan couldn't see the building where their platoon was holed up, but smoke and ash was rising from that direction. His heart sank.

"They got out," said Markus, sensing his thoughts. "They're probably back with the rest of the company by now."

The high-pitched squeal and clatter of tank tracks raked at their ears as more panzers closed in. The dust-filled air obscured their vision, but the monstrous silhouette of the nearest enemy vehicle could still be seen steadily drawing closer.

It was then that something directly in the path of the tank caught Ethan's attention. At first he thought his eyes were playing tricks on him. But another hard look confirmed his initial impression. A man was lying flat on his back, apparently unconscious.

Markus spotted him a moment later and grabbed Ethan's arm,

already realizing what his friend was thinking. "Don't!" he said. "They'll see you."

But Ethan was resolute. He couldn't just hide while an innocent civilian was crushed to a pulp. And he knew that the Nazis wouldn't hesitate to roll right over anyone in their way.

Snatching his arm free, he scampered over the rubble and ran into the street. On drawing closer, he noticed that there was something odd about the helpless man. It was his clothes. His shirt and pants were somehow different – made in a style and from a material he had never seen before. More than that, attached to his belt was a sword. Judging by his gray hair and deep facial lines, Ethan guessed him to be in his mid-fifties.

Markus slid in beside him and seized one of the man's arms. "Idiot. You're going to get us both killed."

Ethan grinned. "Yeah. You're probably right about that."

The man was surprisingly heavy for someone of only medium height and quite slender build. They dragged him as fast as they could manage and had just made it to the sidewalk when there was the sound of German voices shouting out. This was quickly followed by rifle shots. Bits of concrete exploded around their feet as bullets pinged and whizzed through the air. One passed so close that Ethan felt the wind of it on his cheek.

Once they reached the pile of rubble, Ethan glanced over his shoulder. The panzer had pulled forward and the main gun was turning slowly toward them.

"Move!" Ethan shouted. His muscles burned as he tried to go faster. Though conditioned by tough Airborne training and far from weak for his age, he was at his limit.

He felt the blast before he heard it. It was like a sledgehammer striking him in the back, and it took him a moment to realize that he had been thrown forward about ten feet. At first, all he could hear was a hellishly loud ringing banging against his eardrums. This shrill sound smothered out all other thoughts. Then, with a rush, he became aware that his arms and legs wouldn't move. For a terrifying moment he wondered if they were gone. He had seen too many men, stunned from artillery fire, completely oblivious to the fact that they had lost an arm or a leg…or both.

"Are you all right?" It was the voice of Markus coming from within the thick gray dust and smoke.

Ethan tried to answer, but his breath was still gone.

Markus drew closer and shook his head with a smile. "How in the hell do you keep surviving?" he asked, relief written all over his face.

After managing to lift his head and seeing that he was none the worse for wear, Ethan allowed himself a weak grin. He gulped in a deep breath and reached out for Markus' hand.

"Can you walk?" his friend asked.

Ethan nodded and allowed himself to be pulled up. He gripped Markus' shoulder while looking around for the man they had saved.

"We have to leave him," said Markus.

Ethan shot him a fiercely determined look. Markus sighed with sheer exasperation. He knew his friend well.

"A bloody Boy Scout, that's what you are," he grumbled. "Come on then."

They grabbed the man by the arms and continued to pull him down a nearby alley. At the end, immediately before reaching the next street, they spotted a small wooden shed. The roof was gone, but the walls were still intact.

From behind them, more orders in German were being shouted as soldiers began checking the area where they had last been seen. The dust was still very thick, making it almost impossible for the advancing men to have spotted them fleeing. Ethan hoped they would assume that their targets had been buried somewhere beneath the newly created mound of rubble.

The door to the shed was barely hanging by a single hinge. Taking care not to detach this completely, Markus eased it open sufficiently for them to drag the man through. Once inside, they lifted him into the corner. The shed was empty aside from a few crates and a broken broom, and was just large enough to accommodate all three of them.

"If they come looking, it won't take long for the Krauts to figure out where we are," Markus said. "And if this bloke doesn't wake up…."

"If he's not awake by nightfall, we'll leave him here," Ethan told him. "I promise."

The next few minutes were spent tensely listening out for danger. Eventually though, the voices of the Nazi soldiers faded and the shelling doubled in intensity. The Germans were throwing everything they had at the Americans, and were obviously not prepared to give up Carentan without a fight.

As the setting sun began to fade, Ethan noticed a blue glow pulsating from beneath the man's shirt.

"What the hell is that?" whispered Markus.

Ethan reached for the man's collar, but just as his fingers were about to make contact, the stranger's eyes popped open. He shrank back, a frightened and confused look on his face.

Ethan grabbed him firmly by the shoulders. "Take it easy, fella. We're not going to hurt you." But this did nothing to calm the startled man. He wrenched himself free and tried to crawl to the door.

Both Markus and Ethan grabbed him and pulled him back.

"Yemina et alhethra!" the man cried out.

Ethan clamped a hand firmly over the stranger's mouth. "Quiet. You're going to get us all killed."

"I told you this was a bad idea," remarked Markus angrily.

"Do you understand him?" Ethan asked. Markus spoke Spanish and French, and was in the process of trying to learn German.

Markus shook his head.

Ethan locked eyes with the man. "You need to calm down." His voice was soothing and reassuring. "We're not going to hurt you. Understand?"

Gradually, the stranger settled down. Cautiously, Ethan removed his hand.

"Yemina et el atheha?" His voice was much quieter now.

Ethan shook his head and touched his ear. "I don't understand you."

The light from within the man's shirt grew brighter. He reached inside and withdrew a gold chain. Attached to this was a jewel about the size of Ethan's thumb, set in what looked like a silver animal's claw. Its pulsating blue light was accompanied by a low hum.

"Ena mote…" the man said in a half-whisper. Reaching up, he snatched Ethan's hand and pulled it toward the jewel.

Ethan blinked in surprise. "What the hell are you doing?" He resisted the pull, but the stranger tugged even harder.

Markus joined in and grabbed the man around his chest, but there was nowhere to go. His back was already tight against the wall.

Ignoring both of their efforts, the stranger let out a heavy grunt and tried to lean forward. Then, suddenly changing tactics, he grabbed hold of the claw with his free hand. Thrusting that arm out toward their still locked hands, he touched the pulsating jewel onto Ethan's flesh.

Ethan immediately went rigid, eyes wide. It was as though he'd been electrocuted. He fell back hard against the opposite wall, nearly collapsing it with the force. Markus released his hold and caught Ethan's collar, pulling him forward.

"What the hell happened?" he asked.

Ethan took a moment to steady himself before rubbing the bridge of his nose. "I'm okay. Just a little dizzy." He glared at the man, who was looking back at him with a serious expression. "What did you do?" he demanded.

"Only what I had to," the man replied.

Ethan was stunned. Somehow, he now understood what the stranger was saying.

"I am Jonas," he continued, before Ethan could respond. "And I'm here to protect you."

"I'm Ethan." So great was his shock, it was all he could think to say.

"You can speak his language?" asked Markus.

Ethan nodded. "Yeah. But don't ask me how."

"What did he say?"

Ethan did not take his eyes off the stranger for a second while repeating what he had been told.

Markus burst out laughing, then stopped himself when he realized how much noise he was making. "Then he's definitely insane," he said.

"I don't know," Ethan countered. "How do you explain that I can understand him?"

Markus had no reply to that.

It was Jonas who spoke next. "How old are you, boy?" he asked.

"I'm nineteen," Ethan lied.

Jonas scrutinized him for a long moment, then sneered. "You can't lie to me. How old are you really?"

Ethan leveled his gaze. "I'll tell you how old I am, if you tell me how it is I can understand your language."

Jonas shrugged. "I don't know that myself. This amulet was given to me by your mother. It was the only means I had of finding you. Other than that…"

He reached inside a small purse on his belt and pulled out a folded piece of parchment. After running his eyes over the page, he grumbled with dissatisfaction. "This doesn't help very much either. It explains how to get us back home, but nothing else."

Ethan took the parchment. The letters and words were like nothing he had ever seen before. Even so, he was still able to read them.

Jonas,

When the time comes, smash the jewel. It will open a portal that will allow you to return to Lumnia. But you must enter together. I am sorry I cannot tell you more, but they are coming and I am out of time. Tell my son that I love him with all of my heart…and please watch over him.

Illyrian

Ethan returned the note, a heavy frown on his face. "What the hell is all that supposed to mean?"

"I answered your question," Jonas shot back. "Now you answer mine. How old are you?"

He paused. "Seventeen. I lied about my age so I could join the Army."

"You're a soldier?" Jonas asked, with obvious disapproval.

"Am I a soldier?" Ethan scoffed. "Why do you think I'm dressed like this?"

"Soldiers where I…where *we* come from…dress very differently." He noticed the rifle slung across Ethan's back. "Is that some sort of dwarf weapon?"

"What's he saying?" Markus chipped in. "Did he explain what he's done to you?"

"He says he doesn't know," replied Ethan. "But I think you're right. He's nuts. He asked me if this is a *dwarf* weapon."

Markus rubbed his temple. "A dwarf weapon? Brilliant! We risked our necks to save a lunatic."

The sound of tanks rolling down the nearby street silenced them. This was soon followed by the voices of the German infantry. Ethan gestured for Jonas to remain quiet.

"You are at war?" asked Jonas, after the enemy had passed.

Ethan's mouth twisted. "You really *are* crazy, aren't you?"

"I need to get you out of here," Jonas insisted, ignoring the insult. "This is no place for the son of Lady Illyrian."

Ignoring his words, Ethan moved over to the shed door and peered out. The sun was almost completely gone. "We can't stay here," he told Markus.

His friend nodded in agreement. "Are we taking the fruitcake with us?"

Ethan thought for a moment. "I guess so."

Markus sighed, then chuckled. "So he's your good deed for the day, is he? Your scout master would sure be proud of you."

On the far side of the avenue at the end of the alley, Ethan could see a bombed out office building. The top floor was completely blown away, but the large piles of broken bricks and wood would provide them with decent cover. Also, most of the surrounding buildings appeared far too damaged to be of any use to the Krauts.

"Follow us," he said to Jonas. "And keep up."

Jonas looked like he wanted to protest, but Ethan was already moving out. Markus grabbed the older man's arm and forced him to Ethan's back.

The sounds of battle echoed through the streets. Ethan guessed that the enemy's main force was about half a mile to the west. That meant they would need to head south and then try to sneak past their lines, at the same time hoping not to get shot in the dark by their own men.

After pausing to check that both ways were clear of enemy

soldiers, he took a deep breath and set off as fast as he could across the devastated street.

The crossing seemed to drag on forever, though in reality it could not have taken any more than a few seconds. Feeling exposed and vulnerable, for a long time the office building appeared in Ethan's eyes to be getting no closer. With every heart-pounding pace he expected to hear the rattle of a machine gun that would be the prelude to the end of his war.

But he made it safely across, and so did the others, although they were some way behind him. Gasping for air and with sweat stinging his eyes, he watched anxiously as Markus prodded, pushed, and very nearly carried an utterly exhausted Jonas over the rubble strewn ground and into the relative safety of cover.

After a minute or two spent recovering, they began checking the building to make sure there were no enemy soldiers about. Shattered office furnishings, broken plaster and unstable mounds of rubble made moving about treacherous, especially in the rapidly dimming light. Twice Jonas stumbled and fell, the second time opening a deep gash on his left hand. Ethan scolded him with a hard stare, but nevertheless paused to wrap the wound with a bandage from his pack.

A large hole in the office's outer wall gave them access across an alley to the building alongside—a process they were able to repeat several times while making their way to the edge of the next block. Though this wasn't so far in actual distance, the countless obstacles created by the devastation, plus need for caution, made what should have taken them only a few minutes grind on for well over an hour.

Ethan had been hoping that the street would be clear, but it wasn't to be. While peering out of a corner window he caught the sound of German voices in the darkness. He couldn't tell exactly where they were coming from at first. Then the light from a match appeared directly opposite their position.

He listened again, trying to filter out the clamor of battle that now seemed much closer than before. "I think there's either panzers or halftracks to the south," he whispered. "I don't hear anything north."

Markus knew better than to question his friend's hearing. It had saved their skins on several occasions since D-day. "That means we have to backtrack and head north," he said.

"Or try to cross here," Ethan suggested. "I can only see three of them."

He tried to picture the layout in his head. By now the 101st would have stopped the advance, and maybe even gained some ground. But German reinforcements would surely arrive soon. He didn't want to count on their being passed by a second time.

"This is ridiculous," said Jonas. "I can break the amulet and we can be away in seconds."

Ethan growled with exasperation. "Shut up! This isn't the time. You can tell me all about it when we're back with our unit."

Jonas glared furiously, but remained quiet.

They backtracked through two buildings and crossed the road heading north. The structures on this side had suffered far less damage. This meant they could now move faster, but it might also force them into the open more frequently. Not that they had much time to dwell on the matter. As they crept through an abandoned office building in search of a way to the next block that would keep them hidden, the scraping of boots and a guttural voice froze them in their tracks.

"*Mach dir keine Sorgen, du wirst deine Chance noch bekommen. Wir haben sie überrascht aber sie werden früh genug anfangen zu kämpfen.*"

"*Ich bin nicht hier, um anderen beim Kämpfen zu zuschauen,*" replied a much younger sounding man.

The voices were coming from a room just ahead. Both Ethan and Markus unslung their M-1s. In single file they crept down the hall to the edge of a doorway, hoping as they moved that the volume of the battle would mask any sound of their footfalls.

Ethan pressed his ear to the wall. The voices had stopped. They remained absolutely still and silent for more than a minute, but all was now quiet.

After gesturing for Jonas to stay put, he locked eyes with Markus. Holding up three fingers, he counted down. Three...two...one.

Kicking open the door, he rushed in with Markus only a split second behind him. Their eyes darted back and forth, searching frantically for the enemy. The dim light of the half-moon shining through a window illuminated the room well enough for them to see that, aside from a few meager furnishings and a pile of books in the far corner, it was empty.

"What the hell?" cried Markus.

Jonas followed them inside a few moments later. "It would seem that your enemy has gone. Now, if you would just listen to me, you can avoid further problems."

Ethan was on the point of responding when a figure burst through a door to their right that was all but obscured by a deep shadow.

"*Waffen fallen lassen!*" the soldier shouted, his Karabiner 98K leveled at them.

Ethan began to raise his own rifle, but another German soldier came in behind them.

"*Tut was er sagt!*"

Ethan and Markus dropped their rifles and raised their hands. Jonas just stood there, his face contorted in a stricken expression.

The soldier to their rear shoved them one by one against the wall. For a moment Ethan felt certain that his luck had finally run out and mentally prepared himself for the hot burn of bullets. He looked at his would-be killers. One appeared to be no older than himself - fair-haired and with a light complexion. Hitler's perfect man, he thought. The other was much older, battle-worn and grizzled.

"*Durchsuchen!*" said the older man.

His companion nodded and began to search them. When he got to Jonas, he grabbed hold of his sword and began to laugh.

"*Der denkt er wär ein Ritter,*" he sniggered. The veteran did not appear to be amused and made no reply.

Continuing his search, the younger soldier soon found the small purse on Jonas' belt. The jingle of coins when he shook this brought a smile to his face. But when he reached inside Jonas' shirt and tried to grab the amulet, his prisoner's hand shot out to push him away.

Letting out an angry snarl, the soldier struck him on the side of his head with the butt of his rifle. Jonas grunted and slid down the wall, blood already dribbling over his ear.

"*Er ist ein Zivilist. Erschieß ihn,*" said the older soldier. "*Die beiden anderen können wir verhören.*"

The young man chuckled. A malevolent grin crept over his face. He leveled his weapon at Jonas. "*Pech alter Mann.*"

Ethan closed his eyes, a wave of pity washing through him. "I'm sorry," he whispered.

Had the soldier fired immediately, Jonas would have already been dead. But the young man hesitated. Enjoying the power he held over his victim, his eyes searched for any small hint of fear or pleading. Not finding what he was looking for appeared to be a considerable disappointment to him. Eventually, with a small growl of frustration, his finger tightened on the trigger.

The explosion came from seemingly nowhere. A ferocious blast threw the two Germans flat onto the floor, at the same time pinning the other three hard against the wall.

For a moment, silence followed the blast. Then, as the dust began to clear, Ethan felt Markus' arms lifting him to his feet. His ears were ringing and he could feel a trickle of blood running out of his nose.

"Come on!" his friend shouted.

Ethan looked down at the enemy soldiers. The younger man was moaning softly, blood from shrapnel wounds soaking his back. The older man, having been closer to the far wall where the shell struck, was dead.

Jonas was coughing and gasping for air. "What was that?" he asked.

"That was our ticket out of here," Ethan told him. "Can you stand?"

Jonas nodded and struggled to his feet. He retrieved his sword and purse from the wounded soldier.

"Looks like our boys are hitting back," said Markus with a grin.

A bullet whined through the newly made hole in the building, striking the wall just above Jonas' head. A glance outside was enough to reveal at least a dozen Nazi soldiers on the other side of the street. Ethan and Markus hit the floor, searching frantically for their rifles. The first shot was quickly followed by a hail of bullets.

By the time they managed to locate their weapons, two enemy soldiers had already run across to their side of the road, one of them with a grenade in his hand. Ethan fired as quickly as he could, but his shots missed. A moment later the attackers disappeared from his line of sight.

Markus was doing his best to keep the rest of the enemy from advancing. He hit two soldiers in rapid succession, then emptied his M-1, successfully forcing the remaining Germans to take cover.

"Enough of this!" shouted Jonas, ripping the amulet from its chain and placing it on the floor. "We are getting out of here now."

Allied shells were striking with increasing frequency. One exploded only a few yards to their right, shaking the building and obscuring their sight with thick dust.

Ethan knew it would only be a matter of seconds before a grenade flew in. "We need to pull back," he told the others.

"To where?" asked Markus.

"Anywhere but here."

At that moment, Jonas smashed the amulet with a hunk of broken brick. It disintegrated with a blinding flash. When their vision returned, a swirling disk of blue light, six feet in diameter, was hovering directly above where the amulet had just been.

Ethan and Markus stared, dumbfounded.

"We should hurry," Jonas told them. Leaping over the debris, he made his way across to Ethan and gripped him by the arm. But he was only able to pull him along for a few steps before meeting resistance.

"Let go of me!" Ethan shouted, yanking his arm free.

Undeterred, Jonas seized hold of him again. "There is no other way."

Markus moved closer to the light, transfixed. "What is it?"

"A portal that leads to Lumnia," Jonas explained. "But it won't last for very long, I suspect. So we need to go immediately. If we huddle together, we should all be able to fit."

Ethan felt something strike against the back of his leg. He glanced on the floor behind him and caught the unmistakable outline of a German stick grenade. It flashed through his mind that at least it wasn't one of those fitted with a fragmentation sleeve, so the shrapnel would likely be minimal. Not that this would save him. The blast alone would be fatal when standing this close.

Markus saw it too, and was much better positioned to do something about it. Reacting instantly, he kicked it as far away as possible, then shoved both Ethan and Jonas hard down onto the floor. There was no time for him to hit the deck as well. A split second later the grenade went off. Even from the far side of the large room, the force of the explosion sent him flying backwards – back, and straight into the swirling depths of the waiting portal. Ethan watched in horror as his best friend simply vanished into thin air.

He scrambled to his feet, desperately calling out his friend's name. But it was too late. Markus was gone. Ethan made a dash toward the portal, but Jonas leapt up and tackled him hard to the floor just before he reached it.

"We *must* go in together," the older man cried out.

Without a word, Ethan stood up, dragging Jonas with him. "What happened to Markus?" he demanded.

"I told you. This leads to Lumnia."

Disbelief and skepticism were now set aside. Markus had always been there for him. Now it was time for him to return the favor. "Then that's where I'm going too," he stated emphatically.

Wrapping his arms around Jonas, he heaved them both into, what was for him, the complete unknown.

CHAPTER TWO

CONSCIOUSNESS RETURNED GRADUALLY. At first Ethan imagined he was back in New York, safe and sound in his own soft bed. He could almost smell the fresh Italian bread his father had brought home from work. It must be Sunday, he thought. Dad left the bakery every Sunday to eat lunch at home. He listened for his mother. Usually she would be singing Irish folk songs... unless she was in a playful mood. Then it was Louis Armstrong. But try as he might, he couldn't hear a thing - not even the ever-present Brooklyn traffic outside his window.

He struggled to open his eyes, but found that he couldn't. Something was wrong...out of place. Am I dreaming, he wondered?

The memory of Markus being thrown into the strange portal by the force of the grenade flashed through his mind. Suddenly, he recalled everything. This time he was able to open his eyes, though his vision was blurry at first. However, his sense of smell and hearing were as good as ever. Birds were chirping merrily, and the clanking of a hammer on steel rang out repeatedly. The stench of battle had been replaced by the musty smell of horses and tilled soil. It reminded him of the time his father took him upstate to visit his uncle's farm.

As his focus returned, he could see that he was indeed lying in a bed – one made up with fresh linens and a thick blanket. The room was small and furnished with a compact dresser and wardrobe. The window to his right was open and the white curtains in front of it were pulled far back, allowing the brilliance of a clear day to shine in.

Ethan took a moment longer to survey his surroundings. He had no idea how he had gotten here. The last thing he remembered was hurling himself through the portal with arms locked tight around Jonas.

He was just about to get out of bed when he realized that he was no longer wearing his uniform. In fact, he was completely naked. Wrapping the blanket around himself, he walked over to the wardrobe. Inside he found a tan shirt and brown pants, along with a pair of dingy leather boots. The pants and shirt were a bit too big for his thin frame, and the boots a touch tight, but there was nothing else available. At least he found a belt hanging on the door to keep the pants up.

He was about to explore outside the room when the corner of his eye was caught by something moving at the window. A more direct look had him staring in utter disbelief. There, sitting on the windowsill, was what he could only describe as a tiny dragon. It was no bigger than a house cat. Black scales shimmered in the sunlight, and needle-like spines protruded down the entire length of its slender back and along a tail that was nearly as long as its body. White, razor sharp teeth peeked out of its mouth as it cocked its head and looked at him with reptilian shaped eyes that were deep blue in color. It seemed to be regarding him with intense curiosity.

Ethan simply stood there, mouth agape. Then a noise from outside the door caught the dragon's attention. Spreading its leathery, bat-like wings, it immediately propelled itself up and away. Ethan ran to the window and poked his head out, hoping to see where the creature had gone, but it had already disappeared. There was nothing but a cloudless sky and a blazing sun.

The door behind him opened. Ethan spun around to see Jonas standing in the doorway, a look of concern on his face.

"I'm glad you're finally up," he said. "I was beginning to worry."

"What the hell is going on?" Ethan demanded. "Where am I? What have you done with my things? And where's Markus?"

Jonas held up his hand. "Please, one question at a time." He examined Ethan's attire. "I'll get you some better fitting clothes later."

"I don't give a damn about the clothes. Just tell me what's going on, or I swear to God I'll…"

He got no further. All of a sudden Ethan could feel his head beginning to swim and his legs wobbling.

Jonas rushed to his side and helped him over to the bed. "Take things slowly," he said. "The portal must have had a harsher effect on you than it did me."

Ethan pushed Jonas away. "Answer me."

"I told you before we came," he replied flatly. "We're in Lumnia." He could see that Ethan was struggling to accept the situation. "Come with me," he added. "There's food in the next room. I'll tell you what I can while you eat."

At first Ethan didn't move, but after a moment was forced to accept that he had little choice if he wanted to make sense of things. He needed answers, and Jonas was the only one who could provide them. He followed the older man out of the bedroom and down a narrow hallway that led into a large room with a hearth, a stove, and a roughly crafted table with several matching chairs. The walls were bare aside from a few hanging pots and pans, and the floor was covered with a frayed rug that spanned most of the room.

On the table was a wooden bowl containing what looked like porridge, together with a clay cup filled with water. Jonas waited until Ethan had taken a seat, then sat across from him.

"I understand how confusing this must be for you," he began.

Ethan ate a spoonful of the *porridge* and frowned. "Not very tasty."

"I don't doubt it," said Jonas. "The people here are simple farmers and unable to afford much in the way of delicacies."

After washing the porridge down with some water, Ethan pushed himself to try some more. All things considered, it wasn't as bad as what he'd been eating since D-Day.

Jonas leaned in. "As I told you before, you are in Lumnia now. You were sent to Earth by your mother, Lady Illyrian, when you were a baby. I was sent along to protect you."

Ethan frowned. "If you're supposed to protect me, why did you wait seventeen years before showing up?"

"I didn't. I passed through the portal only seconds after you did. But it's unpredictable and dangerous. That's the very reason why it's so rarely used. I was fortunate in that your mother had the foresight to tether you magically to the amulet, otherwise I may never have found you. It must have brought me to your location."

"Magically?" Ethan couldn't help but laugh. "I'm not a kid. There's no such thing as magic."

Jonas fixed him with a hard stare. "If that is so, then how did you get here?"

"I don't know," he admitted. "But you can't expect me to believe in magic."

"From the little I know of Earth, magic doesn't exist there. *Why* is a question for a scholar. And I am just a servant."

"Okay." Ethan pushed back the bowl. "Let's say for a minute I believe you. Why did my mother send me away in the first place?"

Jonas drew a long breath. "Trust me when I say she did not want to. But she had no other choice. Had you remained with her you would have certainly been killed."

"Killed by who?"

"By the Eternal Emperor Shinzan," he replied darkly. "To him, all who wield magic are a threat to his power."

"But I don't wield magic."

Jonas chuckled. "Not yet. But I suspect you'll learn soon enough."

"I'm not going to be learning anything," Ethan told him. "I'm going to find Markus and then get us back home."

"And just how do you intend to do this? How will you find him? Considering what I've learned about the portal, he probably arrived many years ago and is long dead."

Ethan sprang up from his chair. "He's not dead! And I *will* find him."

Jonas held up a hand. "There's no reason to get angry. I'm only telling you the truth."

He waited until Ethan had sat back down. "Let's just suppose that he is still alive. How will you find him? I had the amulet to help me locate you, but you have nothing that connects you to your friend. Lumnia is a vast land. It would take years, and you don't have the faintest idea where to begin."

"I don't care," Ethan said stubbornly. "Markus would look for me."

Jonas sighed. "Very well. If you are determined to go on a fool's errand, I can't stop you. But first you must learn how to stay alive. I've only spoken briefly to the farmer who lives here, but from what I can tell, things are now very different from when we left. How different remains to be seen."

"Different in what way?"

"Back then, Lumnia was divided into the five great kingdoms – Kytain, Malacar, Al'Theona, Ralmaria, and Traxis. All of these had sworn fealty to the Emperor ever since the war was lost and the Council of Volnar destroyed." He noticed the confused expression on Ethan's face. "It was a council of the wisest and most powerful mages in the land. But that's not important right now."

Ethan saw a flash of emotion in Jonas' eyes at the mention of the council. He was hiding something.

"Even the dragons could not endure the Emperor's wrath," Jonas added.

Ethan recalled the tiny dragon-like creature on the windowsill. He was about to mention this, but then stopped himself. Better to say nothing, he thought. If there was one thing he had learned in the Airborne, it was never to give information to someone you didn't trust. And he sure as hell didn't trust Jonas. Even if everything the guy had told him was true, Ethan suspected that he had an agenda of his own. And until he knew what that was, he'd be watching his every move.

Jonas continued with his explanation. "You were unconscious when we exited the portal in Lumnia, but I scouted around and found this farmhouse nearby. I told the farmer and his son that you'd tripped and hit your head and asked them to help me carry you here. I gave the farmer a copper *dractori* so that we might stay the night. He looked at it like he'd never seen one before. When I asked him what was wrong, he told me that he hadn't seen a coin like it since the days of his grandfather."

"So how long has it been since you were here?"

"That, my boy, is a question I desperately need to answer."

"That's all very interesting," said Ethan. "But how does this help me find Markus?"

"It doesn't," he replied. "Your quest to find your friend is not my concern. Keeping you safe and alive is. And if the Emperor discovers that the son of Illyrian has returned…"

"But if what you say is right, and many years have passed, shouldn't the Emperor be dead by now?"

Jonas shook his head slowly and grimaced. "There is a reason he is called The Eternal Emperor. The one thing I know for certain is that he still rules. That much I could gather, even from the short conversation I had with the farmer."

The sound of footsteps approaching from outside the front door drew their attention.

"Until I know more, say as little as possible," Jonas whispered.

The door swung open to reveal a plump woman with shoulder length, mouse brown hair. Her simple, olive green dress was worn and stained from years of labor. Her weathered, sunbaked skin denoted the hard life of farming the land and tending to her home, yet her steps were still nimble and carried a slight bounce. A warm and welcoming smile formed on her face.

"Ah!" she said, her eyes on Ethan. "You're up and about at last. And not a moment too soon. Rodger and Nate could use some help. And your uncle says you've a strong back and willing spirit. That is, assuming you're up to it."

Ethan forced a smile and gave Jonas a sideways glance. "Yes, ma'am. I'm fine. And I'm glad to help."

She walked over to the table, looked at his half-eaten breakfast and frowned. "You'll need to do better than that if you expect to keep up your strength. What's wrong? Don't you like porridge?"

"Yes, ma'am," he replied. "I like it just fine. I'm just not that hungry right now."

"Nonsense," she scolded, sliding the bowl closer. "A young lad needs food to grow strong. She squeezed his right bicep. "And you could do with some meat on those skinny bones."

She turned to Jonas, who was clearly amused. "And don't think you're getting off easy. There's plenty to do around here."

"I'm happy to help," said Jonas. "And we appreciate your hospitality."

She smiled. "Well, Rodger's been going on and on about that bloody copper piece you gave him. Anyone would imagine you'd given him an Imperial gold *korona*. Anyway, I think it earns you a few days' shelter. And I promise you'll find it more comfortable here than the traveler's lodge in town." She gave him a friendly wink. "That's assuming you're not leaving us right away."

"We'll be leaving in a day, possibly two," said Jonas. "But we'd be pleased to stay here until we are ready."

"Good," she said. After giving a quick nod, she moved off to retrieve a small sack of potatoes from the pantry.

"Ma'am," said Ethan. He had just swallowed the last of the porridge.

"Call me Cynthia," she told him, at the same time beginning to peel the potatoes with a small knife. "We're not formal here."

"Yes ma'am…I mean Cynthia. I'm ready to help now."

"Then off you go. Just walk around the house. You'll see Rodger and Nate."

Ethan thanked her and stepped outside. Though the sun was only midway to its apex, the heat was already enough to measure up to any summer he could remember. The exterior of the farmhouse matched the simplicity of its interior, with a front porch boasting two modest rocking chairs but little else. A narrow path led away into the distance, where he could see a line of tall trees.

Following his instructions, he moved around the side of the building and quickly spotted two men repairing a wagon outside a dilapidated barn. The older man saw Ethan and waved him over.

"I see Cynthia's put you to work," he said. "I guess that knock to the head wasn't as bad as your uncle thought." Ethan assumed him to be her husband, Rodger. Leathery skin and a gruff disposition was just what he would expect from someone who made his living by working the land.

The younger man, Nate, still bore the ruddy complexion and bright eyes of youth. In fact, Ethan guessed that they were about the same age, though Nate was a bit taller and far broader in the shoulder. His rippling muscles created by a life of hard labor were obvious, even when covered by his shirt.

"Have you ever worked a farm?" asked Rodger.

"No, sir," Ethan replied. "But I'm no stranger to hard work."

Rodger scrutinized him and scowled. "Couldn't tell that by the look of you. Anyway, just help Nate hold up the wagon while I fit the wheel."

Ethan recalled all the teasing he'd suffered about his build when first arriving for basic training. But he'd soon shown everyone that, though he may be skinny, he certainly wasn't frail.

After they finished work on the wagon, he spent the rest of the morning with Nate, loading it with feed and tools. By midday, he was filthy and tired.

They stopped only to eat a quick lunch that Cynthia brought out to them, and didn't return to the house until the sun was well below the horizon. To Ethan's relief, neither Rodger nor Nate asked him many questions. He found Nate to be a nice lad of good humor and friendly disposition – a trait clearly inherited from his mother. Rodger, on the other hand, was a man of few words and even fewer smiles. He worked the entire day with a sour expression and often mumbled curses to himself.

A large tub of water was waiting for them behind the house, along with a fresh set of clothing. The cold water was refreshing. It had been some time since Ethan had been clean, and he was more than grateful to shed the dirt and grime of both battle, and a grueling day's labor. Working on a farm was every bit as tiring as Airborne training, he considered wearily.

Supper was already on the table when they entered the house. Cynthia kissed her husband on the cheek and hugged her son. As they sat down, Rodger actually smiled for the first time that day. But Ethan's concern rose when he realized that Jonas was nowhere to be seen.

"Your uncle went to town," Cynthia told him, before he could ask. "But don't worry. I'll set his food aside."

This disturbed Ethan. He still had questions, and was impatient to finish their conversation.

The mood at the table was initially light and cheerful. These were simple people with simple cares. The only note of contention Ethan heard was when Cynthia mentioned Nate taking an apprenticeship with a local blacksmith.

"My son's a farmer," Rodger said sternly. "Not a bloody blacksmith."

"But he can do so much better for himself," countered Cynthia.

Rodger snorted. "What are you saying? That farming isn't good enough?"

"For me and you, it's fine," she replied with equal resolve. "But I want our son to have more."

They debated back and forth for some time. Finally, Nate interjected.

"It really doesn't matter," he said. "I'll never get permission from the governor anyway. You know how he is. People need to know their place and stay there."

His remarks brought an angry look to Cynthia's face. "He's an Imperial toad, that one. Doesn't have the brains of a fly."

"That may be," added Rodger. "But if we cross him, Nate will end up being sent east to join the Imperial Army. The only thing stopping that from happening now is the fact that he's our only son." He then noticed Ethan listening and cleared his throat. "We shouldn't be speaking of these things in front of a guest."

Cynthia rose and walked over to Rodger. She kissed his forehead and smiled. "Quite right." After retrieving a pitcher of water from the counter, she sat back down. "So, Ethan. Where is it you are from?"

"Brooklyn," he replied without thinking.

"And is that in Malacar?" she asked.

"Uh, no, ma'am. It's in…" He tried desperately to recall the kingdoms Jonas had mentioned. "It's in Ralmaria. It's very small. I doubt you've ever heard of it."

"You don't sound like you're from up north," said Rodger, a hint of suspicion entering his voice.

"Don't be rude," Cynthia scolded. "If he says he's from Ralmaria, then he's from Ralmaria."

Ethan didn't like where this was going. His mind raced for a satisfactory explanation. "I've moved around a lot," he said, hoping this would get him off the hook. But Rodger's cynical expression told him otherwise.

"And why is that?" the farmer pressed.

Ethan forced a smile and shrugged. "You can blame my uncle. He's the one who's always dragging me along with him."

"I see," Rodger muttered. He was fingering something in his pocket. "And just *what is* your uncle's business?"

"I said that's enough, Rodger," Cynthia cut in, this time more forcefully. "We do not interrogate a guest."

Rodger looked at his wife. She was glaring daggers. Sighing, he withdrew his hand from his pocket and produced the copper coin that Jonas had given him.

"My apologies," he said, turning back to Ethan. "I just think it's odd that your uncle has no money other than this."

"So what?" said Cynthia. "Last night you couldn't stop talking about it. You even said it might be worth more than a regular *korona*. And now you're complaining?"

Rodger shook his head, never shifting his gaze away from Ethan. "I'm not complaining. But it still makes me wonder. Two travelers appear at our door in the middle of the night, one of them unconscious, and with nothing but ancient coins to give. I just want to make sure they're not bringing trouble to our home." His eyes became harder. "You're not, are you boy?"

Before Ethan could answer, the door opened and Jonas entered the room.

"I'm sorry I'm late," he said, giving a polite bow. "Jaobin was further away than I thought."

He immediately noticed the tense mood and took a seat at the table. "Has Ethan been talking your ears off?"

Cynthia popped up and put a plate of food in front of him. "Not at all. My husband was just wondering where you are from."

"I told them I was from Ralmaria," Ethan cut in quickly, before Jonas could say anything to reveal his lie.

Jonas chuckled. "Well, not exactly. He was born there. But I'm from Kytain, and that's where he's spent most of his time."

Rodger turned his attention to Jonas. "Kytain, eh? I can't say I've ever been there. Last night you didn't mention what your business was."

"I'm a grain merchant," he replied without pause. He regarded the coin on the table. "At least, I was. I lost my fortune to the drought last year. All I have left is a purse full of relics bequeathed to me by my father. I was hoping to trade them in town."

"I heard about the drought in Kytain," Rodger said. "I'm sorry for your hardship." His posture began to relax, but not completely.

Jonas bowed. "Thank you. And thank you for opening your home to us. But we must be leaving in the morning."

"I'm sorry to hear that," Rodger responded without enthusiasm. "Ethan is a mere wraith of a lad, but he has heart, and is stronger than he looks."

After finishing his meal, Jonas asked Ethan to join him for a walk. Nate was reading beside the hearth, while Rodger and Cynthia were sitting together on the porch—he smoking a pipe, and she humming softly.

"It's a good thing I picked up that bit of information about the drought while in town," Jonas said when they were safely out of earshot. "Rodger may be an uneducated farmer, but he's a sharp one, nonetheless."

"What were you doing there?" Ethan demanded.

"Trying to figure out where we are and what's happened since we left," Jonas replied.

"I think you just don't want to tell me the things I need to know."

Jonas' irritation flared. "And what is that exactly? What more do you imagine I can tell you? You already know that you're no longer on Earth. You know you can't get back. And you know that, should you be discovered, you'll be in grave danger. What else is there?"

Ethan was unmoved by his display. He'd seen quite a few angry officers, and a whole lot more even angrier sergeants. "First of all, I'd like to know who this Emperor is," he said.

There was a long pause before Jonas responded. He sighed heavily. "Once, all five kingdoms lived in relative peace. Not even the elves were much of a problem in those days."

Ethan raised an eyebrow at the mention of elves, but said nothing.

"That was until a dark power rose in the east, beyond the Shadow

Lands," Jonas continued. "At first, people thought it was just some overly ambitious warlord or mage—the hubris of a lone fool who would be easily put down. Not even the Council of Volnar took the threat seriously." He lowered his head. "But they were all wrong. A man known as Shinzan declared himself to be The Eternal Emperor and began to wage war on the rest of the civilized world. He swept over the land like a plague, destroying everything in his path. The war was lost in a matter of months."

Jonas' voice was faltering more with each word. "After the kingdoms were forced to swear fealty to Shinzan, he declared all those who wielded magic to be enemies of the Empire. He began to hunt down and kill every mage in Lumnia. Only your mother and a few others managed to escape their homes in time. They were trying to reach the dwarves…hoping to save their children." Tears filled his eyes. "They didn't make it."

He wiped his face and cleared his throat. "Now you know who the Emperor is."

"So what should we do?" Ethan asked.

Jonas shook his head slowly. "I don't know. We are at present in Malacar. That much is certain. Miltino is a three-day journey to the north. I think we should head there. In my time it was a large enough city to lose yourself in should you desire to do so." He jingled his purse. "I also need a place to shed these coins. It's all the money I have, and they draw too much attention."

"You've mentioned my mother," said Ethan. "But what about my father?"

"He died fighting in the war," he replied coldly. "I wasn't there, so I don't know the details."

"What kind of man was he?"

"He was a great mage. And a kind man."

Ethan expected more. "That's it?" he said, after it became clear that Jonas had nothing further to add.

"What more is there? He was a noble lord and did not share much with the likes of me. I only know what I saw. And I saw that he treated his wife and you with love and tenderness."

"But what about my family? Is there anyone else?"

"How should I know?" Jonas snapped. "Most likely they're all dead. You come from a family of mages, and like I told you, the Emperor hunted them all down."

"Can you at least tell me my father's name?"

"His name was Praxis Dragonvein." Having said that, he stopped and turned back toward the house. "I'm tired. We can talk more tomorrow while we travel."

Ethan protested, but Jonas ignored him. It would obviously take time to get the full story out of the old man. His eyes swept over his surroundings. *Lumnia.* It was still overwhelming to think that he was no longer on Earth. And without Jonas, there was no hope of finding Markus, or getting home. He needed him...for now. And though Jonas was plainly hiding things from him, it was clear that he was also determined to keep his charge safe.

They returned to the house, and, with the fatigue of the day quickly setting in, went straight to bed. Ethan dreamed of the tiny dragon. But in his dream it became immense—fifty feet from nose to tail, and with a head the size of a truck. Its dagger-like teeth were more than sixteen inches long and gleaming white. Massive wings spread wide as it let out an earsplitting roar.

Ethan woke, drenched in sweat, his heart banging away as if it were about to beat right out of his chest. The roar of the dragon was still echoing loudly in his head.

After a few moments he was able to control his breathing and calm himself. Although it was still dark, he could hear Cynthia already busy in the kitchen. Jonas was asleep beside him, undisturbed by Ethan's restless movements. He lay there for a short time longer and then decided to join Cynthia in the kitchen rather than stare vacantly into the darkness.

"Bad dreams, dear?" she asked. She was already pouring him a cup of hot liquid from a pot on the stove. It smelled like tea, but with a faint mint quality.

He accepted it gratefully and took a sip. It reminded him a bit of the mulled wine he'd tried last Christmas. "It's good," he said. "Thank you."

"I heard you moaning in your sleep. You know, my son has bad dreams from time to time, and it always makes him feel better to talk about it."

He shook his head and smiled. "It's nothing. I can't really remember what it was about."

Cynthia poured herself a cup and sat across from Ethan, regarding him for more than a minute before speaking. "My husband may be an ornery old goat, but he's not stupid. You two are in some sort of trouble. Am I right?"

Ethan didn't want to lie. Her features had the understanding and kindness of a loving mother. "Well...no, ma'am. Not trouble. That's not how I'd put it."

She scolded him with her eyes. "At least will you tell me if trouble is going to come visiting here once you're gone?"

"I don't see why it should," he replied. But the thought then struck him. It might very well. He would hate to see these people come to harm, especially after they had been so open and giving.

She sighed. "Well, it's too late to worry about that now, I suppose. But you watch out. That uncle of yours is up to something. And I'd bet a gold *korona* it's something a nice young boy like you shouldn't be mixed up in." She paused to take a sip of her drink. "Of course, you could stay here with us if you wanted to. Rodger may be a grump, but he could use the help. He says you did a good job yesterday. And Nate needs someone to keep him out of trouble."

"Thank you," said Ethan. "But I honestly can't. I have things I need to do, and Jonas is the only one who can help me." He could suddenly see a reflection of his adoptive mother in the woman's concerned gaze... before his father had died. Before she fell into despair. He desperately hoped he hadn't brought danger here.

"Then you must promise to be careful," she said. "And to visit us if ever you are nearby."

"I promise."

Just then, they heard the shuffling of feet and cracking of joints.

"I see you're keen to make an early start," said Jonas, entering the kitchen.

Ethan thought the man looked twenty years older than he had the day before.

"Well, the two of you aren't going anywhere until you've had some breakfast," said Cynthia. A sharp nod from her told them that there would be no debate over this.

"I would be grateful," said Jonas. "And these old bones need time to get moving anyway."

Soon, the scent of spices and bacon filled the house. Rodger and Nate joined them just as Cynthia was putting out the plates. Both men nodded a greeting and then plopped heavily into their chairs without a word.

"So, you're leaving?" Rodger said, once they were finished.

"Sadly so," replied Jonas. "I'm hoping to reach Al'Theona as soon as possible."

"Al'Theona? Then you're intending to cross elf country alone?"

"I'll try to find a caravan," explained Jonas.

Rodger gave a sarcastic chuckle. "Then you better find one with a lot of protection. The Empire doesn't do much to keep travelers safe in those parts."

"Are you sure you should be dragging your nephew along on such a dangerous journey?" added Cynthia.

"I'll be fine," said Ethan.

"I'm just saying, that's all," she countered with in an innocent smile. "I'm certain your uncle wouldn't want to put your life at risk."

"Leave off," snapped Rodger. "If the boy wants to go, it's not our affair. He's old enough to choose for himself."

"I promise to keep him as safe as I can," assured Jonas. He bowed. "I thank you again for your hospitality, but we must be off."

Reaching into his purse, he took out a silver *dractori* and flipped it to Rodger.

The farmer's eyes lit up and a grin even managed to peak out from the corners of his mouth.

Cynthia shot up and embraced Ethan. "Mind that you remember what I said."

"I will," he promised.

"Oh yes. I nearly forgot," she cried out, suddenly running from the kitchen. She returned a few seconds later with Ethan's military clothing and equipment. "Don't forget this. Odd things you have here, I must say."

Ethan took his belongings and bowed his head in the same way that he'd seen Jonas do. "Thank you," he said.

Nate offered to walk them to the road, but Jonas respectfully declined. After a final farewell, the pair headed out of the door and down the path leading away from the farmhouse.

The road, when they reached it, was unpaved and had deep grooves worn down on either side by years of travel. They turned north and walked along at a leisurely pace. From out of the thin forest surrounding them came the sound of birds greeting the new morning with song.

"You can't keep those things the woman gave you," Jonas said. "They will draw too much attention. Take anything personal and bury the rest."

Ethan scowled but obeyed. There wasn't much he couldn't do without. A picture of his parents was just about it. There were no letters because no one in his family ever knew he had joined the Army. Using his helmet to dig, he buried the rest of the gear as told.

After making sure the freshly disturbed ground was covered with leaves and twigs, Jonas gave a satisfied grunt and set off walking once again. Ethan thought this might be a good time to also dig a little in other ways.

"Tell me more about my family," he said, as casually as he could manage.

Jonas gave him a sideways glance. "There's not much I can add. As I said before, I was just a servant."

"Don't give me that. You got to know something, I'm sure of it."

"I've told you what you need to know," he shot back. "As for your family history...I don't know much. I didn't concern myself with such things."

Ethan abruptly stopped walking. "You're lying. If what you say is true, my mother entrusted you with protecting her only child. No one would just hand over their baby to a servant unless they had complete faith in them."

Jonas also stopped. He faced Ethan squarely, his expression blank and his eyes cold. "I was never meant to do this alone," he said. "Your mother's handmaiden was supposed to come with me."

"So what happened to her?"

"She died." He turned away and resumed walking. "And if we don't want to die too, we'll get as far away from here as possible."

Ethan watched Jonas for a moment and then chased after him. "Why? Do you think the Emperor knows we're here?"

"During the days when he hunted the mages, he had the ability to detect powerful magic," Jonas replied. "And the portal is very powerful magic. There is no reason to think he can't still do the same. Your mother found a way to mask her presence from him...but even that wasn't enough to save her in the end."

A sense of dread washed over Ethan. "Do you think they'll find out where we've been?"

Jonas nodded.

"So what will happen to...?"

"They'll likely be tortured and killed," he replied before Ethan could finish his question. "That's why I told them we were heading for Al'Theona. If they are interrogated, what they say will lead the Emperor's men away from where we are actually going."

Ethan was horrified. "You mean, you knew all the time that we were putting them in danger?"

"And just what should I have done?" he challenged. "Leave you unconscious in a field clothed in garb that would certainly get you noticed and possibly captured? Walk about blindly until we figured out where in the hell we are? For all I knew, those people were our only chance of survival. And though I wish it were not so – *they* are expendable. *You* are not."

Ethan fumed. He wanted to strike the old man, and could not bring himself to speak to him for the rest of the walk to Jaobin.

As they entered the town, Ethan was reminded of the westerns his father would occasionally take him to see at the cinema. Horses were tied to hitching posts in front of simple wooden buildings, and a stench of earth and dung permeated the air. The people were dressed much like himself in simple attire made for work rather than fashion. The horses were identical to the ones found on Earth, making him wonder exactly how they came to be in this world. He wanted to ask Jonas, but was still too angry to start a conversation. He probably wouldn't know anyway. That, or he wouldn't tell him.

Jonas led them down the main avenue and then right along a narrow side street. The ringing of a hammer chimed repeatedly, growing ever louder as they progressed.

They stopped in front of a mud brick building with large double doors. This seemed to be where the hammering was coming from. "Stay here," Jonas ordered. "I won't be very long." He pulled open one of the doors and squeezed inside.

Ethan did as told and waited. About ten minutes later, Jonas emerged with a satisfied look on his face. "I've purchased a wagon and two horses," he announced. "And…"

He took hold of Ethan's hand and placed three copper coins in his palm. "Don't spend this unless you have to. I have enough of the new money to get us a room for the night, plus a meal and a few provisions. But we'll need to wait until we arrive in Miltino before getting any more."

"We're staying the night?"

"No choice," Jonas explained. "The wagon I bought is being repaired and won't be ready until morning. For now, we should head to the inn. You can wait there while I buy the provisions."

"Shouldn't I go with you?"

Jonas shook his head. "I need you to keep your mouth shut and your ears open. I know enough to keep from drawing too much attention, but you know nothing of this world."

"I would if you told me about it," he countered.

Jonas sniffed, then pushed his way past and set off in the direction they had come. He eventually led Ethan to a rickety wooden building on the other end of town with a stable on the side and several horses tethered in front.

"Once I get our room, stay in the common area and listen carefully to anything you hear," he said. "If you're asked, tell people you are from Al'Theona. Make up a town. But do your best to change the subject."

Having issued these instructions, he opened the door and stepped inside. The inn's common area was far from spacious, with room for just two long tables and a small bar. The few occupants looked up at the newcomers with only passing interest before returning to their drinks. The smell of stale beer and unwashed men made Ethan's eyes water. He had thought some of the local pubs in England were bad…but this had them beat by a mile.

Jonas quickly located the innkeeper and had him show them to a room. They were taken through a door at the rear of the common area and down a couple of narrow corridors. When they arrived, Jonas pressed a coin into the innkeeper's hand. The man frowned. This was clearly not as much as he'd been hoping for, but after a long pause he eventually walked away muttering curses under his breath.

The room was bare aside from two cots shoved carelessly into the far corners. Not that such meager accommodations bothered Ethan. He'd slept in far worse since joining the Army. Jonas, on the other hand, looked highly displeased.

"To think I'm reduced to this," he complained.

His remark brought a smile to Ethan's lips that Jonas immediately picked up on.

"Stay inside the inn," he instructed sharply. With a sneer and a huff, he then strode rapidly away.

Ethan returned to the common room and took a seat at one of the long tables. He jingled the coins in his pocket, wondering how much they were worth. A young serving maid very soon approached, her blond curls bouncing with each step. Her tanned skin, twinkling blue eyes and obvious curves had every male eye watching.

She gave Ethan a bright smile. "What can I get you?" she asked.

He wasn't sure. "A beer, I suppose," he finally said, pulling out a coin and handing it to her.

"Planning on getting a bit drunk tonight are we?" she teased. Before Ethan could reply, she sauntered off with hips swaying provocatively.

She returned a short time later with a large pitcher and clay mug. Foam spilled down the side of the pitcher as she placed it on the table in front of him.

"And if you're needing a bit of company, just let me know," she said with a wink. "We don't see too many handsome strangers around here."

"Th-thanks," he stammered.

The girl laughed merrily and spun around, leaving Ethan gawking after her, and uncomfortably aware that the color had risen in his face. He wasn't normally shy around girls. He'd even had a girlfriend for a while back in Brooklyn. But he'd never had one be so forward with him before. Markus would have teased him about it no end had he been there.

Markus… Thoughts of his friend flooded in. At this rate he would never find out what had happened to him. Finding Markus was the only reason he'd come to Lumnia, and yet here he was…lost and at the mercy of a grumpy old man he didn't trust.

He sat alone for more than an hour steadily drinking, though the beer tasted terrible and was far too warm for his liking. The serving maid stopped by from time to time to see if he needed anything…and to flirt a little more.

By the time the pitcher was drained, Ethan's head was beginning to swim. The common room was now almost empty – only a lone drunkard remained slumped in the corner – and Ethan was ready to leave.

"To hell with Jonas," he mumbled. With shaky legs, he pushed himself to his feet. After gripping the edge of the table for a moment, he made his way to the door. "Tell him I'll be back," he called out. He had no idea if anyone had heard him. Nor did he much care.

Not certain which direction to take, Ethan turned left on a whim, taking elaborate care not to stumble as he moved along. Soon he could hear the sound of singing and laughing coming from a building a short distance away.

That's more like it, he told himself.

The door was already flung wide open, and even from outside he could see at least a dozen men and women seated at small tables with pitchers of what he assumed to be beer in front of them. For a moment, the thought of more beer soured his stomach. Then he belched, releasing much of the discomfort. He reached into his pocket to finger the two remaining coins, briefly recalling Jonas' warning about not spending them. But the alcohol already coursing through his veins pushed aside any care for what the old man had said.

The tavern was indeed lively. On stepping inside, he saw that it was virtually full to capacity with a pretty much equal number of men and women, their simple dress and familiar cheer suggesting that they were mostly local townsfolk.

Ethan's entry did not go unnoticed as he made his way across the room to the bar at the far end. His youthful countenance and unsteady steps drew more than a few stares. But no one seemed sufficiently interested to say anything.

He plopped himself down on a bar stool and ordered a beer, careful not to slur his words. The bartender gave him a wary look before turning to a large barrel behind and filling a mug.

"You're not from around here, I take it," he said.

Ethan reached into his pocket to retrieve a coin. "No, sir. I'm not."

The man merely nodded, then handed him five smaller coins. His change, Ethan supposed. He took a sip and raised an eyebrow. This was much better than the beer at the inn. Infinitely better.

He sat there quietly drinking until the daylight coming in through the windows started to dim. At this point, a serving maid began lighting lanterns hanging from the ceiling. He had been trying to listen to what people were talking about, but the sheer number and volume of competing voices, combined with the amount of beer he had consumed, made it impossible to gather anything useful. By now, the five coins he had received in change were all gone. Oh well, he thought. It'll give Jonas another reason to be an asshole.

The serving maid from the inn flashed into his mind, producing a devilish grin. Maybe she was still there. Gripping the bar to steady his legs, he slid off the stool. The beer had certainly bolstered his courage and relieved him of any boyish inhibitions.

Just as he was about to leave, a commotion sprang up two tables away. A stocky man in a sleeveless shirt and rough trousers was clutching hold of a girl who looked to be no more than thirteen years old. He had her wrist pinned firmly to the table top. With thick muscular arms and a shaved head giving him a menacing appearance, he was clearly no stranger to violence.

"Damn little street rat!" the man roared, small flecks of spittle flying from his mouth with each syllable. "Steal from me, would you?"

The girl, her brown eyes wide with fear, struggled in vain. Her straight black hair, tied in a ponytail, flailed wildly back and forth across her thin features.

"Hey, what's the problem here?" demanded the bartender, his loud voice carrying over the crowd. Quickly, he rounded the end of the bar and approached the table.

"I caught this one trying to steal my coin purse," explained the brutish looking man. "Tried to cut it off my belt, she did."

"He's lying!" the girl cried out desperately, tears streaming down her face. "I'm not a thief. I swear it."

"Did anyone else see this?" asked the bartender.

Two companions of the accuser both nodded an affirmation.

The bartender threw up his arms. "Then there's nothing I can do. Sorry, my little dove. A hard lesson is coming."

The man holding the girl bared a mouthful of rotten teeth in what might just have been a grin. With his free hand, he drew a short sword from his side. "Don't worry," he said. "This will only hurt for a second or two."

Horrified, Ethan could barely believe what was happening. This ugly brute was about to cut the girl's hand off. Right here...in front of everyone. And no one was doing a damn thing about it.

"Stop!" he shouted, just as the sword was raising.

The man dropped his arm to glare in his direction. "Mind your own business, boy. Or it'll be you that sees some trouble next."

The horror of what he was witnessing was enough to wipe away at least a small part of Ethan's alcohol induced muddle. Seeing the sword start to rise once again, he reacted instinctively. Racing over to the table, he struck the brute squarely on the jaw with all the strength he could muster. More surprised than badly hurt, the distracted man let out a bellow of rage. At the same time, seizing her opportunity, the girl managed to slip free of his weakened grip. Ducking low under the crowd, she vanished in an instant.

Ethan stepped back, his eyes searching for a path to the door. But the crowd had already closed in, blocking his way. The furious man advanced toward him, sword still in hand.

"Durst!" shouted the bartender. "The boy only punched you. And he's unarmed."

"Durst is it?" said Ethan, using his friendliest tone. "I'm sorry I hit you, but –"

He didn't get the chance to finish his sentence.

The clatter of the sword dropping onto the floor was rapidly followed by a huge, ham-like fist smashing into Ethan's temple. The force sent him reeling back and over a table. He tried to get up quickly, but the heavy blow, together with the effects of drink, were seriously slowing his movements. Durst was on him in an instant, raining down more punches.

Even though he was a mere fraction of his opponent's size, Ethan was trained in hand-to-hand combat. He twisted and shifted with all his strength, trying to avoid being hit while maneuvering into a better position to defend himself.

After receiving a few more heavy strikes, he was at last able to turn to one side and reach into Durst's crotch. The man let out a sharp yelp of pain as Ethan's fingers squeezed tight.

The advantage briefly with him, he pushed Durst hard back and scrambled to his feet. He tried to force his way through the crowd, but before he was clear of them, thick fingers grabbed his shoulder and spun him around. Durst had recovered quickly. Way too quickly.

"You'll pay for that, boy," the furious man growled.

Another bone jarring punch landed squarely on Ethan's jaw. This one sent him crumbling to the floor. The last thing he was aware of as darkness closed in was harsh laughter and the taste of his own blood.

CHAPTER THREE

ETHAN COUGHED AND sputtered, his mouth and nose both suddenly flooded with water. His vision was blurred and his head pounded from a combination of the beating he had taken and the beer.

"Wake up, boy," called a harsh voice.

Slowly his senses began to return. He was in a small room with bars across both the door, and the solitary window. *Great*, he thought as the fog lifted. *I'm in jail.*

Wiping his face with his hands, he struggled to his knees. "What happened?"

"You got the shit beat out of you, that's what," replied a thin, scraggly man holding a now empty bucket. "And from what I hear, you deserved it. Now get on your feet and get out of here. Your uncle's waiting on you outside."

Ethan touched the welts on his face and winced.

"Yeah, Durst sure did lay it on you," the man said, laughing. "If you ask me, your uncle should have left you in here for a few days. Maybe that would teach you some respect."

Ethan reached out and pressed his hand firmly against the wall. "Durst was going to chop off that girl's hand. Why isn't he in here too?"

The man huffed. "Number one – he didn't do nothing wrong. If what I hear is right, the girl was stealing from him. Number two – we've only got one cell. And I don't think you'd really want to be sharing it with Durst. Now get on your bloody feet and get out."

Ethan heaved himself up, the effort compounding the throbbing in his head. He followed the man down a hall and into a room with a small wooden desk and a variety of swords and daggers hanging on pegs directly behind it. The door opposite was flung wide open, revealing the dim light of dawn.

"Your uncle's waiting for you outside," said the man while making his way behind the desk. "I'll tell you what I told him. I don't care how they do things in Al'Theona, while you're here you had better learn to stay out of people's business."

Ethan nodded, but did not bother replying. Stepping outside, he saw a wagon and two horses waiting. Jonas was in the driver's seat, his eyes staring straight ahead, a displeased expression on his face.

"Come on," he grumbled. "Let's get out of here before you cause us more trouble."

Ethan wanted to say something, but the fact of the matter was, he *had* caused trouble. He should never have left the inn. He should have listened and done what he was told. If he had, instead of taking a beating and waking up in jail, he might have enjoyed the pleasurable company of the young barmaid. The thought of the night that might have been caused a wry grin to form. But the pain from the swelling instantly turned the grin into a grimace.

He climbed onto the wagon. "How did you get me out?"

"I had to pay a fine," Jonas replied. "And I had to pay it with the same gold coins I wanted to avoid using."

"I'm sorry," said Ethan. "I only…"

"Save it," he hissed. "We need to get out of here before the whole town is up to watch us leave. I think we've attracted enough attention already, don't you?" He snapped the reins and the wagon lurched forward.

A few people were out and about, and all of them seemed to take notice of their departure. Jonas cursed continuously under his breath until they reached the town's edge.

"If you intend to survive, this cannot happen again," he scolded.

"But I only did it to save a little girl," Ethan protested. "That animal was going to cut off her hand. I had to do something."

Jonas sneered. "Really? You *had to*? They told me what happened. She was a thief and probably deserved it."

"What kind of people are you?" Ethan exclaimed, appalled. "She was just a little girl."

Jonas gave him a sideways glance and sighed. "I admit that things have changed. Such barbarity would not have been allowed in the days of the *five kingdoms*." He then turned his head to look directly at Ethan. "But those days are gone, and you had better learn to do as you're told. Thanks to your heroics, everyone in that blasted town will be talking about us. And as for your farmer friends…it will lead anyone who is interested straight to them. You should think about that."

Ethan's stomach knotted. He squeezed his eyes shut. "I only did what I thought was right."

Jonas sniffed. "And I suppose getting drunk and wandering about a strange town was *right*."

Ethan's guilt was slowly being replaced by anger. "That's enough. If you hadn't brought me here in the first place, I wouldn't be in this mess. It's all thanks to you I've lost my best friend and ended up stranded on this God forsaken world. And even if I do somehow manage to get back home, I'll probably end up in the stockade for desertion."

"You can't blame me for that," said Jonas, unmoved by Ethan's anger. "I only did what your mother asked of me. Nothing more. As for your friend. That was his own fault."

"His own fault? He saved your goddamn life. If he hadn't kicked that grenade, we would both be dead right now." Rising from his seat, Ethan jumped from the wagon.

"Where are you going?" Jonas demanded.

"Away from you," he replied fiercely. But it was only a single road leading north and south. After jogging in front of the wagon until he was several yards ahead, he slowed his pace.

"There's nowhere to go, Ethan," Jonas called out. But his words fell on deaf ears.

They continued like this for more than a mile. Several people passing by gave them curious looks. Jonas tried to speed up and pull the wagon beside him, but Ethan blocked his way.

"You're acting like a child," Jonas told him. "You know you have no chance on your own."

Ethan stopped dead and swung around to glare at him. "I'm an Airborne Ranger," he said. "You may think I'm just a kid, but I bet I've seen more war and death than you ever have. I survived the Krauts. I'll survive this. And I'll do it without your help."

The two locked eyes, neither wanting to blink or look away. Finally, Jonas grunted and shook his head.

"If I was overly harsh with you, I *am* sorry. But you cannot make it on your own. Regardless of how capable you are, you know *nothing* of this world. And though many things have apparently changed, I at least know the lay of the land."

Ethan didn't move for several seconds. *Make him sweat*, he thought. Only after he felt that enough time had passed to make his point did he jump back on the wagon. "You don't have any food, do you?" he asked.

Jonas reached back and produced an apple. "This will have to do until we stop." He also produce a small dagger. "And you should have this."

Ethan examined the weapon and attached it to his belt. He then devoured the whole fruit in only a few bites. The juices helped to cure the dry mouth that had been plaguing him since the moment he'd woken up. Not that he was about to tell Jonas this and give him more ammunition to berate him about the previous night's drinking. But like it or not, the fact remained that he really was much better off in the company of someone who knew the land than he would be on his own.

Jonas took a small glass container from his pocket and tossed it onto Ethan's lap. "Put some of this on your bruises. It will help to heal them."

Ethan opened the lid and instantly recoiled. "This smells awful! What the hell is it?" He dipped his finger into a thick green paste, then wiped it off on the edge of the jar.

"I'm not sure," admitted Jonas. "Normally I would take you to a healer. But as magic is outlawed, this will have to do. The woman who sold it to me said it was good for minor injuries." He glanced sideways and smiled. "Of course, you could always allow them to heal on their own. I must say they are already looking a lovely shade of purple."

Ethan took a long look at the paste before scooping out a large lump with his finger and smearing it over his worst bruises. Jonas waved his hand in front of his nose and frowned.

"Damn barbarians," he muttered. "Humans treating wounds with potions and salves like some sort of wild elf. Even the dwarves are better than this."

"It's not *that* bad," remarked Ethan.

But he soon discovered that it was. As the hours passed, the stench increased. So much so that by early afternoon it was almost unbearable. Ethan tried to wash it off in a stream they happened upon, but this only seemed to make matters worse. By sundown the smell had become so pungent, it was obvious they would be forced to camp outside. There were a few lodges along the road, but Jonas refused to approach any of them.

"We've already attracted enough attention," he growled. He had already wrapped a cloth over his face, but still felt the need to hold onto his nose for long periods. "And if I ever see the witch who sold me that foul concoction again, I'll bathe her in it."

They found a spot a few yards away from the road and made camp. Ethan could tell by the scowl on Jonas' face, and the way he checked his blanket repeatedly for insects, that he did not enjoy sleeping outdoors.

Ethan wanted to build a fire, but Jonas forbade it. At least, he did at first. Less than an hour after they had settled down, Jonas leapt up from his blanket and began jumping frantically about, beating at his chest and legs.

"What's wrong?" Ethan asked. But he already knew the answer.

"Damn bugs!" he cried. "To hell with it. I'm building a bloody fire."

Ethan suppressed a laugh. "Fine by me."

Only after they'd gathered together some dead branches and twigs did Ethan realize that he had nothing to start a fire with. But before he could mention this, Jonas knelt down and placed his hands directly above the heap of wood.

"*Illimiz*," he said, his voice barely audible. A tiny spark shot out from the tips of his fingers, instantly setting the twigs aflame. Within seconds the fire had spread to the thicker branches and a warm glow fell over the campsite.

Ethan gasped. "How did you do that?"

"Don't get too excited," said Jonas dismissively. "I can make a fire and purify water...and that's it. I have no *real* talent for magic."

"Can you teach me?"

Jonas shook his head. "I doubt it. It took me three years to learn that much, and I still don't know exactly how it works. Like I told you – I'm a servant, not a mage."

"Come on," he pressed. "You can at least *try* to show me."

Jonas furled his brow and grumbled under his breath. "Come and kneel beside me then."

Ethan's eyes lit up and he obeyed at once.

Pulling an unlit twig from the edge of the fire, Jonas placed it to one side and adopted his previous position. "Hold your hands above it like I'm doing and say *Illimiz*," he said.

"What does that mean?"

"How should I know?" he snapped. "Fire, I suppose."

Ethan did as instructed and in a clear strong voice said: "*Illimiz!*"

Nothing happened.

He cleared his throat. "*Illimiz!*"

Still nothing.

He tried several more times before sighing with exasperation. "What am I doing wrong? I'm saying it the right way, aren't I?"

"The words are meaningless," Jonas told him. "It's the power that counts. You have to feel it inside of you. The words only focus the thing you want to make happen. A real mage works simple magic without saying anything at all."

"Then can you show me how to...feel it?"

"No."

Ethan let out a loud grunt and returned to his blanket. "Then how am I supposed to learn anything?"

"To be honest, I'm not sure yet that you should," Jonas said. "I was just supposed to keep you alive. And from what I've seen of Lumnia so far, learning magic may not be in your best interests." He could see the frustration written on Ethan's face. "There's no point fretting over it now."

The crackle of the fire almost masked the sharp snapping of a twig that came from just beyond the firelight. Ethan and Jonas both instantly leapt to their feet. Jonas fumbled for his sword, but before he could draw it, a voice came from out of the darkness.

"You had better keep your mind off magic if you know what's good for you." The voice was young and distinctly female.

Jonas finally managed to unsheathe his weapon. It looked awkward in his hand, and the weight had unbalanced his footing.

"Put that away before you hurt yourself," the voice continued.

Ethan felt for his dagger, but didn't draw it. "Who are you? Why are you hiding?"

"I'm not hiding."

The voice was now coming from behind him. Ethan spun around and Jonas very nearly toppled over completely. Standing a few feet away was the young girl Ethan had saved in the tavern. Her jet black hair was bunched together in the same ponytail as before. Her pants and shirt were black as well, enabling her to easily hide in the darkness. She was not overly tall, but her thin limbs and angular features gave her the illusion of height. Ethan thought that she would likely grow into quite a fetching young woman in time. She flashed a toothy grin at Jonas' attempt to look fearsome.

"I'm not here to hurt you, old man," she said.

"Move on," commanded Jonas. "You have no business here."

Ethan glanced at Jonas and scowled. "What's wrong with you? She's just a child. Put that sword away."

After a long moment Jonas complied, albeit hesitantly. "She's the one you took a beating for?" He sniffed and spat. "Worthless street urchin. You should have left her to her fate."

The girl's nostrils flared at the jibe. "Worthless? I'll have you know that I'm worth far more than you." Her initial voice had been laden with the vocal trappings of a commoner. But now all of a sudden she sounded…haughty and somewhat authoritative. "And I know a servant when I see one. So why don't you go kiss a pig?"

Ethan coughed out a laugh before he could stop himself. "That's enough, Jonas. You're too old to fight with children."

Jonas glared furiously. "This one is about as much a child as I am. A thief is what she is."

"What's your name?" asked Ethan.

The girl pulled her eyes away from Jonas and bowed. "You can call me Kat." Her stare then shot back to Jonas. "And I *am so* a child. I'll have you know that I'm only thirteen years old. You should be ashamed of yourself...threatening a little girl."

Ethan had the distinct impression that, despite her youth, Kat possessed the street savvy of someone far older. In fact, she reminded him very much of a boy named Vinnie from his old neighborhood. His baby-faced appearance and the innocent manner he could adopt when caught doing something wrong had got him out of more than his fair share of trouble. Also, coincidentally, Vinnie was a thief. And a damn good one too.

"What can we do for you, Kat?" he asked.

"For me?" She touched her chest and smiled. "Not a thing. You already did it. But a princess always pays her debts. And I owe you my life."

Jonas burst into laughter. "A princess, you say? Princess of what? The street urchins?"

Kat's face turned red and her hands balled up into tiny fists. "Would you please tell your *servant* to shut his mouth?"

"Come on, Jonas," said Ethan. "That's enough."

"Bah..." He waved his hand and sneered.

"I'm sorry, Kat," Ethan continued. "But there's really nothing you can do for me. And we can't be taking anyone along with us."

She waited a few seconds for Jonas to add a cutting remark before replying, but this time he remained silent. "I can do plenty. And I'll start by getting that stink off of you. If you try going through the Miltino city gates smelling like that, you'll never make it." She shot an accusing glance at Jonas. "What happened? Did Miss Jillie con you into buying one of her healing salves?" She reached into her pocket and pulled out a round white disk that she tossed over to Ethan. "Wash with this. It'll get the stink off you. Your clothes are ruined though. You'll have to burn them."

"I appreciate your help," said Ethan. "I really do. But you still can't come with us."

She sat down beside the fire and crossed her arms. "How are you going to stop me?"

Jonas strode toward her, one hand extended. "That's quite enough of this foolishness! Get out of here!"

Kat jumped up, easily keeping out of his reach and laughing at his clumsy attempts to catch her. Ethan couldn't help but smile at the comical scene.

"Stop it," he said eventually. "You two look like the Keystone Cops."

They both stopped short to look at him with confused expressions.

"What's a *keystone cop*?" asked Kat.

Ethan shook his head. "Never mind. Right now, I just want to get this smell off of me."

"There's a stream about a quarter mile off the road," Kat told him. "I'll take you there."

Ethan smiled. "That would be good. Thank you."

With a furious look on his face, Jonas spun on his heels and plonked himself down beside the fire.

After digging out a fresh set of clothes, Ethan followed Kat into the night. She was seemingly unaffected by the near pitch black as she walked briskly along. Ethan, on the other hand, nearly fell on his face three times before they reached the stream.

"Wet the disc and then rub it all over you," she instructed.

Ethan began to strip off his clothing. And though he couldn't see her face, her soft gasp told him that he had embarrassed her. She turned her back and shifted anxiously.

Ethan did as she had told him. The *soap* smelled like old leather, but it was far better than the alternative, and he was grateful for the relief once he'd put on the new clothes.

"You can turn around now," he said.

Kat looked him up and down. "Your servant should get you some clothes that fit better." Reaching for her belt, she withdrew a small pouch. "Take this," she said, pressing it into his palm. "Compliments of Durst."

It took him a moment to realize the significance of her words. "You mean you went back and stole this? After he almost cut off your hand? Are you nuts?"

"I figured he had it coming," she explained without a hint of regret. "There's not much there, but it should buy you a pair of pants that fit. Just don't tell the old man about it. He'll only call me names again."

Ethan couldn't help but laugh. "Don't worry. I won't."

Kat smiled, then pulled him by the sleeve toward the camp. "And just so you know. I really *am* a princess. And like it or not, I *am* coming with you."

Ethan sighed wearily. "I suppose you can come with us as far as Miltino. But don't you have a home to go to?"

"Not anymore. I'm…in exile."

A runaway, he thought. "I see. But I bet if you went home your parents would sure be happy to see you."

"No they wouldn't." She looked directly at Ethan and stiffened her back. "And you should mind your own business."

Jonas let out a loud sigh when he saw them approaching. "So you've agreed to let her come along, I take it?"

"Just until we reach the city," he replied.

Jonas shook his head and wrapped himself in his blanket. "Bloody fool."

Kat retrieved a pack she had hidden nearby and settled down beside the fire. Ethan wanted to question her further about her parents, but the girl was fast asleep before he had the chance to say more than a few words.

Jonas was still awake and brooding, tossing small pebbles into the flames.

"I think she's a runaway," said Ethan.

"An orphan most likely," he replied. "And I would bet that she's trouble for us."

"She's a child, for God's sake. And she's alone."

Jonas sniffed. "And you think having her with us will keep her safe? If you want to protect her you should send her away…tonight. Our path is no place for children to follow. Even one as mature as she pretends to be." He turned his back and laid down. "Princess…bah…"

Ethan glanced over at the sleeping girl. Her waif-like limbs were curled up into a ball as if holding a stuffed toy or favorite pillow. How could she be looked upon as anything other than a child? What did it matter that living on her own had forced her to grow up faster than she should have to? He knew his share of kids back in New York who acted tough on the streets, yet all they really wanted was parents to protect and love them.

But the reality of the situation had to be faced. It was most unlikely that he would be able to do anything to help her. And as much as he hated to admit it, Jonas was right. If people were coming after them, she would be in danger. The guilt he felt about imperiling the farmer and his family was still a raw wound that did not need compounding. All the same, he knew that persuading Kat to leave them would be difficult - perhaps even impossible. She was certainly committed to tagging along, and he doubted very much that she would quietly accept being abandoned once they arrived in Miltino. In that case, he'd have to wait for the right opportunity to give her the slip.

He tried to sleep for a time, but his dreams were filled with images of battle. Not the familiar nightmare of D-Day - that would have been almost pleasant by comparison. What he saw now was ten times more brutal and cruel. Thousands of men were scattered upon a battlefield, moaning and begging for death. Yet death did not come to anyone. They bled and bled from exposed bowels and severed limbs, and still death was elusive. There was only the unbearable pain. Ethan found himself walking among the wounded men and tripping over their mangled forms. Each soldier he passed pleaded for help, but there was nothing he could do.

Then, in the near distance, the figure of a man appeared. The shadows hid his features, but Ethan could feel that his eyes were fixed upon him. The figure spread his arms and black flames spewed skyward, swirling like a vile maelstrom. Ethan wanted to run, but his legs were suddenly too heavy.

The fire soon covered the heavens in black death, spinning faster and faster. He could no longer see the figure, yet he somehow knew that he was still there. Next came a thunderous roar, and red flames split the black sky in two. The two powers battled for control, but the darkness was too strong and threatened to consume the light.

"Help me!" It was a strong feminine voice crying out. But from where, he couldn't tell. "I need you! He'll kill me if you don't help. He'll kill us all."

"Where are you?" Ethan shouted in response. "I can't see you."

But there was no reply. Then another tremendous roar shook the ground. A colossal dragon, this one with blood red scales and black spines all down its back, descended from the red flames and landed twenty yards in front of him. The impact nearly threw Ethan from his feet. Its piercing eyes fixed on him. *Coward.* The word was unspoken, yet he felt it clearly in his mind.

The dragon turned to where the figure had previously been standing and with tremendous strides ran headlong toward it. The creature opened its maw to spew forth a great spear of fire. But the flames had only traveled a short distance when black fire shot out of nowhere to meet it. The blackness quickly overcame the dragon's attack, and an instant later it enveloped the creature in dark flaming hell. Another roar split Ethan's ears; waves of pain racked his body. It was as if he could feel the agony the dragon was experiencing. Screaming, he dropped to his knees and covered his face with his hands.

Coward.

The word echoed in his head again and again.

Ethan sat up, heart thumping crazily and drenched in sweat. It took him a moment to realize that he was now awake. But even when he did, the feeling of dread persisted. The sun had yet to break the horizon and Kat was still sleeping soundly. Jonas, however, was awake with his arms wrapped around his knees, staring at him.

"Bad dreams?" he asked.

Ethan nodded. "You could say that."

"Care to tell me about it?"

"Not really." Ethan couldn't help but feel that sharing such intimate details with a man he didn't trust was a bad idea. "Just dreams about the war in my world."

Jonas curled his lip. "Are there dragons in your world?"

"Dragons? No."

"Then it's odd that you would talk about them in your sleep." He kept his eyes fixed. "There were rumors that your mother could see the future in her dreams, though personally I never believed it."

"I told you," Ethan snapped. "I was dreaming about the war back home."

"If you say so." Jonas stood up and stretched. "We should get moving soon."

A few minutes later Kat began to stir. Jonas distributed a breakfast of bread and some dried apricots. Kat ate greedily and even nodded a thank you to Jonas — a gesture that he did not return. By dawn they were well on their way.

Kat sat in the back of the wagon and crouched down low whenever they came across a fellow traveler.

"Afraid you'll run across someone you know?" asked Jonas.

"I'm afraid to be seen with you," she replied disdainfully.

"Then perhaps you should go your own way," he shot back. "Then you wouldn't have to worry over it."

She curled her knees into her chest. "I told you. A princess always pays her debts."

Jonas shook his head and chuckled. "Ah, yes. I almost forgot."

"How long have you been on your own?" asked Ethan.

"I'll tell you about me if you tell me more about you," she replied.

Jonas shot Ethan a quick glance of warning.

Kat laughed. "You're too nice to be an outlaw. And your servant is too soft and doughy. So I'd say...hmmm...you're on the run from the Empire." She scrutinized Ethan. "And from what I heard last night, I'd say it's because you found out that you can use magic."

Jonas stiffened. "That's enough from you. You should learn to mind your own business."

Kat shrugged. "Don't worry. I won't tell. Not as long as you keep me around, anyway. Of course, if you leave me behind, who knows what I might say? Or to whom?"

"No one would believe a whelp like you," snapped Jonas. "Say whatever you want, to whomever you want."

Kat grinned playfully. "You're probably right. Who would believe me? But I'm not the one trying to hide, am I?"

"Who says we're hiding?" Ethan jumped in quickly before Jonas could speak.

"I do," she replied. "And if you don't want to get caught, you have to promise not to leave me in Miltino."

"Why would I do that?" Ethan asked, feigning ignorance.

"Because you think I'm just a child," she answered flatly.

"You *are* a child," said Jonas. "And if not for Ethan, you'd be a dead one. So show a bit of appreciation."

Kat ignored him and kept her attention on Ethan. "You'll never get in the city without my help."

"What do you mean?" he asked.

"I know all the secret ways into Miltino. You don't."

"And why would we need to sneak in?"

She laughed and laid her head sideways on her knees. "Because you don't want to be found. And you have to register with the magistrate if you enter the city."

Ethan and Jonas exchanged worried glances.

"Oh my," said Kat. "You don't have the proper papers...do you?"

"Of course we do," Jonas lied. "But as you rightly guessed, I would rather we go unnoticed."

"Then it seems you need me after all."

Ethan cocked his head and smiled. "She's right, Jonas."

Jonas huffed but made no reply, instead focusing his attention rigidly on the road ahead.

For the rest of the journey, the time passed pleasantly enough. Ethan noticed that the longer Kat was with them, the more she began to act her age. He figured that she was unaccustomed to being treated kindly by strangers. Even on Earth, life for a street kid could be cruel.

Here, where people were permitted to lop off someone's hand without so much as a hearing, it must be downright brutal.

As the city walls came into view, Kat said that they should pull off the road and wait for night to fall. "I'll go ahead and check that the way is clear," she told them.

Jonas looked displeased but was in no position to argue.

"I don't like this," he remarked, once she'd gone. "Trusting our fate to a child thief is stupidity."

"I really don't get it," Ethan said. "Why don't you like her?"

"She's a thief. I don't like thieves. They can't be trusted."

Ethan smirked. "Well, according to her, she's a princess."

Jonas sniffed. "We'll be lucky if she doesn't turn us in to the guards."

"She won't," he assured. "She thinks she owes me."

"She *does* owe you. And that's the problem. You're going to have a very hard time getting rid of her."

Ethan was already painfully aware of this and did not need reminding of the problem. He gave a flick of the hand. "We'll worry about that later."

It was about an hour before Kat returned. Her little face was twisted into a frown.

"I hope you have gold," she said, a hint of anger in her voice.

Jonas gave a spiteful laugh. "I thought it might come to that."

"It's not my fault," she said. "They've put a sentry near the smugglers' entrance. There's never been one there before."

Jonas narrowed his eyes and scratched his chin. "And you think you can bribe him?"

"No," she replied. "But I can pay someone to create a distraction that will lure him away. The only thing is, you'll have to leave your wagon and horses behind."

Jonas scowled. "Naturally."

"We can get another one," said Ethan.

The walls of Miltino were not exactly impressive. They were old and in serious need of repair. Though roughly fifteen feet high, pits and gouges all over the crumbling facade provided plenty of hand and footholds for a climber.

"Why don't we just go over?" suggested Jonas.

"We could," replied Kat. "But the streets are patrolled at night. Especially near the wall. It's better to get caught sneaking in the back way than over the wall...I promise you." Her final words were accompanied by shudder. "Trust me. This way is much better."

The thin forest beyond the walls was spider webbed by trails and narrow roads. After crossing each one, Kat took great care to be sure no one was approaching before moving on.

As they rounded the northwest corner, Ethan spotted several torches ahead. On drawing closer he could make out a few wagons and a half dozen men lounging beside them. They were passing around a bottle.

"Damn it!" hissed Kat.

"What is it?" asked Ethan.

"Nothing," she replied. "I'll just need a little more gold than I thought."

Jonas dug into his purse and handed her two gold coins. She looked at them for a moment, frowning.

"What is this?" she asked. "These aren't imperial koronas."

"Gold is gold," he said. "Give it back if you don't want them."

She examined the coins carefully. "It had *better* be gold or we'll be in a lot of trouble."

"It's gold, girl," said Jonas. "Now go and do whatever it is you need to do."

Kat shoved the coins in her pocket. "When you see me waving, run as fast as you can toward the wagons. And if you see the sentry, make sure *he* doesn't see you."

Having issued these instructions, she dashed away along the tree line for a distance before crossing over to where the men were gathered. She spoke to them briefly, then disappeared from sight.

"Bloody fool is what I am," muttered Jonas. "Trusting our fate to a child thief."

"You need to ease off her," said Ethan. "She's trying to help us."

"It's not her intent that concerns me."

Ethan could hear the stress in his voice. "She'll be fine. Kat knows what she's doing."

"Does she?" He shook his head. "Do you think she'd be so willing to help if she knew who you really are? Or that the Emperor himself wants your head on a platter?"

"Actually, I do."

"Then you're as much a fool as she is."

"Okay. Then how would you have gotten us in?" he asked.

Jonas gave no reply.

After a few minutes they saw a man in worn leather armor carrying a torch approaching the wagons. He had a long sword on his belt and a studded helm covered his features.

"That must be the sentry," remarked Ethan.

He walked up to the other men and took a seat. Twenty minutes passed before he rose and walked away, only to return again ten minutes later.

"We should have just bribed the guards at the gate," complained Jonas.

"If it were that easy, I think Kat would have said so," remarked Ethan. "And it's a good thing she said something about travel papers. I bet we would have been caught for sure without them."

"That *did* take me by surprise," he admitted. "And it's something we must certainly attend to before we leave Miltino."

For two more hours they waited. Ethan was becoming increasingly concerned. By now, the men had lit a small fire and were passing around several more bottles. Soon the sound of their coarse drunken laughter echoed off the walls. The sentry continued to make regular stops that Ethan timed carefully - a result of his Airborne training.

He was just about to suggest that they move to a better vantage point so they could see what was beyond the row of wagons when Kat reappeared.

One of the men stood up and grabbed her by the arm. Ethan tensed. He tried to hear what they were saying, but was too far away to make out anything other than gruff tones and harsh laughter.

The man threw Kat to the ground. Ethan felt Jonas' hand grip his arm tightly.

"Fool girl," Jonas hissed.

The man drew a dagger from his belt and loomed over her. At that moment, a blond woman in a short skirt and loose blouse that exposed much of her ample bosom sauntered out from between the wagons. Kat's attacker turned to gaze at the new arrival.

The woman, seemingly unconcerned by the dagger, draped her arms around the man's neck and began whispering in his ear. A moment later three more women appeared, all of them carrying a bottle in each hand. Taking seats around the fire, the trio quickly began engaging the rest of the men in lively chatter. After only a brief hesitation, the man with the dagger put away his weapon and joined his companions.

"Now *that's* what I call a distraction," said Ethan.

Jonas relaxed his grip. "Indeed."

Kat moved away from the others and sat just beyond the glow of the fire. After approximately half an hour the women got to their feet, and, with a series of suggestive gestures, led the men away into the night. When the last one had gone, Kat waved Ethan and Jonas over.

Remembering Kat's warning, Ethan kept a sharp eye out for the sentry. But just as they reached her, he heard the soft sound of a woman's laughter coming from somewhere in the darkness. This was followed by the sound of leather and steel falling to the ground.

"The sentry will be occupied for a while yet," said Kat, grinning. "Marian will see to that."

"So you know those women?" asked Jonas with clear disapproval.

"We need to go," she said, ignoring the question. She led them between the wagons. Just on the other side of these was an archway with an open iron gate. Kat crept up to this and peered through. "Come on," she whispered when satisfied that all was clear.

After passing through the arch, they found themselves in a dank, narrow alleyway. Lining both sides were dilapidated mud brick buildings with thin slits for windows. Ethan felt his nerves on edge; he was always uncomfortable in confined spaces.

"Who were those men?" he asked.

"Some of them were off-duty guards," she replied. "The rest were *daiva* dealers."

"*Daiva?*" said Jonas.

Kat glanced back to frown at him. "Don't tell me you don't know what *daiva* is. Where are you from? The Dragon Wastes?"

Jonas scowled. "That's none of your concern."

"*Daiva* is a plant extract," she explained. "It's stronger than wine and makes you feel...well...to tell you the truth I've never tried it so I don't know for sure. But it makes people act like they're drunk."

"Drugs," said Ethan. "They sell drugs." Though he had no personal experience with such things, he was well aware of their existence. Drugs such as heroin and cocaine were everywhere in New York.

Jonas cocked his head. "Drugs? You mean people use it instead of wine?"

Kat nodded. "But it's not really like wine. It makes people crazy after a while. And the more they use it, the more they want it. Before too long they'll do anything to keep getting it."

Jonas shook his head. "Ghastly."

Crossing the end of the alley was a dimly lit street. The stench of urine and mildew told them that this was not exactly a well-to-do part of the city.

Kat gestured for them to stay back while she checked the way ahead. But just as she reached the corner, a hand shot from around the wall and grabbed her by the wrist. Ethan and Jonas sprang forward, but the hand jerked her from the alley and out of sight.

Ethan was first into the street. Just a few feet away was a stocky man with a sleeveless vest, worn trousers, and muddy boots. He was holding on tight to Kat while she jerked and twisted in a vain effort to free herself.

"Let her go," ordered Ethan.

The man flashed a crooked smile. "So this is why you wanted us away from the gate." His voice was high-pitched and raspy. "The girls were a good idea. Too bad for you that my tastes are...different."

"I said let her go," he repeated, this time more forcefully.

The man met Ethan's gaze and winked. "That's more like it. A pity he didn't send you along with the girls too." He laughed viciously. "A bit beat up though. But don't worry, lad. Ole' Hank will tend your bruises for you. Once I've tended to your friends, that is."

"If it's gold you want, I have some," said Jonas.

Hank's smile broadened. "Oh, I have no doubt about that. So many of Jared's girls wouldn't have come cheap." Reaching behind him with his free hand, he pulled out a long knife. "And I'll be having it all." He pointed the knife at Jonas' belt. "That includes that sword of yours."

Ethan assessed the situation. Jonas and Kat would be useless in a fight. Worse still, he was not very good with a knife, whereas Hank almost certainly was.

He drew out his dagger regardless. "We'll give you some gold, and then you'll let us go our own way."

"Or what, whelp?" Throwing Kat to the ground, Hank deftly tossed his knife from hand to hand. "You'll stick me?"

"No," said Jonas. "Let's just give him what he wants."

"Listen to your friend," Hank said. "And you might live to see the morning."

Ethan knew that things would be a whole lot more difficult if they were penniless. God knows what they would need to do simply to feed themselves. No - he had to stand his ground.

Hank shook his head and clicked his tongue. "Bad choice, boy."

Ethan crouched ready, holding his dagger loosely.

The sound of Jonas' sword being unsheathed cut through the air. "I hope you're better with a knife than you were with your fists," he said.

Hank lunged right, but Ethan managed to avoid the blade with surprising ease. A moment later he realized why. His attacker was not trying to cut him...yet. Hank smashed his fist into Jonas' jaw, sending him sprawling. Now the odds were even.

Ethan stepped back and slashed at Hank's chest. But the man merely shuffled away and then brought a knee swiftly up into his abdomen. With a heavy grunt Ethan doubled over, unable to breathe.

He tried to retreat, but steely fingers gripped his wrist and twisted hard. The pain was excruciating and the dagger dropped from his hand.

"Pathetic," Hank chided.

Ethan looked up to see Hank's rotten teeth bared in a vicious grin, his knife hand poised to strike. He braced himself for the killer blow that would surely follow. But it did not come. Hank's eyes suddenly shot wide and the knife slipped from his grasp. A tiny trickle of blood crept from the corner of his mouth an instant before he pitched forward, very nearly landing on top of Ethan.

Kat was standing immediately behind where Hank had been. Her eyes burned as she watched him crash face first onto the hard slates, a small dagger protruding from the back of his neck.

Ethan was stunned.

"Good work," said Jonas, who by now had struggled to his feet and was brushing himself off.

"We need to get off the streets," Kat told them sharply, her eyes still fixed on the body. "As soon as word gets out they'll come looking for us...well...they'll come looking for me, anyway." Her eyes shot to Ethan. "This pays my debt, I think."

Before Ethan could respond, she hurried away. He and Jonas were forced to run to keep up with her as they raced along the deserted cobbled streets lined mostly with warehouses and abandoned single story dwellings. The stench had lessened somewhat, but the filth of decay and poverty was still scattered everywhere.

They crossed nearly three blocks before encountering anyone, and this was only a drunk leaning against a wall, mumbling incoherently. Most of the streetlamps were either broken or missing – for which Ethan was grateful. He had no desire to be seen.

Ahead, the lights of the city were increasing. Kat halted just before they reached the next corner.

"We can stay at a friend's house tonight," she said. "But you need to find somewhere else in the morning."

"If you can just take me to an inn..." Jonas began.

"It's too late for that," she cut in. "The guards will be checking all the inns and taverns for any word on Hank's killer, and they're sure to be especially interested in newly arrived strangers. Tomorrow will be different. Then you can say that you've only just got here."

"How far is it to your friend's place?" asked Ethan.

"Not far," she told him.

They continued on around the corner with Kat just a few steps ahead. The buildings here were in far better repair. Lights in the windows and the sounds of people talking and laughing within gave this area a far better atmosphere. Men dressed in tidy pants and pressed shirts, some of them escorting women in decent looking dresses and with well-kept hair, told Ethan that this was a working class area – not altogether unlike the one in which he grew up. The scent of urine was almost nonexistent, and every lamp was lit and glowing cheerfully. As the wagons and carriages passed by, he was reminded of old pictures he'd seen of New York, taken when his father was a child in the days before the streets had become clogged by cars.

They passed several taverns along the way. Music from flutists and singers carried on the air, helping to ease a little of Ethan's anxiety. But this respite was short-lived. A patrol of armed soldiers marched past them in quick step, their weapons and armor clanking and jingling as they moved along. They were heading in the direction that he and the others had just come from.

Kat was even more aware of the danger. She took hold of Ethan's hand. "We need to move quickly."

They made their way down several more blocks until reaching an area that consisted mostly of modest wooden houses and a few shops. She stopped just across from a two story dwelling on their left. The front was illuminated by a lantern hanging above the door, and a flight of steps on the side of the house led down to a basement.

Kat watched for more than a minute before leading them rapidly across the street and down the steps. As fast and quietly as she could manage, she pushed open the door. The room beyond was pitch dark. For a brief spell Ethan felt Jonas' hand grabbing at his sleeve for support, but in no time at all Kat had lit a small lantern and closed the curtains across the only window.

The interior was spacious enough for them to be comfortable, though a sofa and two cots were the only furnishings. Several cabinets and crates lined the opposite walls, along with two large barrels. Ethan supposed this place was used mostly for storage.

"We can sleep here," Kat told them. She was already making herself comfortable on the sofa. "I don't have any food though."

"We're fine," said Ethan. "Aren't we, Jonas?"

Jonas surveyed his surroundings and frowned. "It will do, I suppose."

Kat huffed, then rolled over.

"Whose house is this?" Ethan asked her, taking a seat on one of the cots.

She reached behind her to dim the lantern. "What difference does it make?"

Jonas laid down on the other cot. "Get some sleep," he told Ethan. "Save your questions for the morning."

Ethan sighed and reluctantly complied. However, just a few minutes later the sound of footfalls descending the steps had them all on their feet. It was at that moment Ethan realized he had left his dagger in the street beside Hank's body. He gave a soft growl of frustration. How could he have been so careless and stupid?

The door opened to reveal an elderly woman. She was dressed in nightclothes, and her silver hair was wrapped loosely beneath a cotton cap. In one hand she held a lamp, and in the other a small knife.

"Get out of here!" she ordered. "Or I'll call the guards."

"It's me," Kat called over.

The old woman strained her eyes into the gloom further back. "Kat? What in blazes are you doing here? If Jared catches you…"

"He already knows I'm back in Miltino," she said.

The new arrival's eyes returned to Ethan and Jonas. "So who are these two?"

Kat introduced them; they both bowed respectfully.

"Well, if you're Kat's friends then you're welcome to stay the night," she said. "I'm Mildred. If you need anything, just ask." She turned back to the young girl. "But why did you come down here? You could have knocked."

"I had some trouble," she explained. "I didn't want to get you involved."

Mildred scowled and shot an accusing glance at Ethan and Jonas. "Did it have anything to do with Jared?"

"No," she answered. "It's nothing to do with him. I swear. And he doesn't know I'm staying here tonight."

Mildred sneered. "I'm not worried about him, my dear. He's all talk. If he comes here he'll wish he hadn't. All the same, you shouldn't have come back. You know what could happen."

Kat reassured her with a fragile smile. "I'll deal with it when the time comes."

There was a long pause. Ethan could see the concern on the old woman's face.

"Are you hungry?" she asked.

"No thanks," Kat replied. "We're fine."

Mildred sighed. "If you say so. I'll bring you something in the morning then." She gave Kat a fond embrace. "But I want you to get out of Miltino as soon as you can."

"I promise," she said.

Ethan and Jonas thanked the woman once again before she left.

Ethan considered asking Kat why Mildred had said she shouldn't have returned, but the girl was already laying on the sofa with her back turned.

Sleep came slowly to him, but it eventually arrived. And when it did, the stress of the day ensured a dreamless slumber.

*

Jonas woke to the sound of stifled sobs. The lamp was still shining, albeit very dimly, and he could see that Ethan was still fast asleep. He could also make out the frail form of Kat laying on the sofa, her body quivering as she tried to suppress her cries. He rose as quietly as he could and crept across the room. Nevertheless, Kat heard him coming and her sobs instantly ceased. Jonas sat on the edge of the sofa and stared down at her.

"Go away," she demanded.

"Why are you crying?" he asked. The harsh tone he had used with her up until now was gone, replaced with one of kindness and compassion.

She turned her head. "What do you care?"

"Who says that I do? I'm just curious."

Kat stared at him for a long moment, trying to look defiant and strong. It was a losing battle. Eventually her tears began to flow again.

"I've...I've never killed anyone before," she whispered.

This struck Jonas. He had not considered how she would feel about causing the death of Hank. Her attitude and resourcefulness made it easy to forget that she was only a child.

"You didn't have a choice."

"I know." She wiped her eyes. "But I can't get the picture of it out of my head."

Jonas brushed her hair from her face. "I really do understand. I've had to kill before as well."

"You?" she said doubtfully. "How?"

Jonas laughed softly. "I may not be very good with a blade, but that isn't the only way to kill someone, my dear."

She looked at him thoughtfully. "So how did you get over it?"

He tilted his head and shrugged. "I didn't. Not really. After it happened, it was on my mind constantly. But as time passed it gradually got easier until eventually I learned to live with what I'd done."

Kat frowned. "So you're saying there's nothing I can do for now? How is that supposed to help?"

"It's not," he replied flatly. "I'm not going to lie to you and say that it will all be better in the morning. You're too grown up for that, I think. But know that the pain *will* subside in time. You'll learn to cope with the fact that we often have to do things we hate in order to survive." He paused. "But that's a lesson you've already learned, isn't it?"

Kat nodded. Her tears had ceased.

"Now tell me one more thing and I'll let you get to sleep." He locked eyes with her. "Who is Jared?"

"No one," she replied, but her lie was obvious as she turned her head away.

"You can tell me," he assured her. "I won't say anything to Ethan if you don't want me to."

After a moment her eyes shifted to Ethan's sleeping silhouette, then back to Jonas. "He runs a brothel. I used to work for him."

His eyes narrowed and his jaw clenched. "Doing what?"

"I'm a thief remember? I used to steal things and give him part of what I took."

Jonas relaxed somewhat. "And what did you get in return for this?"

"Protection," she replied. "The guards and the *daiva* dealers left me alone."

"Why did you run? What changed?"

Kat's lips quivered. "I – I became a woman."

It took Jonas a moment to understand what she was getting at. "You mean, you bled?"

She nodded. "I tried to hide it, but Jared found out anyway. Mildred hid me here for a few days until I was able to slip out of the city unseen."

"And now that he knows you're back, what will happen?"

"He'll try to force me to do *daiva* until I can't live without it." The fear in her voice was increasing with each word. "Then he'll…he'll make me one of his girls."

Jonas grunted with a combination of anger and disgust. "Then Mildred is right. You should leave right away."

"I can't," she replied. "Hank was a member of the Hareesh. No one can get out for now. Not until things calm down."

Jonas didn't bother to ask about the Hareesh. Obviously they were some sort of criminal organization. Gazing down at her frail form, he thought that Kat had told him enough for now.

He stood up and gave her a stern look. "I want you to stay with us until I tell you differently. Understand?"

She cocked her head. "Why? I thought you didn't want me around?"

"I don't," he replied. "But there are some things I just can't abide." He returned to his cot. "Don't think this means I've changed my mind about you. You're still nothing but a thieving street urchin."

"And you're still a worthless, mean hearted servant," she shot back, though without very much conviction in her voice.

Jonas fought back a smile as he lay down. But the moment quickly passed. It was taking a great effort to quell the rage he felt for this Jared fellow. To force a young girl into becoming a whore was… unforgivable. Such crimes would have been severely punished when Lord Dragonvein lived.

He squeezed his eyes tightly shut. *Absolutely unforgivable.*

CHAPTER FOUR

THE MORNING BROUGHT the sounds of a bustling city into the small room. Jonas was already up and waiting patiently for the others to rouse.

Ethan rubbed his eyes and stretched. "I don't know about you, but I'm starving. I hope Mildred remembers to bring us some food. "

Jonas made no reply to this comment. Instead, he said quite abruptly: "I think we should keep Kat with us for a while longer."

Ethan cocked his head. "I thought you said…"

"I know what I said. But we may need her help. She knows the city, and we don't."

"For how long?" Ethan asked.

"Until we reach the next town. She got us in. We might need her to get us out again."

"Have you asked her if she even *wants* to come along?"

"No, he hasn't," Kat's voice chipped in. She was still lying with her back to them. "And being that my debt is now paid, tell me why I should go anywhere with you?"

"You don't have to come if you don't want," said Ethan.

She rolled over to look at them. "And if I don't, you'll both end up dead." She sat up and scratched her head vigorously. "I figure that you lied about having papers, so you'll be needing fakes. I can tell you where to get them. And I know which guards are honest and which ones can be bribed."

"So you'll stay?" Ethan asked.

"For now," she answered through an exaggerated yawn.

A short time later Mildred came down with a tray bearing three bowls of porridge and cups of honeyed water.

"I'm going to the market later," said Mildred. "But I'll leave the back door open for you."

"Don't bother," Kat said. "I won't be coming back."

Mildred nodded. "Good." She turned to Jonas. "Will you get her out of the city?"

"If I can, I will," he replied. "You have my word."

Mildred gave Kat a final embrace. "You take care, young lady."

"I will," she promised.

Ethan and Jonas thanked Mildred for her help yet again before she left, then hungrily set about their breakfasts. Once done, Kat led them back up onto the street. By now it was already mid-morning and hundreds of people were swarming along the sidewalks and avenues.

"Miltino is more populated than I remember," remarked Jonas. He was doing his best to follow Kat as she headed west.

"Lately people have been coming in from the country looking for work," she told him over her shoulder. "Easy pickings for a good thief."

Jonas frowned. "You will kindly refrain from stealing while you're in our company. We don't need the trouble."

Kat flashed a mischievous grin. "I'll do my best." She held up a coin purse. The strings had been cut. "Starting now."

Ethan couldn't help but be impressed. He had not seen her do anything, yet she had been able to swipe a purse with both he and Jonas never more than a few feet behind her.

Jonas grumbled. "Don't make me regret this."

She tossed the purse to Ethan and winked. "I won't."

After a few blocks the houses gave way to small shops and taverns. Vendors of every description were noisily calling out their wares, while street musicians and beggars blocking the walkway made it impossible to move swiftly.

Kat halted in front of a small inn with a sign that read *The Heart's Haven*. "The inn keeper here won't ask too many questions as long as you keep to yourself," she told them. "And the food's not bad either."

Jonas eased past her and opened the door. She stepped in behind him, closely followed by Ethan.

Only a few lanterns hanging from hooks on the wall illuminated the large room, and it took a moment for Ethan's eyes to adjust to the dim light. To his left, three long dining tables had been placed side by side next to a smoke-stained fireplace. The walls were sparsely decorated with faded paintings and placards, and the clanking of pots and pans carried out from a door just beyond the front desk where a tall, thin man stood reading a tattered book.

He looked up and put down his book. "Three of you, is it?"

Jonas nodded.

"Three coppers per night for one room, five for two," he continued. "Breakfast and dinner are included, but if you want midday meals it's extra."

"Sounds fair," said Jonas.

"That's in advance," he added.

Jonas produced two silver coins. "I'm not sure how long we'll be staying."

The man jingled the coins in his hand and shrugged. "As long as you need." He reached beneath the counter and retrieved a couple of keys. "Follow me."

He led them to the far end of the dining hall and through a narrow door. Their rooms were only a few doors down on the right. The innkeeper handed Jonas the keys.

"You've missed breakfast," he said. "And dinner won't be 'til sundown."

Jonas nodded, then gave the man an extra copper who took it without courtesy.

The rooms were barren of décor, each furnished with only one large bed, a chair, and a single dresser. Kat raced inside the first one and jumped on the bed, bouncing playfully on her knees. "I think you two have some shopping to do," she said. "I'll be fine here."

"Shopping for what?" asked Ethan.

"Clothes," Jonas told him.

Ethan took stock of his ill-fitting attire. Yes. It was bad enough that his face looked like he had been in a prize fight. He did not need to give the appearance of having stolen someone else's clothes as well.

After stowing their small packs in the next room, they left the inn together. It didn't take long to find shops well suited to their needs. Ethan still had the coins Kat had swiped, and though he felt a bit guilty, used them to purchase a few comfortable shirts, pants, decent walking boots, and a new dagger.

It was well into the afternoon before they were finished, and the thought of supper had both of their stomachs growling as they made their way back to the inn. On drawing close, they saw a short, thin man with stringy black hair and dark complexion standing beside the front door. He was wearing a red shirt with white pants and well-shined boots, all clearly tailored to fit. In one hand he held a mug, while the other was fidgeting with a small silver knife.

Ethan tensed. There was something about him - something sinister that warned him this was a man not to be taken lightly, in spite of his slight build. Jonas slowed his pace.

The man caught sight of the duo approaching and flashed a toothy smile. "Ah. You must be the companions of my dear friend Kat." He looked them up and down. "You fit the description perfectly."

Ethan now regretted not changing his clothes in the shop. Jonas had suggested that he do so, but the lack of a private changing room had allowed his modesty to get the better of him.

"Kat?" said Jonas. "I don't know anyone by that name."

The man chuckled and drained his mug. "Allow me to introduce myself. I am Jared. She might have mentioned me."

Jonas' eyes were burning. "Like I said, I don't know anyone named Kat."

Ignoring the obvious lie, Jared continued: "When you see her, tell her that she needs to come see me...soon." He glanced at Jonas' sword, his tone now turning dark and menacing. "That's a very nice blade you have there. I wonder...can you use it?"

With the implied threat still hanging, he tossed the empty mug at Jonas and strode briskly away.

Ethan watched as Jared disappeared into the crowded walkway. Jonas threw the mug down, shattering it to pieces.

"Bloody lowlife scum," he snarled.

They hurried inside and headed directly for Kat's room. It was empty.

"She must have gotten out before he arrived," Ethan said, the relief in his voice clear.

"No," came a voice from behind him. It was Kat. Her smile was unable to hide the fear in her eyes. "When Jared came I hid under the bed."

Ethan looked at her incredulously. "Didn't he look there?"

She shrugged. "Nope. Must be my lucky day."

"I need to have a word with the innkeeper," Jonas growled. His face was tight as he stalked away.

Kat jumped on the bed. "It's not the innkeeper's fault. Jared doesn't take no for an answer."

"Well, at least he didn't find you," Ethan said. "What does he want anyway?"

She frowned. "I don't care what he wants. I'm finished with him."

Ethan could sense that she didn't wish to speak further on the matter, so he let it drop. Jonas returned a few minutes later with a satisfied look on his face.

"We need to acquire travel papers as soon as possible," he announced.

Kat directed him to a tavern and told him to inquire with a bartender named Loni.

"It's best you stay here with Kat in case this Jared fellow returns," Jonas said before leaving. "If I don't make it back by morning…well… just get out of Miltino and stay hidden as best you can until I find you."

Once he had gone, Ethan stepped out briefly to collect their meals. They ate together in Kat's room, though conversation was guarded. It was clear that neither of them wished to divulge too much information.

Several hours passed. By now, Ethan was growing increasingly concerned that Jonas had not yet returned. Kat, on the other hand, had fallen asleep with a tiny smile on her face.

Ethan was just about to go back to the common room when the door opened. Jonas entered, his expression unreadable.

"Five days," he muttered while sitting down on the edge of the bed. "He said it would take at least that long to get our papers. And I heard people talking about Hank's murder. The city guards are questioning everyone."

"Then we should stay inside," suggested Ethan.

"Yes," he agreed. "But not here. Jared knows where we are, and I would bet that sooner or later they'll question him as well. He can lead them right to us."

"So what should we do?"

"I checked out a few other places where we can stay," he replied. "We'll move from inn to inn until it's time to leave."

"Then what?"

Jonas reached in his shirt and pulled out a map. He placed a finger on the dot representing Miltino and moved it along a road leading out of the city. We'll go north until we reach Branz. Then northwest across country to the mountains."

"What's in the mountains?"

"Dwarves." He folded the map and tossed it onto the dresser. "At least, I hope there's still dwarves there. But we can discuss that later. Right now, I need rest."

Pulling off his boots, he settled into the room's only chair and within minutes was snoring loudly. Ethan laid down on the bed beside Kat and closed his eyes, but sleep did not come so easily for him. It took more than an hour to finally drop off, and when he did, his dreams were filled with visions of fire and death. Dragons fell from the sky, consumed by dark flames.

In the morning his clothes were drenched in sweat and his muscles ached from a night of constant tension. On glancing around the room he saw that Jonas was already up and packed. Kat, meanwhile, was tying her hair in a ponytail, humming softly.

On their way out, Jonas had a quiet word with the innkeeper, then led them to their next destination. They spent the day in their rooms, only coming out to eat.

For the next four days they moved from inn to inn. Ethan was relieved that they saw no sign of Jared, and that the city guards they encountered took no interest in them. Kat suggested that Hank's death was perhaps now being handled by the Hareesh directly, being that he was one of their own.

It was just after dinner when a message came that their travel papers were at last ready.

"We should leave tonight," said Jonas. "I've had just about enough of Miltino."

Both Ethan and Kat agreed and began packing their belongings while Jonas went off to collect the papers. By the time he returned they were eager to be going.

The way to the north gate took them through a much more affluent section of the city. The streets were immaculate and extremely well lit by highly polished brass lanterns that hung from posts every few yards. Ethan could not help but be impressed by the elegance of the surroundings. The elaborate wrought iron fences enclosing lovingly cared for gardens, and the houses – some as tall as three stories – were every bit as beautiful as the English manors he had seen during his time there.

When they were only a few blocks from the main avenue leading to the gate, three men who at first they thought to be city guards approached from the opposite direction.

"Imperials," hissed Kat as they drew near. She slowed her pace and fell in behind Ethan.

Ethan's heart immediately began to race. He reached back to take her hand, but discovered that she was gone. He quickly scanned the area but couldn't see her anywhere. The soldiers were already upon them and blocking their path. They were clad in chain mail jerkins and polished black greaves. Atop their heads were black leather helms crowned with a crimson raven.

The soldier in the center glared at them. "Destination?"

"Nowhere in particular," Jonas replied. "Just out for a walk."

"Papers," he demanded, thrusting out a gauntleted hand.

Jonas and Ethan produced their false documents at once. Beads of sweat were beginning to form on Ethan's brow as the soldier examined them.

He handed the papers to the man on his left. "And now you can tell me why you are carrying these forgeries." His hand shot to the hilt of his sword.

"They're not..." Jonas began.

He was cut short. "They're good enough to fool those idiots at the gate, but not me. Now tell me where you are going and who you really are...now."

The other two soldiers also placed their hands threateningly on their weapons.

As Jonas struggled to find some authentic sounding story, a voice called out from across the street, cutting through the tension.

"Ah! There you are."

All eyes turned to see a tall, broad shouldered man in black leather armor and with a long sword at his side trotting over to them. He had dark curly hair and a close cropped beard. What could be seen of his face was terribly scarred and weathered, giving him an imposing and somewhat sinister appearance.

"Get back, citizen," shouted the guard.

The man halted in the middle of the street to regard Jonas and Ethan. "Did you try passing off those ridiculous papers to these men?" He shook his head and clicked his tongue. "You are a couple of fools, for certain."

"You know these two?" asked the soldier.

"Of course," he replied. "They are wanted by the Hareesh for questioning."

The soldier spat on the ground. "I should have guessed that by the very look of you. Well, you can tell the Hareesh that they're coming with us. And if they don't like it, they can go to hell."

The man chuckled. "I was afraid you might say that."

The newcomer's hand was a blur as he reached for his belt. Before any of the soldiers could react, a small dagger whipped through the air and sank into the middle soldier's exposed throat. The other two stared at their dying comrade, momentarily stunned.

By the time they had recovered, the man was already across the street with sword drawn. Frantically, they reached for their own weapons, but two swift blows opened up massive wounds in their necks – the second one of these very nearly removing the head completely.

The man stepped back and watched the bodies fall. "You've got to love Imperial arrogance."

Utterly astonished, Ethan and Jonas simply stood there, unable to move or speak.

"Snap out of it," the man told them. His eyes swept around. "Where is the girl who was with you?"

The mention of Kat brought Ethan back to his senses. "What girl?"

The newcomer sniffed. "It doesn't matter. Come with me unless you want to end up in an Imperial prison."

Jonas planted his feet firmly. "We're not going anywhere with you."

He shrugged. "Suit yourself. But you won't get far with the Hareesh on your trail."

"I...I thought –" stuttered Ethan.

"Not a good time to be thinking," said the man. "Someone is bound to walk by here soon. And you don't want to be anywhere near these bodies when they're discovered."

After a few seconds impatiently waiting, he sheathed his weapon and threw up his hands. "Fine. Stay here then."

He strode off with Jonas making no move to follow. Ethan took another look around, hoping to see Kat.

"I think we should go with him," he said.

"Are you insane?" Jonas responded, then quickly shook his head. "Don't answer that."

Ethan glared at him for a second or two. "I'll go on my own then," he said, setting off after what he hoped was their rescuer. Letting out an exasperated grunt, Jonas followed.

"Who are you?" Ethan asked after catching up.

"They call me Specter," he replied.

"Why did you help us?" asked Jonas, full of suspicion.

"Let's just say I'm not a fan of the Imperials. I knew they were looking for someone."

Specter stopped short and pulled them both into the shadow of a tall hedge surrounding a particularly large manor. Three young men in silk finery walked by laughing drunkenly and talking of their night at the tavern. When they were out of sight, Specter continued.

"I heard that they were looking for two strangers leaving Jaobin. And when Hank turned up dead, it didn't take me long to find you."

"We had nothing to do with that," Jonas protested.

"Really?" he mocked. "That's a shame, because I always hated him. Anyway, the girl was the one who really helped me to find you. Jared is going crazy about that one. He's turning over every bloody stone in Miltino. When I spotted her, I knew you'd likely be nearby."

Ethan listened intensely to every word Specter was saying. There was something about the man – his mannerisms and voice seemed familiar. And though his face was badly scarred, his eyes were friendly and kind.

"That still doesn't explain why you helped us," Jonas said. The anxiety in his voice was growing. "Are you with the Hareesh?"

Specter laughed. "Of course I am. But like I said, I have no love for the Empire. And if they want you, I want to know why."

Jonas raised a hand. "In that case we must part ways here."

Specter looked him directly in the eye. "Believe me, I have no intention of allowing the Empire to get their hands on you. And I couldn't care less about Hank. The papers you bought, which by the way, you forgot to take from the guard's body, were worthless. So you can either come with me or wait to get captured. At least with me you stand a chance."

"I'll go with you," said Ethan.

"Smart boy," he replied.

Jonas considered this new situation for a few moments, then his shoulders sagged. "This is a bad idea, Ethan. But if you're going to follow this…person, I guess I must do so as well."

With the matter settled, Specter turned and led them down a series of side streets and narrow alleys until they reached an area not far from where they had entered the city. He pointed to a large brick building at the end of the avenue. Two men were guarding the entrance, and even from more than a hundred yards away they could hear the sounds of harsh laughter and merrymaking issuing forth.

"Stay silent until we're inside," he ordered.

"Where are we?" asked Ethan.

"Home sweet home," Specter replied with a roguish grin.

CHAPTER FIVE

THE GUARDS BY the entrance gave Specter a sideways glance and then moved aside.

He pushed open the door and paused. "Evening boys."

The two men didn't bother to respond. Specter chuckled and continued on inside. Directly beyond the entrance was a long hall with a series of doors on either side. Lamps along the corridor were bright enough to reveal the stains and blemishes on the floor – some of which Ethan easily recognized as being dried blood.

The muffled sounds of laughter and songs increased as they wound their way through the building. Ethan tried to make a mental note of their route, but it seemed as if the place had been designed specifically to be confusing.

Eventually they reached a stairwell that led down into a basement – which was the apparent source of the merrymaking. At the bottom they came to a thick wooden door with a covered slot at eye level. Specter knocked. The slot slid open almost immediately.

"Oh, it's you," came a voice from the other side. "What do you want?"

"To kick your teeth in if you don't open the door," replied Specter.

After a short pause, the door slowly opened. Beyond it was a large room filled with dozens of unpleasant looking men and women all seated at tables, drinking and laughing. At the far end, raised up slightly on a small platform, stood a beautifully crafted oak chair. Though currently unoccupied, Ethan imagined that this was where the leader of this band of miscreants sat.

The man who had opened the door was staring at Specter with a hateful sneer.

"Who's this," he asked, pointing at Ethan and Jonas. "You can't just bring whoever you want down here. Or do you think the rules don't apply to you?"

Specter lowered his head and smiled. "Let me show you what applies to me, Lark." In a blur of motion his fist shot out and connected solidly on the side of the man's jaw. Such was the force, he spun almost completely around before falling hard on his face.

Ethan was dumbstruck by the sudden outburst of violence.

"We should get out of here," Jonas whispered in his ear.

Specter pushed the door closed. "I'm afraid it's far too late for that my gullible friends."

Ethan's heart froze. "What do you mean?"

"I mean you should have listened to your companion." He drew a dagger from his belt. "I'll have your weapons, purses and packs, if you please."

Ethan's eyes darted back and forth. There was nowhere to run. Specter blocked the door and dozens of armed men were on the other side.

"Do as he says," Jonas instructed. He removed his sword and purse.

Ethan glared angrily. "So you lied to us?"

Specter threw his head back in laughter. "Of course I did. Otherwise I would have had to knock you both out and carry you back here all by myself. That's way too much work. Far better to have you walk."

"But why?" Ethan demanded while handing over his dagger and money.

"Gold, dear boy. Gold."

Once Specter had gathered all their possessions, he instructed Lark to have them taken to the cells. Not wanting to risk another thrashing, the man obeyed without complaint.

He gave a loud whistle. Seconds later three armed men arrived and forced them through the crowd to the other side of the room. There,

Ethan saw a large iron door. An older man with a long scraggly grey beard and the creases of age carved deeply into his face was sitting on a stool just beside it. When he saw the group approaching he hastily unlocked the door and stepped aside. One of their escorts gave it a hard shove.

With a loud screech, the door swung open. As they stepped through, Ethan was confronted by a series of small cages, each just large enough to accommodate one person.

"I'm sorry," he murmured.

Jonas said nothing.

They were placed in cells directly across from one another. As the men left and the main door boomed shut, Ethan fought back the desire to weep. His arrogance and dislike for Jonas had led them here. And now they would likely die.

"We're not dead yet," Jonas said, sensing his despair.

The room was lit by a single lantern hanging beside the door. But even in this dim light Ethan could see that there was only one way in or out.

The time dragged by. How long they sat there, he couldn't tell. But after a while the voices outside became quiet. When the door was eventually reopened by a young man bringing them a scrap of bread and cup of water each, Ethan could see that the room beyond was now empty.

"How long are we to be kept here?" Jonas asked. But the boy only shook his head and hurried away immediately after passing them their food.

Reluctantly they ate the meager repast and eventually, when their fatigue overcame their fear, both of them fell asleep.

"Wake up!"

Ethan stirred and cracked open his eyes. Standing just outside his cell was Specter. He was holding two sets of shackles.

"Time to talk to Thrace," he said. He looked back at Jonas who was struggling to his feet. "You too, old man."

Ethan spat on the floor and then held out his hands. Once he and Jonas were both secured, Specter led them back into the main hall.

The tables had been moved against the walls to create space. At least a hundred men had formed a semicircle around the ornate oak chair Ethan had noticed previously. This was now occupied by a muscular man with a bald head and a patch over his right eye. A large gold hoop hung from his left ear, and his face was tattooed with intricate spiraling patterns. A sword with a jewel encrusted hilt leaned casually against the chair's arm. Ethan could only assume that this was Thrace.

"So this is your bounty, Specter?" Thrace asked.

He shoved Ethan and Jonas roughly forward so that they were directly in front of the leader. "It is."

After scrutinizing them for an uncomfortably long moment, Thrace smiled, revealing three gold teeth. "I must say...they don't look like anyone the Empire would burn a whole town over." His eyes fixed on Ethan. "Do you know who I am, boy?"

Ethan shook his head.

"Specter didn't tell you?"

"Only that your name is Thrace," he replied, trying not to sound meek.

"That's right. I'm the leader of this band of vermin." He looked to the crowd. "Isn't that right boys?"

His words were met with shouts of approval and harsh laughter.

"Specter tells me that you're the reason Imperial soldiers burned Jaobin to the ground. Is this true?"

Ethan felt a knot in the pit of his stomach. His thoughts turned to the farmer and his family.

"We had nothing to do with that," Jonas interjected. "We're just trying to head north to find work."

"The look on your young friend's face tells me that you're lying," Thrace remarked. He leaned back in his chair. "Now here's my dilemma. It appears that Specter has taken it upon himself to kill three Imperial soldiers just to get his hands on you. This creates a big problem for me. The Empire doesn't like it when their people are murdered, so they'll be looking for whoever did it. That hurts business. Of course, Specter assures me that the bounty on your heads will be well worth it."

"There is no bounty," said Jonas. "He's a liar."

Thrace smiled. "Oh, I'm sure he is. In fact, he's known for it. But I don't think he's lying about you. Are you, Specter?"

"You know I'm not," he replied sharply.

"Now Specter has not earned himself many friends in the Hareesh," Thrace continued. "But he is a mighty good earner. So what do I do? Do I turn him in to the Empire? Or do I let him take you to the garrison for the bounty?"

"Enough of this, Thrace," barked Specter. "You'll get your cut when I return."

"You're assuming I *want* you to return," Thrace countered. His jaw tightened and his fists clenched. "Your stupidity might bring us all to the hangman's noose. What were you thinking? You don't kill Imperials."

"No one other than the Hareesh knows it was me," he said. "There were no witnesses other than these two, and who would believe them?"

Thrace glared for a moment, but his posture gradually relaxed. "You'll have your bounty, Specter. But there is another matter that must be addressed. Hank's murder."

Specter's top lip curled. "Hank was a dim witted fool. Who knows how he ended up dead?"

"*I* know how," came a voice from the crowd.

Ethan turned and saw Jared pushing his way through.

"Yes," said Thrace. "You said you had information about that, didn't you?"

"I'm not sure exactly who did it," Jared continued. "But I know that these two were involved. Kat snuck them into the city using my girls as a distraction."

Thrace laughed and shook his head. "Well, that certainly wouldn't have worked on Hank. But how do you know they were involved? It could have been anyone."

"I'm not sure," admitted Jared. "But I bet you could get them to talk if you wanted."

"I'll not have my bounty damaged," Specter protested.

Jared shot him a furious look. "They have stolen my property. I want to know what they have done with it."

It took Ethan a moment to realize that he was referring to Kat. "She's not your property," he shouted.

"If I were you, I'd keep that mouth of yours shut," warned Thrace.

"None of this matters," said Specter. "I'm not going to hand over my bounty just so he can find his missing whore."

"She's not a whore," snapped Ethan.

In a single step, Specter spanned the distance between them and struck him hard on the jaw. Ethan stumbled back, nearly losing his footing completely. Pain shot through his head from the blow – pain that was compounded by the stress to his existing bruises that were only now just beginning to fade.

Thrace chuckled. "I warned you, boy." His eyes shifted back to Jared. "Unfortunately for you, Specter is right. A runaway whore is no reason to give up a bounty. And unless you're prepared to fight him for it, I think you're shit out of luck."

Specter flashed a sinister grin. "Yes, you could fight me. I'd enjoy that…very much."

Jared's eyes burned with rage. "This isn't over," he declared loudly. With a final, hate-filled glare at his tormentor, he spun on his heels and stalked out of the room.

"One more thing, Specter," said Thrace. "I want you to take Thaddeus along with you." He plastered on a fake smile. "Just for security."

His displeasure obvious, Specter snatched Ethan and Jonas by their chains and threw them back toward the iron door. Caught out by the momentum, Jonas lost his feet and hit the floor hard. Ethan bent down to help the old man, but Specter pushed him again, this time sending him slamming into the wall. After dragging Jonas roughly to his feet, Specter bundled them both back into their cells.

Ethan held out his hands so that Specter could remove the shackles, but he simply turned and left.

"Are you all right?" asked Ethan.

"I've had worse," Jonas replied.

Ethan gingerly touched his face where Specter had hit him and sucked air through his teeth. "Markus always said my mouth would get me into trouble."

"It would seem he was right," Jonas shot back in a distinctly sour tone.

In spite of the barb, Ethan laughed. He sat down and leaned against the bars, trying his best not to think about what was going to happen next...or the cruel fate that had befallen the people of Jaobin. *These Imperial soldiers are no better than the damn Krauts*, he thought. He closed his eyes and relaxed his breathing. But sleep would not come, and soon the shackles were biting into his flesh.

"As long as we can still draw breath, there's hope," Jonas said softly.

"I know," he replied.

CHAPTER SIX

THE DOOR TO the two story bordello flew open with a mighty crash from Jared's kick. As he stormed inside, the dozen or so girls gathered there gasped in unison at the sight of their infuriated boss and scrambled to get out of his way.

He paused after a few steps to survey the area. To his right was a small waiting room with cheaply made chairs and a few small tables scattered about. Empty mugs and wine bottles left over from the previous night's activities littered every available surface, and the scent of stale beer saturated the air.

"Get off your lazy asses and clean this place up!" he roared. "It's disgusting in here."

The girls instantly obeyed, rapidly clearing the tables and straightening the chairs. Still scowling, Jared continued on until he reached a door at the far end. He tried the handle, but it was locked.

"Brutis is still sleeping," said a tiny voice behind him.

Spinning around, Jared let his hand fly. It connected hard with the cheek of a young blond girl no more than twenty years old. Her thin frame was sent sprawling to the floor. With tears in her eyes, she scurried across the stained carpet into the nearest corner. Jared watched her cower with satisfaction.

"Brutis!" he yelled, banging on the door.

There was the sound of a muffled curse from inside, followed by a loud crash. A few seconds later the door cracked open and a head poked halfway out. Brutis was at least a full foot taller than Jared, with close cropped black hair and a square jaw.

"Get up and get the boys together," ordered Jared.

Brutis rubbed his eyes. "What happened?"

"Specter," he spat. "That's what happened. He's crossed me for the last time."

"You're going to kill Specter?" asked Brutis.

"No," he replied. "You are."

Brutis heaved a sigh. "Are you sure you...?"

"I don't pay you to ask questions, you lumbering moron," Jared snapped. "Just do what you're told."

Having issued his orders, he turned on his heels and headed to the stairs, muttering curses along the way. He paused halfway up and snapped his fingers. The room instantly went silent.

"When I come back down, this place had damn well better be clean," he warned.

With the girls feverishly redoubling their efforts, he continued upstairs and down a long hall lined on either side by poorly furnished bedrooms. After turning right, he unlocked a door at the far end.

His office was as much a mess as the rest of the bordello. Old wine bottles and papers were strewn carelessly all over the tables and floor. A bookshelf positioned in the far right corner doubled up as a liquor cabinet. After snatching a half empty bottle, he plopped down into a chair behind his desk.

"What's wrong, Jared?" came a familiar voice from behind a small couch in the left corner. "Did you miss me that much?"

He leapt up, at the same time grabbing a small dagger from his desk drawer.

Kat stepped into view and took a seat on the couch. "No need for that."

"I should skin you alive!" he shouted. "Do you know how much trouble you've caused me?" He took a menacing step toward her.

Kat smiled. "I'm sorry. I know I've been a pain. But that's over now. I'm back for good."

Jared huffed. "You think you can just walk into my office after what you did and all will be forgiven?"

"If you want me to leave..." She moved to get up.

The dagger came flying across the room, its point burying into the floor right next to Kat's feet. "You're not going anywhere."

She jumped back and hugged her knees.

Jared chuckled while crossing the room and retrieving the dagger. "That's better."

He loomed over Kat until he was content she was sufficiently cowed, then took a seat beside her. "Now then...what to do with you?"

By now, Kat's hands were trembling. "I've heard about a shipment of copper coming in this week. I can..."

He pressed a finger to her lips. "Hush, my dear. Now that you're a woman, your stealing days are over. But you knew that before you came here, didn't you?"

She nodded weakly.

Jared brushed a stray hair away from her face and smiled. "Don't be frightened. You'll like it here. I can protect you...keep you safe." He shifted closer. "You just don't know how upset it used to make me, knowing that you were on the streets all by yourself. There's no telling what could have happened to you out there."

A single tear fell down her cheek. "But I don't...I mean...I've never..." Her voice trailed off.

"Don't worry about that," he reassured her. "I'll show you everything you need to know." He leaned in to kiss her, but Kat jumped up from the couch and backed away.

Jared's face flashed with anger, but quickly softened. "I understand. I've seen this before." He got up and went to his desk. "I have just the thing." Reaching into the drawer, he produced a small tin box.

Kat's eyes shot wide. "Please. I don't want *daiva*."

"All the girls use it," he replied. "A little bit won't hurt you, I promise. It will just make things...easier."

Kat moved behind the couch and picked up a small bundle. "Can't we drink this instead? I got it for you just before I came."

Jared frowned. "Did you now?"

She approached the desk and set down the bundle. Jared stared at it for a moment before unwrapping it.

He picked up the bottle inside and held it at eye level. "Harbor Fields," he remarked. "Twenty years old. Very nice." He studied the cork and seal carefully before removing them.

Kat laughed. "Do you think I'm trying to poison you?"

Jared took two cups from the cabinet. "Perhaps. We'll see soon enough." He poured the wine and handed her a cup.

Without hesitation, she drained it dry and let out an appreciative sigh. Her tongue ran over her lips seductively. "Mmmm! More please."

Smirking, Jared poured her another. He watched with eager anticipation as she drank half of the second cup, her eyes staring into his the entire time.

"You're going to be quite popular," he said. Sitting down at the desk again, he patted his leg.

After another gulp of wine, she settled onto his lap.

"By the way. How did you get in here?" he asked.

"Don't worry," she replied. "Soon you'll know all of my little secrets."

Jared tried to kiss her again, but she put the cup to her lips to prevent him.

"Men don't like being teased, my dear," he scolded, kissing her exposed neck gently.

Kat giggled and hopped up from his lap. "That tickles."

Jared reached out, but she danced away and jumped playfully onto the couch. He stood up and took the bottle. After pouring himself a cup, he ambled across the room and stood over her.

"You know, Kat, some men don't like girls who aren't...how should I put it?" He pointed to her shirt. "Endowed with womanly attributes. Not me, mind you. I like it that way."

She lowered her eyes, her face flushing with embarrassment. It was true that her body had only just begun to develop. Since it had, she had made a habit of wearing loose fitting shirts and blouses to hide the fact.

Jared slipped down beside her. "You can't be this shy when you're working. You know that, don't you?"

Kat met his eyes. "Don't worry. I won't be."

He drained the cup and tossed it carelessly on the floor. "Of course, if you please me, I may just keep you all to myself. Would you like that?"

She smiled sheepishly. "I might. What would I have to do?"

He placed his hand on her leg. "That's what I'm about to...to..."

His words faltered. Suddenly, his brow creased and his mouth twisted into a pained frown.

Kat's smile never faded. "Is something wrong? Don't you think I'm pretty?"

Jared leaned back. His hands were shaking and his face was turning deathly pale. He opened his mouth to speak, but no words came.

She stood up. This time, *she* was looming over him. "I'm sorry, Jared. I don't think I'll be letting you put your grimy little hands on me ever again."

With eyes now wide with fear, he struggled to move but only managed to topple over onto his side. Kat lifted him back into an upright position.

"I have a confession to make," she said. "I *did* poison you. But it wasn't *in* the bottle, it was *on* it. You were done the moment you took the wrapping off and touched it."

Jared gave a soft moan. "Oh, don't worry," Kat continued. "The poison's not lethal. It will only paralyze you for a few hours. You see, I needed your full attention, and this was the only way I could get it."

She knelt in front of him. "When you imagined me on my knees, I bet this wasn't what you had in mind." She rested her chin on his leg and grinned spitefully. "And to think I used to be so scared of you. It makes you feel good when women are afraid, doesn't it? I've seen the way you smile when you beat your whores bloody and make them beg for you to stop."

Kat reached down and pulled a short dagger from her belt. Jared renewed his attempts to move, but his efforts were futile. Slowly, she dragged the tip of the blade along his inner thigh, stopping just before the outline of his manhood.

"Is this what you wanted to put in me?" she asked.

Again he let out a moan, his eyes begging for mercy. She clicked her tongue. "What's wrong, Jared? Afraid I'm going to cut it off?"

She pressed the blade down until it pierced his flesh, but only slightly. "Is this what gives you the right to hurt women? This tiny piece of useless meat? Is that where your power comes from?"

She pulled the dagger away and stood up. Jared breathed a heavy sigh of relief.

"Lucky for you, I'm not as cruel as you are." She walked to his desk and took a coin purse from the drawer. "You don't mind, do you? I'll need some extra gold after I'm gone."

At that moment heavy footfalls could be heard coming down the hall. Jared's eyes darted to the door and then back to Kat. A few seconds later there was a knock. The door slowly swung open to reveal Brutis, now dressed in a black leather vest and pants. He stepped inside.

Jared glared at Kat triumphantly.

"Are you not done with him yet?" Brutis asked.

"Give me one more minute," Kat replied.

Jared's triumph instantly turned to sheer terror.

Brutis frowned. "You sure you can go through with it?"

Kat's eyes settled on Jared and she flashed a wicked smile. "I'm sure."

Brutis gave a sharp nod and left the room.

"I should have mentioned it earlier," Kat said, once he had gone. "Brutis really didn't care too much for what you wanted to do to me. It didn't take a lot to convince him that he would be better off running things around here." She folded her arms. "Didn't it occur to you that someone must have let me in here? I'm a good thief, but your office has a *very* good lock."

She walked slowly across the room and sat beside him. "Right now you might be wondering why I'm doing this. Why have I gone to all this trouble? Well, the reason is simple. After two years of living in fear. Two years of beatings. Two years of dreading the day I would become a woman…I feel I owe you something. And after all – a princess always pays her debts."

She took a moment to gaze at the dagger gripped lightly in her hand. "Goodbye, Jared."

In a single swift motion she slit Jared's throat. The poison kept him from jerking and sputtering as the blood poured from the wound and soaked his shirt. Kat stood up and watched impassively as the light faded from his eyes.

She thought about the moment she had plunged the dagger through Hank's neck. After that she'd been unsure of how to feel. This time it was different. This time she would not be tormented by regret and uncertainty. This time…it was justice.

Kat wiped the dagger on Jared's pants and put it away. She gave one final glance over her shoulder just before leaving the room. Jared's blood was now pooling at his feet.

She sneered hatefully at her one time boss and abuser. "Goodbye… and good riddance."

CHAPTER SEVEN

E THAN SHIELDED HIS eyes from the morning sun that was cresting the top of the buildings. He took a deep cleansing breath. Even the stench of the city was preferable to the smell of stale beer and vomit that permeated the air inside the Hareesh headquarters.

A tall thin man wearing a green cloak with the hood thrown back was waiting in a wagon a few yards away. His black, stringy hair and narrow set eyes made him look almost sickly and frail.

Specter prodded his captives forward. "Don't let his looks fool you," he said quietly, reading Ethan's expression. "Thaddeus is about as deadly as they come."

"You think they'll give us a problem?" Thaddeus asked him when they drew closer

"Not if they want to see tomorrow," he replied.

"We won't cause you any trouble," assured Jonas.

Ethan could almost see the wheels turning in Jonas' mind. For a short time they would be unshackled in order to pass through the city gates without raising suspicion. But he doubted they would remain free for very long after that. Whatever they were going to do, it would need to be done before the chains were put back on.

Specter pointed for Jonas to join Thaddeus in the front and Ethan to get in the rear. "Remember old man," he warned. "If you say one bloody word when we reach the gates, you'll get a dagger through your neck the instant after I gut your young friend."

Thaddeus snapped the reins and the wagon lurched forward. The closer they came to the gate, the more crowded the street became. Soon the wagon was moving at no more than a mere crawl. For a short time Ethan gave serious consideration to jumping off and making a run for it, but Specter was watching his every move. Besides, even if he was lucky enough to get away, he knew that it would likely be a death sentence for Jonas. He could not risk that.

It took them nearly an hour to reach the main gate. There was a line of several wagons and men on horseback on the right hand side of the avenue, while those passing through on foot were to the left. Dozens of armed men, some city guards and others Imperial soldiers, were scattered about checking everyone's cargo and travel papers.

Specter whispered a curse. "Damn Imperials." He retrieved two pieces of folded parchment and gave them to Ethan and Jonas. "These are better than the trash you paid for. Even so, say nothing unless you're asked directly."

A city guard approached their wagon. He looked up at the group with a scowl. "So where are you off to, Specter?"

He jumped down, a broad smile plastered across his scarred face. "Nowhere special, Captain. Off running errands."

Ethan noticed him press something into the guard's palm.

"What's with all the soldiers?" Specter asked.

The guard shot a disdainful glance over his shoulder to where a group of Imperials were searching a large wagon. "You haven't heard? Some idiot killed three of their men the other day. Needless to say, they're not too pleased about it."

"What fool would do that, I wonder?" Specter responded, shaking his head.

The guard shrugged. "Who knows? Probably best that you're leaving the city though. Sooner or later they'll be at the Hareesh's door asking questions." He eyed Specter with sudden suspicion. "You'd tell me if you knew anything, of course."

Specter laughed. "You know I would. I always try to help you and your friends, Captain."

The man held his gaze for a few more seconds before relaxing. "I'd stay out of town for a bit if I were you. Things are getting pretty tense around here."

Specter nodded and jumped back into the wagon. The guard took one final look at the others and then waved them through.

Once beyond the gate, Thaddeus let out an exaggerated sigh.

"What's wrong?" teased Specter. "A bit too much excitement for you?"

He sniffed. "You're just lucky we didn't get searched by an Imperial. I doubt your gold and wit would have gotten us past one of *them*."

Specter grinned. "I'll take luck over skill any day."

"Where exactly are you taking us?" asked Jonas, breaking into their conversation.

"Thinking of escape are you?" scoffed Specter with obvious humor. "In that case, I'll tell you. I'm taking you fifty miles north to the Imperial garrison. Not that knowing this will do you much good."

He reached into a sack just behind the driver's seat. Ethan heard the clank of metal, and before he could protest, a set of shackles had been snapped securely around his wrists.

Specter leaned back with a look of smug satisfaction. "That's better. Flee if you like, old man. I won't even try to stop you. But you'll have to leave your young friend behind."

Jonas turned to look hard at Ethan.

Specter chuckled. "He's thinking about it, boy. Some friend *he* is."

Jonas' shoulders sagged.

Thaddeus was also amused. "Don't feel too bad," he remarked. "He wouldn't have really let you escape."

"Sure I would," said Specter. "The old man is worthless to me. It's the boy they want."

Thaddeus twisted around to face him. "And why would you say that?"

"That's not your concern," Specter replied sharply. "You're just here to see that the boss gets his cut."

Thaddeus grunted. "And mine too." He snapped the reins, pressing the horses to go faster.

For the next few hours they traveled in complete silence. Specter sat with arms folded, his eyes never leaving Ethan. Once again Ethan couldn't help but feel there was something familiar about the man. But he knew this was impossible. Not only would he have remembered meeting someone with such pronounced scars and rough appearance, Specter was from Lumnia, so they could never have met before.

It was now well beyond midday, and Ethan could no longer bear the silence. "What happened to your face?" he asked.

"Way ho!" cried Thaddeus. "Did I just hear what I think I heard? Did someone dare to ask Specter about his scars?"

Specter was not amused. "It doesn't matter how I got them, boy. And if you ask me again, I'll give *you* some to match."

Ethan met Specter's hard stare without flinching. "I didn't mean to offend you. I just wondered."

"Best you hold your tongue," Specter warned him. "So far as I've seen it gets you into nothing but trouble."

"Maybe you should cut it out?" suggested Thaddeus.

"Maybe you should close your mouth as well," Specter snapped back.

Thaddeus mumbled something incoherent, but kept his attention on driving the horses.

That evening they pulled the wagon off the road and built a small fire. Thaddeus produced a bottle of wine and a portion of roasted lamb from a pack, neither of which he offered to share.

Specter secured Ethan to a thin pine tree using a short chain and lock. This done, he tied Jonas' hands and feet with rope and propped him up beside Ethan.

"I'll untie you in the morning," he said. "And I suggest you seriously consider abandoning your young friend. His fate is sealed. Yours is not."

He gave each of them a piece of bread and a flask of water. Ethan hadn't realized how hungry he was and devoured the meager repast in mere seconds.

Specter and Thaddeus sat close to the fire talking in whispers. Thaddeus glanced across at Ethan several times, pointing and shaking his head. Soon it was obvious that they were in a heated, albeit quiet argument.

"What do you think they're talking about?" asked Ethan.

Jonas shifted into a slightly more comfortable position. "It doesn't matter. The only thing I'm concerned with is how we're going to get out of this mess."

"I don't want you getting yourself killed over me," said Ethan. "You should take him up on his offer and go."

Jonas gave him a sideways glance. "I doubt the offer is sincere. And even if it is, I have a duty to perform."

Regardless of what Ethan had felt about Jonas previously, at that moment he was forced to admire his courage. "Thank you," he said.

"Don't thank me yet," he replied. "All of my plans to break free relied on us both being tied with rope. I have nothing with which to loose your chains."

Ethan's heart sank. He had hoped Jonas was just biding his time. He twisted his wrists and pulled, but the shackles were too tight. He looked across at his captors. Specter had stood up and was glaring down at Thaddeus, his hand resting on the hilt of his sword.

"Try it and you won't live long enough to spend your bounty," said Thaddeus, his voice suddenly louder.

After another tense moment, Specter turned sharply away and stormed off into the night.

"Right now would have been a perfect time to escape," remarked Jonas.

"How would you have done it?" asked Ethan.

"I can start small fires with magic, remember? Burning through a bit of rope wouldn't be much of a challenge."

Ethan looked again at the shackles and grunted with frustration. "This is just the sort of thing Markus would know how to handle. There wasn't a pair of handcuffs anywhere in the world that he couldn't get out of."

"I don't suppose he showed you how to do it?" asked Jonas.

Ethan's head drooped. "No. He was going to, but there wasn't time." He pictured his friend's smiling face. "Right now, I'd give anything to have him here."

"Right now, I'd settle for the street urchin," added Jonas, chuckling softly. "I bet *she* could get you free."

"Maybe, but Markus would never have run out on us. I wish I knew what happened to him. It breaks my heart to think about him here all alone."

"I'm sure he was all right," said Jonas.

"I hope so. He was the best friend I ever had." A sad smile formed. "One time, right after we got to England, he saved my life in a South London pub. One of the locals tried to kill me."

"Why?"

"He thought I was hitting on his girl. And let me tell you, this guy was huge – literally twice my size. Anyway, I was trying to explain to him that I had only asked her if she knew the bartender's name, but he didn't believe me. Actually, I think the guy just didn't like Americans and wanted an excuse to fight."

"What's an American?" asked Jonas.

Ethan couldn't help but laugh at the question. "I guess it doesn't matter. It's a dumb story anyway."

"Finish it," said Jonas. His voice was unusually kind. "I want to hear it."

"Okay, if you're sure."

Ethan sighed before continuing. "First of all the guy pushed me up against the bar, so I hit him as hard as I could. But like I said, he was *really* big. It didn't have any effect. He just smiled at me and pulled out a knife. Markus was using the bathroom at the time, so I was all alone and scared out of my wits. I tried to apologize, but this freak giant just spat at me and called me a Yank bastard. He had me by the throat and was just about to stick the knife in when Markus ran up behind and busted one of those big heavy beer mugs over his head. Must have hit just the right spot because it damn near knocked him out cold. Three of his mates jumped up from the bar, but we were already out the door and away down the street before anyone could stop us."

He smiled broadly while picturing the moment.

"It sounds like he was a good friend," said Jonas. "I am truly sorry you lost him."

"I swore I would never let him down," said Ethan. "But I did, didn't I? I left him to die in this God awful world."

"You know that's not true," said Jonas. "What happened to him was beyond your control."

"I know. But I still feel like I should have done something."

The sound of footfalls halted their conversation. Specter appeared and stood over them for a moment. He said nothing, but there was anger still burning in his eyes.

"Come to your senses yet?" Thaddeus called over.

Specter moved away and sat down alongside him by the fire. "Yes, I think I have."

Thaddeus was still smirking over an imagined psychological victory when, in a motion too quick for the eye to follow, Specter thrust a long dagger up under his chin and deep into his brain. The man's muscles seized instantly and he toppled stiffly over onto his back.

Ethan and Jonas stared in stunned horror.

After a few moments Specter got up and walked over to Ethan. Still gripping the bloodied dagger in his free hand, he grabbed Ethan's shackles and jerked him forward.

"Don't!" pleaded Jonas.

"Quiet, old man," Specter growled.

He buried the blade in the ground and produced a key from his belt. "You must be losing your memory," he told Ethan sharply. "I hit him with a wine bottle...not a bloody beer mug."

Ethan blinked and stared, his mouth agape, scarcely noticing that his shackles were being removed.

"Markus?" was the only word he found himself able to utter.

His old friend stood up and turned his back. "My name is Specter."

CHAPTER EIGHT

MARKUS STALKED OVER to the body of Thaddeus and rubbed his chin. "Now, what to do with you?" he mused casually.

Ethan began to rise, but Jonas caught his arm.

"Cut my bonds," he said.

Ethan picked up the dagger and carefully severed the ropes. He then moved toward his friend. "I don't understand," he began. "How is it you are here?"

Markus' hand shot out, halting his approach. "Twenty-five years," he spat out. "That's how long I've been in this shit hole of a world. Twenty-five years!"

"I'm...I'm sorry," Ethan stammered. "I..."

"It wasn't his fault," Jonas cut in. "You have no cause to blame him."

"Don't I?" barked Markus. "Do you know how long twenty-five years is to wait? I kept telling myself that you'd come. But you never did." His eyes bored into Ethan. "I've had a long time to learn to hate you. Now here you are. Not a day older. And me...well just look at me."

Tears welled in Ethan's eyes. "I'm so sorry. I swear I came to find you as fast as I could. It was the portal...it's...well...I'm not sure how it works."

"It's corrupted," Markus said. "I know all about it now. It was forbidden magic, even in the time of the mages. But the old man here used it anyway. Didn't you?"

"That's not how it happened," Jonas protested. "I only used it to save Ethan's life. And I never intended for *you* to come here at all."

Markus sniffed with contempt. "No one ever intends anything. But here we all are anyway. You two – lost and helpless. And me – body scarred and life wasted."

Ethan took a cautious step forward. "What happened to you?"

Markus stared at him for a long time, but made no attempt to answer the question. "There's more food in the wagon," he finally said. "Get it out while I dispose of Thaddeus."

Before Ethan could protest, he grabbed the corpse by the arms and dragged it into the night.

Jonas retrieved a sack of food from the wagon and began sorting it. "Not much here," he muttered.

After a few minutes Markus returned and took a seat by the fire. Ethan sat opposite, staring at his old friend. His heart ached when he thought of the many hardships Markus would have been forced to face. The scars alone bore testament to how difficult life must have been.

"What happened to you?" he eventually asked.

For a moment Markus said nothing. He gazed into the crackling flames, his eyes distant and unreadable. Then he began.

"When I got here I was quite badly injured. That damned German potato masher that blew me through the portal had filled me with a thousand bits of rock and metal. I was bleeding pretty badly and didn't know where I was. The bloody portal dumped me in a field somewhere up north...Ralmaria I think. Anyway, I crawled for as long as I could before passing out. I don't know how long I stayed unconscious, but when I woke up I was in a cage with about twenty other guys. Someone had treated my wounds, but all of my gear had been stolen."

He shook his head. "I was naked as the day I was born and scared out of my wits."

"Why were you in a cage?" asked Ethan, shock showing clearly on his face.

"For the same reason you were," he replied. "Bounty. When the Emperor detected the portal opening, he sent his men to check it out. I couldn't have moved very far away from where I first arrived. They must have found me lying there and put two and two together. I was taken to a garrison and interrogated for weeks." He breathed a sardonic laugh. "The thing is, I would have told them anything they wanted to know. I just didn't speak their bloody language."

"So they did that to your face?"

Markus shot him a furious glance. "No. And stop asking about it."

"I'm sorry," said Ethan.

Markus sighed. "It's not something I like to talk about. People who know me quickly learn it's better to keep their curiosity to themselves."

He leaned back on his elbows and drew in a couple of deep breaths. "So anyway, I don't know for sure how long I was held there, but eventually they gave up and sent me to work in the mines. That was a hellish tough time, but I survived. I learned to speak the language, and picked up a whole lot of other useful knowledge. Eventually, I saw my chance to escape and grabbed it with both hands. After that I made my way south and joined the Hareesh."

Ethan expected him to continue further with the story, but after a few seconds of silence it was clear he was done.

"That's it?" he asked.

Markus shrugged. "What more do you expect? I was alone and having to fend for myself. I ended up in Miltino and did what I had to do to survive."

"So how did you know I was here?" Ethan asked.

"I was at the garrison collecting a bounty when word came in. At first I didn't think too much about it. But when I heard the word *portal* mentioned and that orders to apprehend any new comers to the area had come directly from Shinzan himself, I felt pretty sure it had to be you. Of course, I had a big advantage over the others searching because I was the only one who knew exactly what you look like. Even so, I knew I needed to find you before they did."

Ethan nodded. "So what happened next?

"The rest was sheer luck, actually. I was too late getting to Jaobin, but after I got back to Miltino I went for a drink in the Hanging Man tavern and spotted the old guy collecting those useless false papers. After that, all I needed to do was follow him."

"Why didn't you tell me who you were?"

"Because he intended to turn you over to the Empire," Jonas cut in. He plopped down beside Ethan and handed him a piece of dried beef and an apple.

So far, Ethan had chosen to ignore this fact. Now he was forced to deal with it. "Were you really going to turn me in?" he asked.

"Of course he was," snapped Jonas. He shot an accusing stare at Markus. "Tell him."

Markus spread his hands. "Can you blame me? I was so damn angry with you." He tilted his head and smirked. "I changed my mind, didn't I?"

"But they would have killed me. You knew that. Whatever happened to make you this way?"

"You still have no real idea what I went through. The hell I experienced." His smirk vanished and his voice became hard and dangerous. "The fact that I didn't kill you the moment I saw you is a miracle. Just be thankful you're still alive and free."

There was a long period of silence. Ethan could see the pain dwelling behind Markus' eyes. *Maybe he was right to be angry,* he thought. *How would I have felt if it had been me?*

"Perhaps it would be best to leave the past behind you for the time being," suggested Jonas. "We have more pressing matters to attend to."

"The old man's right," agreed Markus. "Now that I've killed Thaddeus, it won't take the Hareesh long to figure out what happened. And the Imperials are looking for the two of you as well."

"What should we do?" asked Ethan.

"We need to reach the dwarves," Jonas told him. "There was a cave your mother was trying to reach on the southernmost edge of the Gol'Shupa Mountains. We should head there."

Markus gave a short laugh. "The dwarves? You can't be serious. They'll kill you the moment they see you. No one goes there...ever."

"We do," corrected Jonas. "Ethan's family has a special relationship with the dwarves. A blood oath was sworn between Praxis Dragonvein and King Vidar. They will honor it."

"A blood oath?" mocked Markus. "You must be joking? Dwarves won't honor anything except gold. And you'd need a fortune."

"I'm *not* joking," said Jonas. "And I assume that since you've decided not to turn us over, you'll be coming along."

"Into the mountains? Not a chance in hell."

"Then we'll go without you," Jonas said.

Ethan reacted instantly. "We're not going anywhere without Markus."

His old friend let out a long sigh. "You can't stay with me, Ethan. I'm not the man you once knew. Things have changed." He pulled a coin purse from his belt and tossed it at Ethan's feet. "This is the gold I took from you. I suggest you make for San Leon. No one would look for you on the coast. At least, not for a while yet."

"I'm not leaving you," said Ethan. "Not again."

"You won't have to," he replied. "I'm leaving *you*."

"Well *I'm* not," came a voice from just beyond the firelight.

The trio leapt to their feet, Markus instinctively drawing his sword and preparing for an attack.

"Kat?" called Ethan, recognizing her voice.

A second later she stepped into the light, a devilish grin on her face. She removed the small pack hanging over her shoulders and tossed it next to the fire.

"He can run away if he wants," she continued, nodding at Markus. "But I'm still coming with you."

Markus let out a groan and sheathed his sword. "So this is the girl who Jared was so upset over." He scrutinized her for a moment. "A bit young to be working for the likes of him, aren't you?"

"I don't work for Jared," she stated flatly. Her grin had vanished. "In fact, no one does anymore." She flashed a glance at Jonas, who was already scowling. "And before you say I can't come, you should know that there are twenty Imperial soldiers less than an hour behind me."

Jonas' eyes widened. "Are you sure?"

"Yes. And if you don't move fast they'll catch you."

Markus responded quickly by racing over to the wagon and tossing out what little he had brought. "Distribute the provisions equally and douse the fire," he instructed. Without waiting for a reply, he led the horse further away from the road until both it and the wagon were completely hidden by the darkness.

The other three set about doing his bidding. He returned just as the fire was finally extinguished.

"We should go east toward the Traxis border," he said. "I have friends there."

"No," Jonas argued. "We need to make it to the mountains. Regardless of what you think, the dwarves *will* honor their oath."

Markus shook his head. "You're a fool, old man. I've been in Lumnia for twenty-five years, and I'm telling you – whatever oath you think they made…"

He paused. Even in the dim light of the moon he could see Jonas' resolve. "Fine. I'll get you as far as Tulani. But from there you're on your own."

Ethan reached out and touched his friend's shoulder. "Thank you."

Markus brushed his hand away. "Let's just get moving."

He led them southwest for a time. The moonlight gave very little assistance in navigating the rugged terrain; the thin forest was riddled with small rocks and roots that sent both Jonas and Ethan stumbling to their knees on several occasions. Kat, however, stayed at the rear and seemed to have no trouble at all in avoiding the obstacles.

After half an hour of progress, Markus stopped and listened intently. For a few minutes they could hear only the rustle of the wind through the leaves and the chirping of insects. Then, in the far distance, the sound of rapid hoof beats echoed through the forest.

"If they don't smell the campfire we should be fine," he said.

They waited anxiously until the hoof beats faded before moving on.

"How far is it to Tulani?" asked Ethan.

"Two weeks on foot," Markus replied. "Unfortunately, we don't have anywhere near enough provisions to last that long, so we'll need to go into Masi to resupply. As for now, we'll stop in a few miles to rest a while."

Jonas offered no objection to this when Ethan glanced back at him. There were still several hours to go before dawn, and he desperately wanted to talk to Markus some more. So far though, each time he tried, he'd come up against a brick wall.

"Can't you get it through your thick head?" Markus snapped at him after the third attempt. "I'm really not the man you knew before. And if you keep pestering me like this, I swear I'll leave the lot of you alone in the bloody forest."

Ethan opened his mouth to speak, but quickly saw the truth of these words in Markus' eyes, and instead settled for a sharp nod of acceptance.

The rest of the time was spent in silence. When they did eventually halt, Markus made a point of bedding down several yards away from the others.

"What can I do?" Ethan asked Jonas. "All I want is to make things right between us."

Jonas looked away, his eyes suddenly distant. "Some things can never be made right. Best you remember that."

His words only made Ethan even more guilt ridden. Lying on his blanket and staring up at the unfamiliar night sky, he felt truly small and alone.

The part of him that was still a young boy wanted to weep, but the proud soldier he had become kept his tears at bay long enough for sleep to take him.

CHAPTER NINE

THE RUMBLE OF thunder shook Ethan awake. Though the sun was breaking over the horizon, the sky to the west was gray and promising a miserably wet day.

"We should find shelter," said Jonas as he hurried to gather up his belongings.

Markus laughed. "Shelter? There's no shelter where we're going. No soft beds either."

Jonas scowled and eyed the approaching storm. "Why does that not surprise me?"

Kat was the only one who seemed to be in high spirits. She sniffed in Markus' direction and pinched her nose. "Maybe the rain will wash some of the Hareesh stink off you."

"Better the stench of a Hareesh den than a rundown whore house," he shot back. He turned to Ethan. "Why are you taking this girl along with you anyway?"

Kat's chin jutted out. "He's not taking me. I'm choosing to go."

"She'll just slow us down," Markus continued, ignoring her remark.

"Well, at least I won't turn them in to the Empire," she retorted.

Markus' face turned red. He took a menacing pace toward the girl.

"Leave off," ordered Jonas. "Both of you."

Markus growled, but after simmering for a few seconds, strode rapidly away.

Moving close, Ethan leaned down to whisper in Kat's ear. "Try to get along…please. Or at least try not to start a fight."

She held up her hands, eyes wide in feigned innocence. "What did I do?"

He shook his head and sighed. "Just try."

By now, Markus was already thirty yards ahead of them. They hurried to catch him up.

The trees in this part of the forest were widely spaced and thin, giving them little protection from the rain once it began to fall an hour later. Jonas wrapped himself in his blanket looking highly displeased. Soon the wind rose and the rain came down in earnest.

After a time Ethan began to notice that the older man's steps were becoming increasingly unsure. He spoke to him several times, but Jonas insisted that he was fine, even though his pale complexion and trembling hands said otherwise.

The rain persisted until the next morning. They slept – or at least, attempted to sleep – beneath what little cover the trees provided and with their blankets pulled over their heads. Ethan could hear Jonas coughing and wheezing throughout the night. When morning arrived, the combination of chill air and wet clothing was clearly making matters worse for him.

Markus pulled Ethan away from earshot of the others. "I don't think your friend is going to last long out here," he said. "And we can't afford to stop."

Ethan frowned. "What are you saying?"

"I'm saying that if he falls behind, we can't wait."

The sound of Jonas coughing hammered the point home.

Ethan looked at the old man. Kat was sitting nearby, a concerned look on her face. "I can't leave him," he said finally. "If he can't travel, we'll have to find somewhere to rest until he recovers."

Markus scowled and let out an exasperated breath. "I almost forgot what a bloody boy scout you are."

The remark brought a smile to Ethan's face. For a moment he caught a glimpse of the Markus he had once known. But it quickly vanished again with his friend's next words.

"I'm not about to get killed over an old man's weakness," he warned.

"And if it comes to it, you can stay and die with him." Having made his point, he returned to the others.

To Ethan's relief, by mid-morning the rain stopped and the temperature began rising. Not that this appeared to help Jonas very much, who was still struggling badly to keep with the pace. Kat disappeared for a short time, returning with some herbs that she forced the old man to mix with water and drink. The concoction seemed to do him some good for a short time, but by the afternoon his coughing was worse than ever. His balance was deteriorating too, and he nearly fell over completely on several occasions.

As the sun began to set, it became painfully clear that he would not be able to continue for very much longer.

"I'm sure Markus has said that you should leave me if I can't go on," he whispered to Ethan after another long series of throat rattling coughs.

"Don't worry," Ethan assured him. "I won't leave you behind."

"You will if you must," he countered.

Before Ethan could protest, Markus came to an abrupt halt and gestured for everyone to remain quiet. After a moment, the sound of voices drifting through the trees could be heard just east of their position. A few seconds later a soft breeze carried the scent of a camp fire to them.

"Who do you think it is?" whispered Ethan.

"Probably thieves," he replied. "If we're lucky."

Ethan glanced anxiously over to Jonas. The man had both hands clamped firmly over his mouth and his face was turning a vivid crimson. Markus saw it too and shook his head just as Jonas lost his battle for control. A loud, rasping cough escaped.

The sound of voices stopped instantly, replaced by the singing of steel being drawn.

"Perfect," grumbled Markus. "Whatever happens next, do exactly as I say." He drew his sword. "And let me do the talking."

Less than a minute later three men appeared. All were dressed similarly in simple tan shirts and pants, with travel worn boots on their feet. Two were of medium build: one with a shock of red hair, the other by contrast, totally bald. The third man was much taller and broader in the shoulders, with dark wavy hair and deep set eyes. All three carried long swords and wore daggers on their belt. They halted the moment they spotted Markus.

"What business do you have here?" called the larger man.

"Just passing through," Markus replied.

The man whispered something to his companions, then asked: "Is that Kat with you?"

She stepped forward. "Yes, it's me, Jeb."

"These fellows…are they friends of Jared?"

Kat shook her head. "No. They're friends of mine. I don't work for Jared anymore."

Jeb smiled and sheathed his blade. Those with him did the same. "That's good to hear. Now you can become a proper thief. Come. Join us by the fire."

Without giving Markus or the others time to object, Kat quickly set off to follow him.

They were led a hundred yards east to a small clearing. Here, a fire burned cheerfully and three bedrolls were cast carelessly beside it.

Everyone took a seat by the fire. Jonas shivered and stifled his coughs as he rubbed his hands together vigorously.

"Your friend is ill," Jeb remarked.

"We were caught in the rain," Kat told him.

Jeb nodded. "The wilderness is no place for an old man."

"I'll be fine," snapped Jonas. "I just need some rest."

His sharp reaction drew a chuckle from Jeb. "Old *and* stubborn."

He turned his attention back to Kat. "So what brings you so far from Miltino? You finally get caught? Or did that dog Jared run you off?"

"Neither," she replied. "I just wanted to move on."

He eyed Ethan and Markus. "And what of your friends? They don't look very much like thieves to me."

"That's because we're not," Markus told him.

Jeb looked at Kat, then back to Markus. "You know, I heard of a man who fits your description. People call him Specter. That wouldn't be you, would it?"

"Never heard of him," Markus said.

Jeb leaned in, still holding his gaze. "I only mention it because people say he's a bounty hunter for the Empire. Folks like us wouldn't care for him to know where we are...or what we do."

"Understandable," said Markus. "A man like that would be dangerous company indeed. But, like I told you...I never heard of him."

The two men stared at each other for a long and tense moment. Finally, Jeb smiled.

"That's good to hear," he said. "So, Kat. Now that you're not with Jared, I assume you'll join the Corvali. I'll stand for you, if you'd like."

"I'm not going back to Miltino," she replied. "Ever."

"That's too bad," he said. "We could have used someone as good as you."

"What's the Corvali?" asked Ethan.

Jeb looked suddenly suspicious. "You've never heard of us?"

"He's from the coast," Kat said quickly. "The Corvali are a thieves' guild. The largest and richest in all Lumnia."

Her explanation and the flattery appeared to satisfy Jeb. He leaned back on his elbows, grinning. "Can't abide the sea myself. Pirates and smugglers – a sorry lot. Not to be trusted. And if that's where you're headed, young lady, you'd do well to remember that."

Kat nodded and smiled.

"As for us, we're on our way to San Salisio," Jeb continued. "If you like, you can stay at our lodge until your man is well enough to travel. We should be able to reach it by tomorrow afternoon."

Ethan glanced at Markus, who only shrugged and stared into the fire. Jonas hesitated, then nodded his consent.

Jeb leaned back up and clapped his hands together. "It's settled then."

At last able to rest properly, Jonas was asleep well before anyone else. Ethan could not help but notice the worried expression on Kat's face as she sat beside him. Something had changed between the two of them, though he couldn't imagine what had brought this about.

The three thieves huddled together and talked quietly for a time, occasionally eyeing Markus with suspicion. After a while they bedded down, though with their weapons drawn and ready at their sides.

Ethan was just about to settle down as well when he noticed Markus get up and walk quietly into the forest. After a moment, he decided to follow.

He did his best to keep up while at the same time trying to stay hidden, but in moments he was lost and Markus had disappeared from sight. He tried to move faster, but only succeeded in tripping over a root and falling face first onto the forest turf.

He was still muttering a curse when he felt a pair of strong hands pull him to his feet.

It was Markus.

"Why are you following me?" he demanded.

"I wanted a chance to talk to you away from the others," Ethan replied.

"There's nothing left to talk about." His tone was level and unemotional. "I'm still angry with you. It's been too long for me to change that. But if it makes you feel any better, I do understand that what happened wasn't your fault."

"I'm sorry," said Ethan. "If I could change it, I would."

"But you can't. What happened, happened. My life is my life."

Ethan strained his eyes, attempting to pierce the darkness and read his expression, but could see only a dim silhouette. "Would you have really turned me in?" he asked.

Markus regarded him for several seconds. "Just go back to the camp," he said, pointing into the night. "I need to be alone."

With that, he turned away and vanished into the darkness.

Following the direction Markus had indicated, Ethan returned to the others. Jeb was lying on his side, a troubled look on his face.

"You keep dangerous company, lad," he said. "Your companion can deny it all he wants; I know he's Specter. What I don't know is why he's traveling with the three of you."

Ethan sat down on his blanket. "He's my friend."

Jeb chuckled. "Specter? Your friend? Specter has no friends. Not even other Hareesh want his company. And if half the stories I've heard about him are true, I understand why."

"I don't care about that. He's still my friend."

Jeb studied him for a moment. "I'm a pretty good judge of character, and you seem like a nice enough lad. You don't look like the type to keep company with Imperial assassins."

His words sent a chill down Ethan's back. "I don't know what you're talking about."

"You don't? He's your friend, isn't he? If that's true, surely you would know that Specter is an Imperial assassin and bounty hunter."

"He doesn't work for the Empire," Ethan insisted.

"Not directly, no. But he's the only member of the Hareesh who will take the jobs they offer. Nasty stuff, too. I don't imagine that makes him too many...*friends*. Dark rumors surround that man...very dark."

Ethan wasn't sure what to say. Markus was his friend no matter what had become of him. And regardless of whether he refused to admit it, Ethan was convinced that he would have never turned him over for the bounty. Somewhere deep inside - somewhere beyond all the pain and anger - the Markus of old still existed.

"You shouldn't listen to rumors," he said. "And if you have a problem with him, we can go our own way right now."

Jeb held out his hand. "No problem here, lad. Long as he minds his manners, he can tag along with us. I just hate to see Kat mixed up with his kind. She's a good girl. And an excellent thief."

"I suppose you'd rather her *stay* a thief?" Ethan said disapprovingly.

The man puffed his chest and held his head high. "And why not? Thieving is a good way to get by. Especially if you're as talented as she is. It's better than starving in the streets. And now that she's away from that Jared scum, she can make a place for herself in this world."

"There are other ways to get by," Ethan countered. "She's only a thief because she had no other choice."

Jeb sniffed "And you're going to give her one? I doubt that very much."

"She has a family somewhere," insisted Ethan.

"So what if she does? You think she'd be better off with them? She left them for a reason, boy. And whatever it is, I bet it's a good one. You shouldn't go mixing up her head with notions of family. Good friends and stout comrades is the best folk like us can hope for." He sighed.

"But I'm wasting my breath, aren't I? You're going to get that poor girl killed. But here's a warning. If you do, you'd better not let me find out about it."

Reaching down, he jerked his blanket over his shoulders and closed his eyes.

Ethan stared at Jeb, but the man was obviously done talking.

A short time later Markus returned. He glanced at the sleeping thief, fingering the dagger in his belt, with a knowing look in his eyes before laying down beside the fire.

Had he been listening to their conversation, Ethan wondered? Probably. He pushed it from his mind and allowed himself to drift.

Just as sleep took him he thought he heard the flapping of wings accompanied by a catlike growl coming from high above. Real or imagined, the sounds soon faded into the blackness of another weary driven slumber.

CHAPTER TEN

ETHAN WOKE JUST as dawn was breaking; both his blanket and hair were soaked from the heavy morning dew. With the fire completely burned out and a soft westerly breeze blowing, he shivered while hurrying to pack his gear.

To his relief, Jonas looked somewhat healthier, though still quite pale. He was coughing less frequently and his hands had stopped their constant trembling.

"My two companions won't be joining us at the lodge," announced Jeb.

"Why not?" asked Markus.

"The job we've been hired for will take a few days of scouting first," he explained. "They want to go on ahead and get it done. I'll meet them there after I've shown you the way."

He moved to join his comrades who were standing just out of earshot. They spoke to Jeb for a few minutes before departing.

"I don't like it," said Markus. "They could bring soldiers."

"Jeb's a good man," objected Kat. "He wouldn't do that."

Markus regarded her and shook his head. "You're too trusting."

"I'd trust him before I'd trust you," she snapped back.

Jonas hobbled up and rested his arm on Kat's shoulder. "This time I agree with Markus. It would be far too easy for them to betray us. They already suspect that we're on the run. What's to stop them from trying to collect a bounty?"

Kat stamped her foot. "I'm telling you that Jeb wouldn't do that."

"I don't think we have any choice but to trust him," Ethan chipped in. He ran a concerned gaze over Jonas. "If you don't get a few days' rest you're only going to get sicker."

"Are you ready?" Jeb called over.

Ethan waved. "We're ready."

"No one wants to listen to me, but this is a bad idea," complained Markus.

Jeb shot him a sharp glance - a sure sign that he had heard this remark - but made no response before setting off in an easterly direction.

By midday the forest had become much thicker, slowing their pace considerably. Markus kept a watchful eye on their surroundings, his hand never far from the hilt of his sword. Kat stayed close to Jonas, catching his arm on numerous occasions to save him from losing his footing. The exertion was clearly taking a heavy toll on the old man. By the time they halted for a quick meal of fruit and jerky, the frequency of his coughing had dramatically increased once again and his face was virtually devoid of any color whatsoever.

When they finally arrived at their destination, Jonas was on the verge of collapse. In spite of the heat of the day, his entire body was shivering violently, and regular coughing fits had him doubling over and gasping for air. It was only with both Ethan and Kat supporting him that he was able to keep moving over the final few yards.

The lodge turned out to be little more than a dilapidated wood shack with a stone chimney and a narrow covered porch spanning the front. But at least the chimney gave the promise of a warm fire and a hot meal.

Jeb gestured for everyone to wait before approaching the door alone. After listening for a few moments he gave a satisfied nod and called the others over.

"We'll be on our own for a while," he said. "I don't think any of my clansmen will be coming this way soon."

The inside was considerably more accommodating than the exterior suggested. Light poured in from the front windows, revealing a sturdy dining table in front of an unlit hearth. An iron stove was at the far end next to an open door that led through to a dark hallway. On the right was an open area with several comfortable looking chairs around four small, round tables. The walls were bare aside from a few bows and full quivers hanging between the two front windows.

Jeb quickly set to lighting lanterns, one of which he gave to Ethan. While checking the cupboards, he pointed to the darkened hallway. "There are beds in the back."

Ethan helped Jonas through to the first room along. It was furnished with a small dresser and two beds set on opposite walls. Ethan took Jonas' pack and placed it on the floor beside him while he struggled out of his clothing.

"I'll be fine," Jonas said as he dropped onto the bed. "Just tired... just...just need to lay here for a while." His eyes grew heavy and within moments he slipped into unconsciousness.

Ethan pulled the blanket over the old man's chest before returning to the others. Jeb was already getting the fire started, while Kat and Markus waited patiently at the table.

"I have some pork for tonight," Jeb said. "But if you want meat after that, you'll need to go hunting." He gestured to the bows on the wall.

"We don't intend to stay for long," said Markus. "As soon as Jonas is able, we'll be off."

Jeb nodded. "I understand. But he seems very ill. It may be a few days at least."

"I can hunt," announced Kat, proudly. "My fath..." She bit her lip. "I mean, I learned when I was a small girl. I can set traps and snares too."

"You're *still* a small girl," teased Jeb. "What are you going to hunt for? Mice?"

Kat pretended to be offended by glaring at him and folding her arms tightly across her chest.

"I'll hunt if the need arises," said Markus.

"I'll help," added Ethan.

Markus let out a good-natured laugh. "You? You're about as quiet as a thunderstorm. How the Krauts never..."

His voice trailed off. Both Kat and Jeb were looking confused by the unfamiliar reference. Markus' face hardened. "Anyway, I'll go alone if we need anything."

It wasn't long before the fire was burning and the lodge was filled with the smell of roasting pork. After they ate, Ethan went to check on Jonas. Sweat was beading on the old man's brow and he had kicked off his blanket.

Kat joined him a minute later. "Where are you really from?" she asked.

Ethan regarded her steadily. "I'll tell you, if you tell me. I heard you almost mention your father. Don't you still have family?"

Kat ignored the question. "You and Markus sound like you've known each other for a long time. And you say things that…well…they just don't make sense. What are Krauts? And what did you do to him that made him so angry at you?"

She waited for a reply, but Ethan just continued to stare at her. Eventually, she sighed. "If you must know, I ran away from home three years ago before my father could send me away."

"Why would he do that?"

Kat shook her head and wagged her finger. "No, no. I told *you* something. Now you tell *me* something. That's how this works."

Ethan considered his next words carefully. "Okay. I come from a place that's very far from here. Markus is angry because it's my fault he's here instead of back there."

"Your fault?" she repeated. "How could it be your fault?"

He wagged his finger, mirroring her gesture. "Like you said – that's not how this works."

Jonas moaned loudly, capturing their attention and driving other thoughts aside.

Kat placed a hand on his forehead. "He's burning up." Her voice was filled with concern. "I'll get some water and rags."

Ethan hurriedly grabbed a stool from the corner and pulled it beside the bed. The old man's head was thrashing wildly from side to side, flinging droplets of sweat in all directions.

"I'm sorry, My Lord," he groaned. "I'm sorry. I should have never…I didn't know. I'm so sorry."

Witnessing such fevered rambling was not a new experience for Ethan. When he was a boy he had watched his mother nurse one of their neighbor's children through scarlet fever. The poor girl had called for her father over and over, crying out that she was all alone, even though in truth her father had never once left her side. After recovering, she had no memory whatsoever of this.

"It's all right," Ethan said in a soothing tone. He wiped the sweat from Jonas' brow with his sleeve. "I forgive you."

"I'm sorr...I...I didn't..." His voice faded into soft, incoherent mumblings.

A short while later Kat returned with a bowl of water and a rag.

"I'll tend to him tonight," she said.

Ethan got up and returned to the dining room. Markus was sipping on a cup of wine and staring into the fire. Through the window he could see Jeb sitting on the porch, oiling his sword.

"What will you do if he dies?" Markus asked.

Ethan took a seat. "I don't know. I guess I should continue on to the mountains. What else can I do?"

Markus turned away from the fire and cocked his head. "My days with the Hareesh are over. If he dies, you should come with me to Al-Theona."

"And do what?"

Markus paused. "You're going to have to learn to get by in this world somehow." He drained his cup. "But I suppose a boy scout like you wouldn't be interested in the life I have to offer."

"That depends," said Ethan.

As he spoke, he saw Jeb rise from his chair and sheath his sword. A moment later the thief walked in the door. "I'll be leaving in the morning," he told them.

He reached in his pocket and tossed Ethan a round wooden token with the image of a snake engraved on either side. "If any of the Corvali show up after I'm gone, show that to them. They'll leave you in peace."

Ethan nodded his thanks and shoved it in his pocket. Jeb moved on down the hall and into one of the bedrooms.

"You should get some rest," Markus said.

"What about you?"

"I think I'll keep watch for a while," he replied. "You never know who might be lurking about."

Ethan looked in on Jonas just before going to find a room. Kat was still sitting at his bedside holding a damp cloth on his forehead. A little of his color had returned and he had stopped moaning.

"His fever is going down," she told him. "I think he'll be all right."

"You should rest," Ethan suggested.

"I will," she replied. "In a while."

He shook his head, marveling how at Kat could transform from a small girl into a streetwise thief, then in an instant, to a caring mother. "Wake me if you need anything," he told her before leaving.

After finding an empty bed two doors along, he lay down straight away. Sleep came rapidly. The stress of the day had him drifting into a dreamless slumber within seconds of his head touching the pillow.

The next morning he woke to the clatter of pots and the smell of porridge. Even though his muscles still ached, he stretched and got up almost immediately.

In the dining room he was amazed to see it was Jonas busy preparing the breakfast. Kat was at the table blowing the steam from a cup of what smelled like hot tea, while Markus was sitting beside the window staring intently into the surrounding forest.

"Looks like you're feeling better?" Ethan remarked.

Jonas glanced up and sat a bowl on the table for him. "I'm stronger than I look. And Kat is an excellent nurse."

She smiled weakly at the compliment and took a cautious sip from her cup.

"Is Jeb gone?" he asked.

Jonas nodded. "Yes. And we should be going as soon as possible too."

Ethan sat down in front of the bowl. After eating, he began to gather his things.

"Are you sure you can travel?" he asked, tossing his pack near the door.

"The question is, can you fight," snapped Markus before Jonas had time to reply. Leaping up from his chair, he drew his sword. "It seems that you were wrong about your friend, Kat."

She tossed her cup aside and raced to the window, Ethan and Jonas on her heels. At the point where the trees became dense they spotted four men in the same Imperial uniforms as the soldiers they had encountered in Miltino. Two of these were holding vicious looking broadswords, and the other pair, longbows.

"What should we do?" asked Jonas, fear seeping into his voice.

"Nothing," Markus replied. "There's a rear exit, but it's likely being watched." He cast an accusing look at Kat. "I guess we know now why Jeb was in such a hurry to leave."

Her face was red with fury. "I'll kill him. I swear it."

"We have to get the hell out of here first," Markus pointed out caustically.

From the thick of the foliage, a fifth man appeared. He was dressed in black leathers and wore a cloth cap. His keen eyes shifted from side to side as he indicated to the others the positions they should take.

"A bloody Grendil," spat Markus.

"A what?" asked Ethan.

"An Imperial tracker," he replied. "I've dealt with them before. Mean bastards. And good at what they do."

The Grendil took a few long strides toward the house. His voice carried clearly. "Throw down your arms and come out."

While the other three looked at one another with uncertainty, Markus reacted quickly by taking down a bow and quiver from the wall. "I don't suppose any of you are good with one of these?" he asked.

His question was met by silence. Grumbling, he notched an arrow and peered out of the window.

"I'll ask you only once more," shouted the Grendil. "Come out... now."

Markus crept to the door, motioning for Ethan to follow. "Open it on three," he instructed.

Ethan nodded and reached for the handle. Drawing back the bowstring, Markus silently mouthed, *one...two...three.*

The instant the door flew open, Markus jumped out onto the porch and let fly his arrow. The deadly missile streaked toward the Grendil, but it was a hurried shot and Markus' aim was slightly off. The arrow thudded into a tree just to the Grendil's left. With rage on his face, he moved quickly back.

"Burn it!" roared the Grendil. "Burn the place to the ground."

"That was your plan?" Jonas chided as Markus jumped back inside and the door slammed.

He shrugged and tossed the bow on the floor. "I didn't hear you suggest anything."

"So what now?" Ethan asked. His fear was tempered by his training and battle experience.

Markus drew his sword. "We die by fire...or by blade."

Kat was trembling and clutching at Jonas' sleeve. He wrapped his arm around her shoulders and did his best to give her a reassuring smile.

Two or three tense minutes passed without anything happening. Then they heard three loud thumps sound on the roof. A second later the window shattered as two blazing torches were heaved inside. Ethan scrambled to pick them up, but the ends were covered in an oily, tar-like substance that left a trail of flame as it rolled across the floor.

The dry timbers of the lodge went up as if soaked in kerosene. Smoke rapidly began to fill the room. It was obvious they had to get out quickly.

Markus waved everyone toward the front door. "Stay on my back," he ordered. "We'll try to outrun them."

"Or you could just come this way," called a voice from behind them. It was Jeb.

Kat released Jonas and ran headlong into the thief's arms.

"You didn't think I'd leave you?" he asked playfully.

"I knew you wouldn't turn us in," wept Kat.

"Yes," said Markus. "But how did you know they were coming?"

"Explanations can wait," he replied sharply. "Grab your packs and come on. There's a tunnel that will take us a few hundred yards south of here."

He led them down the hall and into the last bedroom on the right. The bed here had been thrown aside, revealing an open trapdoor. One by one they descended down a wooden ladder to a narrow tunnel.

"They won't know what's happened until after they search the rubble," said Jeb. "By then we'll be long gone."

The utter darkness of the passage forced them to advance slowly. When they eventually reached the end, Jeb pushed open a flap just above his head.

Everyone emerged blinking into the daylight and gulping fresh air. But the need to press on was urgent. They made their way due south as fast as possible for a mile or so, then east until reaching a shallow brook. After taking them across, Jeb turned south again, crisscrossing the stream several more times along the way. Three hours passed before they halted.

"That won't fool the Grendil for long," said Jeb. "But it will sure slow him down a bit."

"How did you know about him?" asked Kat.

Jeb's face became tense and his eyes burned. "I found my comrades on the trail early this morning. They had both been tortured and killed."

"They must have told the soldiers where to find us," Jonas said, contempt in his voice.

Jeb flashed him an angry look. "I'm sure they did. Pain can loosen any man's tongue. But I wager they lasted longer than a soft old fool like you would have."

Jonas lowered his eyes. "Forgive me. I spoke hastily. I'm sorry your friends are dead. And I thank you for saving us."

Jeb's features softened. "After what they did to my friends, I wasn't about to let them have you as well. From the look of the bodies, they held out for a long time before talking."

"Brave men," remarked Markus. "You have my sympathies."

"You can keep your sympathies," Jeb retorted. "I want to know why they are after you."

"They're after *me*," said Ethan. "They don't care about the rest."

Jonas shot him a cautionary look.

This did not go unnoticed by Jeb. "You can trust me to keep your secrets."

"As you so rightly pointed out," Markus told him, "Pain can loosen even a strong man's tongue. You're better off not knowing."

Jeb scrutinized Ethan for a long moment, as if trying to see what was going on inside his head. Finally, he nodded. "Very well. But you should at least let me take Kat with me. I have a feeling that your road is far more dangerous than mine."

"I'm staying with them," Kat insisted.

He placed his hands on her shoulders and looked into her eyes. "But why? What do you owe them?"

She smiled up at him. "Nothing. I just…I just know that I must."

"You should listen to Jeb," Jonas eased in. His tone was one of a concerned father. "He seems to be a good man. He'll look after you, I'm sure."

Kat swung around to face him, frowning. "I don't need looking after. I go where I want."

Jonas was unmoved by her sudden sharpness. "Did you not say that a princess always pays her debts? Did Jeb not just save your life?"

"And I *will* repay him," she countered. "But first I have to…I…"

She hesitated, lost for words. Eventually, she flicked a frustrated hand. "I just know I need to go with you, that's all."

Jeb sighed. "You are your own woman now, so I won't force you to come my way. But if you change your mind, you know how to find me."

A tiny smile grew from the corners of Kat's mouth. She embraced him tightly. "Thank you. And I really will repay you one day."

"I know you will, lass." He eased away from her and turned to the others. "You'd better not linger. The Grendil will be on your trail soon enough. But if you press your pace you can stay well ahead of him."

Markus nodded respectfully. "Thank you again."

Jeb chuckled. "You're not as I imagined, Specter. And for that I am grateful. I would speak with you privately before I go."

This time Markus did not deny the name and followed him to a spot several yards away. They talked in whispers for a couple of minutes before returning to the others.

Jonas and Ethan said goodbye to Jeb, and Kat gave him a final fond embrace.

"You see," she said proudly as they watched him vanish into the forest. "Thieves aren't all bad."

"So it seems," said Jonas.

"What did he say to you?" Ethan asked Markus.

"Nothing that concerns you," he said abruptly.

They headed east as fast as they could manage. Markus constantly checked for signs of pursuit, but to everyone's' great relief he could find no cause for concern. Making things even better, Jonas' illness appeared to be completely gone and he was easily keeping pace. Though it was well into the evening before they stopped, he was showing no signs of fatigue.

The meager meal they shared that night was far from satisfying, but their lack of provisions prevented anything more than a small repast.

Jonas positioned himself by the fire directly across from where Kat was settling into her bedroll. After a few minutes she could feel his gaze and sat up.

"How long have you known you could use magic?" he asked.

Kat scrambled to her feet, her eyes wide. "I don't know what you're talking about!"

Jonas smiled and held up his hand. "Calm down. There is nothing to fear."

She took a step back, as if readying herself to flee. "I don't use magic."

"Of course you do," he said. "And if you had the proper training you'd be quite good at it."

"When did she use magic?" asked Ethan. "I didn't see it."

Jonas laughed. "That's because she has become very skilled at hiding it." He turned to Kat. "Haven't you?"

She stood silent, a terrified look plastered across her face.

Ethan moved toward her. For a moment it looked as if she would run, but he held out his hand and gave her a friendly smile. "Come on. You're safe with us. I promise."

Kat allowed herself to be sat back down.

"I suspected it when we first met Specter in the street," Jonas began. "She vanished in an instant. Still, I wasn't certain. It was possible she was just very quick. Besides, a thief would be good at disappearing. But when we were at the lodge, then I knew for sure."

124

Kat wrapped her arms around her knees and began rocking back and forth. "*How* did you know?" Her voice cracked; tears welled in her eyes.

"Because you healed me of course," he replied.

Markus leaned back on his elbows and nodded. "I thought it was odd…you recovering so quickly and all."

"I didn't do anything," Kat insisted.

"Not intentionally, no," Jonas said. "But you have a natural gift. I've felt healing magic many times. And I could feel it coming from you as you cared for me."

Kat was now weeping openly.

"Why are you crying?" asked Ethan. "It's nothing to be ashamed of."

"I'm a monster!" she shouted. "An unnatural monster!"

"You are nothing of the sort," snapped Jonas. "Magical ability is a gift."

"But she's right," said Markus. "People would see her that way if they knew."

Ethan gently lifted her chin and looked into her eyes. "No one will ever know but us."

"Indeed," Jonas added. "As a matter of fact, I was hoping you could help Ethan with his own magic abilities…assuming he has some."

Kat frowned and wiped her eyes. "Why would you want that? He would be an outcast…like me."

"I already am," said Ethan. "We all are. There are things you don't know about us."

Jonas cleared his throat.

"What difference can it make?" Ethan continued. "It's not like she'll go running off to the Empire."

Jonas sighed and held up his hands. "Very well. Do as you wish."

Over the next few minutes Ethan went on to explain how he had arrived in Lumnia, then repeated what little Jonas had told him of his past. Kat stared at him in awe. By the time he finished, her tears had ceased and a fragile smile was lingering on her lips.

"When I was a little girl my mother told me about the time of the mages," she said. "But my father put a stop to it when he found out. He told us the mages were cruel tyrants, and that the Emperor destroyed them so we could be free."

Jonas clenched his jaw. "That is not true. Does this world look free to you?"

Kat shook her head, but said nothing as Jonas continued.

"The mages kept peace throughout the Five Kingdoms. They healed the sick. They fed the hungry. They created wondrous works of art and music, some so magnificent they would take your breath away." His eyes grew distant, and his voice soft and sorrowful. "I didn't fully appreciate it at the time. But the world I knew then was as near to paradise as any man could ask for."

"I don't understand," said Kat, frowning. "This place…Earth. If Ethan was taken there as a baby and you came back with him, how is it you can remember the time of the mages?"

"The magic Lady Illyrian used to take us there was forbidden," he explained. "It seems for good reason. The portal does something to the passage of time – though I don't know how it works. What is only minutes in one world can become years, even centuries, in the other. But I'm afraid I don't know anything more than that."

"And you think the dwarves will be able to tell you?" she asked.

"Possibly," he replied. "We'll find out when we get there."

"*If* you get there," corrected Markus. "You still have to deal with the fact that the Empire wants Ethan dead."

"Then it's fortunate that we have you to protect us," said Jonas.

Markus shook his head. "I told you – I'll take you as far as Tulani. From there, you're on your own."

"You would abandon your best friend?" asked Kat, appalled.

Markus shot to his feet, startling her. "Don't speak about things you know nothing of, girl. And don't presume to know me."

Kat quickly recovered her composure. "You're right. I don't know you. But I *do* know that you don't abandon a friend when he needs you most."

He gave a hollow laugh. "Is that what you think they are? My friends? I *have* no friends. It was friends who landed me in this wretched place to begin with." He pointed to Jonas. "Now this one wants to march into certain death." His finger shot over to Ethan. "And this one is so bloody stupid that he'll follow. Well, I have no intention of being led to my death by a fool and his crazy notions of a world that no longer exists. The mages are gone, and no one can bring them back. The dwarves will either kill you or turn you over to the Emperor. That's a fact. So if my *friend* chooses to ignore my advice, so be it."

"I have no intention of bringing the mages back," said Jonas. "Nor do I think it is within my power to do so. You say the dwarves will kill us. Perhaps. But if the Emperor knows a mage has returned to Lumnia he will *not* stop hunting Ethan until he's dead." He waved his hand dismissively. "So go if you want. Go find some hole to crawl inside and let your hate and anger consume you. Personally, I would rather die than live like that."

His final, contemptuous words sparked a rage in Markus that no one could have anticipated. Grabbing the hilt of his sword, he started toward Jonas. Ethan sprang up and leapt in front of him, but Markus would not be denied. Snarling, he shoved Ethan hard to the ground. Jonas scrambled backward, in his haste tripping and landing awkwardly. His eyes were now wide with fear as Markus drew his sword.

With a desperate cry, Ethan hurried to his feet and threw his shoulder low into Markus' midsection. Markus let out a grunt, but Ethan's slight frame was not enough to do much more than force him to take a single step back.

Quickly regaining his balance, Markus rammed his left elbow hard into the center of Ethan's back. He winced but held on. Markus twisted slightly and landed a second, even harder blow. This one drove Ethan to his knees.

With a face now crimson with fury and thick veins bulging from his neck, Markus smashed the hilt of his sword into the side of Ethan's head. He followed this up with a sharp jerk of the knee that sent him toppling over onto his back. Blood gushed from Ethan's open wound and his eyes glazed over as he struggled to retain consciousness.

Markus sheathed his sword and drew a small dagger. Kat was screaming for him to stop, but his rage was making him oblivious to all but the object of his wrath. Straddling Ethan's chest, he pressed the deadly steel to his throat.

Somehow, Ethan managed to regain his focus, but the weight of his friend had him pinned down and helpless. Kat rushed toward them with a knife in her hand, though to little effect. Markus easily grabbed her by the wrist and twisted. She let out a cry of pain and dropped the weapon. In a rapid single motion, he shoved her away.

By now Jonas was on his feet, fumbling with his sword, trying to draw it. "Stop right now!" he shouted.

His words had little impact. Markus pressed the blade down a fraction, drawing a thin trickle of blood from Ethan's neck.

The hatred etched deep into the scars of his best friend's ruined flesh was terrifyingly evident to Ethan. His heart was racing. "Don't do this, Markus." he pleaded. He held his breath, awaiting his fate. Was this to be his end? For some crazy, illogical reason, the 101st Airborne motto sprang to mind.

"Rendezvous with destiny," he murmured.

He had no idea if his friend had heard him, but Markus suddenly became absolutely motionless for what felt like an eternity. Then his hands began to tremble. A moment later he threw back his head and let out a feral roar that might well have come from a badly wounded animal. With a sharp movement of his wrist, he flicked the tip of the dagger in a shallow line across Ethan's cheek and heaved himself up. After glaring briefly at both Jonas and Kat, he stormed away into the night.

Jonas rushed over to Ethan's side. "Are you hurt?"

Ethan sat up, gingerly touching the wound on his face. "I'll be fine."

Kat tore a strip of cloth from her shirtsleeve and doused it with water. After cleaning his wound, she retrieved her dagger and sat staring outward into the forest.

"I don't think you need to worry," said Ethan. "If he was going to kill me, he would have done so already."

Kat's focus remain fixed. "I don't trust anything that man does."

Jonas looked at her with an amused yet respectful expression. "She certainly came to your defense in a hurry," he said just loud enough for Ethan to hear.

He smiled, even though his head was throbbing like crazy. "Yes she did. And so did you."

"That's my job...you might say. Though I admit that when it comes to fighting, I'm not a very useful protector."

"In France, I saw brave men turn coward and cowards become heroes in an instant," Ethan told him. "You never know what you can do until you're faced with it."

Jonas nodded. "I have found this to be true as well. I sometimes forget that you were a soldier. Your face is so young."

"Markus always said when I'm sixty, I'll still look twenty." He lowered his eyes. "I wish I could have said something."

"Markus is consumed by anger. And only he has the remedy." Jonas sighed. "There was nothing you could have said or done. Once a man starts down the path of self-loathing, the world around him changes. Its injustices reinforce the very thing that eats away at his heart until he can no longer see that good still exists."

"Even so, there must be something I can do," Ethan said. But he knew Jonas was right. He had seen the same thing in his mother – the sadness and anger that ate away at her soul, finally driving her mad. Regardless of what he tried, he had been powerless to help her. That was what Markus was now facing - the same pain and torment.

"The only thing to do now is get some rest," Jonas remarked. "Whether Markus is with us or not doesn't change the fact that we are pursued by the enemy."

The enemy, Ethan considered. At this point he would have preferred the Krauts. At least he knew why he was fighting them.

Jonas checked the gear and cleaned Ethan's wound one more time before they laid down to sleep. It took Ethan more than an hour to still his mind. Kat had eventually relaxed and taken a place near the fire – though her dagger remained in her hand, even as she slept.

Some instinct woke Ethan about an hour before sunrise. Blinking the sleep from his eyes, he saw the shadowy figure of Markus sitting on a felled tree a few yards away. He was hunched over with his arms draped across his knees, staring into the dwindling fire.

Ethan rose and took a tentative step forward. Markus glanced up and made room beside him. Unsure what to say, Ethan simply sat down and folded his hands.

"When you spoke to Jeb the other night," Markus began, "He told you that I was a bounty hunter and assassin for the Empire."

Ethan nodded. He had suspected that Markus was listening at the time, and now tried to recall the exact words of the conversation. "He said you weren't well liked, even among the Hareesh."

"He's right. And for good reason." His friend's voice was distant and filled with pain. "My anger toward you isn't really about my ending up in Lumnia. Or even the hardships I was forced to endure here. Hell, the Krauts were about to get us anyway, so the bloody portal probably saved my life. "

He sat up and held out his hands. "You have no idea what I have done with these. Do you know why they call me Specter?"

At first Ethan thought the question was rhetorical, but soon realized that Markus was waiting for a response. "I assumed it was because you're good at hiding...or something like that."

"It's because I have no soul. Or at least, that's what they say about me."

"That's ridiculous. Why would anyone say that?"

"I've done things...terrible things. Things I never thought I was capable of."

"Like what?"

Markus closed his fingers to make fists, clenching them tight. "These hands...sometimes I wish I could just chop them off. Maybe then I could be forgiven."

Ethan touched him on the shoulder. "Whatever you've done, I'm sure it's not as bad as you think."

He let out a disdainful laugh. "Really? I've killed people. Hundreds of them. And not just men. I've killed women...and..."

He swallowed hard. "And children. I've tortured entire families until they begged for death. I've skinned men alive while their enemies drank and laughed at their pain. I've done things that would make even the Nazi's sick to their stomachs."

Ethan was unsure how to react. "Why?" was all he could think to ask.

"To survive. At least, that's what I tell myself. The first time was hard. I didn't think I could live with myself afterward. I was hired by a merchant to kill his rival's young son. I had just joined the Hareesh and was trying to make a name for myself. No one else would take the job, so I did."

He looked up at Ethan, tears welling in his eyes. "He was only nine years old."

Markus wiped his face and shook his head. "I can barely remember doing it. All I see clearly is the frightened look on his poor little face." He paused to clear his throat. "After that, the Hareesh feared me. And the sad thing is, I liked it that way. I enjoyed how they would step aside when I walked by. It was the first time since I got here that I didn't feel powerless. From then on, I was the one who took the jobs the others didn't have the stomach for. And *that's* why they call me Specter."

After he finished, a lengthy silence developed. Eventually, Ethan said: "I'm so sorry that all this happened to you. But in spite of what you might think, you *do* have a soul. Whatever you've done, it doesn't matter anymore. Not to me. You're not Specter. You're Markus."

"You're wrong," he said. "I'm not Markus. I haven't been Markus for a long time. But I'd like to be him again. When I first saw you in Miltino it reminded me of who I was before I became a murderer. And it was that, more than anything that made me so angry. Not because I'm here, but because I'm Specter."

Ethan got to his feet and held out his hand. "Then let me help you find yourself again."

Slowly Markus cracked a twisted smile and chuckled softly. "A boy scout 'til the end."

He took Ethan's hand and allowed himself to be pulled up. "Jonas was right. Better to die trying. So let's go see the bloody dwarves."

CHAPTER ELEVEN

MARKUS AND ETHAN talked until dawn. Ethan thought it best to avoid any further questions about his friend's past, so he instead focused on discussing practical matters.

He discovered that the travel papers Markus had provided were only necessary when entering a city with a nearby garrison. Local rulers mostly didn't care who came and went, so long as they spent coin while they were there.

He also learned that the former Five Kingdoms were coming under ever increasing hardship, with famine and disease spreading at an alarming speed. The desert that separated the Imperial palace from the rest of the continent was expanding, and had already consumed thousands of acres of rich farmland.

"I started hearing rumors about Shinzan almost from the moment I arrived," Markus told him. "They say he is more than a thousand years old and can never die."

"Do they say anything about how he came to power?" Ethan asked.

"Not much. Only that he defeated the mages and the dragons single-handedly."

This mention of the dragons made Ethan recall his own vivid dreams about them. He decided to keep details of these to himself for now, but he did tell Markus about the tiny dragon he had seen at the farm.

His friend sat up straight and raised an eyebrow. "Are you sure that's what you saw?"

Ethan nodded. "And I keep getting this strange feeling. It's like they're watching me."

Markus thought for a moment. "I've heard stories. Legends really. They say that five children will come to challenge the Emperor for the soul of the world. They will be led by the last champion of the dragons, who will burn the Emperor's palace to cinders."

"And?"

"And nothing. I only heard it a few times from some of the Hareesh wives. It was just a bedtime story they told their children."

Jonas began to stir.

"We'll talk more later," Markus said, getting to his feet.

On spotting him, Jonas scowled and shook his head. "So you changed your mind, did you? Well, at least *Ethan* is happy about it."

"You should be too, old man," he shot back. "You know nothing of Lumnia. The world you left behind has been gone for a long time. It's amazing you even made it as far as Miltino without getting killed."

Jonas began gathering his things. "Then let us hope your decision to come with us isn't just a passing fancy."

Ignoring the insult, Markus walked over to the still sleeping Kat. He gently shook her awake. "It's time to go."

Her eyes popped wide when she saw him. She scrambled for her dagger which had fallen from her hand while she slept and was now on the ground beside her blanket.

"Easy girl," he said, holding up his palms. "I just want to say that I'm sorry if I hurt you last night."

Gradually Kat calmed down, though she continued firmly gripping the dagger and eyeing him with suspicion. "I'm not hurt," she said, touching the bruises on her wrist.

He gave her a curt nod, then moved quickly away to gather up his things.

The pace Markus set for them was at times almost a run. He said that if they were to stay ahead of the Grendil they would need to rest as infrequently as possible and sleep for no more than a few hours at a time. Though he didn't complain openly, it was easy to see that Jonas was less than enthusiastic about what was in store.

"It's not likely he'll try to follow us into the mountains," Markus told them. "The dwarves may trade with the Empire, but they sure as hell don't like strangers."

"The dwarves do business with the Empire?" asked Jonas, clearly disgusted by the idea.

"Of course," he replied. "Otherwise Shinzan would send an army to wipe them out. The only reason he tolerates them at all is that they can make magical items."

"What do they sell?" asked Ethan.

"Weapons mostly."

He recalled Jonas asking him if his rifle was a dwarf weapon. "What kind of weapons?"

"All kinds. Mostly fire blowers and lightning wands. Things like that. Though I've seen some that can make a man's blood boil inside his veins. But we don't need to worry about that."

Jonas gave an understanding nod, but Ethan was confused.

"Why?" he asked.

"Common soldiers aren't given those kind of weapons. Only the high ranking officers. And this far south you don't see too many of them. They prefer the comfort of the larger cities up north."

"The dwarves were always well known for their magic craft," Jonas added. "They were rumored to have constructed weapons that could level a building."

"That's more than just a rumor," Markus said. "The Empire has at least six of them - though I've only ever seen one."

"What did it look like?" asked Ethan.

"It's a long green crystal tube about three feet long and a foot in diameter. They have it mounted on a wooden frame. Looks kind of like an old cannon." Now it was Jonas' turn to look confused. Only Ethan understood the reference.

"Have you seen one being used?" Jonas asked.

Markus shook his head. "All but two are at the Emperor's palace. The others are used more for intimidation than anything else. There's one that sits at the gates of Kytain. The other gets moved around from city to city. Scares the hell out of the locals whenever it shows up."

"To rule by terror is a sign of weakness," Jonas remarked.

Markus chuckled. "It works though. Only those fools in Ralmaria are stupid enough to defy Shinzan. And all they do is raid Imperial caravans, then run away into the hills."

"At least there is *some* resistance," said Jonas.

"From time to time you'll see bands of rebels springing up, especially lately with the drought. But the Empire is quick to crush them. If you're thinking about looking for help, I wouldn't be looking there."

"I don't know *what* or *who* we'll be looking for," Jonas responded. "But it is good to know that someone might be willing to fight with us if needed."

Markus gave a hollow laugh. "If you go up against Shinzan, you'd better hope they're willing to get slaughtered. In the years I've been here I only know of one time the Emperor ventured out of The Eternal Palace. The King of Traxis was having difficulty putting down a rebellion and finally had to ask the Emperor for aid. By the time Shinzan arrived the rebels had grown to an army of almost twenty thousand men. Not that their numbers counted for much. From what I hear, he didn't take a single soldier with him when he went to fight them."

His expression darkened. "That was twenty years ago. I was in Traxis last summer. The field where Shinzan destroyed the rebellion is *still* in ruins. The ground is just soot and ash. Nothing grows for miles around. And incidentally, he also killed the king and his entire family for their failure."

"How can one man take on an entire army?" mused Ethan.

"The Emperor is powerful," said Jonas. "Though such a feat is more than I would have thought possible. It would have taken the entire Council of Volnar to manage such a thing."

"But didn't the Emperor destroy the Council?" asked Kat.

Jonas cocked his head. "So you've heard the story."

She nodded. "When I was a little girl. They say the whole of Lumnia trembled during the battle. All the mages of the world aligned themselves against the Emperor. But he was too strong for them and sent all of their souls into oblivion."

"The world did shake," agreed Jonas. "I remember the day it

happened very well." Kat looked at him in wonder. "And I remember when word came of the Council's defeat." He turned to Ethan. "That was the day I fled with you and your mother."

"If he's so powerful, how do we fight him?" Ethan asked.

"Who says we will?" Jonas replied. "I have no idea what we will do after we reach the dwarves. We'll figure that out when the time comes."

Ethan tried to imagine what could kill so many men. He had seen what bombs and artillery could do. But that was the concerted efforts of soldiers, tanks, and aircraft. What Shinzan had achieved alone was almost impossible to comprehend. The only magic he had witnessed up until now was Jonas lighting small fires, and even that tiny feat had hugely impressed him.

Markus had said that Masi was only a few days away. Once there, they would be able to purchase supplies and mounts – though it was unclear how long they would be able to stay mounted once reaching north of Tulia. From there they would need to leave the roads completely, and the rocky terrain was not suited for riding.

Each night before bed, Ethan asked Kat to show him how she managed to vanish. Unfortunately, she was not fully aware of how she achieved it herself. And there were times when she was completely unable to do it at all.

"It helps when I'm excited or afraid," she told him. "But if someone is in direct contact with me, I can't do it."

Nonetheless, she did her best to show him. But he had no better luck than when Jonas tried to teach him fire starting.

"Magic is something you feel," Jonas explained after yet another frustrating failure. Kat had been patient, but with no frame of reference, she was unable to communicate what it felt like.

"I don't feel anything," he grumbled. "Maybe I just don't have the ability."

"Then you would be the first person in history with two mage parents not to have it," Jonas stated emphatically. He thought for a moment. "Perhaps your time on Earth has affected you somehow." He waved his hand. "Little matter. You'll get it eventually."

"It might be better if he doesn't," said Markus from his bedroll. "Then Shinzan wouldn't be after him."

Jonas shook his head. "He'll kill him anyway. Just to be certain the Dragonvein line is dead and buried. The Emperor would never allow any potential challenge to his power. That was true even in my time."

"You see, Ethan," Markus said, giving a lopsided smile. "Even if you don't learn magic, there's no need to worry. You're dead no matter what."

Jonas was not amused by his remark, but Ethan shook his head and gave a soft chuckle. Markus had always possessed a dark sense of humor and it was good to hear him use it again.

By the time they reached Masi, Ethan had all but given up hope that he would ever be able to use magic. Jonas, on the other hand, had easily been able to teach Kat how to light a fire.

They entered the small village from the south, choosing to appear as if they had taken the road from Santfaliso. Without the shade of the forest, the morning sun was more oppressive than ever. The heat baked the dung strewn streets, filling the air with its stench. The few townsfolk who were about took little notice of the newcomers. Markus explained that Masi was simply a stopping-off point for travelers to resupply, and of little interest to the Empire. The nearest garrison was several hundred miles to the south.

The unpaved main street was riddled with holes and ruts from countless wagons passing through. A narrow sidewalk in front of the single story wooden buildings was in equally poor repair, and much care was needed not to step into the gaps where the wood had rotted away.

They made their way down a side road to a small tavern.

Just before they entered, Markus handed Jonas a scrap of parchment. "Here's a list of what we'll need. You and Kat see to it. Ethan and I will wait here. Try not to be too long."

Jonas stiffened, clearly not liking the way that Markus was giving him orders. But Markus paid him no mind and led Ethan on through the door.

Inside was much as Ethan expected. It was similar to the tavern in Jaobin, though far less crowded. A lone bartender was serving tables.

He looked at Markus and Ethan with displeasure before waving a hand to indicate that they should sit wherever they wanted.

Markus chose a table at the far corner of the room, sitting with his back to the wall. Ethan took the chair opposite and ordered a pitcher of ale.

He told Markus about his encounter with Durst, and the subsequent beating he had received.

"No wonder Kat feels like she owes you," he remarked. He leaned back, scrutinizing Ethan for a long moment. "I can't get over seeing you like this. You're so...young."

"It's been only a few days for me," Ethan said. "I can still hear the Kraut tanks rolling up the streets of Carentan when I sleep at night." He pulled open his shirt collar to reveal a two-inch wound that had only recently scabbed over. "I got this when that mortar shell hit the building, just before you..." His voice trailed off.

"Before I ended up here," said Markus, finishing his sentence for him. "Don't worry. It's all right to talk about it. I'm done with all that..."

He stopped short and leaned in close, his voice suddenly a whisper. "Don't turn around. Three Imperial soldiers just came through the door." He pulled his hood up over his head. "Don't do anything unless I do."

Ethan could hear the stomping of their boots and the rattle of armor drawing closer. He fingered the dagger in his belt nervously.

"You!" shouted a gruff voice. "Turn around! And you, remove your hood."

Ethan felt a gloved hand grip his right shoulder. Markus pushed back his hood and smiled.

"Spirits take me, you're ugly," said the soldier with a jeering laugh.

Ethan turned in his seat and looked up at the guard. The foul stench of the man's breath combined with his body odor caused him to grimace.

"Where are you two coming from?" he demanded.

"Santfaliso," Markus replied.

"What was your business there?"

"Guarding a fat merchant's cargo."

The soldier regarded Ethan and snorted. "This one doesn't look like he'd make much of a guard."

"He's my son," Markus explained. "And he's tougher than he looks."

"Your son is he? We'll see about that. Show me your papers."

Ethan fought to keep his hand from shaking as he reached inside his pocket and held up the papers his friend had provided. Markus handed over his also.

The soldier ran his eyes over them. "Says here you're from Ralmaria."

Markus nodded.

"A long way to go just to guard a merchant's wares."

Before Markus could respond, the door burst open and a third soldier hurried inside. He handed over a folded parchment, then whispered into his comrade's ear.

"I think you two should come with me," the first soldier told them sharply. His hand slipped to the hilt of his sword.

Markus gave Ethan an almost imperceptible nod. "Of course. Whatever you say."

As both he and Markus rose from their seats, Ethan's eyes located a gap beneath the first soldier's armpit where the breastplate of his armor was connected to the back. Here, a thin shirt was all that protected him.

Markus rounded the table and the two other soldiers moved toward him. "Now!" he shouted.

Reacting instantly, Ethan drew his blade and plunged it deep into the first soldier's ribs. He could feel the steel scraping across bone as it sunk in. By now, in a blaze of movement, Markus had already whipped out his own dagger and slashed it across the exposed throat of his nearest opponent. The remaining soldier's eyes shot wide as he fumbled frantically to draw his sword. But panic was making him far too clumsy and slow. Pausing only to flash the man a sinister grin, Markus jammed the dagger up through the bottom of his chin and into his brain. He was dead even before he crumbled to the floor.

Ethan jerked his dagger free from the first soldier, then shoved him onto the table with all his strength. Blood was pouring from the gaping wound in his side. His face was contorted with pain and fear. But there was also a pleading expression in his eyes that made Ethan pause for a split second.

The glint of steel was a blur as Markus came in and finished the man off.

"You can't hesitate," he scolded, pointing to the soldier's outstretched arm. In his hand was a knife ready to plunge into Ethan's back.

Ethan stared, unable to speak. It was a lesson he'd had drummed into him during Airborne training, and one he should never have forgotten. But though he had killed before, he had never done it this way. Up until now his battles had always been at a distance. This was so…personal.

The screaming and shouting from the other customers around them snapped him back into the moment. People were racing from the tavern and into the streets. In seconds they were alone.

Markus unbuckled a scabbard from one of the dead soldiers and tossed it to Ethan. "Put this on," he ordered. It was small – only twice the length of a dagger – yet solid and heavy.

While Ethan did as instructed, Markus picked up the paper the first soldier had been given and read it carefully. A deep frown formed on his face. "It would seem word has spread faster than I imagined. We need to find Jonas and Kat and get the hell out of here."

Having completed the attachment, Ethan drew the sword from its scabbard. It felt awkward and ill-balanced in his hand.

"Just swing it hard," instructed Markus. "If we get out of this, I'll teach you how to use it properly."

At that moment Ethan was dearly missing his M-1 carbine. Hell, a .45 would do.

Markus approached the door and pushed it open just wide enough to peer out. He spat a curse.

"Three more are headed this way," he said grimly. "And this time they'll be ready for us."

"So what do we do?"

Markus gave a pessimistic chuckle. "We fight. What else *can* we do?" He crouched down against the wall next to the door and gestured for Ethan to do the same on the other side. "We'll take them as they come in. Go for the legs."

Focus, Ethan told himself, doing his best to keep his adrenaline from running away with him. He felt much like he had on D-Day. With heart pounding, he gripped the hilt of the sword so hard his knuckles popped.

"Take it easy," Markus said. "Don't lose your head. You can do this."

Ethan had heard these words from Markus before. His reassuring tone and steady nerves had bolstered his courage the very first time they had seen battle together. Now, they were having a similar effect. He drew in a deep cleansing breath. As if to order, his hands ceased trembling and his heart rate slowed to an even rhythm.

It was still beating steadily a few moments later when the door burst open and slammed into the wall just in front of him. As a soldier rushed inside, Ethan swung his blade hard. His steel split the cuisse wide, cutting deep into the enemy's thigh. The man let out a cry and fell forward, his sword falling to the floor.

Markus leapt into the doorway to thrust his blade hard into the second soldier's chest, forcing him outside. After pulling it free, he spun left to attack the third who was just a few feet behind.

Ethan looked back to the man he had wounded. He was scrambling for his lost weapon, a look of pain and terror in his eyes. This time Ethan knew what he had to do – but not exactly how to do it. With a heavy grunt, he struck at the soldier's outstretched sword arm. The blade cut deep and there was the crack of bone breaking. He stepped back and saw that his blow had very nearly severed the limb completely at the elbow. The soldier thrashed and writhed, desperately clutching at his wounded arm. Blood was spewing everywhere, soaking the floor and showering the walls. The stricken man tried to mouth the word *please*, but Ethan struck again, this time at his exposed neck. The blade lodged in his spine and Ethan was forced to plant his foot on the man's chest and pull hard to remove it. The scraping of his blade on bone made his skin crawl. He looked down at his handiwork. The soldier was still twitching and shuddering, blood spurting from his neck in time with the remaining beats of his heart.

The loud ring of clashing steel from outside tore his attention away from the macabre scene. As he exited the tavern he could see that Markus was engaged in fierce battle with the remaining standing soldier. The other was on his knees a few feet away, clutching at the wound in his chest. Ethan moved in to finish him off. He raised his sword high, but the soldier saw him coming and rolled to one side just in time. The blade thudded into the ground and his momentum sent him stumbling forward. Even though the soldier's face was contorted with pain, he still managed to struggle to his feet and lift his weapon. Blood covered the front of his armor, obscuring his crest.

Ethan struck again, but the soldier skillfully deflected his attack and stepped back. After a few more unsuccessful attempts it quickly became clear that, even wounded, the soldier far outmatched him. Had he not been injured, the fight would have already been over.

The soldier countered – and though his blow was accurate, the loss of blood was slowing him down, allowing Ethan to jump clear. However, his opponent's longer blade was preventing him from doing anything more than moving left and right, feigning attacks and then withdrawing.

Frustrated, he reached for his dagger and threw it as hard as he could. The hilt smashed into the soldier's brow. For a moment he simply stood there, stunned. Then his legs wobbled and he dropped to one knee. Ethan charged in, swinging his sword wildly. The blade struck the soldier's collarbone, forcing him down onto both knees. Another swift blow settled the matter.

Meanwhile, Markus was still fighting hard, though by now he had managed to inflict several small wounds on his opponent. Ethan was just about to move around to the soldier's back when he spotted another one appear from the corner of a building a few blocks away. His heart sank. He had only been able to defeat the two men he'd faced so far through sheer luck and surprise. He would not get either of those advantages against this one. But unless he could prevent him joining the fray, Markus would surely be overwhelmed.

The soldier was closing on them rapidly when Ethan spotted a horse galloping along behind him. At first he could see only that the rider was holding a sword aloft. But as the animal drew closer he realized that it was Jonas on its back.

Hearing the rapidly closing hoof beats, the soldier spun around. But Jonas was already upon him. Swinging his blade, he struck the man mightily in the chest, the impact sounding much like a hammer striking an anvil. The sheer force of the blow ripped the weapon clean out of Jonas' hand, at the same time yanking him from the saddle. He landed hard on the street and rolled on for several yards. Some distance behind, the soldier lay motionless on his back – his breastplate split in two and a tremendous wound dividing his chest.

Ethan wanted to run to Jonas, but knew he needed to help Markus first. He moved to the soldier's right and raised his sword high. This alone proved to be sufficient, distracting the man just long enough for Markus to slip beneath his guard and ram his sword into his gullet. The soldier gasped and clutched at the blade. It was his last action. In a single fluid motion, Markus pulled the weapon free and took his head from his shoulders.

Without pause, they both ran to where Jonas was still lying face down in the street. Markus rolled him over.

"Are you badly hurt?" he asked.

Jonas groaned and rubbed his sword arm. "I don't think so."

"Where's Kat?" asked Ethan.

"Waiting at the livery with the horses and supplies," he replied. "We overheard the soldiers asking questions about newcomers. Luckily, they didn't spot us."

Markus glanced up and down the road. "How many did you see?"

Jonas struggled to his feet, "Only two. But I assumed there must be more."

Ethan noticed that Markus was continuing to scan the area nervously. "What's wrong?" he asked.

"If there are this many regulars around here, then officers won't be far behind. And maybe even Rakasa."

Jonas froze, his face suddenly fear stricken.

"What are Rakasa?" Ethan asked.

"Something you never want to encounter," Markus told him grimly. "Now let's get the hell out of here."

After retrieving his sword and horse, Jonas led them to the livery. Along the way, Ethan noticed that the streets were now completely empty. People were peering at them through their windows with dread in their eyes. But to his relief there were no more soldiers about.

Kat was waiting for them just inside the stable doors. A short fat man with weathered features and narrow eyes was standing a few feet behind her with a knife in his hand.

He took a step back as they entered. "You need to leave here at once." His voice cracked and his hands were shaking. "I don't need your kind 'round here."

Jonas took a silver coin from his purse. "For your trouble," he said, tossing it on the ground.

The man hesitated only for an instant before snatching up the coin and hurrying out the back.

They quickly mounted their horses.

"Follow my lead," said Markus. He spurred his steed to a run.

Ethan had only ridden a few times when he was younger, but managed to keep his mount steady and under control. The clatter of hooves, together with the rattling of their gear and weapons, echoed eerily through the deserted streets. He glanced behind him. For a second he thought he saw the cloaked figure of a man standing in the avenue, but when he looked again there was no one there.

They rode hard north for more than an hour before Markus called for a halt and took a long look back. The forest on either side was dense and overgrown with thick brambles and brush.

"We should leave the road," he told them. "There are hunting trails we can follow a few miles to the west."

For more than two hours they were unable to ride and were forced to lead their horses through a labyrinth of pines, oaks, and birch trees. Some were growing so close together that their trunks had fused and twisted around each other. The air was heavy, and even the sounds of the birds high above seemed muffled.

They traveled in silence, with Markus stopping briefly every now and then to listen for signs of pursuit - then with a snort, continuing on his way.

It was well past midday by the time they reached the narrow trail. Jonas took some bread and a water skin from his pack and distributed it to the others. They stopped for a few minutes to eat but did not sit, instead standing beside their mounts ready to flee should the need arise.

With his feet aching quite badly from navigating the bumpy ground, Ethan was grateful when they were all finally able to get back in the saddle. He wondered how Jonas had coped with the difficult walk. Kat had checked the scrapes and bruises from his fall while they ate. On the surface at least, he seemed to be none the worse for wear.

By nightfall the woods were thinning and the trail widening.

"There's a stream up ahead," Markus said, breaking the long silence. "We can at least clean up a bit and wash the blood away."

Ethan looked down at his clothes and hands, only then noticing how badly they were spattered with blood. The thought sickened him. Fear had kept the memory of the fight at bay, but now a vision of what he had done came flooding back.

Markus instructed them to tie their horses to a fallen tree away from the trail and led them to the stream. Ethan did his best to clean his shirt and trousers, but eventually gave up and put on fresh clothing. The water was icy cold and clear as crystal. Once washed and changed, he took a long soothing drink before heading back to the horses.

"We should forgo a fire," Jonas said, after they had all returned.

Markus nodded. "And you should try to sleep. We're still a long way from the mountains. If we're lucky we'll stay ahead of the Imperials. But we'll need to move quickly."

They unpacked some blankets and a small meal of dried figs and jerky.

"How did they find us so quickly?" asked Ethan through a mouthful of jerky.

"That's what bothers me," Markus replied. "The only way is if they have a *sending rod*." He could see the confusion on Ethan's face. "It's like a telephone in a way. It's a rod about a foot long. People can use them to talk over great distances. They're very rare, and only high ranking officers…or a Rakasa would be in possession of one."

"Those Rakasa demons still exist?" said Jonas. "I thought they were all destroyed."

Markus tightened the blanket around his shoulders. "I wish."

"So what do you know about them?" asked Ethan.

"No one knows very much for certain," Markus replied. "Shinzan uses them as his personal guard and assassins. Some say they're cursed elves, others say that they're devils summoned from the fiery depths. The only sure thing is that, if you do ever meet one that's after you, death is guaranteed."

"The council tried to eradicate them just after Shinzan came to power," added Jonas. "He had somehow gained control over their minds and was using them to kill the lesser mages. I thought the council succeeded in wiping them out. But I guess I was wrong."

"I've seen one," Kat interjected. "When I was a little girl we had one come to see my father."

Markus chuckled. "And what business would the father of a thief have with the Rakasa?"

"I don't know," she replied, ignoring the insult. "But I definitely saw one."

"What did it look like?" asked Ethan.

"I couldn't see its face. It was all cloaked in black. But its hands were white as snow, and it had a voice as hollow as the wind. I didn't know what it was at the time, but I knew to be very afraid of it."

"Anyone would have that description," scoffed Markus. "But whether or not you really saw one doesn't matter. If *we* see one, it's all over. Now enough talk. We need to get some sleep."

Kat huffed at Markus and turned her back. "I'm not lying," she whispered.

Ethan rested his hand on her shoulder. "I believe you."

She smiled up at him. "I really am a princess you know. That's why the Rakasa came to my house. One day I'll prove it."

Ethan returned her smile. "Like I said, I believe you."

Kat's smile slowly vanished. "No you don't. No one does."

CHAPTER TWELVE

A SHARP PAIN IN Ethan's ribcage shocked him awake. The clatter of steel and the sound of gruff voices surrounded him even before his eyes were fully open.

He tried to stand, but the blunt toe of a boot thudded into his stomach, forcing the breath from his lungs. Gasping for air, he sank back down.

His sword was missing from its place beside his blanket, but the dagger was still in his belt. Apart from the soldier standing over him, he could see three others in the background. Two of them were holding Markus, and the other was pressing his heel down hard on Jonas' chest. There was no sign of Kat anywhere.

"Don't move, boy," he was told. This order was punctuated with another swift kick.

He looked at Markus, but his friend's eyes were wide and fixed on something else. Risking another blow, Ethan shifted his head to see what could be affecting him so. A few yards away stood a cloaked figure with its hood pulled down low. Although it was impossible to distinguish its face, the ghostly pale hand gripping a long curved blade was all too visible.

Rakasa, he thought.

The thing move forward with unnaturally even strides and stood beside Jonas.

"It's been a long time…Jonas," it said.

As Kat had described, its voice was hollow, yet bore an unnatural resonance that sent waves of fear into Ethan's heart.

Jonas looked up. "Who are you?"

The Rakasa bent down and grasped his left ankle, raising the pant leg sufficiently to expose a ring of pink scar tissue – the mark of a whip. "It really has only been a few weeks for you, hasn't it?" the hollow voice uttered.

Jonas' eyes shot wide as realization dawned. "General Hronso," he gasped.

Hronso hissed a sinister laugh. "Yes. And I see you have brought the young Dragonvein with you." Releasing Jonas' leg, he looked across at Ethan. "I must admit, he's not what I expected."

"How can you be here?" Jonas demanded, his voice a mixture of terror and confusion.

"You were always clever," Hronso replied. "Too clever for your own good, as I recall. Clever enough to elude me. And clever enough to escape with the Emperor's prize. Surely you can figure it out."

He paused, but Jonas said nothing. "No? Well, I'm sure the Emperor will be more than happy to explain it to you. Though I must admit, I think he should just let me kill the lot of you right now. But he's always been a bit sentimental. Why he wants to see you again, I just don't know."

"What are you talking about?" asked Jonas. "I've never met Shinzan."

Hronso's laugh this time sounded more natural...almost human. "Is that right? *He* seems to think you have. And I do *not* question my master's word." He cast his gaze upon Markus. "However, he made no mention of this one. So at least we will have *some* sport today."

Markus glared defiantly. "I'm not afraid of you."

With inhuman speed, Hronso spanned the distance between them. Ethan saw his friend's hands ball up into tight fists, suppressing his fear.

"Of course you're afraid," the general told him. He touched Markus' facial scars with a pale finger. "A very fine piece of handiwork if you don't mind me saying so. It gives you character."

Markus curled his lip. "Don't toy with me. If you're going to kill me, get it over with."

"Ah. It seems that the great and terrible Specter has courage. A pity that you cast your lot in with this rabble. You were a useful tool." He turned to Ethan. "But alas. All things have their time." He waved his hands casually. "Cut Specter's throat, then bind the other two."

"No!" Ethan scrambled to get up. The soldier tried to kick him down again, but he rolled away and managed to gain one knee.

His guard took a step toward him, but Ethan had already drawn the dagger from his belt. Seeing the steel thrusting at his gullet, the soldier attempted to back away but was too late. Ethan threw himself forward. His dagger found flesh and sank in deep.

He tried to pull the blade free, but a crushing blow to the head sent him sprawling. The Rakasa was standing over him, his fist clenched.

"That's quite enough out of you, young Dragonvein," Hronso chided.

He turned away to briefly regard the wounded soldier. "Careless," he murmured, raising his sword with effortless skill. Only the whistle of the deadly steel cutting the air told that he had actually struck.

Ethan stared in amazement. Hronso was so fast, he appeared not to have moved at all.

For a moment the soldier remained utterly still, as if unaffected by the strike. Then, in an almost graceful movement, his head rolled slowly from his shoulders and bounced onto the forest turf. Even now, with blood spurting from its neck, the body continued to remain upright for a few seconds longer before finally collapsing in a heap.

"I can't abide carelessness," Hronso said without a trace of emotion. He glared at the men holding Markus. "What are you waiting for? I said cut his throat."

"Please!" begged Ethan. He attempted to rise, but Hronso moved close, looming over him.

With tears streaming down his cheeks, he watched in horror as the soldier on his friend's right drew a small knife. With the deadly blade only inches from his neck, Markus displayed no fear. Instead, he merely nodded in Ethan's direction and gave him a sad smile of farewell.

A hiss split the air, freezing the soldier's hand. Hronso spun to one side and an arrow buried itself into a tree just behind where he had been standing only an instant before. From all directions, feral yells and unintelligible screams suddenly sounded. Clearly intended to terrify, they reminded Ethan of the Indian war cries in cowboy movies.

The soldiers holding Markus threw him to the ground and drew their swords. A second arrow pierced the throat of the man guarding Jonas. He clutched desperately at the shaft for a moment before falling to the ground, his body still jerking.

"Run!" shouted Markus.

The two remaining soldiers were crouched down low, fearfully scanning the surrounding forest for a sign of their attackers. But Ethan was still frozen with shock.

"No time to argue, damn it," Markus shouted. "Get moving!" He was crawling toward where his sword lay on the ground several yards away. "We'll be right behind you."

Shaken out of his stupor, Ethan glanced over to Jonas. He was still on his back.

"I'll get Jonas," Markus called over. "You run."

Ethan scurried to his feet and did as instructed – though he had no idea of where he was heading. The cries of the attackers seemed to be all around him. He expected to feel the stinging bite of an arrow at any moment. But it never came, so he kept running blindly on. Low hanging branches from the trees clawed at his face and arms, leaving behind dozens of tiny scratches.

Eventually, with lungs burning and legs unable to support him any longer, he collapsed behind a thick pine. The voices were now distant and less frequent. Slowly, he managed to catch his breath and calm down. But every second that ticked by compounded his guilt for having left Markus and Jonas behind. And Kat. Where was she? He fervently hoped that she had heard their attackers coming and used her magic to disappear.

"Fortune smiles on us both it would seem," said a voice just behind him.

He spun around and saw Hronso standing a few yards away. Pressing his back against the tree, he reached to his belt. But his weapon was gone. He cursed himself for failing to retrieve his dagger before fleeing. Not that it would have done him much good against Hronso.

"Don't run, Dragonvein," the general warned. "There is no escape. If you resist I'll be forced to injure you, and the Emperor wants you brought to him in one piece. By now the elves will have slaughtered your friends…and unfortunately my soldiers as well." He let out an insincere sigh. "Poor souls. I suppose I'll have to take you along alone and unaided."

Ethan's eyes darted from side to side, desperately searching for some way of escape. But unarmed and against someone…or something…that could move as fast as he'd witnessed, there was no hope.

Hronso produced a thin rope from beneath his cloak. "You will forgive me if I bind your hands. I have no intention of taking a chance with a Dragonvein. Even one as unimpressive as…"

The sudden flapping of wings cut him short. From above, the tiny dragon Ethan had seen at the farm slowly descended, landing just by his feet. Clearly startled, Hronso took a pace back. The rope slipped from his grasp, but he made no immediate move to draw a weapon.

The dragon craned its neck and let out a high pitched screech. Ethan stared in wonder at the creature. Its black scales glistened in the sun like polished ebony. Its spines glittered like diamonds.

It turned to face Ethan, its piercing blue eyes bearing the look of both intelligence and recognition. Something inside him stirred. Something that he knew had always been there, but only now was becoming aware of. A voice in his mind was speaking to him, though its language contained no words – only emotion and intent. It compelled him to kneel. Hronso was all but forgotten as he stretched out his hand. The dragon moved forward and rested its head on Ethan's palm.

The heat of its flesh was almost painful, yet it filled him with a joy he had never known. It was as if bliss had become tangible – something he could wrap himself within.

The threatening song of steel sliding free from its scabbard broke the spell. He looked up and saw that Hronso had now drawn his sword.

The dragon flicked its long black tongue and let out a contented purr. At that moment, a wave of emotion washed over Ethan. He knew what the dragon intended. He let out a gasp and his eyes shot wide.

Hronso charged, sword held high. Then all was dark.

*

Ethan's eyes fluttered open. At first he couldn't see anything, but slowly he regained focus and a night sky peppered with the twinkling of a million stars appeared. The crackle of a camp fire and the scent of cooking meat helped him to further gather his senses. He tried to prop himself up on his elbows, but a delicate hand touched his forehead and gently laid him back down.

"Be still." It was Kat.

Ethan tilted his head back and smiled. "I'm so glad you're all right. I was afraid that you'd been hurt."

"I escaped just before the Rakasa and his men arrived," she explained. "Sorry I left you, but there wasn't time to give you a warning."

"No need to apologize," he said. "Are the others with you?"

"Yes," she replied. "They're not far away."

With each passing second he was becoming more aware of his surroundings. Something wasn't right. He looked at Kat more closely. Her face was tight and her eyes were darting back and forth nervously. Then something else occurred to him. Cooking meat. They had not brought anything to cook, only dried foods and bread.

He brushed her hand away and sat up. "What's wrong with you?"

The fire behind him was burning gently, a pair of rabbits roasting on a spit above it. Further back, he was just able to make out the silhouetted figures of Jonas and Markus. They were seated and motionless. Ethan's face lit up.

"Thank God you're here," he called out. "I was afraid the elves had killed you."

Neither man moved or responded.

He looked back to Kat. The tension in her expression had increased.

"They may still die," said a voice from beyond the firelight. "And so may you, mage." The voice was musical and clear, yet bore the timbre of neither male nor female.

Ethan scrambled to his feet. "Who's there?" he demanded. "Come out where I can see you."

Kat stood and grabbed his arm. "No sudden movements," she whispered.

"Your friend gives wise council," said the voice. "Twenty bows are trained at your heart. Lift your hands or try to cast a spell and you will all die. Am I understood?"

"I can't cast spells," said Ethan. He kept his arms by his side and remained still. "I'm not a mage."

"Lies will only anger us," it warned. "We saw what you did to the *cursed one*."

Ethan frowned. "The cursed one? I don't know what you're talking about."

"You know him as Hronso. We saw you unleash your magic and drive him away."

Ethan tried to recall what had happened. He could remember the dragon, and then Hronso charging in. But after that his memory was a blank.

"I still don't know what you're talking about," he repeated. "I swear it."

"And I suppose you don't remember the dragon either."

"Yes, I remember that," he admitted. He could still clearly see its tiny head resting in his palm. But there was something else. Something important that he was missing. As he pictured the dragon's eyes staring up at him, he was overcome by a wave of inexplicable sorrow. A tear spilled down his cheek. Suddenly, it was all he could do not to break down and sob his heart out.

"Why do you weep, mage?"

"I…I don't know." He cleared his throat and wiped his eyes.

A tall figure appeared from out of the darkness. Though its voice was not distinctly male, its features most certainly were. He was at least a full head taller than Ethan and much broader in the shoulders. His silver hair was tied into a series of tight braids that fell down his back and over his shoulders. The outside corners of his eyes were turned up, giving him an otherworldly stare. This was compounded by ears that curved into a high point very nearly reaching the top of his head. He was clad in a deep green shirt and pants made from a material that barely reflected the firelight - a feature that allowed him to blend almost perfectly into the background. On his feet he wore what reminded Ethan of Indian moccasins, though without the beads and fringe he had seen in the past. His frame was muscular without being overly so, and his movements were fluid and graceful. Around his waist he wore a long sword with a hilt of ivory, inlaid with gold and onyx. A bow and quiver containing silver fletched arrows was strapped across his back.

Ethan's mouth fell agape at the sight of him. Something completely…inhuman. Strange and terrifying, yet beautiful to behold. The elf stopped a few feet away.

"Does my appearance disturb you, mage?" he asked.

"Yes," he blurted out before he could think. "I mean…no. It's just I've never seen…"

"Why do you weep?" he asked again, cutting him short.

"I don't know. I just…when I thought about the dragon I…I felt sad. I can't explain it."

The elf's eyes narrowed and he folded his hands in front of him. "What is your name?"

"Ethan," he replied. "Ethan Martin."

"Martin?" The newcomer took a step forward and his hand slid to his sword. "I have never heard that name associated with dragons before. Who was your father?"

Ethan glanced over to where Jonas and Markus were sitting. He waited to see if Jonas would speak, but quickly realized he would not.

"Answer me," the elf demanded.

"My father was Praxis Dragonvein."

The elf stiffened, and murmurs could be heard within the forest around him. After several seconds he removed his hand from his sword and took a step back. "I can see that you speak the truth, and yet what you say is not possible. The Dragonvein line was broken long ago. Praxis was the last. Or so we have been told. My people know well the lore of dragons. And we know of the family with whom they were bonded. How is it that you are here?"

"I was sent to Earth by my mother when I was a baby," explained Ethan. "I really don't understand most of it. But when I came back, hundreds of years had passed."

The elf's face twisted into a snarl. "I should have guessed. Portal magic. Stupid humans meddling with what they don't understand and can't control." He glared at Ethan. "And now *you* have come, and with you comes war and death. I should kill you now and be rid of you. But I will wait. Dragons do not reveal themselves without good cause. Even those which have been diminished by Shinzan." He let out a series of high-pitched whistles. "Do not expect mercy should you encounter me or my kin again. If the Mother wishes your continued existence, she will guide you far away from us. But for now, go in peace and fear not enemy eyes. While you are in this forest, none shall harm you."

Having delivered this bizarre combination of dire warning and positive reassurance, the elf burst into a run and quickly vanished into the night.

The moment he was out of sight, Markus and Jonas rose to their feet and approached the fire. Markus had a deep gash over his left eye, while Jonas carried several bruises across his face.

"Are you two all right?" Ethan asked.

Markus sat down by the fire. He nodded, but said nothing. Ethan could tell that he was shaken and felt it best to leave him to his thoughts for a time.

Jonas, on the other hand, looked very much relieved.

"Fortune indeed favors us," he said, smiling broadly. "I was certain they would kill us all. But it seems that the elves hate Hronso enough to keep his captives alive. And from what Kat told me, your display of power helped us as well."

"I really don't remember what happened," Ethan admitted.

"What *do* you remember," asked Kat.

Ethan told them about the dragon, mentioning how he had seen it previously. This soured Jonas' expression.

"You should have told me about this at the time," he scolded.

"I didn't trust you," Ethan countered. "I felt you were holding things back."

Jonas nodded. "I understand. I should have handled matters better in the beginning. Remember though, I was almost as confused as you were back then."

Ethan gave him a forgiving smile. "What did *you* see," he asked Kat.

She drew a deep breath. "I chased after you, but you were too fast for me and I lost you for a while. I found you again just as you let loose a great blast of white flame straight into Hronso's chest. After that you kind of collapsed, like it had drained you of all your energy. I tried to help you, but the elves captured me. They must have been watching the whole time because they knew everything."

Ethan strained his mind, trying to remember, but he could still recall nothing. "Did you see the dragon?"

"No," she replied. "But the elves did. And they seemed pretty upset about it. They kept arguing back and forth over whether or not to kill you. The one you spoke to was against it."

"Why?" asked Jonas.

Kat spread her hands. "I don't know. But he won out in the end. I got the feeling he thinks Ethan is important somehow."

"What difference does it make what those savages think?" growled Markus. He threw a twig into the fire. "They're gone, we're alive, and we should be grateful."

"Indeed we should be," agreed Jonas. "But I think it would be wise to understand their motives."

Markus spat. "Bah! They probably think that sparing us will give them a chance to kill *more* humans later."

"I doubt that," said Jonas, rubbing his chin. "I don't know much about elves. But I was surprised that they knew of the Dragonvein family. Praxis never spoke about them, and as far as I know, dragons never had anything to do with elves either. But then, I only know what little Lord Dragonvein told me."

"You think the dwarves would know?" asked Ethan.

He nodded. "If anyone would, it's them. Elves hate dwarves even more than humans. And I do know that the feeling is mutual."

"What about Hronso?" Ethan asked Kat. "What happened to him?"

She shrugged. "I assumed you killed him. The entire area was burned to cinders and I didn't see his body anywhere."

"The elves seem to think he's still alive," remarked Jonas. "He said that Ethan drove him away, not that he killed him."

There was a doubtful frown on Kat's face. "I don't think anyone could have survived what I saw."

"I hope you're right," Jonas said. "General Hronso was responsible for killing dozens of mages – even members of the Council of Volnar."

He looked directly at Ethan, his jaw tightening. "He also killed your mother."

"My mother?"

Jonas nodded. "It was Hronso who tracked us down. His pursuit forced her to open the portal and send you through."

Ethan wasn't sure how to feel about this new piece of information. The only mother he'd ever known had been on Earth. He had no connection to the woman Jonas was mentioning.

After a short silence, Jonas sighed. "There are too many mysteries to figure out in one night. Like Markus said, for now we should be grateful simply to be alive." He glanced over at the rabbits cooking on the spit. "And it will be nice to eat something other than jerky and bread."

"Why do you suppose the elves left it for us?" asked Ethan.

"Never question a gift," said Jonas. "Perhaps it's just their custom. Better a rabbit in the belly than a knife in the heart."

Once thoroughly cooked, they distributed the meal – though Markus refused to eat any. This did not stop Ethan from enjoying it. The warm meat felt good in his stomach and helped to lift some of the weight from his heart.

He replayed the day's events in his mind while lying beside the fire. What made him so sad every time he thought about the dragon? And what had really happened with Hronso? For now, these would have to join the many other questions to which he desperately needed answers.

He sighed. It was clear that he had been mistaken about Jonas when they first arrived. Though he believed that he was still withholding secrets, he understood now that the old man had been every bit as lost as he was.

His mind shifted to Markus, and how Hronso had taunted him about his terrible scars. Who or what had inflicted these on him was still a mystery. Though there were times when the friend he once knew would surface, far too often it was still Specter who was speaking with Markus' voice. He hoped that once they reached the dwarves, things would become clearer.

Of course, there was always the chance that Markus was right and they simply were marching to their deaths.

CHAPTER THIRTEEN

T HE FOLLOWING MORNING Ethan was the first to wake. The sky was painted in the orange and violet of the coming dawn, while all around large drops of dew rolled off the pine needles and oak leaves. The only sounds aside from the occasional snort from a sleeping Jonas came from the chirping of birds and the gentle rustle of a few small animals scurrying through the underbrush.

He got to his feet and stretched. Yet again his sleep had been troubled by visions of dragons, this time flying high in the clouds and then bursting into flames. As their bodies plummeted he could hear their screams inside his head, begging him for help. But he was powerless. The sadness he felt when thinking about the tiny dragon had lessened somewhat, but the mystery remained as to why he should feel that way in the first place.

"Can I talk to you?"

He hadn't noticed Kat rise.

"Sure."

She led him away from the others to a small patch of thick grass and sat down. For a short time she was silent, as if still contemplating what she would say.

Ethan took her hand. Her fingers were cold and damp, and for the first time he noticed that her eyes were red from recent tears.

"What's wrong?" he asked.

Kat withdrew her hand and met his gaze. "Have you ever been with a woman?"

Ethan stiffened. "What? Why would you...I mean...that's kind of personal, don't you think?"

Her gaze didn't waver. "Have you?"

"Well, yes," he replied. "Once."

"Did you love her?"

Ethan thought back to just before he shipped out for Europe. Sandra Nolan was the only *real* girlfriend he'd ever had. Certainly the only one he'd truly cared about. They had decided to be together a few days before he left – in case he didn't make it home. He had written to her several times after that, but to his dismay, had never received a reply.

"I suppose so," he answered finally. "Why do you ask?"

"You *suppose* so?" she said with disapproval. "Either you did or you didn't."

Ethan could see the seriousness in her expression. He thought for a long moment then said: "Yes, I loved her. At least, I did at the time."

"And now?"

"And now...she's far away. Besides, I don't think she loves me."

"Then why did you couple with her?"

Ethan spread his hands. "How am I supposed to answer that? I was going off to war. At the time it seemed like the right thing to do. Why do you want to know about this anyway?"

"I've never been with a man," she said. Her eyes became distant. "And I don't know that I want to."

"You're too young. There's plenty of time to think about that later – when you're older."

"*Is* there time?" She lowered her eyes. "My mother loved my father very much. I could hear it in her voice every time she spoke to him, and see it on her face whenever she looked at him. I thought that's how all men and women were. But it's not that way, is it? Men don't really care about women at all."

"Of course they do. Why would you say such a thing?"

"Did you know that I murdered Jared," she asked. "I poisoned him, then I cut his throat."

Her admission shocked Ethan into a short silence. "Why?" he finally asked.

"He wanted to have me," she replied flatly. "So I killed him."

"Then he deserved it."

"Did he? Yes. I suppose he did. He was a letch. I wasn't the first young girl he'd tried to ruin; his brothel was full of them. But the more I think about it, the more I realize that's not *really* why I killed him. It's just what I kept telling myself."

"So what was the real reason?"

"Because I needed to. I needed him to be dead. I needed to bury the constant fear in my heart that he would somehow find a way to force himself on me."

Ethan's mouth set in a firm line. "Listen to me Kat. I promise that no one will do anything like that to you. I won't allow it."

"And why is that? Because you care about me?" She threw up her hands. "I've heard Markus call you a *boy scout*. I don't know what that is, but I imagine it's someone honest and good hearted."

Ethan nodded.

"I don't need you to watch over me because it's the right thing to do." She looked up. "I need you to do it because you love me."

Ethan sensed where this was going and began to feel uneasy. "Of course I love you. You've become like…"

"If you say sister," she snapped. "I swear I'll break your nose."

Ethan held up his hands. "All I meant was…"

"I know what you meant. You think I'm a child." She jumped to her feet. "My mother was only two years older than I am now when she married my father. And there are girls even younger than me who bear children."

Ethan got up and tried to place his hands on her shoulders, but she stepped quickly away.

"I'm sorry," he said. "But that sort of thing doesn't happen where I come from. Girls your age are still in school and playing with dolls."

"We're not on Earth," she countered. "And I *don't* play with dolls."

"I know you don't. It's just that in my world you're still too young to be thinking about these things."

"*This* is your world now. And in this world, I *am* a woman."

Ethan sighed and nodded. "I know you are. And I'm sorry. But I just can't give you what you want." He stepped forward and took her hands. This time she did not resist. "One day you'll meet someone. Someone who will be good to you. He'll love you the way you deserve. He'll be kind and gentle and appreciate you for the person you are. You just need to be patient."

Tears welled in her eyes. "And what if I don't live long enough to find him? What then? What if I die and no one ever loves me?"

"You can't think like that. We're going to make it."

Kat pulled her hands away and wiped her face. "Just answer me one question."

Ethan smiled and nodded.

"If I was older, would you feel different then?"

He chuckled. "I'm sure I would."

She returned his smile. "Then I'll just have to wait. I won't be young forever you know. *Then* maybe you'll look at me." She turned and started back. "Don't tell the others what I've said."

"I won't," he promised.

Ethan watched as she began gathering her belongings. He hoped he had said the right things. He had no experience in dealing with young girls. And considering everything else Kat had been through during her life, she didn't need more heartache and disappointment.

A few minutes later, Markus and Jonas stirred. They set off shortly afterward, just as the sun was fully over the horizon. Kat walked beside Jonas for most of the day, but Ethan caught her stealing glances at him several times. It was clear that she had not been deterred; he hoped he would not be forced to hurt her feelings. But the fact remained, in his eyes she was still a child. And if it came to it, he might have to be firm.

When they stopped for a midday meal, Jonas pulled him aside. "I want you to have another go at trying to start a fire with magic," he said.

By now, he had all but given up hope of ever being able to *feel* the magic within him. Even the way he'd driven off Hronso, he assumed, was in reality somehow down to the dragon and not him at all. But the earnest expression on Jonas' face swayed him to try again anyway. He sighed and knelt in front of the pile of twigs that had been arranged.

"Concentrate," Jonas told him. "Picture it in your mind. Let the words transform into action."

After closing his eyes, he whispered the word, "Illimiz," As expected, nothing happened. He tried again, but with the same result. After a few more futile attempts he threw up his hands and let out a frustrated grunt.

"It will come," Jonas assured him.

Ethan glared down at the twigs, disgusted by his failure. His frustration suddenly boiled over. Clenching his fists, he yelled: "Illimiz, damn it!"

To his utter amazement, a thin line of smoke began to rise from the center of the twigs. A moment later a spark popped and a single flame rose. Ecstatic, he jumped up and threw his arms above his head.

Jonas smiled broadly. "There, you see?"

Ethan could only stare at the fire with smug satisfaction.

"All right, great mage," Markus said teasingly. "Put it out. It's time to go."

Ethan took one last, self-satisfied look at the fire before stomping it out. Now inspired, he dearly wanted to try again, but Markus insisted they keep going.

As they walked along, Markus continued to keep a constant eye out for enemies, but saw nothing to suggest they were being pursued. That afternoon he and Kat set snares hoping to catch more rabbits. But to their chagrin, they were unsuccessful.

After three more days they turned due north. Soon after that the forest gave way to an expanse of lush grassland. They crossed several small trails and one well-built road along the way. Although slowing their pace to make certain there was no prying eyes about, they were still able to cover nearly thirty miles each day.

In less than a week the mountains came into view and the flat easy terrain gradually became hilly and difficult to navigate. Some of the hills were far too tall and steep to climb without exhausting themselves, forcing them to take time-consuming detours around them.

"We're fortunate it's not winter," remarked Markus. "By now we'd all be dead from the cold."

The days were indeed mild, but the nights were becoming increasingly chilly. And with wood for a fire now a scarcity, the setting sun was an unwelcome sight.

Jonas spend each evening examining the map. He explained that, although he had a general idea of where the entrance to the cave was, he had never actually been there. Finding it might prove to be difficult. The mages of the past had left markers, but after all these years there was no way of knowing if they would still be there.

They turned west when two days away from the base of the mountains. The terrain was now hard, mostly rocks and gravel, with just a few sickly looking shrubs sprouting up here and there. Steam issued from cracks in the earth, and the smell of sulfur was almost unbearable. The only redeeming aspect was that it was no longer cold at night. Ethan did his best to take advantage of the situation by bathing in some of the various warm springs that dotted the area – though many were way too hot for this and would scald the flesh from one's body. Jonas warned them not to drink any of the spring water, saying that it would sour their stomachs.

"When we arrive there is a fresh spring and fruit trees just outside of the cave," he said. "I can definitely remember Lady Illyrian telling me that."

For another two days they zig-zagged back and forth in the shadow of the mountains while Jonas tried to locate the markers. Having only ever seen pictures of mountains before, Ethan spent most of the time with his head tilted back, staring up in awe at the majesty of the snow covered peaks that were only just visible through the thick grey clouds. Jonas was far less impressed, focusing virtually all of his attention on finding the markers. On several occasions he thought he had succeeded, but each time his hopes were dashed and he would throw up his hands, cursing loudly. But just when he was looking to be on the verge of despair, he finally found what he was looking for. Carved into a tall column of dark granite protruding from the ground was a circle surrounding a five pointed star.

"We're nearly there," he announced, his voice soaked with relief.

Markus though, now appeared to be on edge.

"What's wrong?" Ethan asked.

His friend gave a deep frown. "If we're almost there, then we're most likely being watched. The dwarves are well known for being paranoid and guarded. They will know if someone is approaching their home. If they're going to kill us, they might not wait for us to get too close."

"Don't be so pessimistic," Jonas said. "We've made it this far, haven't we?"

Markus scowled. "Luck is an unreliable companion, old man."

"I'll take what I can get," he shot back with a smile. "Better to have luck than nothing at all."

Markus heaved a sigh. "Then let us pray that our luck holds."

CHAPTER FOURTEEN

FOR ANOTHER TWO days they wound their way gradually closer to the mountain. During this time Jonas found three more markers, and with each discovery Markus' anxiety visibly increased. Ethan did his best to keep their conversation light, but it did little to lift his friend's spirits.

He also took every opportunity he could to practice his one and only spell, and each time delighted in the sight of the tiny flame he was able to produce. Kat once again tried to teach him how to vanish, but he still couldn't feel what she described as: *'a hot coal in the pit of your stomach'*. Jonas suggested that, seeing as how her spell was based on instinct, he may not be able to learn it the same way. But it was of no great concern to Ethan at present. He was still in utter amazement at his newly found fire lighting ability.

On the morning of the third day Jonas started poring over the map yet again, a confused look on his face.

"What's wrong?" Ethan asked.

He shook his head. "We should have found it by now. I've located all of the markers, and followed every one of the directions your mother described to me. The land should have changed from rocky ground to thick green grass." He cast his arm around in a sweeping motion. "But look. Nothing but rocks and gravel."

"We'll find it," Ethan assured him.

Jonas merely grunted and put away the map.

A few hours later, Markus suddenly stopped in his tracks to sniff the air. "There's fresh water nearby," he stated after a few seconds. He shook the near empty water skin hanging from his belt. "And not a moment too soon."

Jonas' expression instantly brightened. "If you're right, then I think we're there."

Ethan looked up at the menacing grandeur of the mountain and began to share Markus' anxiety. He paused to give it a long suspicious look. A finger poked him sharply in the ribs.

"Surely the great mage Ethan Dragonvein isn't nervous?" teased Kat.

He forced a laugh. "I'm not nervous."

"You really need to learn to lie better than that," she said, wagging her finger playfully.

Markus chuckled. "Yes, he does. Come O mighty starter of camp fires. The dwarves await."

Ethan flushed.

They wound their way around large boulders and thorny bushes until the ground began to slope gently downward. After a while they came to a narrow ravine that dropped off roughly six feet. At the bottom of this, a thin stream of clear water trickled gently along.

Markus was the first to climb down, followed by Ethan and Jonas. Kat hesitated, holding out her arms for Ethan to help her. He groaned inwardly at her obvious attempt at flirting, knowing full well that she could easily make it down by herself if she wanted to. Nonetheless, he did the gentlemanly thing.

Markus cautiously tasted the water. Satisfied, he gave a sharp nod to the others and began filling his water skin.

"This should lead us directly to the cavern," Jonas said, now full of optimism.

The ground was smooth and even within the ravine, so they decided to stay down there until forced to do otherwise. At this lower level the air was cool and smelled clean, although it did also serve to make the lingering smell of sulfur on their clothes seem rather more pronounced.

They had only followed the path of the stream for a mile when Markus abruptly stopped. He crouched low and motioned for everyone else to do the same. The sound of voices could be heard from above, though Ethan couldn't tell from which side they were coming.

Warily, Markus peered out, then sat quickly back down with his back pressed against the ravine wall. He pointed to the opposite side, holding up six fingers and silently mouthing: '*Imperial soldiers*'.

Ethan tried to control his rising heart rate. The path ahead disappeared into the distance, so if they were quiet, he hoped they should be able to get far enough away to emerge unseen.

Remaining crouched and with slow measured steps, the group crept forward, staying as close to the stream as they could where there was less gravel to crunch beneath their feet.

"Did you see General Hronso?" a deep, gruff voice drifted down.

"No," answered another. "But I heard he's damn near burned to cinders. How the hell he's still alive I don't know."

"You moron," chided the first voice. "Rakasa can't die."

"That's not what I've heard. Word has it that if you chop off their heads they'll die the same as anyone else. Anyway, whatever the truth, he's liable to be around here any time now, so we better watch ourselves. If it's true that someone's managed to hurt him, he'll be in a killin' mood for sure."

"He's already killed the Grendil who was tracking those fugitives. Hacked him to bits, I hear."

"Let's just hope he ain't got no business with us."

"I don't think the ones he's after will be coming this way. Only thing around here is dwarves, and they ain't the welcoming sort."

"Yeah, well, they won't bother us. And you best mind your tongue if you see the General. A word out of place and you'll end up same as the Grendil did."

Their conversation then turned to more personal matters. After a while the voices faded until they could no longer be heard at all. Markus took another cautious look up and sighed with relief on seeing that it was all clear.

"Where does this stream lead?" he asked Jonas.

"There should be a small pond at the end," he replied. "And the cavern will be just beyond that."

Markus nodded. "Then we should get out of the ravine now. We were lucky they didn't look down here. If they had, we'd have been trapped."

He and Ethan helped the other two up before climbing out themselves. The landscape was somewhat changed. Small patches of grass were scattered about, and a few thin pines had forced themselves up through the rocky soil. Even so, it was a far cry from what Jonas had described.

They reached the pond some twenty minutes later – a circular expanse of clear, icy cold water with a white sandy bottom that extended for several yards beyond the shore. On the far side of this they spotted a worn trail that disappeared behind a low ridge.

They were now almost right up against the base of the mountain. Ethan took a deep breath, hoping this meant they had finally arrived.

Glancing in all directions to be sure that no one was watching, Markus led them around the pond to the trail. As they crested the ridge, Jonas smiled broadly. "This is it!" he exclaimed. "This is the entrance to the cavern."

It was fifty feet across and half as high. On either side stood a cluster of fruit trees, though these were all withered and twisted and bore no trace of fruit.

The air changed almost the moment they stepped inside, becoming thick and humid and filled with a sweet odor that reminded Ethan of spring flowers, only much stronger. So strong in fact, that it came close to being distinctly unpleasant. The light from the entrance seemed incapable of penetrating the gloom within for more than a few yards, so Markus ran out and returned with several small branches to use as torches. But even with these blazing it was only possible to see two or three paces ahead. It was as if the darkness was actually consuming the light.

The cavern floor was smooth and well worn, though with enough inconsistencies in it to show that it had not been fashioned by craftsmen.

With each step, Ethan felt his apprehension rising. The air was growing thicker, pressing in around him, threatening to choke off his breath.

"*This* is where my mother was trying to reach?" he asked incredulously.

Jonas gave no reply.

The sound of water dripping into hidden pools echoed in his ears, punctuating the ominous feel of his surroundings. After a hundred feet or so of progress, the ground suddenly sloped sharply downwards, nearly causing him to lose his footing.

It was immediately after regaining his balance that Ethan first spotted a ghostly green light piercing the darkness ahead. On drawing closer he could see that the glow was coming from thousands of tiny crystals covering the cave wall. In perfect harmony they pulsed like blood running through rock veins, making the mountain seem a living, breathing thing.

"Beautiful," gasped Kat.

"What are they?" asked Ethan.

"I don't know," Jonas replied. He ran a finger over a section of the crystals. As he made contact their light brightened and became steady, then continued to pulse once he withdrew.

They moved on, each one wondering what else might lay ahead. That question was soon answered when the tunnel came to an abrupt end. Ethan could not believe it. He had expected to see something waiting for them – a door, or a clue what to do next – anything that could help. But there was nothing here. Only rock. It was the end of the line.

Markus examined the area several times before kicking the wall with frustration and spinning around. "All right, Jonas. What now?"

Jonas also made an inspection of their surroundings, but with no better results. "Maybe they have to come to us," he said. "I just don't know. Lady Illyrian never told me what was inside."

"I suppose it beats getting killed by dwarves," Markus said, tossing his pack onto the ground.

"Lord Dragonvein would not have sent his wife and son here for nothing," Jonas insisted. "There *is* a way into the mountain. There has to be."

Markus sniffed. "That was over five-hundred years ago, you old fool." He turned to Ethan. "I told you we should have headed for the coast."

"Never mind that. What do we do now?" he asked.

"Well, we can't stay here," Markus replied. "If they find us, there's no way out. We should wait for nightfall, then head west. We can follow the shore north to Barkal or Dragon Bay."

Taking a seat beside his pack, he cast an angry glance at Jonas. "You have until then to find us a way in."

Jonas glared back, then, mumbling curses, resumed his inspection of the walls.

Kat plopped down beside Markus and retrieved a strip of jerky from her pack. "What do you think makes the crystals glow?"

He shrugged. "How should I know?"

"It's probably magic," she said. "I bet this whole place is filled with it. What do you think, Ethan?"

"Maybe."

"I bet that's why we can't find a door. It's been hidden by magic."

"Or maybe it doesn't exist, and we've been led by a fool on a fool's errand," snapped Markus.

"Jonas isn't a fool," Kat retorted. She looked at Ethan. "You don't think that, do you?"

He spread his hands. "I don't know what to think. But I have to agree with Markus. This looks like a dead end."

Kat crinkled her nose and frowned. "You should have more faith. He's gotten us this far."

"*He's* gotten us this far?" Markus scoffed. "If it wasn't for him, we'd already be at the coast by now. Not cornered in a forgotten cave, looking for a door that doesn't exist."

"He'll find it," she shot back. "You'll see." She flashed Ethan a smile. "Then we'll both be able to learn magic together."

"What makes you think the dwarves can teach you magic?" Markus asked.

"I don't know. But if they were friends with Ethan's family, I bet they have books…or something like that."

"Don't count on it," Markus told her. "I don't know much about mages. But I do know that dwarves don't use magic."

"Then how do they make magic weapons?" she challenged.

"You ask too many questions," he growled, then shifted so that his back was to her.

"They'll know something," she said in a half whisper, determined to have the last word.

Jonas continued to scour the walls for another two hours before finally giving up. He refused to make eye contact with Markus, and when Ethan attempted to speak with him he waved him away, muttering incoherently.

They waited until they were confident it must be well past sundown before heading back toward the entrance. Jonas looked sadly over his shoulder and shook his head.

"It's all right," Ethan consoled him. "It was a long time ago. I'm sure there used to be a way inside back then."

Before Jonas could respond, the sudden clatter of steel and stomping of boots echoed loudly down the tunnel. Markus and Ethan both quickly drew their swords.

"I don't suppose you can burn them like you did the Rakasa," asked Markus.

Ethan desperately wished that he could. They could now see the light from a dozen torches as the enemy crested the top of the slope. But they did not advance any further.

"Dragonvein!" The voice of Hronso thundered out, sending fear into Ethan's heart. "I know you're down there."

Ethan strained his eyes, but could not see him. "I'm here," he called back.

"I underestimated you, mage," he said. "I have not suffered injury in many centuries. That is a mistake I shall not make twice."

"Leave my friends alone and I'll come with you," he offered.

Both Kat and Jonas grabbed his shoulders, pulling him back.

"You can't," said Jonas in a loud whisper. "Shinzan will kill you."

Kat simply looked at him with pleading eyes.

Ethan jerked away. "It's my choice."

"I can hear you, you know," Hronso called out. "Specter can live. But your servant has to come with me too. And I think I'll need the young girl as well. Something tells me that she might be of interest to the Emperor."

"You don't need anyone but me. And if you try to take my friends, I'll burn you again." He hoped his bluff would at least buy them a short time to think of something.

"Perhaps you could," Hronso responded. "Perhaps it was your own power and not the dragon's last time. But then again, if you were able to, I think you would have done so already. I, on the other hand, can definitely burn you."

Ethan saw a bright red light begin to flash sporadically, drowning out the torchlight. Markus snatched his collar and threw him toward the rear of the cavern.

"Run!" he shouted to the others.

Kat and Jonas obeyed instantly. But they had only made a few steps when a tremendous roar ripped through the air. Ethan glanced over his shoulder and saw a massive ball of flame streaking toward them.

"Get down!" he cried out.

They all hit the ground an instant before the inferno would have consumed them. Ethan could feel the intense heat from it blistering the flesh of his back. There was the sudden stench of singed hair.

Moments after passing over them, the fireball smashed into the far wall and exploded with a thunderous boom. The cavern rumbled and shook, showering them with dust and debris.

"He's got a dwarf weapon," coughed Markus.

"Indeed I do," affirmed Hronso, sounding pleased with himself.

The pain from his burned skin made Ethan grit his teeth as he stood up. He glanced over in Kat's direction. Her face was a mask of sheer terror and her eyes were filling with tears.

"I will not ask you again," shouted Hronso.

Ethan's heart pounded. *I have to remember*, he thought desperately. He pictured the moment the dragon had placed its head in his hands. What had he felt? Peace. Love. Then something else. Sorrow. But why?

He imagined Hronso charging in, sword poised to strike. But after that, no matter how hard he tried, everything was still as blank as ever.

He saw the red glow of the dwarf weapon begin to flash again. Kat clutched at his arm.

"To the back of the cave," ordered Markus.

Again they ran. The fire burst forth, this time striking the ground where they had only just been standing. The heat blasted Ethan's already burned back and it took all his strength not to cry out from the pain

"Why aren't you fighting back, Dragonvein," taunted Hronso. "You did threaten to burn me again, did you not? Do you lack the power?"

"Why don't you come down here and find out," Ethan challenged.

Hronso responded with harsh laughter. "Bring them to me!" he ordered his men.

The song of steel was quickly followed by the stomping of boots.

"Better than being roasted alive," remarked Markus somberly.

"You should disappear," Ethan whispered to Kat.

She glared at him defiantly. "I'm not going anywhere."

He opened his mouth to argue, but Jonas had already grabbed her hand and pulled her back.

"Stay with me," he told her. He took a few steps further to the rear, allowing Ethan and Markus to stand together in front of them.

"I really wish I knew how to fight with this damn thing," Ethan said, looking at his sword.

Markus smiled. "Just remember that the sharp end points away from you."

He returned the smile and readied himself.

The stomping of the soldier's boots drew closer. Ethan could now make out their ominous silhouettes; they were closing quickly. Yet again his mind concentrated fiercely, searching for a way to produce the same bolt of fire that had dealt with Hronso before. *Try harder,* he kept telling himself. *Try harder.....*

Then he heard a faint rumbling sound. For a moment he thought it was coming from inside his head, a result of the intense pressure he was creating within himself. But the sound quickly grew much louder, and then the ground began to shake violently. Large chunks of rock and debris fell from the ceiling and smashed onto the floor between him and the soldiers. They halted, unsure what to do.

With the shaking growing ever more intense, both he and Markus were struggling to keep their feet. They turned and stumbled toward the rear wall, grabbing Jonas and Kat as they passed. Once at the dead end, the four of them huddled together, unable to do anything more than watch as larger and larger rocks fell. Within moments the soldier's torches had vanished from view.

"Come!" a deep voice called out a few yards to Ethan's right.

He looked across to see that a small section of the wall had opened as if on hinges. Standing just inside was a shadowy figure no taller than four feet, yet extremely broad in the shoulder.

"Come," the figure repeated urgently. "Unless you wish to be buried alive."

Ethan shoved Kat and Jonas ahead. Markus followed close behind. Once inside, the door closed behind them. The clamor of the collapse continued to reverberate, filling the air with dust.

Shielding his eyes, Ethan peered ahead, but the way was too dark to see. He reached up and touched the ceiling. It was only just high enough for him to walk upright, though Markus would undoubtedly need to bend down.

"Hurry," called the voice. "This tunnel is unstable."

Markus took the lead, his sword drawn and ready.

They walked as fast as they could manage for about five hundred yards. The ground was level throughout, and even the walls gradually transitioned from a natural formation to being smooth and neatly squared.

A light beckoned from just ahead. Markus gestured for Ethan to draw his sword as well. Though he was hesitant to show signs of aggression toward someone who had just saved their lives, he did as Markus instructed. This did not go unnoticed by Jonas. He regarded them both with deep disapproval.

The passage ended at a small chamber approximately thirty foot square. Embedded into the walls at regular intervals were stones about the size of a man's fist that glowed dimly with yellow light. At the far end were two iron doors. The one on the left was flung wide. Beside it stood their rescuer.

The dwarf was clad in a dark brown leather vest over a green shirt. His trousers were tan cloth – dingy and torn – and his boots rode high up his short thick calves. Narrow dark eyes surrounded by deep lines stood out clearly in a face that was otherwise ghostly pale. Dense wiry hair which fell down to the top of his chest was divided into three braids, held together at the ends by a silver bead. In his right hand he held a small axe, though a much larger one was strapped across his back. On his belt hung a green glowing rod about a foot in length.

"Which one of you calls himself Dragonvein?" he demanded.

Ethan stepped forward. "I do."

The dwarf scrutinized him for a long moment. "Why did you come here?"

"We seek sanctuary," Jonas interjected.

The dwarf huffed. "And why should I give it?"

"Because you are obliged to do so," Jonas stated firmly. "Will you not honor the agreement made between your people and the Dragonvein family?"

"Ha! You must think me a fool. The Dragonvein's have been gone for more than five hundred years."

"Then why open your door to us in the first place?" Jonas challenged. "It is obvious you heard us speak the name, did you not?"

"I did. And the name Dragonvein is not unfamiliar to me. My grandfather spoke of it often. Yet I do not see how this boy can be of that line. I saved your lives because I was curious, nothing more."

"Will you honor the oath?" asked Jonas.

The dwarf gave Ethan another long look. "If he is not who he claims to be, then you will all wish you had died in the cavern." He jabbed a finger at the drawn weapons. "Do not think me defenseless. Treachery will only guarantee your death."

Ethan put away his blade. After a brief hesitation, Markus did the same.

Jonas bowed low. "I am Jonas. This is Ethan, Markus and Kat. We thank you for your aid."

He gave a slight nod. "I am Birger. And do not thank me yet. I do *not* offer you sanctuary. Only the king can do that, and he may not suffer your presence. Just pray that you can prove this boy to be who he claims."

With that, Birger turned and stepped through the open door.

"You see?" said Jonas. "Our luck has held after all."

Markus shrugged. "For now."

"At least we're still alive," Ethan offered.

"True," Markus replied. "But I wonder how you propose to prove you're a Dragonvein? I get the feeling the king won't just take your word for it."

"You let *me* worry about that," said Jonas.

Birger's voice called out. "I will not wait for you."

Ethan slapped Markus on the back and smiled. "Let's go, buddy."

Markus shook his head. "The Krauts, the Empire...and now the dwarves. Hell, why not?"

CHAPTER FIFTEEN

FOR SEVERAL HOURS they followed Birger through a labyrinth of halls and passageways that twisted and turned ever deeper into the mountain. Occasionally they could hear the clanking of hammers or the echo of distant voices, but Birger paid no attention to these and pressed resolutely on. Everywhere they passed through, the construction was superb. The walls and floors were smooth and highly polished, lit by the same round stones they had seen in the first area. Ethan asked the dwarf what they were, but he did not appear interested in conversation.

"I think they're *rajni* stones," Jonas told him. "Though I've never seen them so big. And I've *never* heard of them being used to light rooms and hallways."

"What are *rajni* stones?" Ethan asked.

"Mages used them to store spells," he explained. "In fact I used one to bring you to Lumnia."

The dwarf looked over his shoulder and snorted. "You know nothing, human."

"I'm sure you know a lot more," admitted Jonas. "But as you have chosen to stay silent..."

"Rajni stones are vessels for magic," he said, cutting him short. "Human mages stored spells, but *we* use them as they were intended."

"To make torches and light rooms?" Jonas gently chided.

"The stones you see here are of a very low quality," Birger informed him. "Not that you would know the difference. Lights are all they're good for. With quality rajni stones we construct objects of great power."

"Like what?" asked Ethan.

"That you don't know these things does not bode well for your case," the dwarf said. "A true Dragonvein would have this knowledge. It was said that Praxis Dragonvein's wisdom rivaled even that of our scholars."

"I never knew my father," said Ethan. "I…"

Jonas squeezed his arm and gave him a warning look.

Birger let out a scornful laugh. "You will need better answers than that when you meet King Halvar. He is not as good natured as I am."

He pressed the pace and was soon several yards ahead of them. Ethan was stunned by how fast he could move on such short legs.

They continued on for two more hours, climbing up and down long stairwells and passing through vast open chambers. Eventually they reached one with three separate tunnels leading out of it. Birger stopped to retrieve a small red stone from his pocket. Closing his eyes, he held the stone tightly in his right hand for about a minute before putting it away again. This done, he moved over to the right hand passage and leaned against the wall.

"Rest here," he said. "We still have four days of hard travel before we arrive in Elyfoss. If you hear anything approaching…arm yourselves."

"Is there danger here?" asked Markus.

Birger made no reply. Instead, he just smiled wickedly and closed his eyes.

Using their packs as pillows, the four of them lay down together – Markus and Ethan with swords drawn and ready by their sides, Kat and Jonas between them, daggers in hand.

"Do you think there's something down here?" whispered Kat.

"It's possible," Markus replied. "Only the dwarves care to dwell in the deep places of the world. Who knows what they might have found."

She shifted close to Ethan and shut her eyes. "I'm not scared. Are you?"

He forced a quiet laugh. "Me? Never."

Markus grunted. "Well, I certainly am."

Kat frowned and clutched her dagger even more tightly to her chest.

Sleep came in small snatches. Unidentifiable echoes from the depths woke Ethan each time he began to drift. On one occasion, a loud thud from deep inside one of the passages had him sitting bolt upright, sword gripped in both hands. Giving up any thought of sleep for a while after this, he tried to pass the time speculating on what a dwarf city might look like.

The tunnels he had seen thus far had been well constructed, but lacked decoration or any other indication of being inhabited. Even the massive chambers they had passed through were stark and dusty – yet the ceilings were well lit by rajni stones, suggesting that they had once been used quite frequently. But for what, he could only speculate.

He was about to make one final attempt at sleep when he heard a sharp tapping sound coming from the passage on the left, as if someone was hitting the walls with a small stone. He listened anxiously to this for a moment. Then, abruptly, it ceased. He strained his ears for another minute or so, but it did not resume.

"Wake your friends," hissed Birger. He was on his feet, the small axe in his hand.

"I'm already awake," said Markus.

Ethan shook Kat and Jonas, who hurriedly rose.

"What is it?" asked Jonas.

"Trolls," Birger replied.

Markus laughed. "Trolls? You must be joking." But the tense look in the dwarf's eyes told him that he wasn't.

"I thought trolls were just a story," said Kat.

"So did I," agreed Jonas.

Birger flicked a hand. "Quiet!" Creeping over to the left passage, he peered along it for several seconds.

The tapping resumed, this time louder than before.

He pointed to the center corridor, indicating to the others that they should take it. Ethan entered first, with Jonas and Kat just behind him. Markus stayed at the rear. Birger waited until they were all well inside before following.

"If fortune holds, they'll not be interested in a fight," he said.

"And if it doesn't?" asked Markus.

"Then I hope you can use those weapons you carry."

Ethan led them down the long passageway, then up a tall flight of stairs. At the top was a small room with a door on opposite walls.

Birger turned and crouched low. "If they come, we can hold them off here."

"I'm still finding it hard to believe that trolls are real," said Jonas.

"Oh, they're *very* real," Birger replied. "Nasty little devils too. They'd kill you rather than look at you."

"How is it they've remained hidden for so long?" Jonas asked. "As far as humans are concerned, they are only stories."

"We've kept them secret from the rest of the world, that's why. There's no need to have you lot fumbling down here, looking for trouble. Besides, trolls never caused any harm until Shinzan became Emperor."

"What happened?" asked Jonas.

Birger scowled. "He decimated my people. Now there aren't enough of us to keep them away."

Jonas stiffened. "I'm sorry."

"Why? Humans never cared whether we lived or died. And they still don't."

He was about to add something further when his hand suddenly shot up to silence the group.

From the bottom of the stairs came a cacophony of high-pitched squeals and guttural growls that sent Ethan's heart racing. He tightened his grip on his sword.

After a short while the sounds faded and Birger visibly relaxed.

"Are they gone?" whispered Kat, trying hard to mask her fear.

"Gone? No. But they must have already eaten. For sure they know we're here."

The dwarf's words sent a chill up Ethan's spine. "What do they look like?"

"What does it matter? Just hope you never see one. Not one of *that* lot, anyway. The adults are docile enough...but the juveniles." He spat and put away his axe.

"You mean they're children?" asked Ethan.

"I mean they'll kill you if they have the chance. So keep your mouth shut and do as you're told. We're not out of danger yet. We need to get away from here as fast as we can, lest they change their mind...or get hungry again."

Having issued this warning, Birger pushed past them all and stepped through the door on the left.

"Actually, he's a bit friendlier than I expected," joked Markus.

"Yeah," agreed Ethan, grinning. "At least he hasn't killed us yet."

Laughing, they chased after the dwarf.

For the next few days their pace was grueling to the point that Ethan feared Jonas would collapse. Several times he considered asking Birger to slow down a bit, but Jonas assured him he would be fine.

"It's just the stairs that get to me," the old man said as they bedded down on the third night. "Why there has to be so many of them is beyond me."

"I wonder how long it took to make all this?" mused Ethan.

"Thousands of years I would imagine," Jonas told him. "Dwarf craft was famed throughout Lumnia in my day. Though what has become of their talents in these dark times, I can only speculate."

The further they traveled, the more intricate the designs of the chambers they passed through became. In one of these, massive pillars towered high to a brightly lit ceiling, revealing incredibly detailed carved images of stars, moons and planets, all of them inlaid with gold and gemstones. The light split within the gem's facets, raining down in a cascade of color and beauty. Everyone apart from Birger, who seemed almost irritated by the scene, had stared up in astonishment. But this chamber, like all the others, was abandoned.

On the day they were set to arrive, Birger stopped and gathered the group together.

"I'm taking us through the west gate," he told them. "No one goes there anymore, so we should be able to pass unseen for a while."

"Why do we need to hide?" asked Ethan.

"We're not hiding," he replied irritably. "I just would rather avoid causing a disturbance if possible. And your presence here will certainly do that."

Jonas cleared his throat. "I hesitate to ask, but I couldn't help noticing that we didn't see any other dwarves along the way. Not a single one. Lord Dragonvein visited your people many times, both here and in the north, and he told me stories of your vast halls and great cities. He said they were always teeming with people and bustling with life. And yet the mountain now seems all but deserted. What happened here?"

Birger's eyes locked onto Jonas', but he did not flinch or falter under the scrutiny.

Finally, the dwarf heaved a sigh and shifted his gaze. "We did not desert our cities, or abandon our halls. There simply aren't enough of us left to fill them anymore. After the mages were defeated, the Emperor set his sights on us. But not even his vast armies could penetrate our defenses. For three years we fought, and for a time it looked as if we might prevail. But then Shinzan himself came."

He paused, his face racked with hatred. "He slaughtered us like sheep. We tried to surrender, but he ignored our pleas and continued his bloody rampage. When he did finally stop, our numbers were but a fraction of what they once were. Our kin in the north, hoping to avoid a similar fate, surrendered at once. But Shinzan didn't care and did the same to them."

He looked up at the faces of the group. "I am telling you this so that you understand the decision my king is now faced with. I have put myself in great peril by bringing you here. But not as much as I bring to my people."

"Then why do it?" asked Markus.

"I have my reasons," he replied. "But enough of that. Come. Soon you will see why our industry and skill was famed throughout Lumnia."

After another twenty minutes, the passage ended with a solid double door made of iron. Birger was forced to lean his shoulder hard into it twice before it screeched open. He then stretched out an arm as an invitation for them to step through.

Beyond was a broad avenue made from polished blue octagonal stones dotted with tiny flakes of silver and white; it was wide enough to easily accommodate six wagons side by side. Lining both sides at regular intervals were twenty-foot tall steel posts, each one capped by a shimmering white rajni stone. The ceiling was now so high that it could no longer be seen, though Ethan caught the sparkle of light here and there – almost like the twinkle of distant stars peeking through a cloudy night sky.

As they walked along they saw, positioned between the light posts, life-sized statues of animals, dwarves…and humans. These were set in various poses depicting acts of heroism, charity, and kindness.

"I thought dwarves didn't like humans," Ethan remarked.

"Those were created a very long time ago," Birger explained. "Things between human and dwarf have not always been as they are now."

They continued for another few miles. At last, rising up in the distance, two gargantuan gold monoliths towering more than one hundred feet high came into view. As they drew near, Ethan could see that they were set on either side of two massive gates made of the purest silver. These had been polished until they shone with an almost heavenly radiance.

"Magnificent," gasped Jonas.

"This is nothing," said Birger, his head held high. "What lies beyond is the true wonder."

When they were only a short distance away, the doors slowly swung outward. Ethan and the others looked for whoever was opening them, but there was no one to be seen.

"Do they open on their own?" asked Ethan.

Birger nodded. "The gate recognizes that I am a dwarf. Were I not here, you could not get in."

"How does it know?" asked Ethan.

"I'm just a simple miner," he replied, shrugging. "If you prove yourself to be a Dragonvein, then perhaps you could ask one of the builders. Though I doubt you'd understand the details, even if they told you."

He paused, and then gave a grand sweep of his arm. "Behold. The great city of Elyfoss."

While moving along, Ethan was dumbfounded by what he saw. The city stretched on for mile after mile in every direction. Towers and spires as tall as the Empire State building reached up, some nearly touching the twinkling lights that danced high above on the colossal ceiling. The buildings were of such elaborate design that they could rival – even surpass – anything he had seen on Earth. He stopped in his tracks, trying to fathom what it would take to construct something of this magnitude.

Birger ushered them on. The streets were constructed of the same material as the road outside the gates, but now featured broad sidewalks of polished white marble veined with deep blue and crimson. The smaller buildings were equally impressive as the skyscrapers. Their stonework was like an artist's canvas; stars and comets in stunning relief, together with mosaics of brave dwarf warriors were so numerous and beautiful, Ethan felt dizzy looking at them.

They walked for nearly five blocks before seeing anyone about. Most of the city's inhabitants were dressed similarly to Birger, though a few wore more elaborate attire with high collared shirts and pants made from a slick cloth that caught the light and gave it a metallic quality. As the group passed by, everyone who saw them immediately stopped what they were doing and stared with a mixture of loathing and curiosity.

Ethan glanced over his shoulder. A crowd had gathered and was keeping pace a few yards behind them.

"It looks like we may not make it to the king," remarked Jonas.

"No one will harm you so long as I am here," Birger assured him. "But I warn you. When you meet the king, speak only when spoken to. And do not lie. If you are found to be false, you will be executed without delay. Do you understand?"

"We have no reason to lie," said Jonas.

Birger muttered something indistinct, then took a left toward the center of the city. After another few blocks, they were suddenly confronted by six dwarves appearing from around the corner, each one of them carrying a huge, fierce looking axe. All of them were clad in polished black leather armor studded with steel. Their beards were tied in a tight braid, and their helms were adorned with black and yellow feathers down the center.

"What is the meaning of this, Birger?" demanded the lead dwarf.

"I have brought these humans here for an audience with King Halvar."

"And why would the king wish to see them?" he asked.

"One claims to be the son of Praxis Dragonvein. I was duty bound to bring him here."

The lead dwarf sneered with contempt. "Then you are a fool. Everyone knows that Praxis Dragonvein is dust and his line broken. You've been fed a lie."

"Perhaps," said Birger. "But that is for the king to decide. Not you, Larrel."

The pair of them stared hard at each other for several seconds. Finally, Larrel snorted and pushed Birger aside.

"You will come with me," he commanded Ethan and the others. "Hand over your weapons."

After doing as instructed, they were surrounded on all sides and ordered to move. The march was quick – even quicker than Birger's pace.

Word of their arrival was spreading, and after only a few blocks the crowd behind them had grown tenfold. Ethan could hear an almost continuous torrent of angry murmurs and hisses. He did his best to ignore these, concentrating his attention on the splendor of the city. The area they were now in consisted of mostly two and three story buildings. The stone used for these had a shine on the surface: not so bright as to give off a glare, but enough to make it sparkle in the light. The windows, both round and octagonal, were set with multi-colored glass that reminded him of a church.

"It's kind of like the West Village," he remarked.

Markus chuckled. "Only cleaner."

"This is true artistry," said Jonas. "To think such glorious beauty stays hidden away beneath the mountains."

"Quiet!" barked Larrel, who was leading the way. "Your foul voices pain my ears."

In the near distance, a massive building peeked out from above the others. Though nowhere near as tall as the towers and spires, it measured at least three full city blocks across. The roof was made from white and gold tiles, and the upper floor was surrounded by a balcony with elaborately designed gold railings. Ethan guessed this must be where the king lived. He was tempted to ask, but thought it best not to antagonize the already hostile Larrel.

As it turned out, the immense manor was not to be their destination. Before reaching it, they were escorted into a small, one story building – uncommonly plain when compared with the rest of what they had seen. It was situated midway down a block and butted up against taller buildings on either side. The room they were in now was completely empty, with just the one door and a window set with iron bars.

I'm back in jail, Ethan thought.

"You will wait here until sent for," said Larrel. "Food and water will be provided later."

Three of the guards searched their packs and then tossed them carelessly into the corner.

"Do you know how long we must wait here?" asked Jonas.

Larrel simply sneered at him, then stepped back outside and slammed the door shut.

The hostile voices of the ever-increasing crowd outside could be clearly heard. Markus tested the door's strength. It was far too heavy to break down, and the bars on the windows much too thick to bend.

"Let us hope the crowd doesn't become violent," said Jonas.

"I wouldn't worry just yet," Markus said, glancing out of the window. "There are a dozen guards directly outside. And I get the feeling the king will want to see us before turning us over to an angry mob."

By now, Kat had sat down in the far corner of the room and was humming softly to herself, a tiny smile on her face. Ethan moved over and settled beside her.

"You don't seem scared," he said.

"I'm not." Her smile widened. "And you shouldn't be either. We made it. We're here, safe with the dwarves."

Ethan chuckled. "I don't know how safe we are. But we certainly made it."

"Everything is going to be fine," she said. "I just know it."

"I wish I had your optimism," Markus remarked from across the room.

"She's right," Ethan told him. "We made it here in spite of everything. I think maybe a little optimism is in order."

"Indeed," agreed Jonas.

Kat leaned her head on his shoulder and continued humming.

Ethan hoped she was right. But though he allowed himself to release a little of his anxiety, he knew in his heart that they had only just begun. Whatever the future held, it would be fraught with difficulty. There would be more danger, more hardship, and more death.

A lot more!

CHAPTER SIXTEEN

E THAN HAD NO idea how much time had passed since they had been locked up; it felt like many hours.

As the waiting for something to happen dragged on, much of his previous anxiety returned. He could see that Markus was faring no better, pacing the room and checking the window every few minutes. Jonas, weary from all the travel, had fallen asleep with his pack under his head. Kat was lying down beside him, though her eyes remained open.

With his back beginning to ache from leaning against the hard wall, Ethan heaved himself up and joined Markus by the window.

The crowd outside had now dwindled to no more than a few dozen curiosity seekers. Ethan was surprised by the look of the dwarf women. Though stockier and shorter than most human women, they were certainly more feminine and graceful than he would have imagined. Some were even quite attractive. Their dress was by far more colorful and ornate than that of the men, the majority of whom wore various shades of brown or gray.

"Perhaps they intend to starve us to death," suggested Markus, trying to maintain a level of lightheartedness.

"And no bathroom," added Ethan.

This drew a dissatisfied moan from his friend. "Well, they better come soon, or else they'll find quite a mess when they get here."

Ethan rummaged through his pack, but only found a few strips of jerky and a small hunk of stale bread. Markus fared little better with just a couple of apricots and a small bag of salted nuts.

"We better hold off until we know how long we'll be stuck in here," Ethan suggested.

Markus nodded and resumed his vigil at the window. Another hour passed before the door finally opened. A very dissatisfied looking dwarf entered carrying a small sack and a pitcher of water.

"The female will come with me," he said.

His few words were enough to wake Jonas and have him springing to his feet. "What are you going to do with her?"

"It is our understanding that it is not proper for human women to be housed with the men," he replied. "We will find her more suitable quarters."

Both Markus and Ethan stepped in front of Kat.

"She will not be harmed," he assured.

Reluctantly, the pair moved aside.

"How long must we wait here?" asked Jonas.

The dwarf shrugged. "Until the king calls for you." Ushering Kat outside, he shut the door.

Ethan looked in the sack and found a loaf of dry bread and a dozen bright yellow fruits. They were about the size of a lemon, though with a fleshy skin rather than an outer peel.

He tossed one over to Markus. "What is it?"

"Mora fruit." His friend's face twisted in displeasure. "Imagine a rotted potato dipped in motor oil. Farmers won't even feed these to their pigs."

Ethan sniffed one, but could smell nothing. Tentatively, he took a small bite.

His taste buds were instantly attacked with the foulest tasting juice he had ever known. After spitting repeatedly and pulling grotesque faces, he rinsed his mouth out with water from the pitcher. Markus could not control his laughter.

Jonas snatched the Mora fruit away from Ethan and took a large bite. Ethan expected a similar reaction from him, but the old man's expression remained unchanged.

"Better this than nothing," he said, finishing it quickly.

Markus laughed again and ate one himself, though with exaggerated swallows and a scowl. Ethan tried again, but very nearly vomited.

His hunger getting the better of him, Ethan finally decided to finish off the remaining jerky and bread from his pack.

Just as he was swallowing the last mouthful, the door opened and Birger entered. His expression was dire. "The king says that he will speak only to Dragonvein."

"With respect," said Jonas. "Ethan knows nothing about this world. There is little the king can learn from questioning him alone."

"King Halvar is aware your claim. I have told him all I have heard."

"Then he must know that Ethan is…"

"He knows only what you have said," Birger snapped. "The truth of your words has yet to be proven."

"When do I see him?" asked Ethan.

"In three days," he replied. "Until then, I have arranged better accommodations for you. But mind that you do not try to leave. You will be killed on sight if you are seen wandering about without an escort." He glanced down at the Mora fruit peeking out from the sack on the floor and grimaced. "Did you actually eat any of those?"

"*They* did," said Ethan. "It was a bit too much for me to handle."

In spite of himself, Birger smiled. "Foul tasting little things. Good for only two purposes. Bat food and troll repellant. Even the young ones won't touch them."

He turned to the door. "I'll have proper food brought to you as soon as I can. If you die here, it will be by steel…not starvation. Now come. You'll be housed in the building next door for now. There are beds and showers waiting."

The dwarf opened the door and led them outside. The crowd was now all but gone. Only a few small groups remained, but the moment they caught sight of the humans their hostile whispering resumed.

The three story building alongside was made from a polished azure stone. It had superbly crafted windows and a small porch. Immediately inside was a staircase leading to the upper floors. To the right was a parlor featuring two sofas and an assortment of comfortable looking chairs. Unlike the prison, which had been lit by a single rajni stone fixed in the center of the ceiling, the room here had brass lamps hanging from silver chains in each corner. The red tile floor had a black rug in the center, while the walls were decorated with numerous paintings of dwarves and animals. Some of these were set in unfamiliar looking landscapes, with plants and trees that Ethan had never seen the like of before. On many of these artworks, the sky was filled with exploding stars, streaking comets, and three blood red moons.

Birger took them down a hallway just beside the stairs with three doors on the right. "These are your rooms," he told them. "There's a kitchen further down, as well as a bath and shower. I have no clothing that would fit you, so you'll need to make do with what you have."

Jonas bowed low. "I thank you, Birger. Your hospitality is most welcome."

The dwarf sniffed. "Enjoy it while you can. King Halvar will not be easily convinced of your intentions."

Jonas smiled. "I appreciate *your* kindness, regardless of what else happens."

Birger frowned. "Be thankful that I am a great fool. If I had a brain in my head I would have left you to the Rakasa. As it stands, I am in nearly as much peril as you."

"I swear that I'm not lying about who I am," said Ethan. "Once the kings sees that, we'll both be out of trouble."

"Actually, the more I think about it, the more I hope you *are* lying. Because if you're not…" Birger shook his head and heaved a sigh. "Well, it's too late for that now. Keep to the ground floor…and *do not* leave this house under any circumstances."

After he had gone, they each took a room. The beds were built for someone of dwarf height and the mattresses were rock hard, but it was still better than a cold floor. Other than a chest and dresser, there was little else furnishing the bedrooms. The kitchen was spacious though, with a sturdy dining table opposite a cast iron stove. Beyond that was the bathroom. Ethan was amazed at how similar it was to those back on Earth. The oval tub in the far corner was equipped with a brass shower head that came down from the ceiling. Two chains hung on either side to control the temperature of the water, and a valve at the head of the tub controlled the flow.

Markus seemed unusually pleased by the sight of this. In fact, Ethan could swear he saw tears forming in his friend's eyes. "I haven't seen a shower since I left England," he explained. "Only the very rich can afford such luxuries in Lumnia."

"Then you can go first," said Ethan.

Markus smiled excitedly. "I will." For a moment there was something uncharacteristically boyish about him.

Not long after they were clean and changed, a dwarf woman brought them a tray of fruits, together with bread and a pitcher of sweet smelling blue liquid. They thanked her, even though she did not so much as acknowledge their presence while in the house.

"No meat," complained Markus, after she had left.

"If memory serves me right, dwarves are vegetarians," said Jonas. "It's the one thing Lord Dragonvein did not enjoy about his visits."

"As long as it tastes better than mora fruit," said Ethan.

In fact, he found the food to be quite good. Though the fruits were unfamiliar, they were sweet tasting and satisfying. The bread was freshly baked, and the blue liquid reminded him a bit of lemonade, though not quite as tart.

"Three days," muttered Markus. "Three days and our fate is decided."

"Is there anything you can tell me that might help?" Ethan asked Jonas, who was clearing the table.

"Not that I can think of," he replied. "Your father spoke often of the dwarves, but our conversations were limited to superficial topics. He never talked about his business here. He was a very private man... even with me."

"When the time comes, just tell the truth," said Markus. "It's what you're best at anyway. If this king is worth a damn he'll know you're not lying."

Ethan raised an eyebrow. "And if he's not?"

"Then we're all dead and the rest won't matter."

Time passed slowly in the house. Without the sun it was impossible to tell night from day. Markus tried to gauge it by looking out of the window to see if people were about, figuring that this would be mostly during the daytime hours.

Ethan spent the majority of the time in his room, staring at the ceiling and going over and over in his mind how he had come to be where he was. One day he was fighting the Nazi's, the next he was being hunted by an evil - and apparently immortal - emperor. He had gone from being the adopted son of a Brooklyn baker, to the son of a dead mage from another world. Of all the ways his life could have turned out, this was one he could have never imagined in a million years.

The others didn't seem to mind their time in the house, though occasionally he would catch Markus running his fingers over the scars on his face, a faraway look in his eyes. Seeing this racked Ethan with guilt. If only he could undo what had happened to his dear friend. But he couldn't. At this point, all he could do was try to make things better in the here and now. That would need to begin by convincing the king he was who he claimed, and keeping them all from being executed.

Birger came by from time to time. With each visit the dwarf seemed a bit friendlier and more accepting of human company, even letting loose the odd laugh here and there. He told them that Kat was in a house not far away and was being well attended. He even suggested that, due to the fact that she was little more than a child, should things go poorly for the others, she would likely be spared. However, Birger's gradual acceptance did not extend to the other dwarf men and women who brought them their food. Each one still looked upon them with suspicion and malice, refusing to so much as utter a single word in their presence.

The day Ethan was due to see the king, the tension in the house was palpable. Ethan hardly touched his breakfast, while Jonas did nothing but pace about the parlor, staring at the door. Only Markus seemed at ease.

"Don't worry," he told Ethan. "Birger said that this King Halvar is a reasonable sort."

Ethan forced a smile. "I'll be fine."

A few minutes later Birger arrived with half a dozen armed guards at his back.

"It's time," he said.

Ethan gave a sharp nod and followed him out of the room, casting a wink and a smile over his shoulder as he did so.

He was escorted through the streets until they were in front of the massive manor he had seen previously. Marble statues inlaid with gemstones and gold were placed at regular intervals along the colonnade which led from the main avenue to the front steps. Considering that they were underground, the gardens surrounding the building appeared surprisingly green and alive. However, after looking closely, Ethan could see that what he at first had taken to be grass, was in fact a thick moss.

The manor itself was five stories high and constructed from a dark green stone. The top floor balcony was crowded with dwarves gathered to watch their approach. They whispered and pointed, their faces awash with suspicion. The main double doors below were made from dark oak; the one on the left had a sun carved in it, the one on the right a moon.

Just as they reached the bottom of the steps, two dwarves dressed in ruffled blue shirts and black pants exited the manor.

"Is this the one who claims to be a Dragonvein?" asked the dwarf on the right.

"He is," Birger affirmed. "And he is expected."

"As are you Birger." His voice bore sinister intent.

Birger grumbled a curse and cast a sideways glance at Ethan. "You had better be who you say you are."

Before Ethan could reply, they started up the steps. On reaching the top, their escorts bowed and lined up three by three on either side of the front doors. The two others gestured for Ethan to enter.

"The king awaits," he was told.

Beyond the threshold was a large receiving hall supported by a series of black columns. The polished white marble floors gleamed from the light of a dozen crystal chandeliers hanging from the ceiling. The walls were covered in beautiful tapestries and paintings depicting stars and various other celestial bodies – a theme that Ethan had noticed was quite common here.

To his left was a spiral staircase leading to the upper floors, and to his right a series of hallways and silver doors. He was taken to the back of the hall where a set of double doors were swung wide open, revealing a room nearly as spacious as the receiving hall itself.

In the center of this room was an immense gray stone table, around which six dwarf men and six women were sat. They were clad in simple yet well-made attire, and were all groomed to perfection. Ethan thought they were probably the ruling class; they certainly had a stately appearance about them. The dwarf seated at the head of the table was clad in a black shirt and vest with a gold robe wrapped around his broad shoulders. A thin circlet of silver with a single ruby set in the center rested atop his weathered brow. His black beard was striped with the grey of many years, and his eyes were deeply set and impossible to read.

This has to be King Halvar, thought Ethan.

The door boomed shut behind him.

"So this is the one who calls himself Dragonvein," remarked the king.

Ethan bowed. "I..."

The king's hand shot up to silence him. "You have not been addressed." His voice was deep and menacing.

Ethan's mouth snapped shut.

"Why did you bring him here, Birger?" asked the king. "Are you not aware of our laws?"

"I am aware, my king," he replied calmly. "I only did what I thought to be right."

Halvar snorted. "And you thought bringing a human...no...*four* humans to our city was the right thing?"

"This one is the son of Praxis Dragonvein," he explained. "The others are his companions."

"And how do you know this?" challenged Halvar.

"I overheard him speaking when they were fleeing the Rakasa."

"So all this is based on something you overheard? What kind of fool are you, Birger?" The king's tone was hard and unyielding. "I also hear you collapsed the west entrance. Is that true?"

Birger nodded. "If I hadn't, the humans would now be in the hands of the Emperor."

"And why should I care?"

"Because we swore an oath to this man's father. And we all know the prophecy."

At the mention of this, the other dwarves began whispering to one another. A movement of the king's hand silenced them.

"You expect me to honor an oath made to a human mage hundreds of years before I was born?"

Birger stuck out his chest and gazed resolutely at his monarch. "Since when does the oath of a dwarf expire? Since when do we forget the honor of our forefathers? Is not a promise given a promise kept, regardless of time?"

The king gave no reply, but his anger was obvious.

"How do we know that this is really the son of Praxis Dragonvein?" asked a dwarf woman seated just to Halvar's right. "All we have is a conversation you overheard. Surely that is not enough to put our people in such danger?"

"The Rakasa called him Dragonvein as well," said Birger.

The woman leaned back and looked to Halvar. "If Shinzan believes him to be the son of Praxis Dragonvein, then I must agree that Birger acted rightly. As impossible as the claim may appear, we should hear what this human has to say."

The assembly nodded.

"Very well," growled the king. He pointed to a chair directly opposite him. "Sit, human. We will hear your story. But be warned, should you be found false, you and your friends will never leave Elyfoss alive."

Ethan bowed, then took a seat.

"You can go, Birger," said the king, waving a hand dismissively. "You are guiltless here."

"With your permission, my king," he said, "I would stay."

After a short pause, Halvar nodded his consent. Birger sat down on Ethan's right and glanced very briefly in his direction. Ethan thought he could detect a hint of encouragement in the look.

The stage was now set. He began telling his tale, starting with his childhood in New York and ending when they first met Birger. The dwarves stopped him every so often to ask for more details, particularly when he spoke about Earth or the dragons. By the time he was done, several hours had passed and his back was aching from sitting in the hard chair.

The king regarded him for an uncomfortably long moment before speaking. "I for one am still not convinced. It is indeed possible that you are from Earth, but I do *not* believe you are the son of Praxis Dragonvein."

"I'm telling you the truth, Your Highness," Ethan insisted.

"I believe him," added Birger. "Who would manufacture such a wild tale?"

"Someone desperate to evade capture," said Halvar. "Someone who would take advantage of our customs and legends to further their own ends."

Several of the assembly nodded in agreement, but others shook their heads. The king raised his hand.

"Your story was well thought, young human," he said. "And it is clear you have convinced some of my more gullible brothers and sisters." A wry grin crept over his face. "Fortunately, there is a way to tell if what you say is true."

Halvar beckoned over a guard who was standing near the door and whispered into his ear. The dwarf saluted and then hurried away, returning a few minutes later with a small wooden box. From this, Halvar removed a silver circlet.

"No!" barked Birger. "You can't."

The king shot him a warning look. "You speak out of turn, Birger. Your advice is not required. Nor is your presence if you cannot remain quiet."

Birger lowered his eyes. "Forgive me, my king. But that was not made to be used on humans. There is no way to know what it could do to him."

Several of those gathered echoed Birger's concerns, but the king would not be moved.

"Human," he began. "I have in my hand a device that when placed upon your head will cause you pain should you speak falsely. Birger is correct in saying that it was not designed to be used on your kind, and I am not entirely certain of the risks. But should you pass this test, I will need no other proof that you are telling the truth." He leaned in. "So, I offer you this choice: Leave here at once. You will be escorted from the mountain and set free to do as you will. No harm will come to you. Or you can place this on your head and answer our questions."

"You should go," said Birger.

"Do you believe I'm telling the truth?" Ethan asked him.

He gave a lengthy sigh and then nodded. "I believe you."

Ethan smiled. "Then I will take the test."

The king rose from his seat and carried the circlet over to Ethan. "The moment you put this on you must tell the truth. For a dwarf, lying results in excruciating pain. But for you…" He shrugged. "Who knows? It *was* used on an elf once."

"What happened?" Ethan asked.

"He died," replied Halvar. "But not before he was driven completely mad."

He returned to his seat. All eyes were now on Ethan.

Taking a deep breath, he placed the circlet on his head. At first he felt nothing. Then, gradually, the metal became warm and a light tingle shot through his body.

Halvar nodded to the others. "Ask your questions."

One by one they interrogated Ethan. Mostly they asked him to enlarge on details of his story, though some presented questions of a more personal nature. When it came back around to the king, his face was twisted in frustration.

By contrast, Birger looked smug and satisfied. "There can be no doubt," he said. "He *is* the son of Praxis Dragonvein."

"What is clear, is that he believes himself to be," Halvar corrected. "I am still not completely satisfied. We will question his friends as well. Particularly the one named Jonas. However, as this young human came to us in good faith, his life will be spared, regardless of the outcome."

"And what about my friends?" asked Ethan.

"Their fate is in their own hands," replied Halvar. "In the meantime, consider yourself my guest. You will be given a room here in my palace. And Birger will attend you."

Birger scowled. "But, my king. I've work to do. I have no time to…"

"You had the time to rescue this human," he retorted. "And you had the time to bring him all the way here. I will send word to your foreman. Considering the circumstances, I'm certain that he will understand."

Birger bowed. "As you wish, my king."

Ethan tried to suppress a smile. He was happy that Birger would be nearby. He had grown to like the dwarf and was grateful to him for his support.

"If you would now excuse us," Halvar continued. "The council and I have private matters to discuss."

Ethan rose and bowed, then followed Birger from the room. The dwarf quickly found a servant and instructed him to prepare a room for Ethan. After a brief hesitation and a sour look, the servant obeyed.

Birger then led him up the spiral staircase and down a long hall to a sitting room. The décor was elegant – much like that of the house he had previously been staying in, with more paintings and etchings of otherworldly places, along with marble busts of stern, powerful looking dwarves.

They sat down in a pair of chairs at the far end. Birger appeared most unhappy and was muttering curses under his breath.

"I'm sorry you've been forced to do this," said Ethan.

He shrugged and leaned back. "I should have expected it. King Halvar does not like being proved wrong. This is just his way of letting me know it."

"What will happen to you if you're not at work?"

"Nothing," he replied. "But I will be leaving my friends shorthanded."

"What is it you mine for?"

"Rajni stones mostly. But sometimes we find gems and precious metals."

"And you trade them to the Empire?"

Birger shook his head. "We trade what we make with them."

"Weapons," muttered Ethan.

"Don't think we do it because we want to," snapped Birger, now on the defensive. "It's the only thing that keeps Shinzan from wiping us out completely. As it stands, we have to trade gold and gems with human smugglers simply to get enough food to eat. In case you didn't notice, there is no sunlight here. And without that, plants won't grow. Our only other choice is to live off tunnel rats and mora fruit. Personally, I'd rather die."

"I didn't mean anything by it," said Ethan. "It's just that all this is new to me."

Birger held up his hand. "No need to apologize. It's not your fault. My people have allowed this to go on for far too long. The truth is, when I heard the Rakasa shout out your name, I dared to let myself hope. That's the main reason why I saved you."

"Hope for what?"

"Hope that your coming heralds the end to Shinzan's reign. Hope that my people can once again feel the sun on our faces and the wind in our hair."

"Are you saying that you used to live on the surface?"

"No. Well, a few did, though most of us have always dwelled in the mountains. But we also possessed vast stretches of rich farmland and bountiful orchards. Some dwarves would choose a life of farming to provide our people with the food we needed. And it was our pleasure to leave our mountain homes from time to time and spend our days in the sun and our nights gazing at the stars. We love the deep places of Lumnia. But we also love the freedom of being able to visit what lies beyond occasionally."

Ethan lowered his head. "How am I supposed to do this...to beat Shinzan, I mean?"

"We were given a prophecy just after our defeat," Birger replied. "Well, *given* isn't really the right word, I suppose. *Taken* is more like it. My people captured an elf trying to escape Imperial soldiers and... interrogated him."

"You mean you tortured him?" There was obvious disapproval in Ethan's voice.

"Do not judge us," Birger warned. "Elves have committed terrible crimes against my people. And at the time, we were still reeling from what Shinzan had done to us."

He sighed. "In any case, the elf told us that his people were given a prophecy from the very heart of Lumnia. It said that one day, the children of magic shall rise again to do battle with the stain that blackens the soul of the world. We will know that time is at hand when the dragons return to herald their arrival."

"Anything else?" asked Ethan.

"Sure, but I don't remember it anymore. Even though I knew it by heart as a child." Birger shrugged. "Anyway, that's basically what it says."

"And you believe it."

"Elves have an uncanny way of knowing things before they happen. They claim it comes from their connection to the planet. And who knows, it might be true. But if *they* take it seriously, it would be foolish to ignore it."

Ethan wasn't so sure. He found it difficult to imagine relying on mystical prophecies and things like that for hope. He well remembered the men in his unit just before D-Day. Chuck Marshall had nearly gone insane when he couldn't find his lucky rabbit's foot. He was convinced that he wouldn't survive the jump without it. As it turned out, Markus, who did not like Chuck one bit, had hidden it behind the barracks. He returned it an hour before they took off. Chuck was so happy that he forgot to be angry with Markus for taking it in the first place. Not that getting it back helped him very much. Chuck was killed even before arriving at the drop zone when an anti-aircraft shell tore through the plane he was in. So much for lucky charms.

Birger could see that Ethan was doubtful. "So, there is no magic on Earth at all?"

Ethan shook his head. "Not that I've ever seen. No need for it really. We have machines that do work for us. Cars and planes to take us where we want to go. And radios to listen to for news and music."

Birger rubbed his chin. "My father used to tell me stories about how our people once built incredible machines that could reach the very stars themselves. He said that long ago we could fly through the air like birds whenever it took our fancy. If your people can build such things, perhaps we could have done so as well."

Ethan smiled. "I don't know about going to the stars, but we can sure fly through the air easy enough." He began telling Birger about his time in the Airborne. A short while later, the door opened and a young dwarf woman in a red and green dress entered.

"Lord Dragonvein's room is ready," she said. "The king sends word that your friends will be brought here tomorrow."

Lord? Since when am I Lord?

They both stood and followed the woman along a series of hallways and up to the next floor. After walking for what seemed like miles, they arrived at Ethan's room.

"*Your* quarters are just across the hall," the woman told Birger. "Meals will be brought to you. Please stay in your room until the king tells you otherwise." Without waiting for a reply she sped away.

"Do you think my friends will be all right?" Ethan asked.

Birger opened the door to his own room. "As the king said – their fate is in their own hands. Just hope that they choose to speak the truth."

After the dwarf disappeared, Ethan stood in the hall for a moment longer, his mind turning to Jonas. Even after everything that had happened, he was still certain that Jonas was holding back some secrets. Markus felt it too. What would happen to the old man when they placed the circlet on *his* head? He shook off the thought and entered his room.

It was by far the most luxurious place he had ever stayed. To his left was an expertly crafted wardrobe of richly stained and polished wood. Beside it, a matching dresser and vanity. The bed opposite was wide enough to easily accommodate three grown men, and, Ethan gratefully noticed, long enough to allow him to stretch out comfortably. There was also a small table surrounded by four chairs, and a splendid bookcase filled with leather bound tomes.

On the far wall were two doors, both slightly ajar. The left hand door led to a formal dining room, while a peek to the right revealed a bathroom complete with sink, toilet, and shower.

He pressed down on the mattress and sighed with relief. Soft...but not too soft. Spreading his arms wide, he allowed himself to fall back onto it, bouncing several times before letting out a satisfied moan.

He lay there for a short while, trying to clear his thoughts. Just as he felt himself beginning to drift off, there was a light rap at the door. Before he could move to answer, Kat stepped inside.

She looked at him, smiling. "Did you miss me?"

Ethan struggled up into a sitting position. "Are you all right?"

She ran over and jumped onto the bed. "Of course I'm all right. Why wouldn't I be? Don't tell me that you were worried."

He rubbed his eyes and yawned. "Of course I was worried. We all were."

"There was no need to be. The dwarf women took good care of me. Not that they spoke very much."

"How did you get here?"

"They brought me just now. They said you were staying here, and being that I wasn't under suspicion, I could stay here too."

Ethan cocked his head. "Not in this room?"

"Down the hall," she replied. Her smile became an impish grin. "Unless you want me to, of course."

Ethan groaned and pushed himself to his feet.

"I was only joking," she said, giggling. "I just wanted you to know I was here." She hopped off the bed and danced playfully to the door. "I'm three doors down if you need me."

Ethan nodded. "I think I'm going to get some rest. And you should be careful. They said that we should stay in our rooms until the king tells us otherwise."

She opened the door and looked over her shoulder. "You worry too much. We made it. We're here. What more do you want?"

After the door closed behind her, Ethan checked it for a lock but wasn't able to find one.

What more do I want?

He answered himself aloud. "A hot shower and a good night's sleep."

Just then his stomach growled. "And maybe something to eat."

CHAPTER SEVENTEEN

THE FOLLOWING MORNING, the first thing Ethan saw when opening his eyes was Kat sitting at the table, legs crossed, nibbling daintily on a piece of bread.

"It's about time you woke up," she said. "I've been sitting here for almost an hour with no one to talk to."

He yawned and stretched. "You should really knock before you come in here."

"I *did* knock. You didn't answer."

Groaning, he sat up. "Have you heard anything about Markus and Jonas?"

"No. But Birger was here earlier. He said he'd be back in a few hours."

Ethan wiped the sleep from his eyes. There was a plate of fruits and berries placed on the table in front of an empty chair.

"No meat here at all," complained Kat. "I asked the woman who brought our food if they had any bacon and she looked at me like I'd asked for horse dung."

He chuckled and sat down. "Bacon *would* be nice. Unfortunately, I doubt we'll be seeing any for a while." The mention of bacon made the breakfast seem far less appetizing than it had a moment before. He closed his eyes, imagining the smell of Sunday breakfast back home in New York. He recalled how their apartment held the scent of bacon and coffee all day long.

After eating, Kat asked him to tell her more about Earth. And with little else to keep them occupied, he was happy to oblige. He'd just got to explaining how a subway operated when Birger entered. His face was grim.

"What's wrong?" asked Ethan.

"Your friend…Jonas. Things did not go well during his questioning."

Both Ethan and Kat sprang to their feet.

"Is he all right?" asked Kat, anxiously.

"It's hard to say," Birger replied. "The circlet…well, it seems that with humans, refusing to answer a question is the same as a lie."

"What do you mean?" pressed Ethan, his concern deepening.

"When the council questioned him on personal matters, he refused to answer."

"What kind of personal matters?"

"I don't know. I wasn't there. All I know is that he's unconscious."

Ethan stepped toward the door, but Birger barred his way.

"There's nothing you can do," he said. "Our physicians are treating him as we speak. You should also know that before he was injured he confirmed your identity to the king and the council. However, this has caused even more debate."

Ethan tried to calm himself. "How so?"

"Now that there is no question of your identity, the king fears that when the Emperor learns of it, he'll send his armies."

"But didn't Ethan's father make a deal with your people?" asked Kat. "They have no choice but to help him. Right?"

Birger lowered his eyes. "It's not that simple. Praxis Dragonvein did indeed make a pact with my people. But King Halvar fears for our very existence. He argues that, seeing as how I saved you from the Rakasa, the oath has been fulfilled and we have no further obligation."

"So he's going to make us leave?" asked Ethan.

"I don't know," Birger admitted. "The king doesn't have unlimited power. The council must be with him on this. And right now, they're divided."

Ethan thought for a moment. If there was a possibility that his presence could destroy these people, perhaps he *should* leave. "And how do you feel about it?" he asked.

"I'm not sure how to feel," Birger replied solemnly. "I share some of King Halvar's fears. We cannot stand against the power of Shinzan. Not alone. I have family…friends…a life here. Most of us were killed the last time we defied the Emperor. If we try again, there may be no one left to tell our story."

He looked up at Ethan. Now though, rather than sadness and fear, there was unremitting determination in his eyes. "Then I look around at how we are forced to live. The way we cower like frightened children at the mention of Shinzan's name. Forced to bow to the very demon who slaughtered us without pity. How long can this go on? How long before our spirits wither and die completely? How long before there is nothing left of us but our empty, broken bodies? No…I think I would prefer death. But I have no right to choose that fate for everyone else."

"Do you really think I can help you?" Ethan asked. It was one thing to look to the dwarves for a place of refuge. But now, here was someone looking to *him* for salvation. He suddenly felt very small and inadequate.

"I don't know for sure," Birger said. "Yet it was no accident that I came upon you and your friends. Before that, I'd never put much faith in the elves' belief in a greater power. However, something that day compelled me to go to the cave where I found you. I've never gone there before. But that day I did, and without even knowing why. I arrived the same day…the very minute in fact, that you needed me."

Ethan had never been religious – though more than once during the heat of battle he had prayed for God to keep him alive. To think that some *'greater power'*, as Birger put it, was guiding him, was more than he could accept. Even so, the conviction in the dwarf's eyes was enough to make him wonder.

"When can we see Jonas?" asked Kat.

"He's at the other house. The king will not permit him to stay at the manor for now. I'll look in on him later and let you know if there's any change."

"What about Markus?" asked Ethan.

"He's with the council now. If all goes well you'll see him in a few hours. Now I must leave. I have errands to run. I'll be back as soon as I can."

Once Birger had left, Kat and Ethan sat at the table silently for several minutes. Ethan's mind was reeling from the sheer magnitude of the events that were transpiring. Even trying to imagine what the future might bring was taking him to the brink of panic.

Kat moved her chair close to Ethan and rested her head on his shoulder. "Do you think Jonas will be all right?"

He gave her a reassuring smile. "Jonas is a tough old man. I'm sure he'll be just fine."

"You know, he's not as mean as he pretends to be."

"I know."

Just as Birger had told them, a few hours later Markus arrived. His eyes were distant and his hands were trembling. Ethan and Kat rushed to his side.

"Before you ask, I'm okay," he said. "I'm just a bit shaken. Some of their questions were pretty damn uncomfortable for me."

"I'm just glad you answered them," said Ethan. "Any word on Jonas?"

"None. But I have a feeling the old man isn't done yet. I was right though. Even his secrets have secrets. Makes me wonder what the dwarves asked him about."

"I don't care what they asked," said Kat, frowning. "*Everyone* is allowed to have secrets. I'd bet you have a few."

"Not anymore," Markus said bitterly. "At least, none that the dwarves don't know about." He forced a smile at Ethan. "There's never a priest around when you need one."

Ethan returned his smile and offered him a seat, but Markus refused.

"I'm tired," he said. "I think I'll go to my room and get some rest." He made his way to the door, halting just long enough to add: "But not before I enjoy another one of those hot showers."

Kat also left a few minutes later. Ethan stretched out on the bed, but no matter what he tried, he couldn't quiet his mind sufficiently for sleep to come. Frustrated, he took a random book from the shelf and started reading. It was a compilation of dwarf poems that he found difficult to understand. The imagery was confusing and largely unfamiliar. By the time he finished the third poem, his head was throbbing.

Birger returned just as his evening meal arrived.

"Jonas has regained consciousness," he told him. "It looks like he'll recover."

Ethan sighed with relief and thanked him for the good news. He suggested that Birger join him for dinner, but he politely refused, saying that he still had things to do.

Kat came in a few minutes later, a plate in one hand and a cup in the other.

"Markus is still sleeping," she said, plopping herself down at the table.

After they finished eating, Ethan told her that he was still tired. Reluctantly, Kat left, though not without first making him promise to have breakfast with her in the morning.

It took some time, but eventually he managed to drift off. His dreams were troubled: filled with dragons battling dark fire while dwarf cities burned in the distance. He woke twice with heart pounding and the roar of the flames and the cries of dying dragons still echoing clearly in his mind.

The next morning after breakfast, Birger arrived to say that the king and his council wished to see Ethan. Kat asked to come along with them, but Birger quickly told her that this could not be allowed.

Outside in the hallway, they bumped into Markus. His friend looked rested and in good spirits following his much needed and well-earned sleep.

"Mind what you say," he warned Ethan. "I get the feeling that the king would like nothing more than to have a good excuse to hand us over to the Empire."

"King Halvar would never do that," Birger protested. "He is a dwarf of honor."

Markus shrugged. "Whatever you say. But I know when someone's plotting something. And I could see it in his eyes."

Birger sniffed and muttered a curse.

"I'll be careful," Ethan promised.

As they approached the council chambers, even before the doors had swung open, Ethan could hear loud angry voices coming from within. Then, the moment he stepped inside, all went disturbingly silent. King Halvar was standing with his hands planted firmly on the table. His face was red and his mouth twisted in anger.

"Ah," he said, not masking his disdain for Ethan. "The son of Praxis Dragonvein has arrived. All hail, the bringer of our doom." He pointed to the empty chair at the far end of the table. "Sit."

Such was the malice and judgment bearing down on him, Ethan had difficulty looking the king in the eye. "Forgive me, Your Highness. But I didn't come here to bring doom."

"Of course you did," Halvar retorted. "Did you not come here seeking our aid? Are you not asking my people to honor your father's request?"

"It was not a request," countered an elderly dwarf woman. Though the years showed in the creases on her face and gray in her hair, her voice was commanding and her posture regal. "It was an oath. Do not pretend it is otherwise."

"And you, Lady Thora, do not presume to educate me in history," the king shot back furiously. "I know full well what King Vidar promised. And I also know that many of you believe the arrival of Praxis Dragonvein's son heralds the coming of our deliverance. But I ask you this: Is it worth risking all we have? Is it worth the lives of our children? We know what will happen if we defy Shinzan. It will be the end of everything."

"Then you are content to have us living as slaves?" barked a dwarf with a close cropped blond beard and long braided hair. "Shinzan is *not* mortal. He will *never* die. We cannot pretend we can simply outlast him. I say that if the choice is between a slow death and a quick one, I'll take the edge of a sword."

This was met by nods of agreement from four others.

"You speak like a courageous fool, Lord Olaf!" shouted a dark haired woman opposite him. "Have you no sons or daughters? Do you believe in your heart that our children would wish to follow us to their end?"

Olaf glared. "My sons would be proud to follow me if it meant dying with honor."

"And could you watch them die?" Halvar interjected.

Olaf slowly nodded. "If I must. My heart would break, but at least they would die as I have *never* lived…as free dwarves."

"You don't know what you are saying, my dear friend." The king's voice had become soft and reserved. "If the consequences were merely death at the point of an Imperial sword, I too might be swayed to fight. But that is not what would await us."

Reaching under his chair, he picked up a small, red-leather bound book and placed it on the table. He opened it with great care. "This is the journal of King Vidar, given to me by my father on the day of my coronation. I have read it many times. But only once did I read his final entry. I have tried many times, but have never been able to read it again."

A hush fell over the room.

"Ethan Dragonvein, son of Praxis. I will read it to you now. What you are about to hear was written moments before King Vidar was slain within these very halls by Emperor Shinzan. Once you have heard it, I hope you…"

He paused to cast his eyes over the assembly. "I hope all of you, will consider the cost of your actions here today."

He bowed his head for a moment, then began reading aloud.

Fourth Day of Red Harvest

This will be my final entry and final minutes as king. I will attempt to give as full an account as I can, but my time is short. Shinzan is coming and there is no escape.

After two days I have managed to drag myself back to the manor. My left leg is shattered beyond any hope of repair and my left arm is all but useless. But these injuries are trivial compared to what I have witnessed.

My beautiful city is lost and her people all but extinct. In our arrogance we thought our mighty gates could withstand any foe.

The armies of the Emperor have broken against them like waves on rocks for three years, and for three years we believed this made us invincible.

When the humans fell, I should have known that we would soon follow. I should have heeded the words of my dear friend, Praxis. He was always the wiser of us. He urged me to form an alliance with the Council of Volnar. But I was too proud; too blinded by arrogance. Then, when word of his death came, it was too late. The mages were being exterminated, and I was helpless to intervene. For this I am deeply sorry. I abandoned my friend and his people to their fate, and for that I am ashamed.

At this moment, I am sitting in my bed chamber beside the window looking out at countless pillars of black smoke. They serve to remind me that it was my actions - and my inaction - which have brought us to this end. When Shinzan arrived fifteen days ago and demanded that we open the gates, I all but called him an addle-brained fool. The entire Council of Volnar could not have hoped to breach our defenses, and his vast armies had failed utterly. What threat could he pose to us? I stood atop our great wall and mocked him openly. His face was covered, but I remember feeling as if he was smiling up at me. I should have known in that moment I had made a terrible mistake. With a single wave of his hand, Shinzan smashed our mighty gates to ruins. It took only seconds.

Had he wanted to, he could have taken the city in a day. But his wrath was beyond reckoning and his cruelty unimaginable. Our soldiers did everything they could to stop him. But Shinzan unleashed magic the like of which, even after having seen it, I still find hard to believe. In an instant, a thousand stout dwarves fell screaming to their knees, blood pouring from their ears, while Shinzan simply watched and laughed. It took them more than an hour to die, and they were all begging for death until their final breaths.

Even though in my heart I knew it was useless, I then ordered every soldier in the city to push him back. But it was as if I had sent children to slay a dragon. Wave after wave fell to his power. Never had I conceived that magic could be used to such horrific effect. Some were torn apart by unseen beasts, while others had their eyes and tongues set aflame so they could neither see nor cry for mercy. Five hundred of my finest soldiers died with their blood boiling inside their veins. There were no quick deaths. Not a single one. I pray that the spirits of my people can find a way to forgive me.

Those who fled only prolonged their end. Shinzan sealed the city, trapping all who still remained. I sent word of our surrender and begged his mercy. But when my messenger returned he fell face down at my feet, screaming in agony, then burst into flames before my eyes. When the flames died away the words 'No Mercy' were scorched into the very rock where the body had been only moments before.

For the next two weeks Shinzan continued his monstrous work, wandering through the city and killing everyone he encountered. Those who thought they had escaped his notice found that they were only being toyed with. I will not describe the horror they suffered. It was as if murder to him was nothing more than a source of amusement. His laughter boomed and echoed, mingling with the screams and pleas of his victims.

It mattered not if they were male or female...old or young. All were objects of his murderous desire. I watched helplessly as my people were being slaughtered. He knew I was there. He knew I followed him as he casually strolled through the streets. I even heard him humming. I think he did this only to taunt me. To make me pay. Again and again I tried to attack him, if only to have him kill me and end my own suffering, but he wouldn't allow me to get close enough. He wanted me to watch. Now the city is quiet. He has saved me for the very last. This is my punishment for defiance. I welcome it.

Should these words manage to escape the hands of Shinzan, know that I am sorry I have failed those who looked to me for protection. I am to blame, and no other. The door to the manor is smashed and I can hear him coming. In this last moment I know only one thing. I deserve what is about to...

Halvar closed the book and set it down. Tears were welling, not only in his eyes, but in those of several others sat around the table. "Shinzan must have killed him before he was able to finish writing that final sentence."

He looked hard at Ethan. "Are you prepared to do battle with that? Are any of you?"

There was a long and heavy silence. It was Lady Thora who spoke first.

"My King," she began. Her voice trembled slightly, but her back was straight and her head held high. "I do not question your love for our people. Nor would I have you suffer the fate of King Vidar. You have been a wise and just ruler. There is none who would dispute that."

She paused while the entire council nodded in agreement. "I am as frightened by what I have just heard as I think the rest of us are. To face such enormous power and evil is enough to wither the heart of the bravest dwarf. But we cannot continue as we are. You must know this."

"What I do know is that I am charged with the protection of my people," Halvar responded. "And harboring the son of Praxis Dragonvein is certain to bring death to us all. There is no oath that can be sworn by anyone that will make me ignore my duty."

"But do not forget that we are seeing the fulfillment of the prophecy," Thora countered. "That alone is enough to give us hope. When you read from King Vidar's journal I was deeply moved. But not by the horrors he witnessed. It was by the regret he felt for abandoning a friend and ally. For not joining in the fight sooner. Would you make the same mistake?"

"We have no allies," Halvar said. His tone was hard and unyielding.

"The humans now serve Shinzan, and as for the elves…they serve only themselves. You might claim to see prophecy in what has happened. I do not. One tiny dragon is not enough for me to abandon my reason. The prophecy says that the dragons will herald the return of the mages and the fall of Shinzan. I have seen no dragons, have you? Also, the prophecy clearly states that five mages are needed before freedom is restored. Five. Not one."

Thora sat back down and sighed.

"I would like to hear what the son of Praxis has to say," Olaf interjected. "It is his fate we discuss here as well. What say you? Are you willing to fight this evil?"

"Indeed," agreed Halvar. "What say you? Surely you have heard enough by now to know where you stand."

A host of grim faces turned to Ethan in anticipation. He cast his eyes around the table. Some softened their expressions as he looked into their eyes, but others turned colder. He had no idea what to say. These people were debating the future of an entire race. And everything hinged on him. For a moment he felt dizzy from the weight of it all and needed to grip the arms of his chair to steady himself. After taking a deep cleansing breath, he rose slowly to his feet.

"First, I want to thank you," he said. His voice trembled slightly, but he managed to keep his composure. "Birger saved my life. And after he brought me here, instead of killing us, you allowed me and my friends to stay. Without your kindness, I don't know where we'd be right now. Probably dead."

He cleared his throat. "As you know, I've only recently arrived in this world, so all of this is very strange to me. I don't know anything about magic or dragons, and there are no dwarves or elves where I come from. But I do know about evil. And in my world we fight it to the end. Even when it looks like it can't be defeated.

"You say you want to know what I think. But I can't really tell you. This is all too big for me. I can't decide what the best thing to do is. Stuff like that should be left to generals…and kings. What I can tell you though, is how I feel in my heart."

His gaze fell directly at Halvar and his nervousness melted away.

"On Earth, my people were faced with a great evil. His name was Hitler. He didn't have magical powers like Shinzan, but his armies were said to be unstoppable. And for a while it looked like they were. But you know what? The freedom loving people of Earth joined together... and we bloody stopped him. We took the beaches at Normandy and we pushed that bastard back.

"A lot has happened to me since I arrived on Lumnia. I've seen things I could never have imagined in a million years. And to tell you the truth, most of it scares the hell out of me. But that's all right. I've been scared before. Fear didn't kill me in France, and it won't kill me here. You all want to know what I plan to do. Well, I've been wondering that myself, and I've come to realize something. No matter how I look at it, I only have three choices."

He raised a finger. "First off, I can hide - though it doesn't look like there's anywhere I can go where Shinzan won't find me." A second finger rose. "Second choice is to run. Well, I've already tried that, and I can't seem to run fast enough to get away. Anyhow, you can't run forever. Eventually the road ends."

The two fingers dropped beside the others to make a fist. "The third option is to fight."

He straightened his back and held his head high. "Your Highness, I'm an Airborne Ranger. That may not mean anything to you, but it means a whole lot to me. It means running and hiding is not an option. I keep thinking about the Airborne motto – *rendezvous with destiny*. I used to think I knew what that meant: that whatever is supposed to happen, will happen. That our destiny is unavoidable and we should accept it with honor. But the more I see, the more I think I was wrong. What it really means is that our destiny is out there waiting for us. We can choose to avoid it. Or we can have the courage to meet it head on...even if it means dying."

He looked at each member of the assembly again. The cold stares were now fewer in number. "Whatever you decide here today, I will understand. I know that you have families and friends you want to protect. This can't be an easy choice. But know that if you want to fight, I'll fight with you. If not...then I guess I'll fight alone."

He sat down, folded his hands on the table, and allowed his gaze to settle on Halvar.

The king's jaw clenched. "Thank you. Unless someone has a question for...*Lord* Dragonvein, we still have much to discuss."

Ethan stood and bowed. "Your Highness, I would like to see Jonas, if that's all right."

Halvar waved his hand. "Very well, go. Birger can take you. But *only* you."

Ethan bowed once again before leaving the chamber.

"That was very interesting," Birger said as they exited the manor. "I think you might have even changed a few minds."

"I wasn't trying to. I just said what I was feeling."

"And that's what did it. My father always said that you can only change a person's mind if you speak from the heart."

"Sounds like a smart guy," said Ethan.

"He was. And very wise."

"So he's dead?"

Birger nodded. "For many years now." He gave Ethan a sideways look. "I've been wondering lately if he would have thought I was right to bring you here."

"And what did you decide? Would he?"

Birger shrugged. "Perhaps. I know what he would say though. He would tell me that if I acted with pure intent, then I should be satisfied with what I have done." He chuckled softly, a faraway smile on his face. "Of course, then he would tell me that even the well-intended can make foolish decisions. He was always good at confusing me when I asked him for answers. I used to think he did it just to annoy me. But now I understand that he wanted me to work it out for myself. He was wise enough to know that I had the solution within me the entire time. I just needed to realize it."

Ethan thought of his own father on Earth. He had been kind and gentle...in his own way. What would *he* say about this? He laughed inwardly. He'd never have believed it. He was far too grounded for the notion of magic, elves, and dwarves. Of course, Ethan had always thought that he had taken after the man in this respect. But now he didn't even know what his real father was like. The little that Jonas was willing to divulge had left him with an incomplete picture. It was no wonder the circlet had hurt him.

When they arrived at the house there were two guards standing outside, talking casually. Upon seeing Ethan they stepped aside and stood smartly to attention. He glanced at Birger, who only smiled and shook his head.

"What was that about?" Ethan asked, once they were inside.

"You're staying in the king's manor," Birger explained. "And it's no secret that you are the son of Praxis Dragonvein. Rumors about the prophecy being fulfilled are already spreading."

"I have a feeling King Halvar isn't happy about that."

"I don't imagine so. But you mustn't judge him too harshly. If it wasn't for him, my people would have starved by now. The little Shinzan gives us in trade for weapons and tools isn't nearly enough. So King Halvar has made deals with human smugglers and merchants to provide us with what we need. And he does this at great risk to himself. If the Empire found out, things would go hard on him."

"What would they do?"

"Demand that he step down and turn himself over to the Emperor."

"Would he agree to this?"

"If he didn't, they would blockade the mountain and cut us off completely until he did. King Halvar would not be able to watch his people starve to death, so refusal wouldn't be an option for him. He may be flawed and stubborn, but his love for his people is without bounds."

Ethan could hear the sincerity in Birger's tone. Even so, what Markus had said to him earlier still resonated. The king was plotting something. And from what Birger just told him, there were no lengths he would not be willing to go to if he thought it would keep his people safe.

The door to Jonas' room was open. Ethan poked his head in and saw him sitting in his bed, reading. He smiled and put down the book.

"How are you feeling?" Ethan asked.

Jonas sighed. "Like an old fool. I should have known that damn dwarf device would hurt me."

"If you had answered their questions, nothing would have happened," Birger chided.

"They had no reason to know such personal things," Jonas said. "I told them what they needed to know. That Ethan is the son of Praxis Dragonvein, and I was his father's servant. That should have been enough."

"The king has his own ideas about what is or is not enough," Birger told him. "I would suggest you get used to that fact."

Jonas curled his lip and crossed his arms. "They can ask me as many questions as they want. But I will not answer unless they are relevant. My personal affairs are my own and belong to no one else. Not even the king."

"No wonder you're not allowed in the manor," teased Ethan.

"I am perfectly happy here, thank you." He paused. "Have you seen Kat?"

"She's with me and Markus. She asked about you."

Jonas tried to hide a smile. "Just tell her to stay out of trouble."

"I will."

They chatted for a while longer, but Ethan could see that Jonas was still not completely recovered. He began politely excusing himself.

"Can I speak to Ethan alone for a moment before he goes?" Jonas asked Birger.

The dwarf eyed him suspiciously, but left the room anyway.

"Something is wrong," whispered Jonas once he caught sound of him descending the stairs. "I've been around nobles and kings most of my life. King Halvar is planning something."

"Markus thinks so too," said Ethan.

"Then you should be careful what you say, and who you say it to. You and Markus should try to find out as much as you can about the city. It might help if we need to flee."

Ethan nodded. "I'll do my best."

On their way back to the manor, Ethan spent most of the time recalling his meetings with King Halvar. But no matter how hard he tried, aside from the monarch's general animosity, he could find nothing else in his words or actions that invited suspicion.

After returning to his room, he told Kat and Markus about his audience with the king, and of Jonas' condition. Markus was deeply concerned that Jonas shared his suspicions. Kat, on the other hand, insisted that all serious talk be put aside, commenting that she hated being confined to just a few rooms and how it would be nice to explore the city.

As if a prayer had been answered, Lady Thora arrived at Ethan's room just before dinner. He and Markus bowed, while Kat gave her a formal curtsy.

"I see you have some training in etiquette, young lady," Thora remarked. "That is good."

"To what do we owe the pleasure?" asked Markus.

"Which of you men is this girl's guardian?"

The pair looked at each other, then back to Thora, neither knowing how to respond.

"I see," said Thora. "Then I take it you wouldn't object if she spent some time with me and my family."

"I – I suppose not," stammered Ethan. "That's really up to her."

Thora fixed her gaze on Kat. "Well?"

"Well what?" Kat responded.

"Would you like to spend some time with me and see a bit more of the city?"

She shot a look at Ethan, then shook her head. "I had better stay here."

"I assure you that he will be just fine without you," Thora said. "You can return here each evening if you wish to see that he's being taken care of."

Kat looked again at Ethan, as if expecting him to object, knitting her brow when he didn't.

"My dear," Thora continued, "The council's debate is likely to go on for several weeks, and King Halvar will not allow you to leave this area until it has concluded. I can't imagine that a young girl like you would prefer to remain cooped up in here the entire time."

"You should go," said Markus. "It beats sitting around doing nothing."

"What will I be doing?" asked Kat.

"I've read much about humans over the years," she replied. "I would be very interested to spend time with one. That you also happen to be a young lady is more than I can resist. I can show you the city, and in return you can tell me about human customs. When I'm forced to take part in the council meetings you can spend time with my two granddaughters. They are excited to meet you as well."

Kat thought for a moment, then nodded. "Thank you, Lady Thora. I would be pleased to accept your invitation."

Thora smiled. "Then it's settled. I'll send for you in the morning."

She bowed and left.

"Sounds like fun," Ethan said to Kat. "That's just what you wanted."

The remark was meant to be encouraging. But her response was far from what he expected. After glaring furiously at him, she stormed out of the room, slamming the door behind her.

"I'm eating alone," she shouted from the corridor.

Ethan stood there with a perplexed look on his face. "What the hell was that all about?"

"She has a crush," said Markus. "She wanted you to say she should stay here with you…and you didn't."

Ethan groaned. "I wish she'd leave it alone. She's way too young for me."

Markus laughed. "Too young now, maybe. But you wait. There's only a few years' difference. I bet she'll grow up to be a real beauty. Then you'll be wishing you had been nicer."

"I *am* nice," Ethan protested. "It's just that I don't want her to get the wrong idea."

His friend slapped him on the back. "Poor little Romeo."

Ethan shot him an irritated look. "That's not funny."

Markus laughed even harder. "Sure it is."

CHAPTER EIGHTEEN

AS THE DAYS passed, Ethan felt himself becoming increasingly anxious. With only dwarf books to read and his movements confined, the room that had at first impressed him so much was now starting to feel more and more like yet another prison cell.

To make matters worse, his dreams were becoming ever more vivid. No matter where they were supposed to be taking place – Earth, Lumnia, or those in-between places that only make sense in a dream – they would be filled with visions of dragons dying and people being slaughtered. Each time he woke he would be gasping for breath, still feeling the intense pain of the dragons in his heart.

Kat was spending most of her time with Lady Thora and her two granddaughters. However, she did still make sure to spend at least a short period each evening with him.

From what she had heard while outside the manor, the city was utterly divided. Some believed that Ethan was indeed there to fulfill the prophecy. Others refused to accept it. Tensions were rising, occasionally erupting into open hostility.

Kat told him Thora was growing concerned that the matter should be settled soon, otherwise things might even turn violent. If that were to happen it would give King Halvar more reason than ever to oppose Ethan and those dwarves who were willing to fight.

"We should just go," he said to Markus one morning over breakfast after nearly two weeks of isolation. "You said you could find us work on the coast, didn't you?"

Markus frowned. "I doubt they will allow us to leave now. This prophecy of theirs has everyone in an uproar. It looks to me as if we're stuck here until they can figure it out."

"I guess you're right," Ethan sighed. "But it makes me uneasy the way they're all looking to me for their salvation. They seem to think I'm some sort of all powerful mage like my father. But I'm not. And who knows if I ever will be."

"You'll never convince them otherwise," said Markus. "Belief is a funny thing. If they *believe* you can save them, there's not much anyone can do to change their minds. From what I've heard, these people have suffered for so long, they're desperate for hope. *Any* hope. And that's what you are to them. Hope."

He regarded Ethan for a moment, then cracked a smile. "You've just been sitting around here too long. It's not good to be looking inside your own head every day. It can drive a man crazy."

That night, while Ethan lay staring at the ceiling, dreading another nightmare that sleep would surely bring, a light knock sounded on his door.

He growled with irritation. "I'm trying to sleep, Kat! Go to bed!"

The door opened, revealing Lady Thora. The sight of her entering jerked Ethan upright. He immediately scanned the room for sight of his clothes.

"Kat is spending the night at my home," she said. "Get dressed. We must talk. Time is short."

Ethan hesitated. But it soon became evident that Lady Thora cared little for human modesty. Grabbing his blanket, he wrapped it around his waist. His clothes were piled up in a corner beside the dresser. Doing his best to keep himself covered, he slipped them on.

"Your boots as well," she instructed. "You'll be leaving in a few minutes."

Thora took a seat at the table while Ethan donned his boots.

"Where are we going?" he asked.

"*We* are not going anywhere," she replied, gesturing for him to sit.

"Then where am *I* going?"

"I'm afraid King Halvar has decided to take matters into his own hands. Actually, I think he intended to all along and was just waiting for the right time. He has sent assassins to murder you and your friends. If you stay here, you will be dead by morning."

The hair on the back of Ethan's neck stood up. "Why would he do that?"

"He is convinced that you will bring an end to the dwarves. When he brought you before the council last time, he had hoped your words would sway more members to his side. Unfortunately for him, your youth and inexperience was overcome by your heart and conviction. At this point, only two others still support him. And as his support on the council fades, so does his support among the people. Soon he will stand alone and be forced to concede."

"Can't *you* stop him?"

"I'm afraid that King Halvar is determined. He is willing to risk his throne to see you dead."

She leaned in and focused her gaze. "I am not warning you now because I am convinced you are the answer to our problems. In fact, I have to admit that the king has a valid point. There are no dragons heralding the end of Shinzan's rule. Your arrival may be a false hope. And though brave you may be, you are no mage. You cannot find victory without magic – and there is no one alive who can instruct you."

"So what do you want me to do?"

"Flee," she replied. "Take your friends and flee as far and fast as you can. I ask only one thing of you. Leave Kat here with me."

Ethan furled his brow. "With you? Why?"

"She has no business on such a perilous journey. And wherever you go, death is sure to follow. I can protect her. King Halvar would not dare to harm a child, human or no. Particularly one protected by a member of the council."

Ethan thought for a moment and then nodded his consent. "Please see that she is safe."

Thora smiled and bowed her head. "You have my word. You know, she's quite taken with you. A pity she is not a bit older. She would make a devoted wife in time. And unless I miss my guess, she possesses a few magical talents as well."

"Yes, she does," he confirmed.

"All the more reason for her to stay. She would be hunted in the human world." Thora rose from her seat. "Now gather your belongings. Birger has already taken the one called Jonas near the passage where you will be leaving. He is waiting with your other friend outside."

Just as she turned for the door, Ethan stopped her. "Can I asked you something?"

Thora nodded.

"Why are you helping us?"

"Because King Halvar is wrong," she replied flatly. "Even if you are not the one to fulfill the prophecy, you bring us hope. That is something we desperately need. And I'm helping Kat because I'm a grandmother, and that's what grandmothers do."

The moment Thora had left the room, Ethan quickly packed his things. As she had told him, Birger and Markus were waiting just outside his door. Markus appeared calm, but Birger was obviously on edge. His eyes darted back and forth nervously and his hand was planted firmly on the handle of the axe hanging from his belt.

"It's about time," he complained. "They'll be here any minute."

After taking one final look down the hall, he set off at a fast walk. "There's no way to depart from the manor unseen," he told them. "But it will take time for the king's guards to figure out which way you've left the city. Hopefully by then we'll be far enough ahead of them to escape."

"So you're coming with us?" asked Ethan.

"Only as far as the exit to the mountain," he replied.

"Are you going to get in trouble for helping us?"

"Possibly. But I think that once news of King Halvar's attempt on your life gets out, I'll soon be forgiven."

While making their way through the manor they passed a fair number of servants and various other dwarves. All took notice of them, their eyes drawn especially by the rapid pace that Birger was setting. So fast was it, Ethan was forced into a jog several times just to keep up.

After they were clear of the manor he could see Birger relaxing somewhat. They first headed east, then south through a series of side streets and alleyways until Ethan was hopelessly lost. There were a few dwarves about, but Birger was able to spot them in time to alter their course and avoid detection.

After more than an hour they reached the outer edge of the city. Beyond was an area of flat rock, which ended in a sheer cliff wall that rose high beyond Ethan's sight. In spite of their peril, his mind boggled at the thought of how long it must have taken to dig out a cavern large enough to house such a grand city.

Jonas was waiting near a small building. As well as his pack, he had with him all of their weapons.

"I was getting worried," he said. He put on the short sword that Ethan had taken from the slain soldier and handed him his own elegant blade. "You'd better take this. You'll get more use out of it than I ever will."

Ethan strapped on the sword. "Let's hope not."

Birger led them right up to the cliff face, then over to a spot where there was a small opening in the rock. "This way is not widely known to anyone but the miners," he said. "It should buy us some time."

"I think not," called a voice from inside the tunnel.

The group instantly drew their weapons and backed several steps away from the entrance. A few seconds later a lone dwarf emerged. His red beard was tied in a single braid, as was his waist length hair. He wore black leather armor and carried a large, two-handed axe. He glowered at Birger while resting the weapon on his shoulder.

"Rumhold," said Birger. "Why have you come?"

"To stop you from making a terrible mistake. I knew where you would go the moment I saw you leaving the manor. You're not the only dwarf who knows the secrets of the mountains."

"So you would support King Halvar's decision to assassinate an innocent?" Birger challenged.

"Innocent?" Rumhold scoffed. "He brings with him certain death for us all. The council members who refuse to see this are fools. They should trust in our king's wisdom."

"There is no wisdom in murder. And the king has no right to do this. There is a reason why we have a council. To prevent a king from falling from grace when his mind becomes clouded."

"It is not the king's mind that is clouded. He sees quite clearly what this false hope will bring down upon our heads. I implore you to turn back, Birger. I will say that you had a change of heart. Leave the humans to me. I'll deliver them to the king's guards."

"I think you may find it's not so easy to take us," cut in Markus. His tone was dark and dangerous. "Unless you have an army behind you, we'll be leaving now."

Rumhold drew a short wand from his belt. "I don't need an army, human. So unless your sword can halt a bolt of lightning, I suggest you keep your mouth shut."

"Leave this to me," said Birger.

"So you would fight me?" A heavy frown creased Rumhold's face. "For the sake of these humans you would bear arms against your own kind? Against a friend?"

"No," he replied sadly. "I would do it for the sake of our people's honor."

"Honor will not save us from Shinzan."

"You're wrong. In the end, honor is the *only* thing that will save us."

Putting away the wand, Rumhold gripped his axe with both hands. "So be it."

Birger crouched and broadened his stance. Ethan could see the muscles in his powerful arms quivering with tension, ready to burst into life.

With uncanny speed, Rumhold charged in, swinging his axe upwards from the hip. Birger spun left, easily avoiding the blow and brought his own much lighter weapon down in a deadly backhanded strike. Rumhold only just managed to dive away in time, rolling and instantly regaining his feet.

Rumhold nodded approvingly. "You've practiced." Without waiting for a reply, he feigned right and then stepped left, thrusting the axe head at Birger's midsection.

Birger swatted the heavier blade down and jumped back, poised to parry. But Rumhold had already matched his movement and was striking at his legs in a tight arc. Birger tried to evade this, but the tip of the blade slashed across his left thigh. In a wild flurry of strikes, he drove his opponent back, then limped out of range. Blood was pouring from the wound and soaking the leg of his pants.

"Don't make me kill you," said Rumhold.

Birger glanced down at his injured leg and spat. "I'm not beaten yet, my friend."

Ignoring the handicap and pain of his wound, he let out a feral roar and ran headlong at Rumhold who, caught off-guard by this unexpected display of aggression, could only raise his weapon and block a series of blows with the flat of his blade. Birger drove him back several paces before planting his boot hard into Rumhold's chest. A human would have been sent sprawling, but Rumhold's sturdy legs and low center of gravity kept him on his feet.

Birger advanced again, pressing his advantage. In another hail of strikes he managed to open a deep gash in Rumhold's right shoulder. Clutching at his wound, the dwarf dropped to one knee.

Seeing an opportunity to finish it, Birger moved in. But the instant he came within striking distance, he realized his mistake. It was a ruse. Rumhold rolled right and jerked the handle of his axe up hard. It thudded flush against Birger's jaw.

With legs wobbling, Birger staggered back. Rumhold sprang up and swung at his neck. Birger ducked, but not quite low enough. The massive blade swept above his head, shaving a thin layer of skin from his scalp in the process.

Desperate to get at close quarters, Birger ran in and wrapped his arms around his opponent's waist. Rumhold smashed the axe handle into his back three times before Birger was able to lift him from his feet and tackle him to the ground.

Scrambling forward onto Rumhold's chest, he raised his axe. But before he could strike, Rumhold gave a desperate heave, forcing Birger to drop both hands behind him and push hard into the ground in order to prevent himself from toppling back. Once steady, he then squeezed his legs tight around Rumhold's torso and regained his position.

Rumhold tried to lift his weapon, but it was too long and bulky to be of much use. Now in total control, Birger raised his small axe again, but after hesitating for a moment, tossed it aside. Instead, he produced a short dagger from his belt and pressed the blade to his opponent's throat.

As the steel touched his flesh, Rumhold ceased to struggle. "You've won, my friend. Now finish it."

Birger shook his head. "Just go back. Tell the king what has happened. Tell him I'm a traitor if you must. But leave."

"You know I can't do that. If you release me I will be forced to take up my axe and try again." He locked eyes with Birger. "You must choose between us."

With conflict and indecision contorting his face, Birger glanced briefly over to Ethan and the others. No one said a word.

Once again he gazed down at his helpless friend. "Forgive me," he whispered, moving the blade away from the dwarf's throat and instead placing it directly over his heart.

"You will doom us all," said Rumhold. His voice was clear and without a hint of fear.

"I pray you are wrong."

Birger plunged the dagger hard down. Rumhold gasped and clutched at his sleeves, but after only a few seconds went limp.

For a long moment Birger lay motionless on top of Rumhold's body. Eventually, he rolled to one side and onto his back.

Ethan started toward him, but Jonas caught his arm.

"Give him a moment."

The dwarf clambered to his knees and placed his head on Rumhold's lifeless body. He remained like this for several minutes, his body shaking from a series of great sobs. Finally, he sat up and struggled to his feet. The tears on his face had mingled with blood from the wound to his scalp, creating a grotesque kind of war paint. His pants and boots were completely saturated.

"Are you all right?" asked Ethan, knowing full well what a damn fool question that was.

Birger blinked at him. "I've known Rumhold since I was a small child. My father was one of his first teachers. That I was forced to take his life has broken my heart. But he left me with no other choice. I will have to find a way to live with what I have done."

"Can you continue?" asked Jonas.

He nodded. "My injuries are not as bad as they might seem." Hobbling over to his pack, he retrieved a small phial of green liquid and poured a few drops of this over each of his wounds. Once finished, he tossed the phial over to Ethan. "You may need this. It will heal minor cuts and scrapes in hours."

Ethan thanked him and stuffed it inside his pack.

"We should go quickly," Birger told them. He picked up his axe and attached it to his belt. "The fight may have attracted attention."

As he stepped toward the entrance to the tunnel, Jonas cleared his throat.

"I don't want to be indelicate," he said. "But are you going to leave your dagger behind?"

Birger glanced back at the body of his dead friend. "When they find him, my dagger's presence will tell them it was I who killed Rumhold... not one of you. If there is to be any hope, it cannot be believed that you have spilled dwarf blood."

"I understand," remarked Jonas thoughtfully.

"I'm truly sorry about your friend," said Ethan.

Birger frowned at him. "I am a murderer of my own kind now. I just hope that my crime is worth it."

His words struck Ethan to his core. He felt as if a massive burden had been dropped onto his shoulders. It was one thing to talk about fighting evil and self-sacrifice. But Birger had showed him the true meaning of sacrifice. He suddenly longed to disappear completely, and found that he could not bear to look at the dwarf...not even for a moment.

Silently, they walked to the tunnel.

Once through the narrow entrance, the path widened considerably. However, unlike the passages that had brought them to Elyfoss, this one was unlit. Birger produced a silver rod with a round green stone on one end. He held this aloft. Light immediately began emanating from its core, illuminating the way.

"Interesting torch you have there," said Markus.

"A toy," remarked Birger. "Nothing more."

"Useful though," said Jonas.

"We won't need it by tomorrow," he told them. "The tunnels are lit by shantara stone."

Jonas raised an eyebrow. "Really? How do your people dig through it?"

"Such things are no challenge for us," he replied. "Our tools are far superior to anything you humans possess."

"What's shantara stone?" asked Ethan.

"It's like a diamond," answered Markus. "Only it glows. Hardly anything can break it. You won't see it much in Lumnia, mainly because it doesn't come in small pieces. You have to cut it from much larger rocks. Most mines can't even lift them from the ground, let alone cut pieces off. And as for digging tunnels through the stuff...forget it."

"You have some experience in mining?" asked Birger.

"Some," Markus affirmed. "A long time ago when I first arrived."

"I thought most human miners were slaves."

"They are," said Markus.

Birger nodded with understanding. "Slavery is a dreadful practice. Dwarves would never do such a thing. Not even to a human."

"It wasn't always like that," Jonas said. "In the time of the mages, *all* people were free. Slavery was outlawed."

Birger picked up his pace. "Let us hope that those days will soon return."

CHAPTER NINETEEN

"WAKE UP, SWEETHEART. Time for breakfast."

Kat smiled at the thought of sausage and eggs. But she wasn't ready to open her eyes. Not just yet. The bed was too warm and soft.

"Please, mother," she whined, burying her face in the pillow. "Just a few more minutes."

"Wake up."

Kat groaned. "Just a little while longer. I'm still tired."

"Wake up, Kat."

Slowly, the dream faded. But another voice was now demanding her attention.

"Wake up, sleepy head."

Kat forced her eyes open. Lady Thora's granddaughters, Asta and Maile, were lying on either side of her, grinning and giggling.

Asta was the younger of the two, with a fair complexion and curly red hair. Her frame was nearly as thin as a human girls might be. By contrast, Maile was far stouter, with thick black hair and olive skin. Both girls were still in their nightgowns and caps.

"Come on, Kat," said Asta. "Breakfast is ready."

She covered her face with her hands. "I don't suppose there's any sausage and eggs, is there?"

Asta mimicked a retching sound. "Yuck!"

"How do you know, until you tried it?"

"No burned animal flesh for me, thanks," chipped in Maile.

Kat rolled on her side and pulled the blanket over her head.

"Get up," insisted Asta.

Kat shook her head defiantly.

At once, both girls began poking her sides and tickling her arms. Kat jerked and jostled in a useless attempt to fend them off.

"All right! All right! I'm up!" she said, finally yielding.

The girls slipped out of the bed and skipped across the room to the door.

"We'll meet you downstairs," Maile said. "Grandmother's already left, so she said we could play all day today."

Kat waited until she heard the door close before peeking her head out from beneath the covers. This had been the first night she had spent away from her friends since they'd left Miltino. She had protested at first, but Lady Thora pleaded with her, saying that her granddaughters had begged her to ask and would be extremely disappointed if she refused.

Her first thought now was to wonder if Ethan had noticed she hadn't returned to the manor. Getting out of bed, she stood in front of the dresser mirror, straightening her back and placing her hands on her hips.

"He's never going to notice you," she hissed angrily. "Not looking like this."

She ran her hands along her sides, longing to feel the curves of maturity, but experiencing only disappointment. A sudden urge to smash the mirror was only just resisted.

Feeling depressed, she removed a pair of pants and a shirt from the wardrobe. Hanging nearby was a lovely blue dress Lady Thora had made for her. But while she appreciated the gesture, Kat had no intention of wearing something that just hung there loosely off her shoulders. When Thora had first showed it to her she had said that it was a proper way for a young woman to dress. Even so, how women could stand to be in such things was beyond Kat.

She reached in to feel the fabric. It was soft and smooth. Was she perhaps being unreasonable? She tried to picture herself in it, but it had been more than three years since she had worn anything other than clothes fit for a thief.

"I bet Ethan would like it," Thora had told her.

This had embarrassed Kat to no end.

Her thoughts were broken by Asta calling out from downstairs.

"Come on, Kat. Hurry up."

She liked Asta and Maile very much, and enjoyed the time she spent with them. Though they acted a bit childish at times – in fact most of the time – they were fun to be around.

Since she had first arrived at the house, Lady Thora had made a point of seeing to it that the girls had plenty of time to play together. It had been a long time since Kat had done anything so frivolous as playing. At first she found it difficult joining in. Soon though, she was laughing and giggling as much as the other two while looking for clever places to hide or running through the halls trying to get away from whoever was '*it*' at the time.

All this reminded Kat of her life when she was a little girl; sometimes thinking about it made her quite sad. Asta and Maile would pick up on her mood immediately and do their best to cheer her up. Occasionally they would ask her about things in the human world, or what she had done before coming to Elyfoss. Unwilling to tell them that she had been a thief, Kat refused to answer anything about her past – although she did so as politely as possible. Thankfully, the girls didn't pressure her, so she was never forced to be openly rude.

Though not as vast as the king's manor, Lady Thora's home was every bit as elegant and well-furnished. The art on the walls, the intricacy of the fixtures, and the polished silver rails along the broad spiral staircase all indicated a person of great wealth and power. Yet in spite of the lavish nature of her surroundings, the warm way that Lady Thora had opened her home made Kat feel comfortable and relaxed. It was all too easy to forget that only days before they had been running for their lives from the agents of the Emperor.

She made her way downstairs to a small parlor where Asta and Maile were sitting at a round breakfast table. A bowl of steaming porridge and a glass of cold juice had been placed in front of an empty chair. The girls had already started eating when she arrived.

"Sorry," said Asta. "We couldn't wait."

Kat smiled and took a seat. "That's all right. I eat faster than you anyway."

After breakfast they played a game of hide and seek, then took turns reading stories from one of Maile's books. Kat didn't care so much for this particular activity. Dwarf stories were confusing, and she could never quite get the point to most of them.

When it was time for lunch, Kat suggested that they go to the king's manor. "You can meet my friends," she said.

Asta and Maile looked at each other, mouths open and eyes wide.

"What's wrong?" Kat asked. "I'm sure Lady Thora won't mind."

"We can't," said Asta, wringing her hands. "Grandmother said we should stay inside today."

"Besides," added Maile. "It's much too far. I don't feel like walking all that way. Let's just stay here."

It was obvious that the girls were becoming increasingly uneasy.

"What's going on?" Kat asked. "You can tell me."

The pair looked at each other again, then said in unison: "Nothing."

"Tell me!" Kat repeated, this time more forcefully.

Asta lowered her eyes and kicked her feet. Maile also tried to look away, but Kat stepped forward and bent down to her eye level.

"I...I...," Maile stammered. "It's not our fault. We overheard grandmother talking. She made us promise not to tell you."

A chill shot down Kat's spine. "Tell me what?"

"Promise that you won't be angry." Maile was nearly in tears. "Promise, and I'll tell you."

Kat took a deep breath. "I promise."

"They're gone," she said.

Kat's eyes narrowed. "Who's gone?"

"Your friends. You know, Ethan, Markus and Jonas. They left Elyfoss last night with Birger. Asta and I heard grandmother talking to my uncle about it right after bed-time when we came back down for a glass of water. She made us swear not to tell you."

Kat felt like she had been punched in the stomach. She staggered back, her head swimming.

"I'm sorry," said Asta. "We wanted to tell you. But we swore not to. Please don't be angry."

Tears were streaming down both girls' cheeks.

Something inside Kat snapped. "They had no right!" she screamed. "They had no right to leave me behind!"

Maile reached out to comfort her, but Kat brushed past and set off at a run toward the front door.

"Please wait," Maile begged. "They're already gone."

Kat did not even hear her. She burst through the door and raced as fast as her legs would carry her to the king's manor.

Normally the guards at the entrance would let her in without question. But this time they barred her way.

"Lady Thora is occupied at the moment," one of them said. "She left word to say you must wait for her at the house until she returns."

"I'm not here to see Lady Thora," said Kat, trying her best to sound calm. "I just need to get something from my room."

The guard crossed his arms and shook his head. "I'm sorry, but whatever it is will have to wait until Lady Thora is finished in council."

With fingernails biting into her palms, Kat forced a smile. "Of course. If you see her, please tell her I came by and that I'll see her later."

The guard nodded, watching closely as she headed back in the direction of Lady Thora's house. However, once safely out of sight around the corner of the next block, she stopped and placed her back flat against the building. Her heart was pounding and her breaths came in shallow gasps.

How could he do this to me?

It took her a full minute to regain her composure. Then, once she was sure that no one was looking at her, she concentrated hard on a point deep inside her mind. Within seconds Kat could feel a heat and power throbbing to the rhythm of her pulse. When she was badly afraid, this only took a fraction of a second to happen, but now the process was taking quite a bit longer. Only when she was certain that it was completely done did she step out from behind the building and walk back toward the king's manor.

The guards were talking quietly about how they wished the council would hurry up and decide what to do so they could get back to their regular duties. They had no idea that Kat was walking silently in front of them.

The doors were shut. If she tried to open them the guards would notice and the spell would be broken. She'd be caught for sure then. She moved along the building a short way and tugged at one of the first story windows, but it was locked on the inside. There was an open window on the second floor, but the walls were too smooth to climb.

It was hard to stop herself from crying out with frustration. Normally she did this sort of thing under the cover of darkness. But it was never dark in Elyfoss. She looked left and right. The manor was massive. It would take way too long to search the entire ground floor for an unlocked window.

The front door opened and three dwarf women walked out. The guards snapped to attention as they passed, then relaxed again the moment they were on the avenue. Slowly the door shut with a muffled thud.

That's it, Kat said to herself.

Creeping close to the guards, she crouched down between the pair of them. She knew this was risky. If someone looked directly at her with too much curiosity or intensity, it might cause the spell to break. It was how that oaf Durst had caught her.

"What was that?" asked the guard on the left. He glanced briefly down in her general direction.

The other guard looked across at him, but his eyes were passing over her head.

Don't look down. Don't look down. Don't look down, she repeated over and over in a silent prayer.

"I don't see anything," he said.

"I could have sworn…" His companion shrugged. "I guess it was nothing."

The door opened again. This time a young male dwarf and an older woman stepped out. Once again the guards snapped to attention. Kat waited just long enough for the way to be clear, then scuttled through. It began to close just as she was safely inside.

She gave a brief smile of satisfaction. Jeb would have been proud.

After hurrying up the stairs, she headed straight to Ethan's room, still clinging to the vain hope that the girls might have been wrong. But they weren't. His room was empty. So was Markus'.

The hollow ache in the pit of her stomach turned into a sharp pain. She fell to her knees, weeping uncontrollably.

A stern female voice sounded. "What are you doing here?"

Kat glanced up to see a dark haired dwarf woman with a broom in her hand standing in the doorway. She was looking very displeased.

"Answer me," the woman snapped.

The sorrow tearing away at Kat's insides suddenly boiled up into a blind rage. Jumping to her feet, she shoved the woman aside and stormed her way directly to the council chamber. By the time she reached it, her tears were completely dry. Flinging the door open, she walked boldly inside.

The council was in the middle of what looked to be a highly heated argument. King Halvar was pounding his fist on the table and shouting at the top of his voice - something about liars and traitors.

A sudden hush fell over the room as Kat appeared.

Halvar then found his voice again. "What the bloody hell is she doing here?" His face was bright red and his knuckles scraped and bruised from pounding them on the stone table.

Lady Thora sprang up and was at Kat's side in an instant. "Come with me, child."

"Why did you do it?" Kat shouted at her, ignoring all else.

Thora leaned close to whisper in her ear. "Not here. Please. I'll explain everything later, I swear I will."

"Will someone answer me?" demanded Halvar. "Why is this child here?"

"She's upset, my king," explained Thora. "And for good reason, as you well know. I'll take her back to my home and return as soon as I am able." She gave the assembly a slight bow. "I'm sure you can all shout and yell at each other perfectly well without me for a while."

Before the king could say another word, she ushered Kat from the chamber and closed the door. "You shouldn't have come here," she said.

Kat's eyes were still blazing. "Don't you dare tell me what I should or shouldn't do. You lied to me."

"Yes," she admitted. "And if you will just come back to my house, I'll explain why."

"Explain to me now." Kat crossed her arms defiantly.

Thora sighed and pinched the bridge of her nose. "My dear, if you don't come with me right away, we will both end up in a whole world of trouble."

"Fine. But I want answers as soon as we get there."

As they exited the manor, the guards gazed at Kat in shock and alarm.

"How did you get in here?" one of them demanded.

A harsh look from Lady Thora silenced him. Both guards then quickly snapped to attention.

Kat didn't utter a single word during the walk back to the house. When they entered the front door, Asta and Maile were waiting, their faces bright red from crying.

"We're sorry," each of them wailed.

Thora gave her granddaughters a loving smile. "Dry your tears. You did nothing wrong."

"But we promised you," said Asta.

"It's fine, darling," Thora gently assured her. "I know you only did what you thought was right. The fault is mine. I shouldn't have asked you to lie to a friend. Now go upstairs and wash your faces. You both look a complete mess."

The girls paused to look at Kat, but she was still too furious to speak.

"Go on," said Thora, a touch more firmly.

The girls burst into a run and were up the stairs in seconds.

Thora waited until she heard their door slam shut before speaking again. "You shouldn't blame them."

"I don't. I blame you."

She held out her hand. "Come. Please. Let's sit and talk."

Kat refused to take Thora's hand, but the woman simply smiled and walked toward a door leading into the library at the rear of the house. Kat followed…but not closely.

The library was stocked to the brim with hundreds upon hundreds of books and scrolls. A glowing rajni stone hung from the ceiling.

Thora sniffed the air and sighed as she entered the room. "I love the smell of books, don't you? I used to spend hours in here when I was a girl."

"I don't care what you did when you were a girl," Kat retorted. "I only care about why I was left behind."

Unmoved by her rudeness, Thora laughed softly to herself. "You are so much like my daughter. Headstrong and stubborn. And when she was angry...well, you had better get out of her way."

She walked over to a masterfully carved wooden table at the center of the room and gestured to one of the chairs placed beside it. Kat gave a curt shake of the head.

"Suit yourself," said Thora. "But I'm sure you'll be more comfortable sitting. We have a great deal to discuss."

Kat huffed and growled, but finally sat down. "Now tell me where they are or I'll...I'll..."

Thora suppressed an amused grin. "You'll do what, my dear? Hit me? Kill me? Run away? What is it you think you'll do?"

Kat balled her fists. "You'll find out. Don't think I can't."

"Oh, I'm sure you could. Very sure, in fact. I don't doubt for a second that you are capable of amazing things...*and* terrible things. But I also think you have no intention of hurting anyone. Least of all someone who only wants to help you."

"You don't know anything about me."

"You may be surprised. You're not as careful as you might think when you try to hide your feelings."

Kat leaned back and sneered. "So tell me what you think you know then."

"I know you were a thief," Thora began.

Kat shifted uncomfortably in her seat, but said nothing.

"I also know you've taken at least one life...possibly more," Thora continued. "And I know that you were once loved and cared for, but something tragic happened. My guess is that it has something to do with magic. Oh yes, and I know you're in love with Ethan Dragonvein."

With each word, the cold empty feeling Kat had felt before anger had taken over, began returning. A single tear spilled down her cheek.

"How could you...?" she began. Her voice cracked.

"I may be old, but I'm not blind," Thora told her. "Over the years I've learned how to notice things that people are trying to hide. Call it a talent."

"How could he leave me behind?" Kat's voice was little more than a whisper.

Thora gave her a motherly smile. "Because in his heart he knew there was no other choice. Ethan's path is one fraught with danger and death. I offered to keep you safe. If it helps, he took quite a bit of convincing before agreeing to let you stay."

Kat wiped her eyes. "It doesn't matter. He doesn't love me anyway."

"Of course he does. Just not in the way you want him to. And that's not even the saddest part of all this."

"What do you mean?"

"I mean, if he did love you that way, then he wouldn't be the man you love."

Kat cocked her head and wiped her face with her hand. "I don't understand. Of course he would be."

Thora smiled sweetly. "I've already said what I know about you. Now I'll tell you what I know about Ethan if you like."

Kat nodded slightly.

"I may not look it these days, but when I was a young woman I was quite the beauty. Or so I was told. When I was about Asta's age my body began to develop. In less than a year I looked every inch a grown up."

Kat glanced down at herself and frowned. "I don't have that problem."

"No," said Thora. "And though you may not think so right now, that *is* a blessing. When it happened to me, I wasn't mature enough to fully understand the sort of attention I was getting. I don't mean from other children, but from grown men. I have to admit that after a while I learned to enjoy it. They were practically tripping over themselves for a chance to talk to me and were constantly bringing me presents. It made me feel special. But I was still far too young to desire *them* in the same way they desired *me*. I didn't feel like that about men until I met Tadeus."

Her eyes became distant and a faint smile hovered on the corners of her mouth. "He was a young builder's apprentice who used to come to my father for advice. His father and mine were friends, so he came quite often. The first time I saw him, I knew he was the one. He was everything I dreamed about. He was handsome, kind, considerate, generous, and most of all, honorable.

"Each time he visited, I would make sure I was in the house that day. He didn't seem to mind the barrage of questions I asked about his work, his life, or whatever else I could think of to keep him talking. He answered them all. He even asked me about my studies and what I hoped to be one day. And I could tell that he wasn't just being polite. He was *genuinely* interested. Finally, I built up the courage and told him how I felt."

Kat was captivated. "What happened? Did you marry him?"

Thora laughed. "Of course not. I was still little more than a child. He was far too honorable and good to take advantage of me like that. Naturally, I was devastated. I didn't leave my room for days."

She sighed. "After that, Tadeus stopped coming by. He sent me a letter telling me that he could not bear to see me in pain, and that one day I would make a wonderful wife. And though sadly it could not be him, he hoped that whomever I married was deserving of my love."

A tear fell down her cheek and she took a deep breath.

"Who *did* you marry?" Kat asked.

Thora's smile vanished. "My father died soon after that and I married a foul brute of a dwarf. He didn't care that I was too young and innocent for marriage. He could only see me from the outside. The day he died was the happiest moment of my life – aside from when my daughter and grandchildren were born of course."

She reached out to touch Kat briefly on the cheek. "The point is this, my dear. If Tadeus had taken me for his own, he would *not* have been the honorable and kind person I had fallen in love with. But he was. And *that's* what I know about Ethan. He is too good and kind to return your love. Tragically, it's the very thing you love about him which prevents him from loving you back."

Kat considered this for a moment. Slowly, she nodded. "What happened to him...Tadeus I mean?"

"Oh, he married some dainty little mouse of a woman. I hated her intensely. Even after we became best friends."

Kat laughed, in spite of herself.

"That's better," said Thora. "I want your days here to be filled with laughter."

"Thank you," said Kat. With a sudden rush of emotion, she sprang up from her chair and wrapped her arms around Thora's neck in a loving embrace.

Thora patted her gently on the back. "You are very welcome, my dear."

Kat sat back down, still wiping away her newly shed tears. "Why are you doing this for me?"

"Ethan asked me the same question," she replied. "So I'll tell you exactly what I told him. I'm a grandmother. And that's what grandmother's do."

It was an answer that touched Kat's heart. But the renewed mention of Ethan's name reminded her that she was still angry with him.

"I can see the truth in everything you've told me," she said. "But I still don't understand why Ethan could not at least say goodbye."

Thora's eyes looked directly into her own.

"Would you honestly have allowed him to leave without you if he had?"

CHAPTER TWENTY

I T WOULD TAKE three days of rapid marching through the tunnel to get them to the road that descended the mountain. From there they would head west to the coast.

At the end of the first day Birger had nearly exhausted the rest of the group with his intense pace. Jonas had already stumbled and fallen twice, but luckily suffered only minor scrapes.

"The faster we go the better," the dwarf told them. "King Halvar's guards will not tire, nor slow. We must cover enough distance to stay ahead of them. If they figure out our route too soon then they could be on our heels by tomorrow."

"Jonas can't go on like this forever," Ethan pointed out. He was still unable to look Birger directly in the eye, so focused his attention on the old man.

"If they catch you, they'll kill you all," Birger told him sternly. "They'll hide your bodies and no one will ever know what happened to you. So he had better find a way of keeping up."

"I'll manage," Jonas said, gulping for breath.

"If you don't, you'll be left behind," Birger added.

"We're not leaving him," snapped Ethan.

The dwarf looked at Ethan and shook his head. "In days to come you will need to make hard choices. It is an inevitability of war. Sometimes you must look to the greater good."

"Isn't that exactly what King Halvar did?" challenged Ethan, a flash of anger surging through him. "Isn't that why we're running for our lives?"

Birger threw up his hand and muttered a curse.

"It doesn't matter," Jonas interjected. "I said I'd manage."

He was as good as his word, though when they finally halted he was pouring with sweat and flushed from fatigue.

"Three hours," announced Birger. "Then we start out again."

Jonas wasted no time in laying down right in the middle of the pathway. He was asleep in seconds.

"I must admit," remarked Birger while rummaging through his pack for some fruits and a water skin. "He is stout for someone so old."

"What will you do when you return?" asked Markus, changing the subject.

"I must face the king," he replied solemnly. "I have committed murder and must answer for that."

"But Rumhold attacked you," Ethan pointed out. "It's not like you wanted to kill him."

Birger sat down and leaned against the wall. "That may be. But I must still present myself to the king. He will decide my guilt or innocence."

"And if he finds you guilty?" asked Markus.

"Then my life is forfeit."

"Are you kidding?" Ethan exclaimed. "The king is the reason you had to kill in the first place. You can't just let him judge you. He'll find you guilty for sure."

"Perhaps," said Birger. "Perhaps not. I cannot let the actions of others dictate my personal morality. Our laws are clear. I must trust that King Halvar will honor his duty."

"And if he doesn't?"

He smiled up at Ethan, a look of deep sincerity in his eyes. "Then I will die with my honor intact."

Markus sniffed.

"You disagree with my reasons?" Birger asked him.

He nodded emphatically. "During the time I've lived in Lumnia, I've seen many a brave man throw his life away to satisfy some misguided code of *honor*. The graveyards are filled with men who thought it was worth dying for. And there's one thing that they all have in common… they're all dead. Honor is just another word for surrender. You'll march off and face someone who in all likelihood will kill you. Of course, you could decide to fight for life. But for some reason people like you see living as being dishonorable." He sneered contemptuously. "You can keep your so-called honor. I'd rather stand with the living than sleep with the dead."

Birger regarded him for a moment. When he spoke, it was in a calm and measured tone. "Unless I miss my guess, those are words spoken by a man who has been betrayed many times, and suffered much hardship and loss. I pity you that your spirit is so broken and stained that you can find no value in honor. I truly do."

Markus sniffed. "I've seen men like you before. You look at me and think you're somehow better. And maybe you are. But I'll be around long after you're nothing but a tear in a loved one's eye. So you can keep your pity too."

Birger gave Markus another sad look and then closed his eyes.

It had been a difficult debate. Markus had a point, Ethan considered. Was honor really a good enough reason to throw away one's life? The part of him that took pride in doing the right thing said yes. But lately, honor had seemed increasingly less important than seeing the next day arrive. Could there be some middle ground, he wondered?

The soreness in his body and the need for sleep pushed such complicated thoughts from his mind. Hard choices could wait.

He woke to find Jonas shaking him roughly.

"Time to go," the old man said. He looked thoroughly reinvigorated.

Ethan pushed himself up. "What's with you? A few hours ago you looked like you were about to die."

"I have Birger to thank for that," Jonas replied.

"You must be careful though," the dwarf warned. "I've never heard of humans taking it before. Only use it if you must."

Jonas gave him a sharp nod. "I will."

Before Ethan could ask, Birger tossed him a small stone bottle.

"I went looking for hanging druidia after you fell asleep," he explained. "It sometimes grows in this area and I managed to find some about a mile further down. Mixed with water it will give a fully grown dwarf enough energy to work all day without rest. I wasn't sure what it would do to a human, but I didn't see any other choice but to try."

"And I'm glad you did," said Jonas, giving an almost childish grin.

"A small sip should do if absolutely necessary," Birger continued to Ethan. "But you have to be careful. If you take too much your heart can burst. And it only works for about three days. After that your body will simply stop and you'll fall asleep wherever you happen to be at the time. And like I said, it's used by dwarves, not humans. So your body might shut down sooner."

With that said, he hurried off once again, forcing the others into a run in order to catch up. This time however, Jonas had no trouble keeping pace, even overtaking Birger a few times.

Occasionally the dwarf withdrew a small red stone and gripped it tightly. Ethan recalled seeing him use it when they were on their way to Elyfoss and he took this opportunity to inquire what it was.

"It can sense life nearby," Birger told him. "Not from too far… about a mile or so. It tells me if anyone is coming."

"Another useful tool," Markus remarked.

"Indeed," Birger agreed. "It has steered me clear of many a danger over the years."

They paused only briefly to eat. Though Jonas showed no signs of tiring, Ethan and Markus were by now both grimacing regularly from sore muscles and aching feet. Ethan considered taking a sip from the bottle, but eventually thought better of it.

The tunnels wound and twisted in snakelike patterns, as well as forking off in multiple directions. Ethan was again grateful that Birger was among them. Without him they would be utterly lost, likely condemned to wander around in the dark until the food in their packs ran out and they starved to death.

He reckoned it was close to early evening – though it was hard to know for sure while they were within the mountain. Ahead, he could see a soft glow illuminating the passage.

"Shantara stones," said Markus.

Birger put away his light. "They go on for many miles."

On drawing close, Ethan stopped in his tracks and gasped in awe. From floor to ceiling the clear stone glowed with a warm blue light. He gazed into the wall and ran his hand along its flawless surface. Countless individual embedded facets sparkled like captured stars, shooting rays of light from one to another, creating a vast web of perpetual radiance.

"This is incredible," he whispered.

From the look on their faces, Jonas and Markus appeared to be sharing his feelings.

"There's no time for gazing at rocks," Birger scolded.

"But it's just so…beautiful," Ethan remarked.

Birger grumbled with irritation. "Unless you think it a beautiful enough place to die in, I suggest you move your bloody feet."

He quickened the pace – Ethan thought it was a punishment for making them stop. It worked. Soon, his multiple aches and pains were making the beauty of the Shantara seem far less important.

After another hour of rigorous progress, just after turning a bend, they spotted a large figure lying on the ground a short distance ahead. Birger immediately took out his axe. Ethan and the others also drew their weapons.

After gesturing for them to stay put, Birger crept forward until he was only a few feet away from the figure. On returning, he put away his axe and shook his head.

"It's just an injured troll," he said. "Nothing to worry about."

Ethan's nerves were instantly on edge. "I thought you said trolls are dangerous."

"The young ones are. This one's almost fully grown."

"I don't get it?" Ethan scratched his head in confusion.

"When trolls are old enough to leave their mother, they become wild and vicious," Birger explained. "The adults drive them away until they get older and are calm enough to return to the herd. However, from time to time, a young troll will stay away too long and become docile. When that happens, the younger trolls attack it."

He glanced back over his shoulder. "It seems that is what's happened to this poor creature. Don't worry. As adults they are harmless enough. It won't hurt us."

"Shouldn't we try to help it?" asked Ethan.

Markus let out a moan. "Here we go again."

"There's no time for that," Birger said.

Just as he finished speaking, a loud guttural cry echoed down the tunnel. The troll tried to stand, but was only able to get to its knees before collapsing again a few seconds later.

"You see," said Birger. "It's too badly wounded. The kindest thing we can do is put it out of its misery."

Ethan shot him a furious look and pushed his way past.

Another groan, this one much louder, escaped from Markus. "I do wish you hadn't said that. You should have just lied and said the bloody thing would heal on its own. You don't know him. He'd try to save Satan from the pits of hell if he was given the chance."

Ethan grinned over his shoulder while still advancing. "Damn right I would."

Throwing up his hands, Birger followed him. "The rest of you wait here."

Ethan approached the wounded troll cautiously. He was immediately taken aback by the sheer size of the creature. He guessed it would stand at least eight feet tall, with shoulders twice as broad as a normal human. Its dark green flesh and bald head was so caked with mud and grime, he couldn't be certain if its flesh was really that color or just tinted that way by the layer of filth. Around its waist hung a skirt made from what looked like a combination of moss and bark. These materials had also been used to fashion the crude shoes on its enormous feet.

The troll turned to face Ethan. Its features were flat and unusually large, even on a head of such great size, giving it an almost comical appearance. The creature's narrow-set brown eyes were filled with terror and its face contorted in pain.

Ethan held out a hand. "Take it easy, big fella. I'm just here to help."

The troll cowered against the tunnel wall, letting out a frightened whimper. Ethan could see deep gashes on its arms and legs, and several more across its back.

"What are you waiting for?" said Birger, pushing his way past.

The troll began to tremble as he squatted down beside it.

He waved Ethan over. "This was your bloody idea. I'm not doing it by myself. Don't worry. It won't hurt you."

Ethan knelt beside the dwarf while he rummaged through his pack.

He removed a copper tube and a blue shirt. The latter was handed to Ethan. "Tear this into strips," Birger instructed, then scowled as Ethan complied. "That was my favorite bloody shirt," he grumbled.

Putting this major annoyance aside, he opened the tube and scooped out a thick yellow salve. The air filled with a sickly sweet odor as he began applying it to the various bites and gashes covering the troll's body. The torn remains of his shirt were then used to bandage the most severe of the injuries. As Birger was wrapping its legs, the creature let out an ear-splitting howl.

Ethan fell on his backside, stunned.

Birger spat a curse. "Its leg is broken."

"Can you set it?" Ethan asked, after recovering from the shock of the troll's cry.

"Yes," Birger replied. "But I'll need your help."

Taking hold of the troll's foot, he motioned for Ethan to do the same. "I don't have anything to use as a splint, but hopefully this will be enough for it to get back to its herd." He took a long deep breath. "Ready? One. Two. Three. Pull!"

Ethan yanked as hard as he could. The troll let out a howl so loud that he had to fight an urge to cover his ears. Then, after a few seconds of straining, he heard a loud crack as the bone shifted back into place.

Birger and Ethan scrambled up and backed away a few yards. The troll sat there for more than a minute, staring blankly at them. Eventually, it pushed itself to its feet and tested the broken limb. Its face grimaced with pain, but this time it was able to remain standing. After giving the pair one final lengthy look, it hobbled away. They watched until it was out of sight.

"I hope your kindness didn't just kill us all," remarked Birger. He then waved for the others to follow him down the tunnel.

"I'm impressed," said Markus after catching up. "That took guts."

Ethan smiled. "A gentle giant. That's all it was."

"Yeah. But a gentle giant that left you covered in muck."

Ethan looked down. There was green grime and dirt all over him. He groaned and tried to wipe his hands clean on his trousers, but only succeeded in making matters worse.

"Even being a boy scout comes at a price," Markus teased.

He raised a hand to slap Ethan on the back, then stopped himself. "On second thought, I think I'll stay clean."

CHAPTER TWENTY-ONE

WITH ONLY BRIEF stops in between long grueling marches, by now even Birger was beginning to show signs of fatigue. Jonas, fueled by the dwarf concoction, was the only one unaffected.

Even so, despite aching muscles and painful blisters, Ethan was becoming cautiously optimistic. Birger had been using the stone he kept in his pocket regularly, and was as certain as he could be that they were not being followed – at least not too closely. They'd also had the good fortune to run across an underground spring where Ethan was able to wash off at least some of the grime left by the troll. However, a musty odor persisted.

When they were only a few miles away from the end of the passage, Birger called for a halt. "I think we can risk an extra hour's rest," he announced. "Your descent down the mountain will be easy enough, but you'll need to get to the forest ten miles north of the base before you stop."

Ethan needed no further prompting. He immediately plopped down on the ground and pulled off his boots. Markus did the same. Even Jonas seemed grateful for the respite.

"I may need just a little more druidia," he said, rubbing his legs as he leaned against the wall.

"You should wait," Birger told him. "If your body reaches its limit then we'll have to carry you. I would say you'll be left behind, but I've come to realize that's never an option when you're in Ethan's company."

Ethan expected to see a sour expression on the dwarf's face, but instead he saw a grin.

"It wouldn't be the first time we've carried him," said Markus. He went on to tell Birger how they had first come across Jonas in Carentan, and of their escape from the Germans.

Birger threw his head back in laughter. "He really thought you were using dwarf weapons?"

"I didn't even know what a dwarf was," said Ethan. "At the time I thought he was completely insane."

"Think about how I felt," Jonas said. "I wake up from one war and find myself in the middle of another. The baby I had been holding only seconds before was now grown, and there were two men in strange clothing whispering to me in a language I didn't understand. It's a wonder I *didn't* go insane."

They talked for a time, laughing and joking about the follies and narrow escapes they had experienced together. Markus told Birger how he and Ethan had met and become friends. Ethan enjoyed seeing him in good spirits. For the very first time since arriving in Lumnia, he didn't feel quite so far away from home.

Following a brief nap, they gathered their packs and continued. However, when they were only a mile from the exit, Birger came to an abrupt halt. Quickly, he produced the red stone and closed his eyes. After only a few seconds, his eyes shot wide.

"They're here," he said. "Less than a mile back."

"How many?" asked Markus.

"It's hard to tell with this," he replied, shoving the stone back in his pocket. "At least twenty. Possibly more. And they're moving fast. Curse my carelessness. We should have never stopped."

"We're almost there," said Ethan. "If we run, we can probably make it."

Birger nodded unconvincingly. "Then let's get to it."

They all burst into a dead run. Ethan glanced at Jonas and prayed that the effects of the druidia would not expire before they reached the end. If they had to carry him, they'd be caught for sure.

This concern faded as he saw sunlight pouring in through the tunnel entrance. They had made it.

Birger slid to a stop and shielded his eyes. "I can go no further," he said.

"Thank you, my friend," said Ethan. "For everything."

Markus and Jonas bowed low.

"Go quickly," he pressed. "I'll do my best to keep them from following you."

"You think they will?" asked Markus.

"I...I don't know. They may leave you in peace once you're away from the mountain."

Ethan could hear in the dwarf's tone that he thought otherwise. *They'll chase us even after we're outside,* he thought. *We didn't get away after all.*

They could hear the clatter of weapons and the barking of orders echoing from the darkness.

Markus gave Ethan a wry smile. "Looks like our luck has finally run out."

"Not yet it hasn't," said Jonas. His eyes were aflame with determination. "Let's see how fast they really are."

"Faster than you, I'm afraid," said Birger.

Markus shrugged. "Let's give it a go anyway."

Without waiting for any more words, Jonas raced from the mouth of the tunnel. Ethan was right on his heels. The full glare of the sun nearly blinded him, even with it shining on their backs. Judging by its fairly high position, he guessed it was mid-morning.

The path was wide and smooth, flanked on either side by sheer rock walls. Ethan had no idea of how far it was to the bottom of the mountain; the twists and turns were making it impossible to see more than fifty yards ahead.

He glanced over his shoulder. Markus was grinning from ear-to-ear, clearly unafraid that they would shortly be overcome by their pursuers. *I suppose there's worse ways to die,* he thought.

Ahead of him, Jonas suddenly slid to a halt, arms waving in a signal to fall back. He quickly joined Ethan.

"Imperial soldiers," he said. "There's a whole line of them on their way up."

They listened for a moment. The sound of voices talking casually carried easily up the path.

"It doesn't sound like they saw me," said Jonas.

"Not that it matters," said Markus, who by now had caught up. His smile was gone. "They'll see us soon enough."

"*Now* I think it's safe to say that our luck has run out," remarked Ethan.

The other two looked at him, then burst into laughter, covering their mouths to muffle the sound.

"Well, lads," said Markus. "Who should we fight? The dwarves or the Imperials? I leave it to you."

"I think I'd rather die killing Shinzan's men," said Jonas. He held out his hand. "I'll have that dwarf potion now, if you please."

Ethan handed it over and unsheathed his sword. Jonas took a sip from the bottle, then drew his weapon as well.

Behind them they could hear the sound of the dwarves descending the mountain. The Imperials heard it as well and began shouting orders to form ranks.

"So much for a surprise attack," said Markus. He gave Ethan's arm a fond squeeze. "Thank you, my friend."

"For what?"

"For bringing Markus back to life."

Ethan embraced him in a final farewell.

This done, he turned to Jonas and spread his hands. "We tried."

"You did well," Jonas told him. "I only wish I could have done more to help."

"We all did our best," said Ethan. "It was a pleasure to know you."

Markus slapped his thigh sharply twice. "Enough of this mushy talk. I think it's about time we got on with it."

"Indeed it is," agreed Jonas.

Ethan strode out into the middle of the road and squared his shoulders, sword at the ready. Markus and Jonas took up positions on either side of him.

The advancing soldiers quickly came into view. There was at least a hundred of them, all bearing the raven crest of the Empire. They paused for a second, then seeing only three men standing in their way, burst into harsh laughter.

"This is going to be easier than I thought," called out one of them.

A man with a bright red sash draped over his armor stepped forward. "You wouldn't be Dragonvein by any chance, would you?"

"I am," Ethan replied proudly. "And if you know what's good for you, you'll turn back now."

His words prompted another round of laughter.

"Take the boy alive," ordered the soldier. "Kill the others if they resi…"

A thunderous roar shook the ground, reverberating through the cliff walls as if a great stone bell had been struck. The advancing soldiers instantly halted.

Ethan looked everywhere for the source of the sound, but could see nothing apart from the cliffs and blue skies above. Another roar erupted, this one so deep and booming that he could actually feel it vibrating deep within his chest. He saw one of the soldiers pointing up at the sky behind him, a terrified expression on his face. Before Ethan could turn, a vast shadow blotted out the sun and what felt like a gale force wind threw up swarms of choking dust, forcing him to cover his eyes.

Seconds later, something hit the ground just in front of him, shaking the earth and forcing him to his knees. He was still blinded by dust, but could hear the terrified cries of the soldiers.

"*Dragon!*" they screamed repeatedly.

Ethan wiped his eyes and blinked hard, finally regaining his vision. It was true. Standing there before him was an enormous dragon, its jet-black scales glistening as if set with highly polished opals. Pure white spikes ran all along its back and right down to the tip of its tail. It was at least fifty feet long and as tall as three large men. Even though it was at present facing the soldiers, Ethan could make out a series of curved horns along both sides of its head.

The soldiers were already running back down the mountain as fast as they could. Ethan got up and offered his hand to Markus and Jonas. But they were unable to move, clearly overwhelmed by the spectacle.

The dragon heaved its massive body around to face Ethan. As it turned, its twelve-inch long talons scraped across the stone road, throwing up large hunks of rock. Its eyes were a deep blue, yet reptilian in shape and appearance. Rows of razor sharp teeth peeked out from within its closed maw.

Ethan wanted to speak, but could find no words. Hot breath blasted out from its nostrils, blowing back his hair and scorching his face. It was truly the most magnificent creature he had ever beheld. Even those he had seen in his dreams paled when compared with the majesty of what was now before him.

Ethan could feel the beast peering into him, probing his mind. He felt a desperate need to move closer as its voice called out from the recesses of his soul - from places that, until this very moment, he never even knew existed. His steps were slow and deliberate, each one deepening his connection between them until he could hear the dragon's thoughts clearly. It wasn't words or language – not in the way he understood it. It was something far more complex than that. All at once he knew why the dragon had come. He knew what it wanted.

Coward.

The word spoken to him in his dream.

It was not an accusation. It was a question.

"No, I'm not," he whispered. Though he wasn't sure if he had said it, or thought it. But he knew the dragon had heard him.

Ethan reached out his hand and the dragon lowered its head. He placed his palm on the tip of its long, scaly snout. The instant he made contact, a blinding flash of light tore through his mind like a streak of lightning. Faces of men and women - hundreds of them - raced through his head as though frames on a reel. All were unfamiliar, yet somehow he knew they were a part of him. For what seemed like an eternity he stood stricken and paralyzed. Then, as quickly as they came, the faces were gone. He felt his legs giving way and his vision starting to fade.

Then there was nothing but utter blackness.

*

For a moment Ethan thought he was dreaming. There was the sound of many hushed voices, along with the friendly crackle and pop of a fire. The air was cool and felt nice on his face. The dragon's breath had definitely given him a burn, though how severe it was he couldn't be sure. At the time, he didn't care.

The dragon, he thought, forcing open his eyes. The night sky was a dark canvas showered with tiny jewels. Someone had placed his pack beneath his head and covered him with a blanket. He struggled up onto his elbows, his muscles and joints protesting from lingering fatigue and stiffness.

All around him were dwarves, and the fire he had heard was a few feet to his left. Jonas' sleeping form was directly below his feet near the mouth of the tunnel that led back into the mountain.

"Good. You're up."

Markus plopped down beside him and slapped him fondly on the shoulder.

"What happened?" asked Ethan. "How did I get here?"

His friend stared at him in disbelief. "Don't tell me you can't remember."

Ethan tried to piece events together. The last thing he recalled was touching the dragon and the barrage of strange faces. After that, there was nothing.

"Did I pass out?" he asked. "I remember touching the dragon then...well...I woke up here."

Markus gawked at him for a moment, then laughed so hard he fell over backwards. Wiping his eyes, he propped himself back up and said: "You *really* don't remember?"

Ethan shook his head.

"Well, old buddy. I can promise you that no one will ever question again whether or not you're a mage. That much is certain. When you touched that bloody dragon, you collapsed like a sack of potatoes. I thought the damn thing must have killed you. Then it jumped twenty feet in the air and flew off. All I could do was watch until it was out of sight. After that I went to check on you, but you were already on your feet."

Ethan cocked his head. "I got up?"

Markus nodded. "Oh yes. You got up all right. You looked over at me and Jonas with this strange little smile on your face. It was like you knew something that we didn't. Then…well…it's hard to describe what happened next."

"Tell me," pressed Ethan.

"You turned away and…I can't believe I'm saying this…but it looked like you flew. What I mean is your feet…they never touched the ground. You were gone before I could even blink."

"Gone where?"

"After those soldiers. The only way I knew that, was by the trail of dust you left behind. I've never seen anything move so fast. Me and Jonas took off after you, but by the time we got there you were almost done with them."

"Done with them how?" Ethan was almost afraid to hear what Markus would say next.

"You killed *every single* one of them. And I don't mean that you just killed them. You roasted them alive. They had only made it a half mile down the mountain when you caught up with them. By the time we got there, most were already dead. The few still alive were screaming bloody murder while you threw what looked like spears at them. Only these things were made of fire. Each time one hit a soldier, his entire body lit up. When it was over, there was nothing left but smoldering corpses all over the place. Jonas actually laughed out loud and clapped his hands. He looked like a kid on Christmas morning. Anyway, a few seconds after doing all that, you collapsed again."

Ethan was horrified. Had he really burned a hundred men to death? The idea made him grateful that it was gone from his memory. Though soldiers of the Empire were without a doubt his enemy, what Markus described was gruesome beyond imagining.

"Yeah," said Markus, as if hearing his thoughts. "I wouldn't want to remember that either. But something tells me it wasn't really you. When you looked at me, it was like someone else was seeing me through your eyes. I mean, you were you. But not you. Does that make sense?"

Ethan shook his head, though Markus' account did help a bit.

Perhaps the dragon had somehow possessed him? He pushed it from his mind for the time being.

"And the dwarves?" he asked.

"You don't have to worry about them anymore. After what they witnessed, they think you're their savior and to blazes with what the king says. Right now a group of them is disposing of the bodies at the foot of the mountain."

Markus' eyes shifted to just beyond Ethan's feet. "Jonas over here finally gave out. I guess that last sip of dwarf potion did him in. He fell asleep about two hours ago and hasn't moved a muscle since. Birger said that if he doesn't wake up by morning they'll have to carry him."

Ethan was relieved to hear that Birger was safe. "Where is he?"

"Helping with the bodies. He'll be back soon."

Ethan's head was spinning. He knew Markus was telling him the truth, but his mind simply couldn't take in the enormity of it all. He rested back down on his pack and closed his eyes.

"Are you all right?" his friend asked, sudden concern in his voice.

He nodded without opening his eyes. "I think I just need to sleep a bit more."

Markus gave his arm a squeeze "You do that. Take as long as you want. I don't reckon the dwarves will be going anywhere without you."

CHAPTER TWENTY-TWO

*W*E'RE HERE. WE'RE *waiting.*

"Where are you?" cried Ethan. A dense fog surrounded him and the stench of scorched earth was burning his nostrils. "I can't see you. Help me."

Come to us. We have waited so long. We need you.

"I don't know where you are."

Time is running out. He knows you are here. He will move against you. You must *come soon.*

The fog lifted and he found himself atop a grassy hill overlooking a vast plain. Flying high above were six dragons. Two were black, one crimson, one blue, and two pure white. They circled for a few moments, then went into an almost vertical dive. Their beastly roars shook the ground and forced the breath from Ethan's lungs. When all six were only a few feet from impact, they exploded in a hellish fireball.

Ethan sat up gasping, drenched in sweat, heart thudding in his chest.

The sun was not yet cresting the horizon, but the orange and purple sky stated that it would be appearing very soon. The dwarves were gathered in several small groups near the tunnel entrance, speaking in hushed whispers and stealing glances at him.

"That must have been quite a nightmare," said Markus. He was sitting nearby, alongside the smoldering ashes of the fire.

"It was," Ethan said. "Or I think it was. I didn't really understand what it was about." He knew the voice in his dream was that of a dragon, but the rest was chaotic and confusing.

"After everything you've been through, I'm not surprised you're having bad dreams."

"And there is more to come," added a different voice.

It was Birger. The dwarf took a seat beside Markus and stared at Ethan. There was a bandage wrapped around his head.

"What happened to you?" Ethan asked.

Birger smiled. "My kinsmen weren't exactly happy to see me. It got a bit rough. But there's nothing to worry about now."

"So they've really changed their minds about me?"

"After what you did, even King Halvar will be forced to admit he was wrong."

"Assuming he doesn't kill me when I return."

Birger sniggered. "He wouldn't dare. Besides, you now have quite a few dwarves willing to protect you. Even if he was foolish enough to try, *they* wouldn't allow it."

This gave Ethan a good degree of comfort. Though he wasn't actually looking forward to seeing the king again, at least this time he wouldn't be defenseless – something he had felt all too often since arriving in Lumnia.

It wasn't long before the dwarves began to grow restless. They wanted to be off as soon as possible, but none appeared willing to say anything directly to Ethan. From the snippets of conversation he could hear, they were uncomfortable about being exposed and in the open. Most of them had only been outside the mountain a few times in their life, and then only briefly. The brighter the morning became, the more agitated they grew.

"I suppose someone will have to carry Jonas," Ethan eventually announced.

Two young dwarves stepped forward and bowed low.

"We will carry him, Lord Dragonvein," said a young dwarf with a short blond beard.

Apparently, in anticipation of this possibility, they had already weaved a makeshift net from some rope. It was looped on each end and long enough for Jonas to fit in the middle. Within moments he was swinging limply between the two volunteers, who easily bore his weight.

"Not exactly a feather bed," laughed Markus.

"He'll live," chuckled Birger.

At a normal pace, the journey back to Elyfoss would take almost twice as long as their flight out. Jonas awoke the next day, embarrassed and sore. It didn't help his mood when both Markus and Birger teased him relentlessly about being carried along: *"like an old sack of turnips".*

Ethan's dreams were becoming ever more confusing and surreal. He could feel the dragons reaching out for him. And even though his actions after touching the creature were hidden from his memory, the events leading up to it were becoming clearer.

The old dragon who had saved them had not wanted to reveal itself. But it could not allow Ethan to be taken to Shinzan. It had been watching him from afar through the eyes of the tiny dragon he had first encountered. But something had happened. At first only the sorrow returned after recalling the moment when Hronso cornered him in the forest. But then the truth washed over him like a massive wave. The creature had sacrificed its life for him. It had destroyed itself to unlock Ethan's dormant abilities. *That* was how he had driven Hronso away. Through the death of a dragon.

After this revelation, he wept for more than an hour. The dwarves looked at him with concern and confusion. Markus did his best to console him after he'd explained what was wrong.

"There was no way for you to know what it intended," his friend said. "And if it hadn't done what it did, you'd be dead right now. I don't know what these dragons want from you, but whatever it is, they obviously think it's worth dying for."

"The Dragonvein family has always had a deep connection to dragons," said Jonas, who had been listening to their conversation from his bedroll nearby. "It's in your blood. And your particular connection seems to be extraordinarily strong. Stronger than I would have thought possible."

"Was my father's connection strong too?" asked Ethan, wiping away the last of his tears.

"I believe so. That's what he said, though I never actually saw him *with* a dragon. He told me that he could hear them whispering to him. He didn't talk about it often, but I do know there have been times in the distant past when the Dragonvein family actually lived amongst them."

"Where are they now?"

"They live on the other side of the world in a land of vast jungles and rolling hills. They prefer to stay away from everyone – elves, dwarves, and humans."

"There's no jungle now," said Markus. "The Dragon Wastes are about as inhospitable as it gets. From what I hear, Shinzan destroyed everything there after the war. Most people think he killed all the dragons too. But I guess they were wrong. Makes me wonder though. How many of them are left?"

"That would be something well worth knowing," sighed Jonas.

They both looked at Ethan, as if expecting him to have the answer. He spread his hands. "How should I know? I'm still trying to understand all this. I suppose we could go to the Dragon Wastes and find out."

Markus laughed. "Not a chance! Ships won't go there. None that I've heard of, anyway. And even if you had your own ship and a crew willing to risk it, the trip would take months. It's on the other side of the bloody world."

"First things first," said Jonas. "There's still the matter of King Halvar and the prophecy. Once that's sorted out, then we can move on."

"Speaking of moving on," observed Markus.

The dwarves had begun to gather their gear, ready for another march.

Ethan spent most of his time during the journey in quiet thought. The voices in his dreams were continuing to grow stronger and ever more urgent.

Come to us. Time is running out.

By the time they arrived in Elyfoss, his nerves were completely frazzled. He'd hardly slept for more than a few hours at a time and was finding it increasingly difficult to concentrate. He hoped he would not be forced to confront King Halvar in this condition, but knew it was likely. The king had sent out assassins, who were now returning as protectors of the very person they were meant to kill. This was sure to cause something of a sensation.

The former assassins surrounded him and marched through the street as if they were an honor guard on parade. People rapidly gathered on the sidewalks and followed them as they made their way to the king's manor.

On reaching it, the two guards at the door stepped forward and shouted for them to halt.

"You have no business here," one of them said, his eyes centered on Ethan. "The council is still in session."

"Step aside," commanded Birger. "We come bearing important news."

"I don't care what news you have," he shot back. "You're not getting in. King Halvar was very clear that…"

Birger took a menacing step forward. "King Halvar will see us now whether he wishes to or not."

The guard's eyes shifted past Birger and moved along the line of armed dwarves staring at him unflinchingly. The crowd in the street behind them was growing by the second. It was an intimidating scene.

"Wait here," he said after a brief hesitation, then turned sharply and disappeared inside. He returned a few minutes later, pale-faced and with an uncertain expression.

"Only Ethan Dragonvein may enter," he said.

The dwarves lurched forward, shouting their objections. Ethan held up his hands until they had calmed.

"It's fine," he told them. "I will meet with King Halvar alone."

"He's already tried to kill you once," objected Jonas. "Who's to say he won't try again?"

"I don't think he will," said Birger. "He knows what will happen if he does. All the same, you should be careful."

"I will," promised Ethan.

He allowed the guard to usher him inside. The council chamber door was already wide open with a line of council members filing out. Ethan spotted Lady Thora among them. She gave him an almost imperceptible nod and a smile.

When he stepped inside, the chamber was completely empty apart from King Halvar, who was still sitting in his chair. The monarch's eyes bore dark circles beneath them and he was rubbing his chin as if in deep thought.

He pointed to a chair on the opposite side of the table and took a deep breath. "I see that in spite of my best efforts, you are still among the living."

Ethan nodded, but remained silent.

"I hear that the dwarves I sent after you have actually escorted you back, and at this very moment are ready to charge in should they suspect your life is in danger."

Ethan nodded again.

"Then it is safe to assume that something extraordinary has happened to change their minds."

Ethan considered his words for a moment. "Your Highness, I understand why you tried to have me killed. If I were in your position, I might do the same thing."

The king huffed a disdainful laugh. "You would, would you? Let me tell you something, boy. You can't begin to imagine the responsibility I bear. I live to see my people endure. And regardless of what anyone says, *enduring* is the best we can hope for. The life my people are speaking of, now that you have appeared, is not possible. Even so, they are beginning to believe that it is. You have them preferring death to the life we have. The life we have had for centuries. The life that has prevented us from being driven from memory."

He leaned in and narrowed his eyes. "Now, tell me why my men parade you through the streets as though you had cast down Shinzan himself."

Ethan thought for a moment and decided to hold nothing back. He told the king in detail everything that had happened to him since leaving the manor – including what had occurred during his memory lapse.

"I never intended any of this," he finished off. "And I don't want your people to die. But I can't control how they feel. If they want more from their lives, then there's nothing I can do to change that."

"You can leave," Halvar shot back. "You can leave and never return."

He regarded Ethan for a long moment and then shook his head. "But you won't, will you? Now that the dragon has revealed itself, you're going to stay and be the doom of us all."

"To tell you the truth, I haven't decided *what* I'm going to do," Ethan told him. "Ever since arriving in Lumnia, I've done nothing but try to stay alive. I haven't had much time to think ahead. So far, almost everyone I've met has tried to kill me."

Halvar chuckled. "I suppose that would be a bit off-putting. Well, you don't have to worry about me any longer. I won't pose a threat to you again. I swear it."

"Thank you, Your Highness."

"I also give you leave to remain here as long as you wish…whatever the consequences may be. You already appear to have the protection of my people. So I will bend to their will and give you mine as well. I just pray that neither of us will live to regret it."

The king paused then fixed his gaze. "Regardless of what I have done, or what you might think, I believe you to be a good and honorable person. And know that I felt my honor was sullied when ordering your death. But at the time I believed I had no other choice. I still foresee disaster looming, though for once in my life I want nothing more than to be proved wrong."

He rose and walked toward Ethan. "Come with me. There is something you need to see."

Ethan followed the king out into the receiving hall and through a door on the far right side. After making their way through a series of long hallways, they eventually came to a narrow stairwell that led into an empty basement roughly the same size as the council chamber. Moving over to the far left corner of the room, Halvar pulled on a brass handle set in a recess on the floor. In response, a trapdoor with a metal ladder attached to the side slowly opened. Halvar stepped onto the ladder first, then called for Ethan to follow.

Ethan looked down the shaft. The king had already vanished into the darkness by the time he had his foot on the top rung. While climbing down he could feel the air getting dramatically colder. After what he guessed to be about thirty feet, his boot touched solid ground. There was still no light, and the cold was causing him to shiver.

"I suppose if I really wanted to kill you, this is where I should have brought you."

The king's voice was somewhere off to his right. For a second Ethan wondered if he was simply having fun with him, or had really set up a trap.

"You're fortunate I didn't think of it before," Halvar added. A dim glow appeared above where he was standing a few yards away.

Ethan forced a half-hearted laugh. "Yeah. I guess I am."

The light gradually grew in intensity. Soon, several others appeared on the ceiling of a long but quite narrow passage.

"What I am about to show you is known only to myself and a very few others," Halvar said. "You are not forbidden to speak of it, but I urge you to give this knowledge only to those you entirely trust."

Ethan nodded. "I promise."

Satisfied by his response, the king led him several hundred yards down the passage until it seemingly came to a dead end. There, he placed his finger in a small recess in the top left corner. With a sharp crack, the entire wall blocking their further progress slid to the left.

Beyond was a natural rock cavern, roughly fifty feet wide and double that in length. The small rajni stones set at regular intervals gave off a much dimmer light than those in the manor.

At first, Ethan was confused. The cavern appeared to be completely empty. But then Halvar strode to the far wall and touched a second control. A section of the stone opened as if on hinges. Ethan stepped closer. Halvar's body was blocking his view, but he could see a light shining from within.

The king stepped aside. "This is Lylinora," he announced.

Placed inside a recess was a six foot tall crystal. Much like the Shantara stones, its perfect facets glowed with pure white light. But it wasn't the crystal that was capturing Ethan's attention.

He blinked to make sure his eyes were not deceiving him, then gasped.

"It's a...girl."

Totally encased within the crystal was a young woman. With flaxen hair and ivory skin, she looked to be only slightly older than himself. A silken blue dress tied at the waist by a white sash hugged her feminine form, while on her delicate feet were matching slippers. Her eyes were closed as if sleeping. For a short time Ethan could only stand there, slack-jawed and amazed by her sheer beauty.

"She's gorgeous," he finally managed to say. "Who is she? And why is she inside this crystal?"

Halvar sighed. "She is the daughter of Lord Killian Jaymonte, the only mage ever to make it to our mountain at the end of the war. He left her here for us to watch over, protected within this crystal."

"Is she alive?"

"Of course she is."

Ethan ran his finger along the surface. "Can you get her out?"

"No. Whatever magic her father used to seal her inside is unknown to us. He left her this way in the hope that one day Shinzan would fall and she would be safe again."

The king placed a hand on Ethan's shoulder. "If the prophecy is true, you must free her, then find the others. That is the only way you may defeat Shinzan."

"What others?"

"There are supposed to be five in total. That is what the prophecy states. But it doesn't say who or where the others are. I'm hoping that King Ganix will know more. He's by far our greatest scholar."

"Where does he live?"

"He rules in the north under the Salisar Mountains. Lady Thora sent for him more than a week ago. I suppose she thought he'd be able to change my mind about you. Unfortunately, travel on the surface is very dangerous for a dwarf, so there's no way to tell when he'll arrive."

Ethan stood there for several more minutes just staring at Lylinora. She was perfect in every way. He began to imagine what her voice would sound like, what color her eyes were, how she looked when she walked. Only when hearing Halvar clear his throat did he snap back to reality.

"Come," said the king. "The council will be getting impatient."

By the time they returned to the chamber, Ethan could hear

hundreds of voices seeping in from outside the manor. The idea that he may have to talk to a large crowd produced a rush of nervousness. This didn't go unnoticed by Halvar.

"If I'm still king, I'll address them on your behalf if you would like," he said.

"What do you mean, *'if you're still king'?*"

"I tried to assassinate you. That was in defiance of our own laws, and against the will of the council. They must now decide if I am to remain on the throne."

Ethan watched the king closely as he returned to his seat. He was showing no sign of fear.

Soon after, the council returned and took their positions around the table. It seemed that word of the dragon had already reached their ears, for they all stared at Ethan in wonder.

Once everyone was settled, he could see that Halvar was about to speak and knew he had to act fast. Jumping up from his seat, he slapped the table twice to gain attention.

"I'm sorry if this is out of place," he announced. "But before we get started, I want to thank King Halvar for sending his guards to find me. Also, I wish to apologize for my temporary lack of courage. I shouldn't have run away. Thanks to the king, I'm back and now confident that I can face whatever comes next." He bowed low.

Halvar looked at him, absolutely stunned. For the moment, he seemed unable to speak.

Lady Thora took up the responsibility. She spoke in a strong, clear voice. "Indeed, our king was most wise to bring you back. Let us hope this lesson has been well learned and the incident is not repeated."

Halvar's eyes moved between the pair of them. Finally, he lowered his head and smiled. "I'm sure it won't be."

Ethan took his seat feeling very satisfied with himself.

Following this, several of the guards along with Birger were summoned to tell the council exactly what they had seen.

When they were done, the king stood to address the council.

"Although I am still uncertain as to the wisdom of the course we are preparing to take, there is no denying that the dragons have returned.

This holds true to the prophecy. I still believe that it will be the end of our people should we challenge Shinzan, but perhaps Lady Thora was right when she said that our people died long ago. That we now only breathe air and occupy space, bereft of culture and purpose. If that is so, then we *cannot* die. We can only be resurrected."

He drew a deep breath. "So, unless there are any objections, I say we should begin to make preparations for war."

Thora was the first to applaud, quickly joined by another and another, until the entire council was clapping vigorously. Ethan felt the hairs on the back of his neck rising. What would be his role in this? Would he be expected to lead? The enormity of the situation slowly began to press down on him.

Halvar held up his hands and the room settled down. "There is no more we can do here today. And I'm sure Lord Dragonvein is tired from his journey. So, until tomorrow."

Each member bowed to Ethan before departing the chamber. Lady Thora gave him a friendly smile and squeezed his hand fondly.

"I'm not used to that kind of treatment," he said to the king once everyone had left. "It feels a bit strange."

"You had *better* get used to it," Halvar told him. "My people will be looking to you for courage in the days ahead. I pray you can provide it."

So do I, Ethan thought.

"Your room is still at your disposal," the king continued. "And you may move about as you wish. Though I would ask that you take an escort whenever you leave the manor, just to be on the side of caution."

Ethan nodded his agreement and turned to the door.

"One last thing," called Halvar. "Thank you for keeping my honor...and my throne intact."

He smiled and bowed his head. "Your people need you far more than they need me."

On returning to his room, he found Markus and Jonas already waiting there. He told them what had transpired, and about the girl in the crystal.

Jonas was elated. "She lives?! That's good news indeed! Can you take me to her?"

271

"Tomorrow," said Ethan. The sight of his bed was making him keenly aware of the fatigue in his muscles. "Right now, I really am tired."

Markus grinned and slapped Jonas on the shoulder. "Come on you old bag of turnips. Let the boy rest. I think we should find ourselves a few bottles of wine."

Jonas scowled. "I'd kindly ask that you do not call me that."

A sudden loud bang at the door grabbed everyone's attention. Before Ethan could answer, it flew open and Kat stepped inside. Her face was red with anger.

Beaming, he held out his hands. "So you heard we're back."

Whatever reaction he was expecting, it was far from the one he received. Spanning the distance between them in two long strides, she punched him squarely on the nose. Ethan staggered back, a thin trickle of blood spilling over his lip.

"That's for leaving me behind!" she shouted. Message delivered, she rounded on Markus and Jonas who were wide-eyed with shock. "I'll deal with you two later."

Her furious gaze remained fixed on the pair until they finally took the hint and hurried from the room. Ethan heard both of them bursting into laughter the moment they were outside.

"How could you?" Kat demanded.

"I had to. It was too dangerous."

"No. How could you leave without saying goodbye?"

Ethan looked into her eyes. Though still burning with fury, they also contained a deep hurt. "I'm sorry," he said. "I should have said something. But I was afraid you would find a way to follow us. At the time, it didn't look like we'd be able to stay alive much longer. I…"

Before he could finish, she threw her arms around him, burying her face in his chest. "I know you don't feel about me the same way I feel about you. And that's fine. I understand now. But that's no excuse for abandoning me without as much as a word."

Ethan stroked her hair. "I promise. I'll never do it again."

Kat looked up at his face and began to laugh softly. She reached into her pocket and pulled out a small cloth that she used to wipe the blood from his face.

"Now I want you to tell me everything that happened," she insisted. "People are whispering and gossiping that the dragons have returned. Is it true?"

"It's true."

Ethan sat down at the table and gave her the full story.

"I knew the dragons would come," she said.

"Yeah. But now I have to figure out a way to find them. They're calling to me in my dreams, but I don't know what they want me to do."

"King Ganix will know. Lady Thora told me that he's the wisest dwarf alive."

"King Halvar said the same thing."

"In that case, I suggest you do some studying while you wait."

Skipping to the door, she picked up a bundle that was lying on the floor just outside and placed it on the table. Ethan unwrapped it to find four books with strange looking symbols etched all over the covers.

"Lady Thora gave these to me," Kat said. "They're the only books she could find on human magic. She told me most of them were destroyed when Shinzan came. I tried reading them, but I can't understand hardly any of it."

Ethan ran his hands over the covers and traced the symbols with his index finger. "Thank you. And thank Lady Thora for me."

"I will."

Kat then went on to tell him about her time with Lady Thora and her granddaughters. In spite of his fatigue, he listened attentively. When she was finally done, she stood up and hugged him goodbye.

"I'm glad you're safe," she said quite seriously, then gave a mischievous smile. "But you really did deserve that punch in the nose."

Once alone, Ethan took a few minutes to flip through the pages of one of the books. He was excited by the possibilities of what they might contain. But for now, it would have to wait. The exhaustion was overwhelming. Even the walk to the shower felt like it was up a steep hill.

He was asleep seconds after slipping beneath the blanket.

CHAPTER TWENTY-THREE

ETHAN SPENT MOST of the next few weeks in the underground chamber alongside Lady Lylinora. The first time he showed her to Jonas, the old man had wept openly.

"She is just as I remember," he said. "Radiant, isn't she?"

Ethan agreed wholeheartedly. "She's breathtaking. No doubt about it."

"You *must* find a way to free her," he urged. "She was a very talented mage, especially for someone so young. She could teach you much."

Sadly, the books given to him by Kat had thus far been of little use. They were confusing and vague. Ethan guessed they were written for someone who'd already learned at least the basics of magic. It was like trying to study physics without knowing simple addition and subtraction. Nevertheless, the possibility that hidden somewhere within the pages was the key to freeing Lylinora was enough to keep him trying. For hour upon hour he sat in front of the crystal, reading and re-reading each book.

The fact that he spent so much time there did not sit well with Kat, and she made her displeasure obvious. Frequently Ethan would venture down to the cavern only to find that the door to where the crystal was kept had a pile of rubbish shoved in front of it. Every time he asked her about this she would just throw up her hands and bat her eyes innocently.

Some nights he would simply sit in front of Lylinora and stare at her dreamily. Whenever Kat saw him doing this she would sneak up behind him and topple his chair. One time, his head struck the ground so hard it almost knocked him unconscious. After that he made a habit of placing a bottle in front of the door so he could hear every time it was opened.

The voices of the dragons persisted. Their desperate calls were now echoing in his mind even when he was awake. He tried to talk back, but was never able to make them hear him. The only time they were truly quiet was on the occasions he fell asleep studying in the cavern. This prompted him to take a small cot down and begin sleeping there as much as possible. Naturally, Kat hated this, and frequently he would wake in the morning to find Lylinora's crystal smothered over by blankets.

King Halvar spent his time making preparations. Ethan attended the first few council meetings, but they dealt mostly with matters of supplies and defenses. By the end of the third assembly he decided not to return unless called for.

The king visited him frequently and kept him updated on progress. And though it was clear that he did so out of courtesy rather than need, Ethan was happy that the king's melancholy was beginning to lift. Whether this was due to seeing his people smiling and laughing with renewed hope, or possibly the calm acceptance only understood by those destined to meet their end, Ethan wasn't sure. Either way, he had grown to enjoy the king's company.

"You should go out into the city more," Halvar often suggested. "You spend too much time in that cavern. A young man like you should not be looking so weary all the time."

But Ethan was totally focused on his study. In response he would smile politely and nod, yet with no real intention of taking up his suggestion.

Halvar had ordered all tunnels leading to and from Elyfoss be set with special rajni stones that would seal the mountain completely if activated. Shinzan, he reasoned, may be able to shatter their gates, but blasting through mile upon mile of solid rock would be an entirely different proposition. Only the dwarves themselves possessed the tools to cut through the mountain rapidly enough to be a threat. The downside was that, once sealed in, even with their superior equipment it would take them more than a year to get out again. This meant that provisions would need to be stockpiled and new ventilation shafts drilled. The undertaking was enormous, but the dwarves were undaunted. Ethan thought back to the way they had looked when he first arrived. They were a worn and beaten people then, filled with fear and anger. Now, although fear still remained, a new life had been breathed into their hearts.

When news came that King Ganix would be arriving in less than a week, Elyfoss erupted into a beehive of activity. Ganix was well loved and respected amongst the dwarves. Even more so than King Halvar. The council thought that a celebration was not only appropriate, but would also ease the mounting pressures put upon the people as they readied their beloved city for war.

It was just two days before the expected arrival of Ganix when Ethan burst into Markus' room, his face alight with excitement. His friend was sitting with Jonas, teaching the old man how to play chess on a makeshift set he had pieced together.

"What's got into you?" Markus asked.

Jonas didn't bother to look up. So far, he had been beaten in every game they played, and he was not willing to admit that the *scarred brute* as he liked to call Markus when irritated, could outwit one as educated and cultured as himself...even in a game he had only just learned.

"Come on down to the cavern," panted Ethan. "There's something I have to show you."

When they arrived, Kat was already there. Predictably, the covers and pillows were missing from Ethan's cot and a blanket was draped untidily over Lylinora.

Moving the table and chairs aside, Ethan stood in the center of the room. "You should stand back," he warned.

Once they were well clear, he held out his right palm and closed his eyes. After several deep cleansing breaths, he opened his eyes again and whispered: "Alevi".

A ball of green flame appeared, hovering a few inches above his hand.

"Very nice," said Jonas. "A good start."

"Yeah," said Markus. "But did we really need to stand back?"

Ethan never took his eyes off the fire. "That's not what I wanted to show you." A roguish grin grew from the corners of his mouth. "Alevi Drago!" he shouted.

This time there was a blinding flash and a loud roar that threw all three of the spectators hard against the nearby wall. They stared in a combination of terror and wonder as the flame took the form of a massive pair of dragon wings spanning the entire width of the cavern. The heat was so intense that they were forced to shield their faces. Kat screamed and tried to run, but the fire blocked the way out.

"Enough!" cried Jonas.

The flame instantly vanished, leaving Ethan standing there, completely unharmed and with a smile stretching from ear to ear.

Markus was trembling, unable to speak, while Jonas was looking only mildly pleased.

"Not bad," he said. "I'm not sure how useful it is…but not bad."

Ethan was crestfallen by his lack of enthusiasm. "Not bad? What do you mean? You know how long it took me to figure that out?"

"I once saw your father conjure a flock of fire-breathing eagles to chase off bandits that were plaguing a village," Jonas told him. "And he did so with very little effort. You'll need to show me more than a pair of flaming wings before I'm impressed."

Ethan was about to say something back when he noticed Kat on her knees, weeping into her hands. He hurried over and touched her on the shoulder.

"Are you all right?"

Her eyes shot up. An instant later she slapped him hard across the cheek. The crack of the impact bounced loudly off the stone walls and left a bright red mark on his face.

"You should have warned us!" she yelled, wiping her eyes.

"I'm sorry," said Ethan. "I was just excited. I didn't think it would scare you so badly."

Kat pushed herself to her feet and stiffened her back. "I wasn't scared. It just surprised me."

"Don't worry," said Markus. By now he had regained much of his composure, though was still looking a touch shaken. "It scared me too. How did you do that?"

"It was right at the end of one of those books," Ethan explained. "Most of it is too confusing for me. It's not like it just tells you to say something definite. It talks mostly about the essence of magic, how it combines with the elements, where you draw the power from…stuff like that. And even when it does give you words, it's not specific words. It's a series of possible words or phrases that may or may not be right, depending on what you're combining them with."

He shook his head, as if to clear away the muddle. "But then I found this one…and I understood it. Don't ask me why, but it just made sense."

"What was it?" asked Kat, doing her best to look calm again.

"Dragon fire," he replied. "And you're wrong, Jonas. It *is* useful. I only made wings because we're inside this cavern. But I can make it into any shape I want. Well, I think I can. I can't see any reason why not."

"Then we should make arrangements for you to go somewhere with more room," Jonas said. "What you've achieved may not be much compared with an experienced mage, but you could certainly stop a few soldiers with it. Or at the very least, scare them away."

"I say that you should get the hell out of this dungeon and celebrate," added Markus.

Ethan glanced over at the still covered crystal. "I think I should stay here and keep on working."

"I think you spend enough time ogling that little b…" Kat stopped herself from uttering the next word. "Just for a little while. Please."

Her pleading eyes and Markus' inviting smile soon forced Ethan to give in – on the condition that Jonas came along too. The old man groaned unhappily but agreed.

"So long as this oaf of a bandit stops calling me an old sack of turnips," he said.

"You make fun of my poor scarred face and then complain about that?" cried Markus, trying hard to sound offended.

"It wasn't me who started with the insults," Jonas countered.

Kat blew an exasperated breath. "And *I'm* the one who's supposed to be a child."

They headed upstairs and quickly came across an unused parlor. Markus found some wine and a few bowls of fruit to get them started, and soon they were talking and laughing as if the world around them had never gone awry. Even Jonas looked like he was having fun, especially when telling them stories of some of his boyhood misadventures. Birger stopped in briefly to tell Ethan that King Halvar would like him to join the council the next day. Ethan asked him to stay with them for a while, but the dwarf politely declined.

After another hour or so, Ethan struggled to his feet.

"If I have to see the council tomorrow," he told them, moving toward the door on rather unsteady legs. "I need to sleep off all this wine."

"You always were a lightweight," teased Markus. "Even Kat here can outdrink you."

She pursed her lips. "He just wants to get back to Lylinora."

"She *is* quite the beauty," Markus chuckled.

Kat snarled and punched him on the arm. "She's not *that* pretty."

His chuckle turned into a loud laugh. "Is that why you cover her with a blanket?"

"She looks better that way."

Jonas wagged his finger. "Jealousy is unbecoming in a young woman."

"I'm not jealous," she protested, then promptly stamped her foot.

Smiling to himself, Ethan waved goodnight.

"Maybe I'm just a *little* jealous," Kat admitted, once he was gone.

"Ah, the bitter sting of young love," remarked Jonas.

She glared at him and growled. "Just give me some more wine you old sack of turnips."

*

Ethan very nearly fell down the ladder on his way back to the cavern. He cursed himself for drinking too much: the morning was sure to bring a dry mouth and a sore head. He regretted not bringing some water with him, though on reflection, he knew he would have fallen for sure, and probably broken his neck as well, if he'd tried to climb down with a pitcher in one hand.

On reaching the cavern, he pulled the blanket away from Lylinora and plopped down on the floor in front of her. "I'll get you out," he promised softly. "Whatever it takes."

After a few minutes, he crawled over to his cot and rolled on top. The lack of a pillow, and the fact that he'd left his blanket on the floor beside the crystal, was annoying. Then the room began spinning. For a minute he thought he might vomit. Slowly though, the impulse subsided and he managed to drift off.

He had no idea how long he'd been asleep. But Birger would come to get him if he was late for the council, so he guessed it must still be early. As expected his mouth was dry and his tongue felt like used sandpaper. With a pounding head, he groaned and forced himself into a seated position.

"Too much wine?" said a kindly male voice.

Ethan scrambled to his feet and pressed his back against the wall. "Who's there?"

His vision was still blurry, allowing him to make out only shadows at first. He shook his head and blinked several times. Slowly the haze cleared to reveal an old dwarf wearing a red satin robe. He had a long silver beard and hair, and was sitting in a chair just a few feet away from Lylinora. His bright green eyes twinkled in the light of the crystal. There was a warm smile on his face as he folded his hands in his lap.

"If you need a moment, I'll wait," he said.

"Who are you?" Ethan demanded. "And what are you doing down here?"

"A bit grumpy I see. No matter. I can fix that." He reached in his sleeve and pulled out a silver flask. "Drink this," he said, tossing it over to Ethan.

Ethan regarded the flask suspiciously. "What is it?"

"It's not poison, if that's what you're worried about. Drink. It will make you feel better."

Ethan unscrewed the lid and sniffed. It was odorless. He took a cautious sip. Tasteless as well. But cold. Ice cold. Almost instantly, his dry mouth went away. He took another, much larger sip. His head had now stopped pounding. He suddenly felt fully refreshed, as if having enjoyed a good night's sleep.

"What *is* this?" he asked.

"It's an extract from a rare mushroom that grows deep in the mountains near my home."

The dwarf stood and bowed. "I am King Ganix. It is a pleasure to meet you."

Ethan's jaw went slack. "I...I mean...well...I'm sorry if I was rude."

Ganix laughed and waved his hand. "The fault is mine. I was anxious to meet you. I should really have waited until later in the morning."

Ethan bowed awkwardly. "No. Not at all. But I thought you weren't due for a couple of days."

Ganix sat back down and offered Ethan an empty chair nearby. "I don't care for fanfare. This gives me a chance to observe without distractions. I knew they would have a celebration planned, so I sent word that I was arriving a little later than I actually was."

Ethan took the chair and placed it in front of the king. "I have so many questions for you."

"And I have many answers," Ganix told him. "But I doubt most are the answers *you* need." He looked at Lylinora and sighed. "Lovely, isn't she? Personally, I prefer my women to have a bit more girth to them. But she is still quite lovely."

"She's beautiful."

"All these long centuries trapped in a crystal prison, poor thing. Completely unaware that the world she once knew is gone."

"King Halvar said you might know how to get her out."

"Possibly. But first you must decide if it is time to release her." He tilted his head and regarded Ethan for a moment. "Tell me about the dragons. Can you hear them? Are they calling to you?"

"Yes," he replied. "Constantly. But I don't know what to do about it?"

"You must go to them, of course."

"But how?"

Ganix placed a finger on the side of his nose and winked. "Let me worry about that. First, tell me about your dreams. I presume the dragons are in these as well."

Ethan nodded and told him all he could remember. "Down here, the dreams are less intense and the voices quieter," he concluded.

"The scenery is rather nice as well." Ganix smiled. "Who is that young girl who tried to cover Lylinora with a blanket?"

"That's just Kat. She doesn't mean any harm."

"I'm afraid I frightened the poor child when she came down here earlier. I'll have to remember to apologize."

"Can I ask you a question?"

The king nodded.

"Why do the dwarves hate humans?"

"Well now, that *is* a question," Ganix responded. "One for which there is no easy answer. Before I try, I would correct you by saying that dwarves do not *hate* humans. Well, some do, I suppose. But mistrust would be a better word for it. There is a long and not always pleasant history between our two peoples. No one knows it in its entirety, and only a handful know as much as I."

His expression became very serious for a moment. "I *am* willing to tell you some of what I know, but I would ask that what I say stays with you alone."

Ethan suddenly felt uneasy. "Is it *that* bad?"

"Not bad. Just unexpected and confusing. This sort of knowledge could strip some dwarves of their pride and self-worth."

"Then you have my word," said Ethan. "I won't tell anyone. Not even Markus."

Ganix smiled. "I will begin by asking you whether you have seen the artwork that decorates much of Elyfoss."

Ethan nodded.

"Then you might have noticed that there is a common theme in the older sections."

"I honestly can't tell the new from the old," Ethan admitted. "But I have noticed paintings and carvings of stars and planets. There seems to be a lot of them around."

"That is because they were created many thousands of years ago by dwarves who knew our true origins. You see, the dwarves are not really from Lumnia. Once, long ago my people traveled the stars."

Ethan's eyes popped wide. "Birger said he'd heard stories like that. But he wasn't sure if they were true."

"His father was a wise dwarf – one of my teachers actually – and well aware of our history. As a youth, Birger was studying to be a scholar. Unfortunately, he and his father had a falling out, which resulted in Birger choosing a different path. But that's a tale for another time."

He drew a deep breath. "As I said, we traveled the stars. We built mighty vessels and set out across the heavens in search of a new home. Where we came from originally is not known, but we eventually found Lumnia. Drawn by its energy, which we quickly discovered was able to power our technology, we settled down and claimed it for our own.

"However, the elves were already here and did not exactly welcome us. We looked upon them as superstitious primitives, and they regarded us as unwelcome interlopers. It wasn't long before tensions between our two peoples became unbearable and eventually war broke out. We had our superior weapons, but were hopelessly outnumbered. We knew that sooner or later we would be forced off the planet, so we made plans to evacuate. But something happened. How it was done, I don't know, but the elves found a way to destroy our ships. Fearing that more of us would follow, they had decided that none of us would ever leave to tell others about Lumnia. It was during this time that the portals were discovered.

"Using these, we scanned the heavens for a way off the planet… and found Earth. Your people were little more than barbarians at the time – even less advanced than the elves in fact. But rather than escape to Earth, we decided to bring its inhabitants over by the thousands to help us in our fight against the elves. Soon the tide was turned and the elves were driven back."

"Why didn't you just live on Earth?" asked Ethan. "Why keep fighting?"

"Because, dear boy, we were greedy. The energy you know as magic didn't exist on Earth, and by then we had become dependent on it. We couldn't use it ourselves – not in the way a mage does – but we could channel it through our bodies to create wondrous objects of fearsome power. It ran our machines, constructed our buildings, and enabled us to live in lavish comfort. We tried bringing it to Earth, but the power dissipated too quickly. In the end, the elves were sent running and the humans became little more than our slaves."

Ethan leaned back, appalled. "Your people enslaved us?"

"Not in the sense you might think. We didn't force you to work. But we did nothing to help you either. And if you complained, we made you suffer for it. Not our proudest moment, to be sure. But don't worry. The humans repaid us well. They were already having problems with the elves. Another war seemed inevitable. The elves, fearing the flood of humans would continue to come through, corrupted the portals, making travel between worlds far too unpredictable and dangerous to attempt.

"By then, humans had already discovered that some amongst them could use magic. Not just channel it, but alter the world around them using nothing more than their bodies. The most talented among them grew strong and defiant. Where we thought they would make war on the elves, they attacked us instead."

Ethan could not resist a tiny smile.

It did not go unnoticed. "Yes. We deserved it. The war went on for years. And thanks to the power of the mages, they drove us underground and cut us off from the surface. Eventually, we made an agreement and were permitted outside our strongholds to farm and trade, but the days of dwarf supremacy were well and truly over.

"Since that time our people have steadily declined. The knowledge to build the great machines which were the *true* power of my people slowly faded to dust. Our cities are all that now remains of my ancestor's industry and might."

Ethan rubbed his temples, trying to come to terms with the fact that the dwarves were from some distant, unknown planet in outer space.

"Why did you ask for my silence?" he asked. "Why wouldn't you want your people to know all this?"

"To spare them the shame. If they knew how far we have fallen - the wonderful things we were once capable of that are now beyond

284

our abilities – there are many who could not accept it. I would fear for their sanity. And seeing as how there is nothing we can do to regain our former glory, it was decided long ago to let the knowledge fade. Only a selected few of us keep that particular candle lit."

"And the dragons?"

"I don't know much. Only that, like humans and dwarves, they are not from Lumnia. Humans supposedly brought them here from Earth, and your family above all others have a special bond with them. Dragons were a big part of the human victory over the dwarves, and they remained a powerful reason we feared your kind…that is, until Shinzan came."

"Do you know anything about him?"

"No more than anyone else. Just that he's supremely powerful, and that his desire for death and destruction knows no bounds."

Ethan's head was spinning. Nothing was as he'd imagined. Burying his face in his hands, he tried to slow his thoughts.

Ganix leaned forward and gripped him on the shoulder. "First, I must teach you how to free Lady Lylinora. But that will take time. So for now, be glad that you and your friends are safe. Nothing can harm you here. Take pleasure and comfort while you can and enjoy what the dwarves have to offer. For your moment of peace will be fleeting. Soon, war will come."

Ethan looked up and squared his shoulders. He could feel the heat of determination growing in his belly. Lylinora must be freed.

"How soon can we start?" he asked.

King Ganix flashed an enthusiastic smile. "Will right now suit you?"

CHAPTER TWENTY-FOUR

GENERAL HRONSO STOOD at the base of the immense staircase, his eyes fixed on the archway peeking out just over the top. The gold raven perched atop the keystone seemed to mock him every second he stared at it. It was a constant reminder of his hatred, and the source of his torment.

The echoes of hushed voices he had heard throughout the palace upon arrival continued to haunt him, swelling both his anger and his fear. Word of Dragonvein's escape had not yet spread among the common soldiers; those who would have known had either been slain by the elves or buried alive in the mountain. But the most trusted of Shinzan's inner circle were already well aware of his failure. The look in their eyes and the satisfied grins on their faces told him that. They hated him...almost as much as he hated *them*. Simpering fools, he thought. Sitting here, surrounded by their own ruin. Ignorant to the fact that, in the end, they will be no better off than the fools tending the fields or laboring in the mines.

"*I* know what you are," he said in a whisper. "They don't."

The air grew suddenly cold. Shinzan had heard him. Hronso cursed himself for his stupidity. He squeezed his eyes tightly shut and clenched his fists.

"The Eternal Emperor Shinzan the Great demands to know why you delay."

At the sound of the voice, Hronso's eyes snapped open again. At the top of the stairs stood an old man in purple robes with gold trim: the attire of the Imperial Household. His eyes, although riddled with the lines of many years, were razor sharp, while his hawk-like nose and protruding jaw gave him a naturally haughty appearance.

Throwing back his hood, Hronso glared at the man. "And I demand to know when a servant has license to speak to the Emperor's General without so much as a bow. Or has your status changed, Ional? You are still the Emperor's court messenger boy, are you not?"

Ional lowered his eyes and took a step back.

It was all too easy to cow these vermin, Hronso considered. They were courageous when whispering in dark corners, but when facing him in person their fear had them whimpering like dogs. He could almost hear their gossip as he ascended the stairs.

Hronso was driven away by a mere boy.

Hronso had to run home with his tail tucked firmly between his legs.

Not that any of this was untrue. But no one knew the way in which events really unfolded. Not even Shinzan. Not that he would care.

As the general reached the top, Ional, refusing to look him in the eye, spun on his heels and walked away as quickly as he could through the archway. The black and red marble floor beyond was split down the center by white tiles that led directly to a raised dais. Atop this stood one of Shinzan's thrones – he had three others scattered about the palace. The room itself was massive, spanning more than one-hundred feet across and twice as long, together with fifty-foot high ceilings. Black columns, so large that five men stretching hand-in-hand still wouldn't be capable of reaching around their circumference, flanked the white tile path. Gold ravens as tall as a man hung on the walls every ten feet, with a five-pointed gold star set within the marble between each one of these.

The intricately carved throne was pure white ivory and gold – or that's what people believed. Hronso knew better. What was imagined to be ivory, was in reality the bones of the Council of Volnar. Often during an audience he would notice the Emperor running his finger along the arm of the throne, an odd little smile on his face. Some claimed that he actually talked to it, even having entire conversations as if it were speaking back to him with a voice that only he could hear. Naturally, no one ever dared mention this in his presence.

On either side of the throne were two smaller archways, both of which led through to a courtyard at the back. Seeing that the throne was currently unoccupied, Hronso knew this was where Shinzan would currently be. The Emperor spent much of his time there sitting alone by the fountain, or perhaps with one or two of his concubines.

His long strides quickly overtook Ional.

"Wait," the old man cried. "I must announce you."

Hronso stopped short. Without turning around he said: "You will run as fast as you can, as far away from me as you can…now. Or I will present our beloved Emperor with your head."

Ional paused for a moment. Then, on seeing the general's hand drift into the folds of his cloak, ran for all he was worth from the chamber. Hronso did not move on until hearing the echo of his footfalls exit the archway.

Just as he reached the entrance to the courtyard, he stopped to see where the Emperor was located. If he was beside the fountain, this might just go well. If not…

The courtyard itself was nearly as large as the throne room itself, only without a ceiling. The fountain was crafted from a rare green stone found only in the mines of Syrius in the northern regions of Kytain. The dwarves had built it for him as a tribute several hundred years ago. It was made in the shape of a giant raven with wings spread and head tilted skyward. Water poured from both its beak, and the tips of its feathers, into a deep octagonal pool. Several benches surrounded the area. This is where Hronso was hoping to see the Emperor. But all the benches were empty.

Rows of rare flowers and neatly trimmed bushes created a series of narrow walking paths around the rest of the yard. But Shinzan was not to be seen on these either.

He took a few cautious steps forward. "Your Majesty?"

Pain ripped through his right shoulder, sending him lurching forward. Instinctively, he reached for his sword and spun around.

"I wouldn't do that if I were you."

There stood Shinzan, dressed in a white silk open-necked shirt and loose fitting trousers. His blond locks fell just past his shoulders in tiny ringlets, held back by the gold band on his brow.

Hronso instantly dropped to one knee. "Forgive me, Your Majesty. You surprised me."

The Emperor loomed over him in silence. Slowly Hronso looked up. Shinzan was smiling. His chiseled jawline and perfect nose were neatly complemented by his deeply set blue eyes. In fact, many of his servants often spoke of the Emperor's allure and charm. Handsome was not quite the word. *Striking.* That was what the women would whisper as he passed by.

Shinzan placed his hands on his hips and laughed. "Please, old friend. No need to grovel."

Hronso rose and bowed. "You wanted to see me?"

At a signal from Shinzan, a young dusky-haired woman came through the archway toward them. She wore a sheer silken blue gown stitched with circular gold patterns, which in the light of the sun revealed that she had nothing else on beneath.

"Have you met Kariel?" the Emperor asked. The girl lowered her eyes and bowed respectfully to Hronso. "One of my agents rescued her from a brothel in Traxis and brought her here. Lovely, isn't she?"

"Yes, Your Majesty. She is."

Shinzan led her to a bench beside the fountain and sat down. "So, you are here to tell me more about your failure. Am I right?"

"It's not as simple as that," said Hronso, trying hard to keep any hint of irritation out of his tone.

Shinzan kissed Kariel's hand and looked into her eyes. "Did you know that General Hronso was the very first Rakasa I created?" She shook her head. "It's true. He is the first and the best. I thought it was good fortune that he was nearby when a portal opened in Malacar. I thought that surely the great General Hronso could handle such a simple matter for me."

He turned to the general. His face darkened. "But I thought wrong, didn't I?"

Hronso could see that the girl was trembling. Shinzan was squeezing her hand tighter and tighter. Then, all at once, his demeanor brightened and he relaxed his grip. Kariel let out a soft whimper.

"I'm sorry my dear," he said, stroking her injured hand. "I'm afraid I allowed my temper to get the better of me." His own hands then glowed with a radiant blue light.

Kariel gasped.

"All better?" he asked.

She nodded. "Yes, Your Majesty. Thank you."

His attention returned to Hronso. "Tell me, old friend. Where is the son of Praxis Dragonvein?"

"He is being protected by the dwarves."

"And why did you not catch him for me?"

Again, the air grew cold.

"There was no way to breach the mountain," Hronso explained. "I sent one hundred soldiers to demand that they turn him over, but they never returned."

"And why did you not go there yourself?"

"I didn't think it was necess…"

Before Hronso could finish, Shinzan waved his hand. A line of black smoke sprang forth from the ground at the general's feet. In a flash, it coiled itself around him like a foul serpent. He was instantly frozen in place. The pressure on his body mounted as the smoke tightened its hold. He gasped for air, but each time was finding it more and more difficult to breathe.

Kariel stared, fear stricken.

"There, there," said Shinzan, stroking her hair. "No need to be afraid. This won't kill him. Fortunately for the general, your considerable…talents have put me in a rather forgiving mood."

He turned to Hronso, whose eyes were beginning to bulge far out of his head. "You should really thank Kariel, old friend. You know how I detest failure. Even from you."

In a sudden puff, the smoke vanished.

Hronso fell to his knees, gasping. "I…will…go…at…once."

"That is no longer necessary," the Emperor told him. "Events have already been set in motion. I have other work for you."

Hronso struggled to his feet. "I am at your command, Your Majesty."

Shinzan regarded him, his eyes shining with an unnatural red light. "Yes, I know you are."

End Book One